I0788707

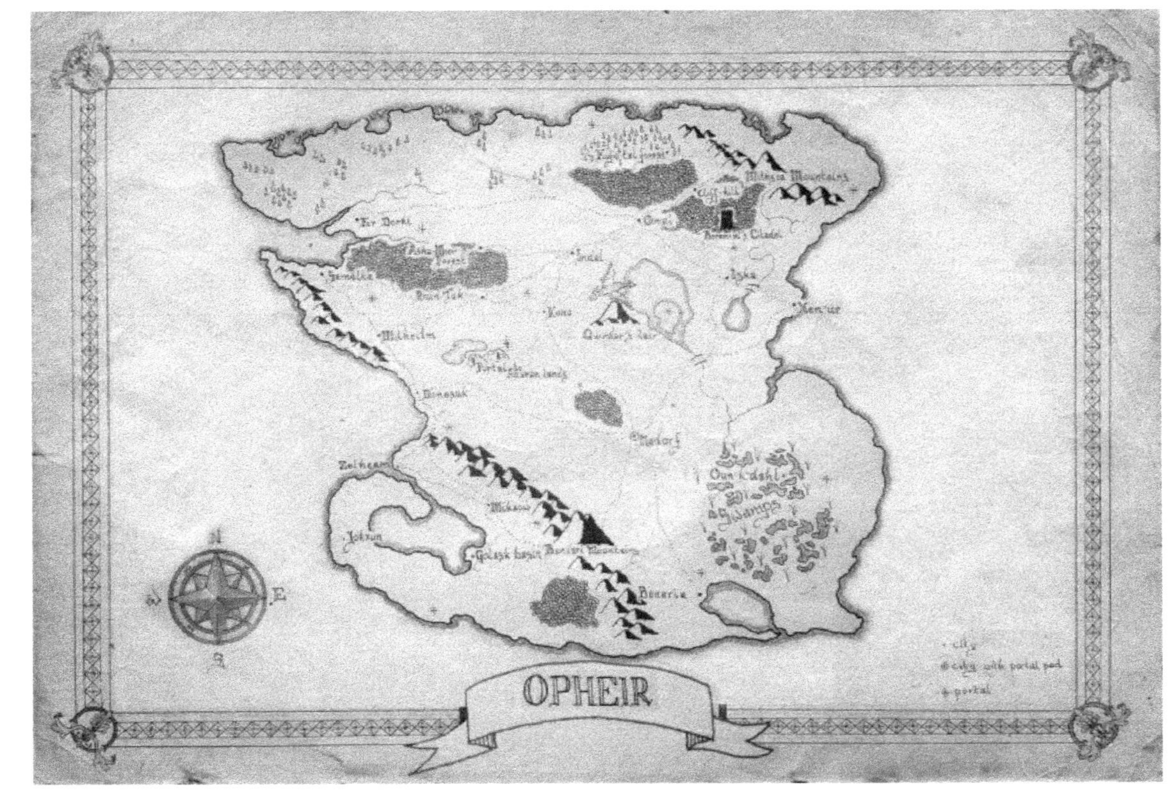

Mithan Mountains
Armen's Citadel
OPHEIR
• city
city with portal pad
+ portal

Meluki
Hagar
Fjeld
Bernhal
GUDALO KINGDOM
Per Volt Islands
ORC AND GNOME LANDS
SOUTHERN REACHES
N
W
E
S
GUDALO

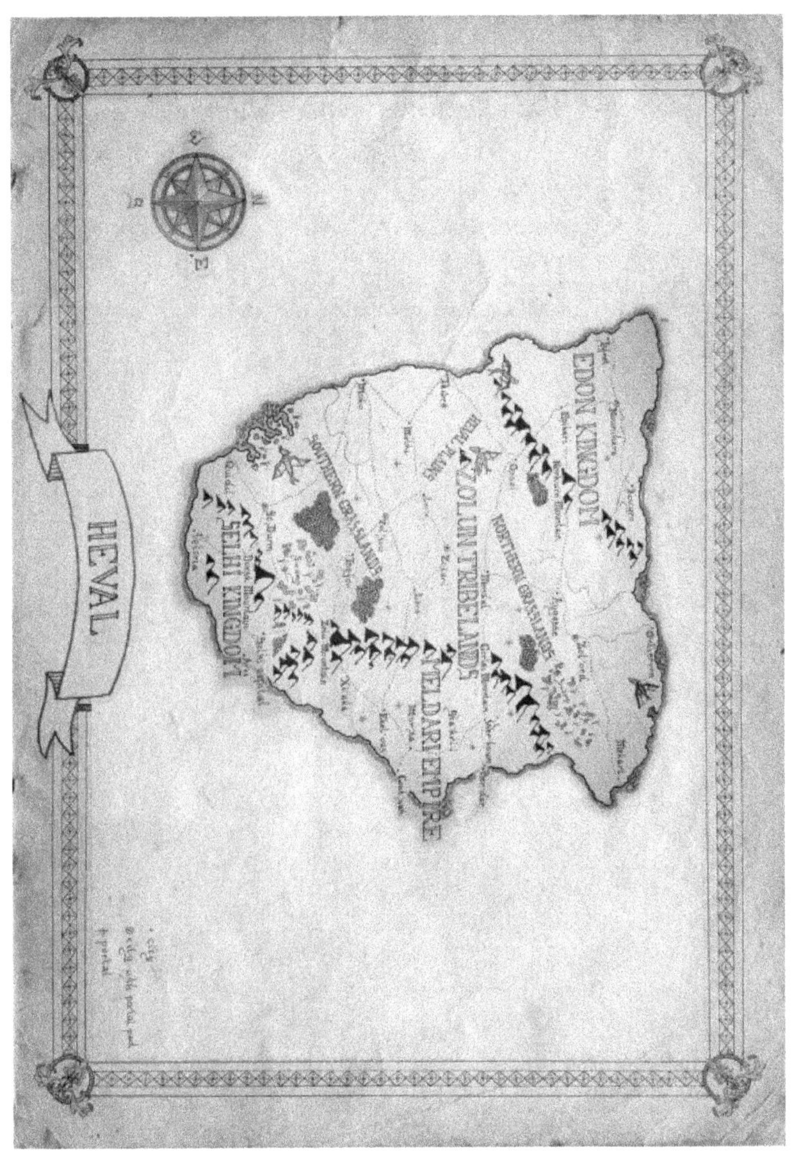
HEVAL
EDON KINGDOM
SELHI KINGDOM
ZOLIN TRIBELANDS
NORTHERN GRASSLANDS
SOUTHERN GRASSLANDS
VELDARI EMPIRE

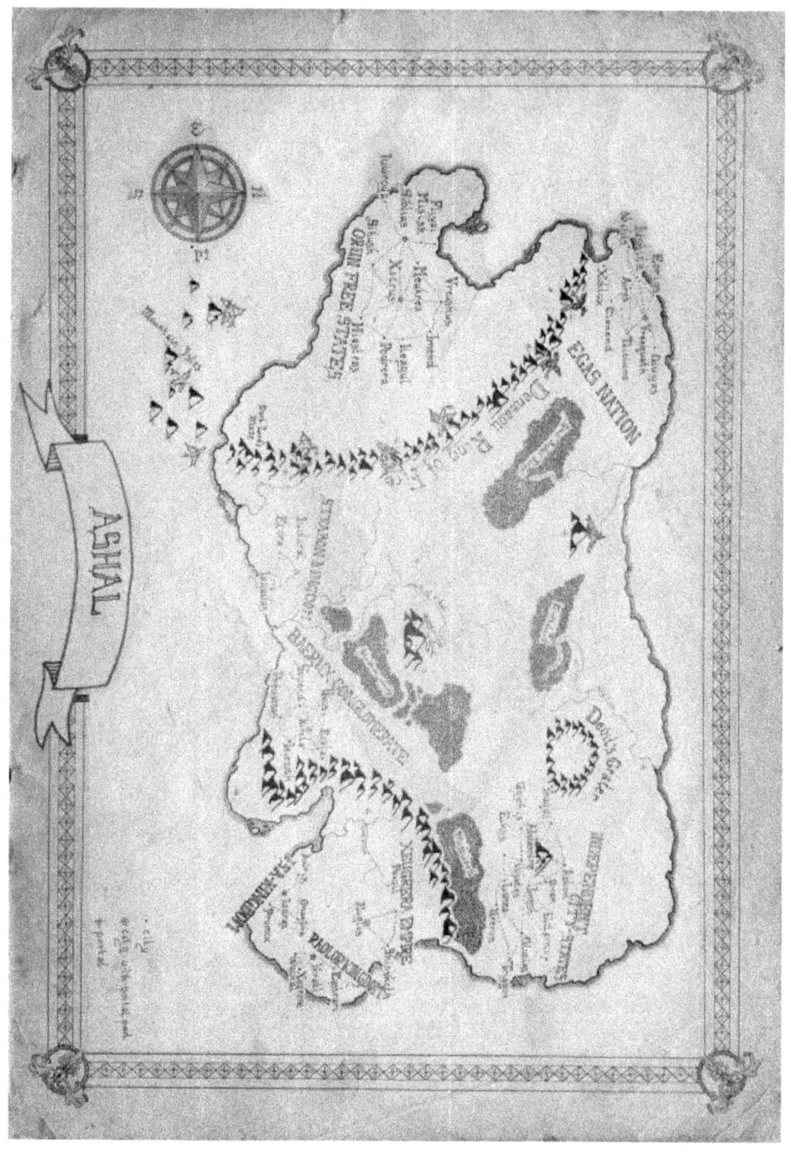
ASHAL
ODIN FREE STATES
EGAS NATION
STERNSON KINGDOM
PANDARAN CONFEDERATE
ALVA KINGDOM

Want a bigger map of Emerilia and the continents? Check out **http://theeternalwriter.deviantart.com/**

Character Sheet is located in the back of the book for reference.

Emerilia

Beyond All Expectations

Chapter 1: Beyond the Expected

Dave looked upon the Weapons of Power vault. As the various fighters had made their way in, he and the other dwarven master smiths had also ventured into the room to look upon the items that they and past masters had worked on, as well as look for inspiration for later projects.

Even as the dwarven master smiths smiled and talked in excited tones to one another, there was a shadow in their voices and eyes. They all knew what opening this vault meant, the impact that it would have on the world.

Dave heard a commotion as a few items were knocked over.

"Where is he? I can sense him!" an old voice said. Just by the tone of the voice, one could tell that the person speaking was slightly eccentric.

A staff flew out from between the racks.

Dave's eyes widened at the staff. With his Touch of the Land, he could sense the Mana that seemed to pour from the staff.

Its body was made of crystallized Mana. Along its length, there were carved scenes from every Affinity: flames, waves, bark, smooth as polished metal and rough as raging air currents Light glowed out from it symbolizing the final affinity. These six different surfaces all intermingled together, coming to form six different pillars that extended out of the top of the staff, turning into red, green, black, white, blue, and gold to create a cage around a perfectly spherical gray crystal.

This staff halted in midair, pausing before it rushed toward Dave.

"You're not him! Who are you?" An old voice filled with suspicion came out of the staff as it stopped in front of Dave. It revolved around him, studying Dave.

"A talking staff?" Dave muttered to himself, looking at the creation in front of him.

"Archmage Jekoni, this is Dave Grahslagg," Kol, who was nearby, said in a respectful tone, seeing Dave at a loss of what to do.

"Why can I read Jung Lee's Mana signature on you?" A light was emitted from the staff. A wizened old gnome, about five feet tall with a classic wizard hat and robe, floated up to look at Dave face-to-face.

Dave's eye twitched at the gnome's appearance.

The robe was much too long and the gnome, although trying to be serious, had to flip his head so that the tip of his well-used wizard's hat didn't fall in his eyes. "Even in my damned spiritual form, this hat can't stay straight!" The gnome pulled the hat off and threw it on the floor. "I'll deal with you later!" He pointed at the hat. It started to use the brim to try to escape!

Even the damn hat's animated!

Dave looked to Kol in confusion.

"So—Jung Lee? Where is that medicinal nut?" Jekoni asked.

"Umm, er, well, we rescued him from the Six Affinities Temple," Dave said.

"Rescued him?" Jekoni frowned.

"He was trapped there with six different Free Affinity spirits fighting for control of his body," Dave said, recovering from the shock.

Just then, the hat started to climb his leg, as if hiding from Jekoni. Dave shook his leg, but the hat clung on for dear life.

Jekoni's face was dark as he stroked the faint hairs that made up the wisp of a beard he had. "Well, let's go see the old bugger. Been awhile since I was able to talk to anyone from my time period! Those old elves have always been an uppity and boring bunch. You dwarves only got interesting after the last couple of centuries. Quite the improvement, if I do say so myself!" Jekoni announced.

Dave looked to Kol.

"Best to go take him to Jung Lee. He's harder to reason with than an enraged goblin," Kol advised.

Dave made to open his mouth.

"We can handle the rest here." Kol waved down his words.

"Well, let's be about it! Also, have you got any soul gems? Old charge is a bit low," Jekoni said.

Dave sighed, feeling something on his shoulder. The hat now rested on his left shoulder, seeming completely happy with itself.

Dave pulled out a grand soul gem and passed it to Jekoni.

Jekoni didn't make any sign of taking it. Instead, a force pulled the soul gem to the staff. The glow of the gray crystal and blue staff became brighter as a stream of multi-light was pulled from the soul gem.

The soul gem was exhausted in a few moments.

"Hmm, interesting, a rechargeable soul gem. Holds a bit back to maintain the structure of the soul gem. Smart, that. What is this? Magical Circuitry, or some kind of variation?" The soul gem rotated in front of Jekoni as he stared into its depths.

"It's called magical coding, a simplified version of Magical Circuitry." A smile appeared on Dave's face at Jekoni's words.

Jekoni made an impressed noise. With a wave of his hand, the soul gem disappeared. A ring around the shaft of the staff glowed. It was an integrated spatial ring within a smooth area on the staff that someone could hold onto.

Dave was impressed with the staff. Even with his current skills, making something similar would be a massive undertaking.

"Lead on to Jung Lee! Been in here too long." Jekoni's eyes moved to the hat on Dave's shoulder. "Hat!" Jekoni said in a firm tone.

The tip of the hat moved from side to side, giving off the feeling of a petulant child saying no to its parent.

"Hat." Jekoni snapped his fingers as his voice lowered.

The hat resisted for a few moments before reluctantly leaving Dave's shoulder and floating over slowly to Jekoni. It seemed to pout the entire way before it landed on Jekoni's head.

Jekoni settled the hat on his head when the tip of the hat promptly fell down in his face. "Hat!" Jekoni flicked the tip out of his face, only to have it come back and fall on his face again.

Jekoni mumbled some angry curses and promises before the hat reluctantly flipped the peak backward and out of Jekoni's face.

It seemed to be amused with itself and Jekoni's reaction.

Dave sensed Jekoni's annoyance and moved to leave the vault. The staff floated next to the gnome, following Dave.

Dave nodded to the dwarven masters guarding the door. Their looks turned slightly fearful as they saw the staff following Dave. These Hidden Masters who could have been the top fighters in the dwarven tournament shivered in the mere presence of the staff and accompanying gnome.

They quickly moved back through Aldamire. Jekoni looked around the mountain, an unreadable expression on his face.

Dave also looked around. The city within the mountain was suspended on wires, much like the dwarven Benvari Mountain.

Refineries added a deep orange glow to the lowest levels in the mountains. Greenhouses coated the inner walls of the mountain; light was reflected through a series of mirrors and tunnels into the light globes, which were glass spheres with metal fragments held within. They created miniature suns that lit up the inside of the mountain.

Unlike Benvari Mountain, there was a greater number of armed shield bearers wandering around. Aldamire might be the greatest stronghold of the dwarves, but that didn't mean it couldn't run without the support of a dozen warclans.

If one was to look closely, they could see where the massive dwarven artillery rested, hidden within the mountain so that they couldn't be seen by approaching armies.

Aldamire had one of the longest histories on Ashal. Few people could live on Ashal without being overturned, either by a beast horde or an opposing force.

"Things have certainly changed while I've been relaxing in the vault, going over the dwarves' information," Jekoni said. Instead of sounding pensive, he seemed excited, as if once again returning to a world filled with new experiences and adventure to be grasped.

Dave looked at Jekoni with interest as their elevator stopped. A large corridor led to the exterior of the mountain and the areas where the final arenas were located.

"It is indeed a strange and wonderful place." Dave walked forward.

Jekoni floated alongside him, the staff to his side.

As the doors opened, Jekoni's eyes seemed to shine with joy and the corners of his lips turned into a smile. Realizing his facial expression, Jekoni's face changed once again into a gloomy expression.

Dave smiled slightly and led Jekoni toward a restaurant that Party Zero and their friends said they'd be eating at. There were people all over the place, partaking in the festivities at the end of the dwarven tournament.

Dave passed through the crowds, people remarking about Jekoni and the staff as they passed. Although some coveted the staff, seeing Dave's necklace that displayed his status as a dwarven master smith made them quickly avert their eyes. Dwarven master smiths were rare and revered people among the dwarves. Taking something that belonged to a master smith or their friends while within a dwarven mountain was just asking to get your ass kicked.

Dave's smile grew wider as he heard Dwayne, Josh, Kim, Alkao, Steve, Anna, Gurren, and Lox all in a loud argument about the last fight in the dwarven tournament.

They sat outside, enjoying the warm early summer weather, half of the table in quiet conversation and nibbling on food, while the other side argued and counter-argued about how the fight could have gone differently or how it would have had the same result regardless.

Jekoni's eyes thinned, looking through the group before his eyes fell on Jung Lee's back. He raced forward, a mischievous smile on his face. His staff followed.

Jung Lee frowned, making to turn around as he heard a voice from behind.

"Where is that homework, Mister Jung! I thought you said you'd have that thesis on the combination of medicinal formulas and strength increase over time on my desk three centuries ago!" Jekoni said in a furious tone.

Jung Lee whipped around, spilling wine that he had been drinking. "Archmage Jekoni?" Jung Lee's eyes latched onto the floating gnome before he let out a hearty laugh. "Looks like your spiritual integration worked, you gnarled sapling!" Jung Lee pronounced. His proper manner of talking disappeared in front of the gnome.

The gnome let out a laugh, his lined face breaking into a smile. "Was a right pain in the flesh, but once I started, I finished!" Jekoni's eyes narrowed as he looked over Jung Lee with interest. "It's as the boy said. I can sense all of the Affinities and none of them within your body. Seems that you've kept your youth!"

Dave's appraisal of the gnome went up slightly when he heard these words. Even though Jekoni knew that Jung Lee had every kind of Affinity within his body, much like Dave, he couldn't sense their power or type.

It took not only mastery of arcane sight but arcane skills to be able to see Jung Lee's Affinities.

Jung Lee simply nodded and scratched his head awkwardly.

"Looks like you suffered greatly to command that power." Jekoni's tone softened.

"It was a long time," Jung Lee replied with a sad smile. "What great things do not come with great suffering?"

"Hmphf. Sounds like you've become a bit more refined in your time away. Bit too boring for my tastes!" Jekoni said.

"I've spent enough time in one place. If it was not for this upcoming event, I would be wandering freely. In fact, my friends have been helping me to understand what is going on in Emerilia." Jung Lee waved to the people at the table.

Jekoni had a thoughtful expression on his face. "I have heard something of this event." Jekoni's tone was dark.

"It will indeed be a battle, the kind of which we have not seen before." Jung Lee's face was solemn, though there was a hint of excitement in his eyes.

Jekoni tugged at the corner of his mouth, a fire in his eyes as his staff started to vibrate with power. "Well, I couldn't let you have all the fun. It's been some time since we went into battle. Shall we do it again?"

"You're a spiritual body," Jung Lee said, confused.

"I'm also a Weapon of Power." Jekoni smiled as runes started to glow over his hat as it went upright.

The hairs on Dave's neck rose as Mana gathered in the air. People looked over in interest as a glow started to envelop the magical staff.

The cage of different-colored Affinities opened, releasing the gray sphere. As it separated, a domineering feeling of wild Mana filled the air.

Dave recognized this feeling—it was the same as his own Affinity! Wild and Affinity-less Mana.

The staff shook as the crystal started to move and change shape, as if it were a liquid.

The staff formed into the shape of a sword with only one sharpened edge and curved at the end. It looked like a thicker katana, with no guard between the blade and hilt. The blade was covered in a sheath that matched the hilt. Where there would have been a string for a grip, now there were six different threads, each the color of a different Affinity as they reached for the end of the weapon. The six pillars that made up the gray sphere's cage extended as the gray sphere turned into an ovoid, inserting itself once again into the cage, embedding itself into the blade's hilt within the six pillars.

The sheath made from crystal dimmed as there were three lines on either side, each showing the same symbol of the threads.

Jekoni looked much older after the light dimmed and the sword moved to Jung Lee.

Jung Lee received the blade with both hands.

"Well, what do you say?" Jekoni asked, his breathing hard as the runes on his hat dimmed and the peak slowly started to fall backward.

"Are you sure?" Jung Lee asked.

"You were a good student. Even though you didn't aspire to be a mage, you went further than many who underestimated you to develop the field of alchemy. I am an archmage who has practiced with gray Mana for three lifetimes. Where am I going to find another student able to learn how to control all of the Affinities with ease and with the drive to persevere?" Jekoni asked in a soft voice and a smile on his lips.

Jung Lee's hands tightened around the sword, Jekoni's life's work and the container for his spiritual body. "If you would teach me, I would be honored to be called your student." Jung Lee held the sword out as he got to both knees and bowed his head.

Jekoni smiled and coughed; Dave saw the flash of emotions on Jekoni's face before he was able to hide them.

"Get your knees out of the dirt, will you," Jekoni grumbled, but even his serious tone couldn't hide the glow in his eyes.

Jung Lee rose to his feet.

Jekoni's hat flipped over and fell in his face.

"Oh, you damn hat! I'll recircuit you, I swear!" Jekoni yelled, pointing at the tip of the hat, cross-eyed as he looked at it.

It flipped back over as people laughed at the comical sight.

Jekoni glared upward, an annoyed expression on his face.

Jung Lee laughed, his eyes filled with mirth.

"I can't believe you added in that hat to your spiritual body. I knew that you couldn't part with that thing." Lee grinned.

"Damned nuisance is what he is!" Jekoni said.

The tip of the hat stood up from its slumped position, as if arguing with the indignant words of its owner.

Lu Lu squawked, as if agreeing with the hat.

Jekoni's eyes swept through the bar, looking at where the noise had come from. His wrinkled face went flat as his jaw dropped. Faster than one could blink, he was next to Suzy and Lu Lu.

"A lightning phoenix. I only heard of this in lore passed down by the Pantheon and the Grey God!"

Jekoni looked over Lu Lu; the phoenix eyed the spiritual body of the gnome in confusion, her head cocked to the side.

Jung Lee smiled and shook his head. He pulled out his old sword from his waistband. He smiled and put it into his pouch of holding.

He pulled the new blade free from its sheath. Its blade looked as though it were from a soul gem. It glowed with moving motes of light. There was a sharpness and strength to the weapon, despite its beautiful and fragile appearance.

Many people around the Stone Raiders' table looked on in envy at the magnificent blade held within Jung Lee's hands.

Dave pulled out a couple of grand soul gems as Jung Lee studied the blade, weighing it in his hands.

Jung Lee looked up from his daze.

"Looks like it could use a charge." Dave smiled.

"Would you do me the honor?" Jung Lee returned the smile.

"Are you sure?"

"We both know you've wanted to study this blade as soon as it was made." Jung Lee laughed.

Dave didn't try to deny it as he held out his hands. Jung Lee passed the blade to him. Dave looked it over, a screen appearing in his vision.

Blade of Gray

Formed from the Staff of Gray, this Legendary item was created by Archmage Jekoni from his own spiritual body's container. This weapon is best suited for a six Affinity user, or gray Mana practitioner.

Quality: Weapon of Power

Abilities:

Can retain spiritual body of holder. Current spiritual body: Archmage Jekoni and companion "Hat."

Increased command of all Affinities making up the sword (+20%)

Wielder's Willpower increased (+25%)

Spells are 5% more powerful when used with the Blade of Gray. Affinities stack. (ie, using 2 Affinities=10% power increase. All Affinities=30% power increase)

Grows in power through use

Soul Bound

Two as One (Legendary ability)

Charge: 15,700/1,000,000

Durability: 1,247/1,247

Dave looked at the blade in shock. Even with his mastery as a blacksmith, he wasn't able to understand the material that made up the blade. He saw elements of heavy metals as well as soul gems and Mana. It was as if someone had taken solid Mana, and melted it together with a soul gem to contain the power and heavy metals to direct it. He shook his head.

Even with everything I know and have done, I still don't know everything.

Dave smiled to himself, taking the grand soul gems, pouring power into the staff, and bringing it up to half charge.

He didn't notice Jekoni's look of interest as his staff, now sword, was getting charged.

Dave handed the sword back to Jung Lee once he'd charged it.

"Thanks for letting me study it," Dave said sheepishly, knowing his face had probably been filled with childish awe as he looked over the sword.

"With all of your machines and different items you and the others have been able to show me, it feels good to surprise you." Jung Lee chuckled.

"That reminds me—when we were attacking the Six Affinities Temple a second time, when we got to the Affinity spirit-controlled shades, they attacked us outside of their range," Malsour interrupted.

Jung Lee tilted his head and looked to Malsour. "I think it might have been because I wasn't there. Was there someone on the throne?"

Malsour looked to Dave, who closed his eyes, thinking back to what his Touch of the Land had sensed.

With his high Intelligence, his mind was like a computer with past saved files of all he'd done.

"I think that there was," Dave said after a moment.

"When I was sitting on the throne, I had some command over the Affinity spirits. There was less control over the Free Affinity shades as they were stronger and had more will.

"I never tried to exert any control over these creatures as I was fighting my inner Affinities. However, if someone has spawned in to take my place on the throne, then it might be said that they could control creatures of less power than themselves. While the Free Affinity spirits are indeed powerful, they are not sentient. If they were, they would have left the Six Affinities Temple long ago. They are strong beasts with incredible reflexes and power. As with all beasts, they submit under the power of the strongest."

Dave and Malsour glanced at each other.

"I wonder what the mob that replaced you would be like," Dave said.

"What would happen if you were to return in your current state?" Malsour asked.

Jung Lee opened his mouth to reply, before closing it. It was some time before he replied. "I am not sure." Jung Lee shrugged. "I might be able to exert some control over the creatures that reside in the Six Affinities Temple. I might equally have to fight them in order to gain access to the temple once again."

"Control them? Could you possibly move them out of the way?" Dave asked.

"It is possible," Jung Lee said, not sounding as if he truly believed his words.

"Would you be willing to try?" Anna, who was nearby, asked.

"For those who rescued me from that prison, I owe many favors. I would do this for you. It would also give me an opportunity to vent my inner frustrations," Jung Lee said. "However, I have one condition."

"Name it," Anna said.

"I am new to my current body and power. I might have to go all out to test it out and remove the one at the peak of the temple. I do not want too many people to see my new true strength. As such, I would only like the people of Party Zero to be with me," Jung Lee said.

Dave looked to Anna and Malsour in the conversation, all of them nodding to the other. "We can agree to these terms. The rest of the party will agree, too," Dave said, vouching for the others who had become akin to his family. He would naturally know their reactions.

"I look forward to it." Jung Lee gave a faint unsmiling smile, a hint of coldness in his dark eyes. Finally, after uncountable years, he was going to be able to unleash his strength and vent his rage at the very place that took his freedom away for so long.

Jekoni circled Steve, his eyes glowing as he did so. "I never thought that so many things would change while I was within the vault." Jekoni tapped his chin as he inspected Steve.

"Who's the floating midget?" Steve said, a big finger making to push Jekoni's head away. Instead, his finger went through Jekoni.

A complicated expression appeared on Steve's face.

"You're a ghost! I knew that they were real!" Steve cheered, jumping up and down, sending tremors through the resturant

"I am not a ghost. Those are just animated ectoplasm with a faint animalistic reaction system," Jekoni chided. "I am a spiritual body incarnation," Jekoni said in a haughty manner.

"Sooo, high-class ghost?" Steve said, a confused look on his face.

"If I'm a high-class ghost, then you're an upgraded garbage can!" Jekoni waved a thin and gnarled finger at Steve.

"That'd be cool—mean I'd get some more storage." Steve grinned.

Jekoni let out a frustrated noise as Jung Lee cleared his throat.

***

First elder Houx'Rei looked up from her meditation as a bright golden light flooded her senses. *Who dares attack me within the first elder chambers of Markolm!*

Markolm, the island of elves—the majority of which were high elves—was controlled by a council of elders. The strongest and most powerful was the first elder.

Every eight years, the position of first elder was vacated and one on the council of elders was elected into the position of first elder. It was largely based on the strength of the elf and their overall age.

A terrifying aura filled the floor, causing Houx'Rei to be unable to move from her seat. If she had been standing, she would have been struck to the floor under the power of this aura.

Cold sweat ran down her back. She was a Level 1500 talent! Someone suppressing her to this degree must have been at least a hundred levels more powerful. Her eyes widened as the golden light faded slightly to reveal a woman who would have stirred many men's hearts and a number of women's with her beauty.

That outward beauty was only further refined by her serious expression and the displeased look on her face.

People would sacrifice their lives in order to make her smile again.

Her golden eyes looked upon Houx'Rei with distaste, her golden armor shining in the approaching nighttime.

Houx'Rei's eyes were not wide because of her beauty or the armor that exuded its own powerful aura. Her eyes were glued to the twin, blindingly white and pure wings that extended above and to either side of the angel.

"Khan...un...dra," Houx'Rei said. The combination of massive wings, the three powerful beasts released from captivity, the woman's beauty and power: all of these things allowed her to make this guess.

"Seems that you have not forgotten everything," Khanundra sneered, as if looking at an unsightly blemish on an otherwise perfect landscape. "I have come to pass on a warning." Khanundra's words were cold as she looked at Houx'Rei. Her aura decreased slightly, leaving Houx'Rei panting.

"This warning is to all of the believers who have been turned away from the Lady of Light, the rightful goddess of Emerilia. They need not fear as their goddess has returned." Khanundra's eyes sparkled with fanaticism and belief in her goddess.

Houx'Rei had seen all manner of people. Of them, those like Khanundra were the worst, in her mind. They believed that everyone had been led astray from their right and proper religion. That once everyone followed the teachings of her deity, that they would be forever grateful.

They called it bringing people to their religion, finding them purpose. Instead, it was just their way of acquiring more power and feeling as if they had accomplished something. They didn't really care about their religion as much as they showed their devotion to it. They were devoted to the idea of power, power that came from having others follow their ideology.

If anyone was to argue against them, or take on another religion, there was nothing that would change their mind. They were losing the basis of their power! If they didn't have it, then they didn't want anyone else to have it.

"Those who follow the Lady of Light are free to do so. I will not tell them who to hold in their hearts," Houx'Rei said.

Khanundra's eyebrow rose as her golden eyes turned cold. "Are you not the leader of the people on Markolm? Do you not command this nation's armies and fleets?" Khanundra said, her voice icy.

"I might control the military power, but it is my position to try to carry out the people's will. Not be the one to determine it." Houx'Rei's voice tightened as Khanundra's aura pressed down on Houx'Rei once again.

"The Lady of Light was right when she said that the people of Emerilia had lost their way in our absence," Khanundra spat.

"We found it, out from under the control of the Pantheon and their tools." Houx'Rei wheezed after spitting out the last word. Her body pressed into her chair once again.

"If you're not with us, then you're against us." Khanundra slowly stepped forward.

Houx'Rei could sense the boundless anger she was faced with. "In all that time, you still remained blinded. At least the demons found their way." Houx'Rei's voice held a note of sympathy within it.

"Demons? You think demons are better than me and my kin!" Khanundra yelled, her voice filling the room, her wings expanded out in fury.

"You may kill me, but you will not kill the spirit of my people. We might have been blinded in the past, but now we can clearly see. You and the gods do not determine our fate or our paths. It is our strength of will to fight against our circumstances, to push ourselves forward that makes us strong." Houx'Rei propped herself up on her seat, her calm and collected features now red as veins popped out across her forehead and down her neck.

"Then, there is no need for you," Khanundra sneered. She turned her wing and lashed out. Its white feathers left a red line on Houx'Rei's neck as she slumped into her chair, blood staining her simple robe.

The strike had been so fast that not a drop of blood had landed on Khanundra's wing.

She looked down on the first elder of Markolm as if wanting to spit on the dying woman's body.

Houx'Rei never thought that she would die this way. Her thoughts ended with hope and anguish. *I hope my people and Emerilia are strong enough to resist these angels and the monsters that will be released upon the lands.*

With that, the first elder of Markolm died, her lifeless eyes looking toward the ceiling of her office, where she'd worked for her people for six long years.

Chapter 2: Pandora's Box

It had been three days since the dwarven tournament. Jekoni and Jung Lee were following Dave and Malsour as they entered Terra's power station facility.

Jekoni had been in a state of curiosity since entering Terra. Now that he was a spiritual entity, he didn't need to sleep. He'd taken the sword and headed off across the city to look at different systems and areas.

Now, he was looking at the power station in interest.

Malsour grinned at Dave.

Dave snorted at Malsour's expression. *I wonder what he'll do when he sees the things we've been working on?*

They entered through the secret entrance into their laboratory, nicknamed Pandora's box.

Jekoni's severe expression turned into slack-jawed amazement at everything within the laboratory. Magical tech that had never been seen on Emerilia was out in the open, displayed in its full glory. Jekoni muttered to himself as he seemed to teleport to different areas of the laboratory.

Dave and Malsour grinned; Jung Lee had an amused expression on his face.

"Who's there?" Bob's voice came from one of the private workrooms off to the side of the large work area.

"Bob, what are you up to?" Dave asked.

"Ah! I did it! Well, at least part of it!" Bob yelled.

"Part of what?" Dave asked.

"Making the bodies!" Bob said. There was the sound of things being dropped on the floor and swearing before Bob's gnome face appeared from the workroom.

"How?" Dave asked, all of his attention focused on Bob.

"We grow them!" Bob clapped his hands together.

"I know that much." Dave waved his hands for Bob to elaborate.

"Okay, so we're thinking we're going to have to mass-produce these people's bodies as soon as the Jukal find out. Well, what if we were able to grow their bodies, without any imprinted memories, then upload the memories to their minds when the Jukal do find out? That way, we don't need to make their bodies all at the same time. We've got them all stocked up and ready!"

Dave and Malsour looked to each other.

"Can we actually do it?" Malsour asked.

"What materials are we going to need?" Dave added.

"We can do it. I've got a few things pulled together. Had to use Jeeves to do the heavy coding. As for materials, we're going to need tons of organic materials. The power consumption is going to be massive—and that's not even including the metals, soul gem constructs, and other items we'll need to make the machinery to not only create and store these bodies, but transfer the player's consciousness from the player vaults over to their bodies." Bob grimaced. They were running low on every kind of resource. Bob's resources were being used up at an alarming rate and their mining projects were only just slowing down the consumption rather than meeting their needs.

"Well, making a few million bodies is going to be hard work," Dave said with a wry smile.

Malsour gave Dave a smile. He knew that Dave was in charge of producing most of the materials.

"With the resources we have left, we can maybe get a third of everything set up," Bob said.

Dave's face looked pinched. The resources Bob had at his disposal were not inconsiderable. For them to only make up a third of everything that was needed, Dave didn't think that he'd be able to get the resources through normal means.

"I haven't wanted to do this for a long time as I know that it will bring attention after a while. Though, is there a way to trick the AIs and use my money in the Earth simulation here to speed things up?" Dave asked.

Bob let out a breath. "It's going to have to be small amounts. Maybe endorse the Stone Raiders, buy ad spots. Then that can reflect back on you in-game," Bob said. "I can have a look at it, but as you said, we can keep it up for maybe a year or two in Emerilia, before they start figuring out that you're playing the entire time that you're also supposed to be in the simulation."

"When they figure that out, then there's going to be hell to pay," Malsour said.

"Well, let's do what we can in the meantime. We're putting miners in Ashal around the outpost. We're building more ship bays as well as extensions for Terra." Dave shrugged. "If we have enough time, then we should be able to get all of these bodies made before the empire figures it all out."

Jekoni and Jung Lee looked at each other in confusion.

"Dave, you going to introduce us?" Bob asked.

"This is Archmage Jekoni and the man who was captured in the Six Affinities Temple, Jung Lee," Dave said. "Jung Lee, Jekoni, this is Bob, the Grey God, or Neut."

Jekoni and Jung Lee had alarmed looks on their faces. They'd heard of the Grey God, the seventh member of the Affinities Pantheon who oversaw the others and tried to balance things out. However, it was hard to associate that name with Bob, a simple-looking gnome wearing simple clothes and working on rows of machinery.

"Good to meet you. Seems that Dave trusts you and thinks that you might be able to help us on our insane little projects! I guess I should show you what we've got going on here." Bob waved them to his workshop.

There were several tanks to one side, a console of sorts. Then, banks on banks of metal plates that had been coded with runes. The whole room was warm with the multiple grand soul gems and three vault soul gems that were littered around the room.

In the center of the mess, there was a pod with runes and tubes running into it.

"So we take the DNA of the brains that are stored within the different facilities. We then get Jeeves to break it down, input it into this thing and then it can grow a body from that. This essentially uses the same idea as a tree. Feed the cells with the right kind of growing energy and wait till it forms the right shape. Once they're fully formed, they'll be just a toddler. We take them from this incubator to a growth chamber. In a couple of days, they go from being a toddler to a full grown adult. Then, they go into a dormant phase where they're maintained at the age they are within the Earth simulation, ready to have their mind and their memories uploaded in a moment," Bob said.

He made it sound simple, but he was essentially cobbling together systems that would be able to do the same thing as an Altar of Rebirth.

This was only based off his own knowledge and experience. Unlike the Aleph and Dave with teleportation, where they had been able to work off the portals to some degree, Bob was making this up as he went along.

It was much more impressive than the Aleph and Dave's cobbling together of different ideas. He'd come up with ideas, turned them into working machines, and replaced a system that people had used and understood for nearly fifteen hundred years.

"Now then, we just need time to infiltrate a moon," Malsour said.

"No time like the present!" Dave thrust his forefinger into the air. "Bob, this is—well, it's damn incredible. With this, we've got options and a path we can take. Have you figured out a way to automate this all?"

"I had Jeeves sort that out. Thankfully, for the heat sinks, we can use a heat-absorbing series of runes like the power stations and cycle it right back in so that we shouldn't show anything on the Jukal ships or AI's sensor sweeps." Bob sounded excited.

"With our Pandora's box, we're not opening up disease to the universe but bringing back the human race." Malsour shook his head.

"Well, it's not going to open itself! Shall we check and see if reversing the teleport array will work? I think we've got enough data from the nearly three hundred summons that people have gone through already." Dave rubbed his hands together, a wide smile on his face.

They had been recording data from the summoning halls that allowed people to soul bind a creature to them. In the last week, people had gone nuts and most Stone Raiders were eager to gain a companion that could increase their fighting ability.

Others went for the cute factor or a mix of both. The end result was a whole lot of summoned creatures in a very short time. People outside of the Stone Raiders had also paid for the privilege. It was expensive, but doing it through a summoner was not a guaranteed thing.

"Worth a try." Bob shrugged.

"Well, first we create an anchor point, then we ship over a portal. Open it there and in the seeder so we have a direct line. We can also add in onos from the Pandora's box facility to the seeder, which is going to turn into our portal and teleportation hub," Dave said.

"Well, we won't need to work it that much at the beginning. Later on, when we start expanding outward and need to reach more places, we'll have to move more items over there," Malsour said.

"Then we need to get working on the factories for mass production," Bob said.

Jung Lee, who had been listening to the entire conversation, sighed and shook his head. These three men were talking about technology and exploits that they were arranging as if it were nothing more than another day at work.

They were smart, driven, and more than a little willing to do something crazy, all of which came together to make them all the more impressive and dangerous. He might be the highest leveled person in the room, but at that time, he felt as if he were the weakest one. These three people would change not only the world, but the universe with their machinations.

Dave, Malsour, Bob, Jekoni, and Jung Lee went to the teleportation array to gain access to the different "summoning realms" they needed to change a lot of the array's settings over to.

After a few minutes, Jung Lee created a few dozen spirits that moved beyond his body to help move the different items.

"Hmm, they're similar to summoned creatures as they follow their soul-bound master's commands. Though, there is no loss in Willpower to send them out and control them. It's more like they're an extra limb than anything else." Malsour studied the spirits moving around the teleportation array.

"I have noticed that I feel as if there is less power that I am able to draw from," Jung Lee said.

"Would make sense. They're splitting off from the source. These are much more docile creatures compared to the true Free Affinity spirits. If they were to stay away from you like the other Free Affinity spirits they would then disappear. Regaining the strength that they took to form would take awhile," Bob said.

"What if they were to die?" Dave asked.

"Well, I think that they would lose a portion of their power, but most of it would make it back to Jung Lee." Bob shrugged.

"Though, I'm not sure. I've never seen someone who has a Free Affinity spirit from every Affinity in their body. It's pretty exciting!"

The spirits finished their work and returned to Jung Lee.

"Okay, there might not be air on the other side, so create big Mana shields so that you retain some air from here." Dave moved out of the teleportation array room.

"Where are you going?" Malsour yelled after him.

"I need that damn anchor!" Dave said.

Jekoni floated into the room. "This magical coding system is amazing!" Jekoni declared, waving his hands out wide.

"It certainly makes things easier," Malsour said.

"What's this?" Jekoni rushed around the room.

"Teleport array and general gravity manipulation chamber," Bob said.

"Hey, who's talking about my baby?" Dave returned to the room.

"You got it?" Malsour asked.

"One portal anchor ready and waiting." Dave tapped his faithful bag of holding.

"Well, let's fire her up!" Bob clapped his hands together.

"One trip to Emerilia's moon coming up!" Dave smacked the console in front of him.

The teleportation array hummed with power as runes lit along the walls and in the racks around the room.

Jung Lee looked around, his eyebrows rising. The power running through the room was not inconsiderable. He doubted someone with fifty grand soul gems would be able to support the high Mana output.

"Why is the output so high?" Jekoni asked.

"Well, this is supposed to be a one-way transition point. We're basically using the power from the teleportation array to lock onto that transition point and punch a hole through space. Think of a slide. We're at the bottom of it. With the teleportation array, we're punching from the bottom of the slide to the top without us having to try to climb up the slide. It's much more power to climb up a slide than just go down it," Dave said.

Jekoni and Jung Lee shared a look.

"There really are no limits to people's imaginations and things they can do," Jekoni said in quiet praise.

"If these people were alive when we were, they would have been knocked out and locked up," Jung Lee said.

"Heh, those were good times." The corners of Jekoni's mouth twitched upward.

The power reached the center of the teleportation array. One moment, they could see to the rune-covered wall on the other side of the room. The next, they were looking into a pitch-black room of some kind with a shimmering light surrounding it.

***

A screen appeared in front of Dave's face.

Quest Completed: Master of Space and Time Level 14

Come up with new possible theory (2/2)

Rewards: Unlock Level 15 quest

+15 to Willpower

+15 to Intelligence

+15 to Endurance

+15 to Agility

1,400,000 Experience

Quest: Master of Space and Time Level 15

Come up with new possible theory (2/3)

Rewards: Unlock Level 16 quest

Increase to stats

Class: Master of Space and Time

Status: Level 14

Greater understanding of Space and Time.

+210 to Willpower

Effects: +210 to Intelligence

+210 to Endurance

+210 to Agility

Quest Completed: Master of Gravitational Anomalies Level 10

Come up with new possible theory (2/2)

Rewards: Unlock Level 11 quest

+10 to all stats

1,000,000 Experience

Quest: Master of Gravitational Anomalies Level 11

Come up with new possible theory (2/3)

Rewards: Unlock Level 12 quest

Increase to stats

Class: Master of Gravitational Anomalies

Status: Level 10

Effects: Greater understanding of Gravitational Anomalies.
+100 to all stats

Quest Completed: Librarian Level 4

Use research to prove a theory

Rewards: Unlock Level 5 Quest

+10 to all stats

400,000 Experience

Class: Librarian

Status: Level 4

+40 to all stats

Effects: Read 5% faster

Understand 10% more of the information that you read

Quest: Librarian Level 5

Use research to prove a theory (1/2)

Rewards: Unlock Level 5 Quest

Increase to stats

> **Active Skill:** Teleportation
>
> **Level:** Master Level 4
>
> **Effect:** Able to create a device to teleport across distances.

Level 238

You have reached Level 238; you have **5** stat points to use.

"Yes." Dave put the five stat points directly into Intelligence and quickly checked his new stats.

Character Sheet

Name:	David Grahslagg	Gender:	Male
Level:	238	Class:	Dwarven Master Smith, Friend of the Grey God, Bleeder, Librarian, Aleph Engineer, Weapons Master, Champion Slayer, Skill Creator, Mine Manager, Master of Space and Time, Master of Gravitational Anomalies
Race:	Human/ Dwarf	Alignment:	Chaotic Neutral

Unspent points: 0

Health:	48,100	Regen:	24.02 /s
Mana:	15,780	Regen:	57.95 /s
Stamina:	5,320	Regen:	50.15 /s
Vitality:	481	Endurance:	1,201
Intelligence:	1,578	Willpower:	1,159
Strength:	532	Agility:	1,003

He quickly dismissed the screen.

"We're stable for now." Dave pulled out metal plates from his pocket. "These are called Band-Aids. They can disrupt Jukal signals to your interface. This means they can't activate the kill switch in our bodies and has the added benefit of making them unable to see where we are or what we're doing. While on Emerilia, it will be hazy. On the moon, they won't even sense us."

He tossed them out and everyone took one.

"Hey, where's my invite?" Steve asked from the doorway.

"Well, you've been cooped up in your workshop for so long we didn't know what you were doing in there." Malsour shrugged. Dave and Bob both let out short laughs at Malsour's hint.

"Hey, just gotta knock first." Steve winked.

"I don't think I want to even think of what you're doing in there." Dave sighed and tossed Steve a plate.

"Shall we get going?" Jung Lee asked.

"Did the voices tell you to say that?" Steve's eyes thinned.

"Voices?" Jung Lee asked, confused.

"Well, you've got like seven creatures inside you. Might be a bit full in there." Steve shrugged.

"You need to stop referencing the bad movies you've been watching." Dave sighed as he moved for the wormhole in the middle of the room. A gray shield extending a few feet outside of his body solidified.

"Hey, well, at least I'm ready for an exorcism or two! And a zombie plague! Which would be *soo* cool, by the way!" Steve said.

"Seems he hasn't changed much," Bob said to Malsour as they followed Dave, who'd disappeared through the wormhole.

"I think he's getting worse the more time he spends around the Stone Raiders," Malsour complained.

"You are a Stone Raider." Jung Lee followed them as Jekoni continued to study Steve as Steve poked his spiritual body, his finger going through Jekoni's face.

"Boop," Steve said.

"Will you stop that?" Jekoni's eyebrow twitched as he fought with his emotions. He was a great archmage of Per'Ush and now he was being poked by a rune-covered trash can that acted no different than an interested five-year-old.

"Never seen a ghost before. You're a rather noisy one. Thought that they just said boo?" Steve said.

"You're one to talk! Nothing you've said has made any sense since I met you!" The two of them continued to bicker as Malsour turned to Jung Lee.

"I call it the Stone Raiders effect. You learn to relax to the max when you get free time and then in a serious situation, you can immediately focus on the task at hand," Malsour said.

Jung Lee nodded. The Stone Raiders were a lively bunch when they weren't exploring, raiding, or on various quests. He'd seen how they acted on a raid. Working together, they were a force to be taken seriously.

Malsour and Bob both created shields around themselves. Jung Lee did the same as he passed through the teleport array's wormhole.

Jekoni's spiritual body disappeared from Emerilia and reappeared on the moon.

Jung Lee looked around.

Dave had cast mage light spells, filling the area with light.

Party Chat invite

You have been invited to the private party: One small step for man, one giant leap for mankind.

Do you wish to join?

Y/N

Jung Lee accepted the request.

"Leap for mankind? Really? That's a crap name," Bob said as Jung Lee joined the chat.

"Hey, it was a great quote, and we're the first people from Emerilia to ever be on this moon, so I'd say that it's pretty accurate," Dave said.

The atmosphere on the moon was thin, meaning that they had to rely on the air they'd brought with them and it also made talking impossible other than through the private party chat.

Steve entered the chat with Jekoni.

Jung Lee looked around the large storage area.

There were automated robotic limbs waiting along the roof on runners that would allow them to move freely. Along the walls, there were multiple crates with barcodes on them. The storage facility was massive, extending into the distance.

Nearly a kilometer in the distance, a circle lit up, showing a creature within a shield before they disappeared.

A limb that was over the circle lifted upward, carrying a box that was identical to the ones on the wall.

"This is the storage and distribution area for the summoned creatures. As someone summons a creature, it activates this system here. A creature is pulled from the storage racks, placed on the circle, and then transmitted to the summoning circle.

"There are also growing facilities that make these creatures as well as fusion reactors and material storage areas for the different nutrients and substrates needed to create and maintain these creatures," Bob said.

"Well, we don't have much time till our air runs out. We should get working," Dave said. Everyone seemed to be pulled into the air as they raced off, leaving the shimmering wormhole that showed the teleportation array on the other side.

They raced through the storage facilities, ducking into a large hallway with multiple sealed doors. Bob opened them ahead of time. They closed behind them.

It wasn't long until they came out into an area filled with storage bins.

They swung away from where they'd entered.

"Malsour?" Dave asked.

Malsour held his hand out. As it looked as if they were going to fly into a wall, the bland gray walls opened for them. The wall closed behind them; darkness surrounded them until Bob created a mage light. The rock ahead of them seemed to dissolve as the rock behind them reformed.

They went a few hundred meters before Dave brought them to a halt.

Malsour moved his hands, black shadows covering his body as he went to work. Jung Lee could sense what he was doing. He pulled all manner of resources from the surrounding area, and then compacted and firmed up the rock, creating massive supports as a facility started to form. They were on the ground floor of it. Every fifty meters, there were massive compacted and reinforced stone supports, creating squares through the area.

Cylinders flew from Dave. These automated carvers were nearly five hundred strong as they spread outward. White Mithril tips came from one end, cutting into the walls and leaving lines of runes across the growing open area.

Malsour pushed the ceilings up fifty meters while Steve tossed out mage lights that attached to the pillars, lighting up the massive area.

Bob moved to where the right edge of the facility would be. With a wave of his hands, a complicated number of runes were laid out around the open space. He unfolded a bag of holding he was carrying until it was nearly ten meters wide.

He held the edge. Like a magic trick back on Earth, as he lifted the bag from the floor, a ten-meter-wide metallic stand appeared on the floor. On top of the five-meter-tall stand, there was a metal sphere with a radius of ten meters.

The two metallic objects were covered in runes, as well as pipes and different lines.

Jung Lee and Jekoni looked on in awe as in front of their very eyes, a facility was being born.

Bob pulled out what looked like a box created from soul gems. Inside there was an ebony box with glowing runes.

Jekoni and Jung Lee's eyes stuck to the box. The rich Mana signature of the item was alarming.

Bob threw it to Dave.

He took the box and placed it against the wall. His army of carving cylinders were making short work of the walls.

The soul gem box expanded outward and grabbed onto the wall. The soul gem expanded across the wall, like frost rapidly forming on a window.

The soul gem filled in the different runes that had been formed, glowing with power.

Dave floated over to Bob while Malsour walked forward. As he did so, the stone in front of him parted, moving up and down, to reveal solid stone pillars and piles of resources on the ground.

"The runes are so that no one can sense what we're doing in here, an added safety precaution. Also, they'll allow people to walk around with some gravity. The only reason we're not floating off is because Dave's orbs are exerting the same gravity on us as we would have on Emerilia. That box-looking thing that the soul gem sheet is growing out of is a Mana well. The soul gem will power the runes. Later on, it can be commanded to grow the different machines and items that Bob will need to create people.

"That sphere-looking thing on the pedestal is a fusion reactor. It can pump out more power than a dozen Aleph power stations." Steve pointed to Bob, who was with the same massive bag of holding, revealing what looked like big metal lockers. "Those are factories to make the repair bots and mining drills this place is going to need."

Jung Lee looked at it all. In less than fifteen minutes, they'd pulled out these artifacts and they had built a facility two hundred meters wide, one hundred long, and growing.

Steve walked over to where Bob and Dave were; Jekoni followed as the soul gem sheet spread under their feet.

Steve listed off the things that Bob pulled from his bag of holding.

"That's a sensor package. It will allow us to make an image of the whole moon so we know the best place to mine. Also, it will have the ability to allow us to see outside of the moon to map the things surrounding it. That's an automated mining drill. It's small now, but those factories will be able to make bigger ones with enough resources, power, and time. That's a small refinery—got a couple of those. Automated carts and a few repair bots."

The different items kept falling out of the bag. Bob placed them along the right-most wall, creating an area filled with equipment and machinery.

Some things, like the repair bots and automated carts, were activated.

Steve gestured and they started to move.

"You're controlling the automated machines?" Jekoni asked.

"For now. Once Jeeves's module is set up, he'll take over everything. Right now, I'm just going to collect the resources Malsour has identified, and pour them into the small refineries so that we can start putting the factories to work," Steve said as they reached the fusion reactor, where Dave was working on a console that was connected to the pedestal of the massive machine by lines of glowing soul gems that were inlaid into the floor.

The soul gem sheet filled in the runes around the fusion plant and continued to spread outward. Its speed was slowing down, but it had still covered a massive area in just a few short minutes.

As the sheet reached the factories and other stationary machines that Bob had placed down, the soul gem sheet created lines from the machines to the fusion plant in the ground.

"This should help out a bit." Dave pressed a command button on the console in front of him.

A line that connected the Mana well mounted in the wall through the soul gem sheet and into the fusion plant glowed with power as energy was fed into the fusion plant.

The soul gem sheet's progress halted. All of the power that was stored in the sheet and coming from the Mana well was now poured into the fusion plant.

Slowly, runes along the pedestal started to glow with power, finally reaching the sphere. There was a faint whirring noise as the runes on the sphere lit with power even slower than the ones on the pedestal. The power line from the Mana well reached its limit as light spilled out from it.

Dave was completely focused on the console. Over his shoulder, Steve watched everything that was happening.

"Hydrogen read is good; gravity is ramping up. Good increase in pressure," Dave muttered. Steve nodded behind him, his playful attitude gone as they went through the fusion reactor's start-up.

The *whoump whoump* of the fusion reactor sped up, becoming faster and faster as it seemed to become one continuous noise. Slowly, the sphere started to rise from the pedestal. The top of the pedestal where the reactor core had rested was covered in various runes that glowed with Mana.

The runes over the reactor continued to climb as the noise coming from it reduced. As it did, faint distorting waves seemed to form around the core.

As the sound died, these distorting waves grew. As the noise disappeared, the waves halted and then started to converge on the reactor once again. They stopped when they were just a few inches from the exterior of the reactor.

The last runes started to light up faster and faster until they reached the peak of the sphere.

The light that connected to the Mana well dimmed and then went out.

Dave and Steve checked over various different readings on their console.

"Even though that power is contained, it's stronger than anything I've ever come close to seeing. Even more vicious than a ley line," Jekoni said in a solemn voice.

"With great power comes great possibilities." Dave pressed another switch on the console. The runes across the floating core and pedestal underneath flared with brilliant light.

Jung Lee blinked his eyes a few times to try to get rid of the bright afterimages. As his sight recovered, he noticed the lines within the soul gem sheet branching out from the fusion reaction glowed with power. He looked to the factories and reactors that were spreading out in the space that they had, unfolding themselves and readying their various systems for operation.

The fusion reactor was now sending power to the soul gem-constructed floor, walls, and roof. Its rate of growth climbed, racing to cover where the army of carvers had been as they filled the ground, and tried to catch up with Malsour, who had expanded the facility until it was two hundred meters wide, forty meters tall, and four hundred meters long.

The room vibrated with power. It had been less than thirty minutes since they had entered this area when it had been nothing more than rock and stone untouched and unseen for centuries.

"Looks good. Now, time to get that portal set up," Dave said. The group followed him as he floated over to near the center of the facility. Malsour finished off the farthest wall as mining drills approached him. They'd take what he'd started and build on it to expand the facility.

The refineries weren't that large, but they still were ready to accept the materials Malsour had pulled from the stone where the facility had been and were now in the process of being picked up by the automated carts and repair bots wandering the area.

Bob was busy working on a console, referencing his interface as he worked.

Dave pulled components from his bag. Steve took some of the parts. There was a central pillar that was connected by a series of rune-covered metal bands that reached four smaller metal pillars.

"This is the anchor?" Jung Lee asked.

"Yeah. Basically, it will act as a focal point for me to connect to when bringing back a portal." Dave looked over the construct. He checked a few things before the pillars and runes activated. The pillars started to spin faster and faster until the runes on them were just a faint blur of light.

"Be back in a minute." Dave disappeared.

"Teleportation magic?" Jekoni said, his voice a shocked whisper.

"Yeah, he figured it out awhile ago, but he can't use it anywhere where the Jukal have eyes. If he was to do so, then they'd catch on and we'd have to advance all of our plans," Steve said.

"All of your plans?" Jung Lee asked.

"Well, you didn't think that just making a moonbase was our only plan?" Steve smiled.

Jung Lee looked around as he sensed something changing.

The soul gem sheets in the areas that weren't occupied started to grow. They formed multiple capsules stacked closely together while entire sections expanded with rune-covered soul gem sheets inside.

Jung Lee recognized these from the items within Bob's workshop.

However, there had only been one capsule in that room. Here, there were thousands being created, as well as machinery meant to move the capsules.

The progress was slow because of its complicated nature. Even though it was slow, with the power of the fusion reactor and Mana well, they were growing at a rate visible to the eye.

Malsour returned from his work. The mining drills were already looking to expand the facility.

"The mining drills will open up more areas, while the soul gem construct will fill the inside, making it impossible for the Jukal to detect this place as well as compacting the pillars, ceiling, and floors so that the whole thing is structurally sound," Steve said.

"Is Bob pulling out plants?" Jung Lee saw Bob working in an area that was growing a series of floors on top of one another, with a series of bins on each floor under what looked like strip lighting.

"I was wondering how they were going to get the materials to make the bodies." Steve sounded impressed.

"They're going to use these plants to make bodies?" Jekoni asked.

"Why? Looking to possess one, ghost?" Steve asked.

"Why did I ask?" Jekoni muttered.

There was a flash of light where the anchor was located. If one was able to see the origin of this light, they would have seen a complicated spell formation in the middle of the anchor point.

Everyone stepped back under the blinding light.

"Seems that his teleportation ability has become more refined," Steve said.

Jung Lee was surprised at Steve's words. *Seems that in the last couple of weeks, I have been met with nothing but surprises.* Jung Lee smiled as the light faded away.

The anchor was gone, but in its place there was a massive portal, the kind that linked Emerilia to a number of different realms with different creatures.

Jung Lee looked at it, remembering the portal that he had guarded for centuries.

This one had four identical clamps at the northwest, northeast, southeast, and southwest points. They were thick with magical coded runes.

Another massive clamp also rested at the top of the portal. Each of them was connected by a band of soul gems that ran between them. At the bottom clamps, they connected to the soul gem sheet.

A thick power line grew through the soul gem sheet, connecting the reactor to the portal.

As soon as it connected, the portal flared to life. A grinding noise came from the portal.

Jung Lee stepped backward. Unlike the fusion reactor, the Mana that powered the portal wasn't contained; it was wild and powerful.

The runes on the overlaying clamps activated, lighting up.

He sensed the different Magical Circuits were rotated into place and then moved within the massive circular housing of the portal.

Hundreds of pieces moved at the same time before finally the first locked into position. It was a ripple effect as, piece by piece, the Magical Circuit that was the portal locked in the different circuits.

The last one came online and the power surged once again.

Jekoni stepped backward as Steve laughed wildly.

Runes along the portal's ring lit up from the outer band, reaching inward. When they reached the inner band, they were no longer looking through the facility. Instead, they were looking at Dave, who stood in a warehouse-looking facility with all manner of materials behind him.

He walked through the portal. "Like the show?" He smiled.

Jung Lee and Jekoni didn't know what to say. These magical artifacts were well in excess of anything that they had ever seen in their lifetimes. These four people had combined these artifacts and their knowledge to make a facility that they could never have dreamed of making in their previous lives, even at the peak of their careers and positions.

"Bob, once you're done with the greenhouse, I want to connect this place to the *Datskun*. Then I want to set the miners and bots to making our exit before returning to work on the different facilities here. How long do you think until we can start growing bodies?" Dave asked.

"I'm going to need to do a number of test runs to make sure everything works. I'll have Jeeves set up soon." Bob poured items out of his bag of holding into the different growing bays of the greenhouse he had created in a few of the fifty-meter-by-fifty-meter squares that rested between the spaced-out supports.

If one was to look closely, they would see that a Mana shield covered the greenhouse and that it was slightly hazy inside as Bob had released canisters of stored air within the enclosed area.

"I can get started on the exit right now. Going to need the components sooner or later, but we can leave that to the bots here. I'd feel more safe if I do the mining. Don't want the Jukal seeing us, especially with it needing to be so close to the moon's surface," Malsour said.

"Okay, sounds good. I'm going to go to Pandora's box, shut down the teleportation array and set up a portal there to connect to moonbase, shipyard one, and *Datskun*."

Dave looked to Jung Lee and Jekoni. "If you need more air, just release your shield here, step through the shield, and grab some from the other side. We're going to need to fill up this place. I have to move automated carts to the seeder, then capture air there, and move it to the moonbase. We've never connected the facilities together properly. Having them all accessible is going to really speed things up!" Dave smiled as Jekoni and Jung Lee could only look at each other.

"All of this is a bit...insane," Jekoni said.

"Ah, just a bunch of ideas that came together." Dave smiled.

Just came together? I doubt anyone would have the resources, drive, or balls to do something on this scale! All right under the noses of a race that has an entire planet filled with one of the races that they conquered, for entertainment!

Chapter 3: A Melding of Ideas

Dave wiped his eye, a faint tiredness still pulling at them. He found Deia next to him, his knee experiencing a number of kicks from her large belly.

"Seems that someone is antsy this morning." Dave gently put his hand on Deia's stomach. The latter was asleep, only faintly moving with the kicks as she tightened her grip on her pillow while her legs tightened on Dave's.

He smiled, looking at her cute face as she tried to get a few more minutes of rest.

A buzzing noise came from within his head. It was his interface's alarm. He opened it up, finding a reminder about a meeting he had with Commander Sato and his developmental engineer Edwards. They were the leading military officers of the only group of humans outside of Emerilia that Dave knew about.

Seeing as he wasn't going to make it out of bed without a crowbar and waking up Deia, he pulled out a small Mirror of Communication from his bag of holding next to his bed.

After his work on the moonbase, the place was nearly self-sufficient. The portal network was set up and Bob was working in the moonbase on creating bodies for the players who were stored in the north and south poles until the current players needed to be replaced.

He felt a deep relief now that the moonbase was set up. Even now, it was currently growing with mining drills and soul gem constructs expanding outward. Automated carts were shifting in materials from shipyard one, and mining drills had been sent to the Ashal outpost to begin mining within the week.

Things were coming together slowly.

Dave touched the small Mirror of Communication. It connected to the large one that he had gained so long ago when he'd found that hidden cabin in the woods.

The room he was in disappeared as he accessed the conference room. This one was a modern-looking place, much like the kind of place Dave had seen every day when he had been Austin Zane, the CEO of the Rock Breakers Corporation.

Sato and Edwards were waiting for him. Both of them looked to be in high spirits.

"Hey you two, what's up?" Dave asked.

He'd been wrapped up in so many projects that he hadn't had much time to spend with the two. Instead, he had been funneling them all of his information on different magically coded systems that he had come up with.

Shard, the rune-coded AI of the Aleph, had also been keeping them updated on the situation on Emerilia.

"We think that, for a change, we might have a solution to one of your problems," Edwards said with an excited look on his face. He looked as if he wanted to jump up from his seat and run around the room.

"Okay." Dave leaned forward, curious.

"We've noticed that you've got a few problems with inertia and gravity management. Right now you know how to control gravity yourself, but can't find a system to manage it for you. We've got plans for a gravity sensor that would allow a stable gravity field within an accelerating gravity field. It would constantly be feeding information back to your systems so that the two fields would cancel out each other. Then, we've also got a more general inertia system that you could adapt or use. Might be useful to have as a backup, redundancies and all." Edwards opened his interface and sent files over.

Looking at the files, Dave realized that he was not just looking at systems. These were coded from runes. Adapting them from technology to runes was time-intensive, either requiring multiple different magical coders or an AI to translate everything over. With this, Dave could save weeks of time.

With his high Intelligence, he was able to look over the different items and figure out how they would work by the runes and their diagrams.

Tense silence spread through the conference room as Dave continued to look at the plans.

Finally, he sat back, a great weight lifted from his shoulders as he smiled. "Thanks. I was looking to tackle that system in the near future. It was going to be a pain in the ass to sort out. With this, we can leap ahead and start working on the drive systems and other subsystems. This will accelerate my plans quite a bit."

"What is your plan, Dave?" Sato asked, even as Edwards and Dave had large smiles on their faces. Their joy dimmed somewhat with Sato's cold voice.

Sato was a good man and one Dave had come to trust and value. However, he could feel that Sato in this moment was not his friend, but rather someone who was looking to protect himself and understand the motivations of a possible ally.

The weight of this simple question was not something to be brushed off.

"My plan." Dave let out a breath through his pursed lips. "Right now, we don't have a plan but a number of contingencies. We're building habitats and ships, a way for people to survive the Jukal kill switches and plans to wipe us and Emerilia out. For that, we need to survive against the creatures that are unleashed from whatever prison they've been held within.

"If we can do that, then we can start seeing about which plan of action we can take against the Jukal. Or, there is always the possibility that for us and the POEs to survive, we might need to use or do something that would bring the Jukal's attention down on us. As much as I wish we had a plan, we can only ready the parts that we might need," Dave said solemnly.

"When the time comes when you fight the Jukal and you do have a plan, my leaders might be swayed if it was good enough. As much as I and my people are thankful for all you've given us and helped us, we don't want to expose where we're located and surviving right now. If we can hold out longer and build our strength, then we can hit them later on. Though, if you give us a way to hit them back, then it is possible that my leaders would allow me to assist you," Sato said in a strained voice.

Dave nodded and smiled at Sato. He could see how much Sato wanted to help him, though he had people he had to answer to. In the end, going to war wasn't his decision. It was only when war was declared that he would be able to move his forces and people to assist Dave and those on Emerilia.

"Don't worry, Sato. When the time comes, you'll know and the Jukal won't know *what* hit them." Dave smiled.

***

Mal hummed slightly as he swayed back and forth. Mal watched as his son's eyes fought against sleep, his hands curling up slightly as spit trailed down his chin and onto Mal's shoulder.

There was a slight rumbling in the other room. Mal didn't move from his position, continuing on. He knew if he paused, then his little boy would more likely than not wake up in a foul mood and he'd have to start all over again.

He heard light footsteps approaching the room. He turned slowly to find Fire in the doorway to the nursery.

Her face softened into a smile. "How are my two boys doing?" she said in a hushed tone, moving to Mal.

"Just about ready to go for a nap," Mal said back, in a low voice.

Fire smiled at Mal as his arm wrapped around her and they both looked down on their little Desmond, who had fallen asleep, oblivious of his parents and the world.

Who would have thought that the infamous elven Fire mage Oson'Mal would once again be the nursemaid to his second child?

Mal's smile grew. He had raised Deia mostly by himself as Fire had been too scared. Now, with Fire by his side, he couldn't be happier.

Deia and Fire acted more like sisters than mother and daughter, but that was normal with elves after a certain age. After their time apart, they were now finding common ground and their bonds were becoming strong. The fact that they had both been pregnant at the same time had also helped in bringing them closer.

If it wasn't for the upcoming event, then Mal would have been the happiest man on Emerilia.

"How did things go?" Mal's voice hardened as he looked to Fire.

She took a deep breath and rested her head on his shoulder. "Water's advancing his knowledge on spells at an incredible rate. He's going to be one hell of a force to contend with in the future. As for the rest? I've told Jelanos and Alamos to call on the mage's guild and college.

"When these creatures start appearing, the college will move to its guild duties. I told them to go and talk to the Stone Raiders. With them, they can make the mages even more effective."

Mal kissed her forehead, hearing the frustration in her voice.

She took a deep breath again, as if trying to push those frustrations and fears from her mind. "Bob says that he has a safe place for everyone to hide." Fire's eyes lingered on their baby.

Mal didn't have to be a mind reader to know what she was thinking. His face hardened. Letting their boy be taken away somewhere while they looked to fight for Emerilia would be a struggle. "Everything we do is for our family and the countless other families on Emerilia."

Fire didn't say anything as her arms wrapped around Mal and tightened. Her eyes became cloudy with emotions as his arm tightened around her. "Then it's time that you started training again. You might be one of the strongest elven mages, though I know you've fallen out of practice in your later years," she said.

"I'd say I'm pretty active." He gave her a saucy look.

She pouted and hit his chest lightly so as to not disturb her boy resting on Mal's shoulder.

Chapter 4: First Marker Opens

"People of the Jukal Empire, today we bring you a special event!" The Jukal announcer's purple fur-covered, toad-like body moved in excitement as his words were transmitted across the Jukal Empire.

"An event never seen before in the history of Emerilia! That's right—the event Of Myths and Legends! The creatures that were sealed away by the Affinities Pantheon or by the people of Emerilia will once again return to Emerilia! Will the humans survive or will they be torn apart? Will these returning creatures destroy Emerilia or be destroyed by it as we saw with the Dragon King Akatol? Let us find out! The first group have remained undetected before their spawn-in. We have the name of the first released creatures! They are the Elsoom spores! Please refer to your Emerilian encyclopedias to know the stats on the Elsoom spores."

A male Jukal laid in bed, looking at a screen above his bed as tens of beauties from every single race in the empire, all dressed in sheer clothing that left little to the imagination, attended his needs.

Even with all these beauties, this Jukal, who had only experienced the finest items, lived for one thing: the brutality and entertainment of Emerilia.

His eyes thinned as the announcer faded away and a map appeared, showing where the Elsoom had spawned.

He ate the offered food with little interest. This powerful Jukal was the emperor of the Jukal Empire. From him, all decisions were made for hundreds of races and trillions of people.

He was also the biggest supporter of Emerilia. While his advisers ran the empire, he cared only about the biggest game in the universe—where the humans fought among themselves.

***

Dave was working in the Terra smithy when he got an alert from his interface. His face paled as he looked out into the smithy. All of the dwarven master smiths had stopped working as they, too, had received the same message.

They put down their tools and moved to the conference rooms that held Mirrors of Communication. The Council of Anvil and Fire had been called to a meeting of war.

As they arrived in the conference room that the council always used, the normal laughter and cheerful chatter was missing. Endur sat at the head of the table; there were four dwarves around him, two on each side. These dwarves were the leaders of the military council, they also commanded the warclans across the entirety of Emerilia.

"It seems that the event has started," Endur said.

An interface appeared in front of everyone. A marker appeared in the forest at the base of Norkurn Mountain, which bordered on Ossai, a Zolun tribe city that bordered the Northern Grasslands and Heval plains on the Heval continent.

"We had people reporting that they were being affected by a corrosive poison on the southern side of the mountain. The wind was passing through this forest when it reached the mountain. We've since sealed the mountain and sent out messengers to the surrounding area. The corrosive poison is not only powerful but it has a parasitic element to it. One of the infected had their forearm affected, which attempted to then kill him and wound others to pass on," Endur said in a grave tone.

Fighting an enemy straight up was one thing; fighting an airborne pathogen was hell.

"Do we know if they have any weaknesses?" Dave asked.

"Fire seems to do the trick," a war council member said.

"Are we in contact with Ossai?" Kol asked.

"They are evacuating, for the most part. Others are staying behind. I'm scared that they will simply pass on the infection," Endur said. "The only good news is that it seems after two minutes, the poison loses its effectiveness unless it has gained access to a person's body. Even then, if someone is to take an anti-effect or poison potion, then they could defeat the poison."

"I think it's best that we hold up and we take this to Terra. We are mostly skilled in Dark and Earth Affinities. If we can get people with Fire Affinity to aid us, as well as the strength of Terra, it would go a long way to firming that alliance, as well as showing everyone how we're in this together," Dave said.

Endur looked to the war council leaders and the dwarven master smiths. "Very well. Send a message to the Stone Raiders in Terra. If they do not act within a day, then we will combat this ourselves." The latter was said to the war council, who nodded their heads. It was on them to come up with a backup plan to defeat this poison and whatever was behind it.

"Dismissed!" Endur said.

Dave exited the Mirror of Communication and reappeared in Terra. Immediately, his messages popped up with a full report from Endur.

He sent the message to the Stone Raiders' leadership, as well as Party Zero, Fire, Bob, and Jung Lee.

Dave ran to the top of the smithy. As soon as he was on the roof, he shot off toward the Stone Raiders' tower.

An emergency message flashed across the city.

Stone Raiders and the armed forces that various embassies had brought to Terra all stopped what they were doing and moved to their staging positions. The air was filled with people flying from one place to another. The roofs had a sea of bodies rushing over them as squads on the ground bellowed for people to move out of the way as they moved.

Dave passed through a barrier around the Stone Raiders' towers. His amulet, made to look like a simple rock, allowed him entry. Doors opened ahead of him as he quickly made his way to the conference room.

Leaders from all of the different higher-leveled parties came in as they could. The guild leadership also rushed in from wherever they had been.

"Shut up and listen up!" Dwayne's voice cut through the room after ten minutes. People were still drifting in but Josh and Lucy stood from their seats, ready to start the briefing.

"It seems that the first of the spawn points has opened somewhere in the vicinity of Norkurn Mountain and the city of Ossai in Heval. I will let Lucy get into the details." Josh sat down.

"It seems that the creatures or whatever has been released excrete a kind of corrosive poison that has an added parasitic effect. The poison can reduce your hit points slowly. If one is to have an open wound, then the poison can get into the body, increasing the rate that one will lose hit points as well as take over their limbs."

"Elsoom spores!" Jekoni yelled, his face a mass of angry wrinkles as he floated cross-legged, with his arms over his chest.

Everyone looked to him as Jung Lee seemed to teleport behind him with his great speed. Jung Lee didn't even have a touch of sweat on him after displaying that speed.

"Elsoom spores?" Lucy asked.

"They were around while I still had a body. They look like five-foot-tall mushrooms. They release spores all over the place. Given time, they'll make a spore field around themselves that no one can get through without being infected. You have to burn the bastards out. They're weak creatures but their poison and its effects are powerful. The spores can take over a person, turning them into a mad beast. Many called them zombies. Once the spores have bodies that they control, they'll multiply within and move to attack other living creatures. Once they get spores into open wounds, then the creature has just hours before they lose control. Creatures that have been heavily infested can explode from being hit, turning into a mass of spores," Jekoni said.

Dave shivered at his words.

"How did you defeat them?" Kim asked.

"We Fire bomb spelled the hell out of the infected cities and then burned everything that was close to them," Jekoni said in a dark voice.

"Is there a way to cure the infected?" Jules asked.

"Well, as long as a person gets a Health potion before they're fully infected, they can stop the spread and start fighting back. Otherwise, once infected, removing the infection would take a powerful healer," Jekoni said.

"I might be able to make a potion that could counteract the effects of the poison, allow people to enter this spore-ridden area for some time, as well as destroy the infection within people," Jung Lee said.

"Anything you need, let us know," Josh said to Jung Lee, who nodded. "Jekoni, anything you know, we're going to need to learn." A prompt stopped Josh.

Event: Of Myths and Legends

You have figured out a race of the first creatures to spawn in!

Elsoom Spores have once again returned to Emerilia. These spores control armies of living creatures. Letting them run rampant will lead to infected cities that you must retake or destroy.

Objectives:

Stop the spread of the spores and infected.

Defeat the Elsoom Spores

Remove the infection

Failure:

Emerilia becomes overrun with infected

Become infected

Rewards:

Experience

Resistance to all poisons increase by 10%

Change in relationship with Dwarves/Zolun tribes depending on actions.

"Well, at least we know what they are for sure," Dwayne said.

"The dwarves are ready to fight back in any manner. Is it possible to make potions to kill off the spores and rain them down on the Elsoom spores?" Dave asked.

"I can make the potion. I do not know about how to disperse it," Jung Lee said.

Dave and Malsour looked to each other.

"We can take care of that," Malsour said.

"I will inform the other races and embassies that are within Terra," Josh said.

People moved from their seats, looks of excitement on their faces. The event had finally started!

"I will need to go to Ossai," Jung Lee said.

"We have a number of onos on standby for just this thing. Dave, get one placed in Ossai," Lucy said, overhearing Jung Lee.

"Can do." Dave nodded. Unlike the other members of the Stone Raiders, the leadership all had solemn expressions on their faces. They knew the reality of the situation.

***

Just twenty minutes later, Jung Lee stepped through a teleport pad in Terra and exited an ono into Ossai.

"Time we get to work," Jekoni said.

Jung Lee sniffed the air. The spores had spread here but they weren't that thick yet. The infection would start off slowly within these people.

Waiting for him was the city's tribe leader, as well as a number of tanned men and women wearing polished bronze armor and holding spears.

"Mister Jung Lee, thank you for coming." The tribe leader of Ossai extended his hands in greeting.

"Thank you. I must go to the point closest to the edge of the city. I can sense that the spores have made it here in limited numbers. I would advise that you lock the city down. If people with even a slight infection are to leave the city, it will grow slowly at first before taking over their bodies. I will have a cure made soon enough," Jung Lee said.

The tribe leader paled at Jung Lee's words. "Seal the city!" the tribe leader ordered without hesitation. With the tribes, infections and disease were common, their effects enough to cripple entire tribal towns. Passing it on or allowing it to spread to the other tribes would cripple the Zolun tribes.

People with spears ran off as the tribe leader waved for Jung Lee to follow him. "I will show you to the wall closest to the forest," the tribe leader said.

"Thank you." Jung Lee tilted his head as they quickly moved through the streets. No one stopped them as they moved.

Jung Lee stood on the wall, his eyes closed as he took in the smell and taste of the spores. It was much thicker at the wall. If one was to see, waves of heat emanated from his body, killing any of the spores that made it into his body or rested on him.

After five minutes, Jung Lee frowned. "I will begin." With a wave of his hand, an alchemist's table appeared with all manner of objects on it. He pulled out ingredients from a pouch of holding on his waistband.

"Jekoni, could you screen people and put protections in place?" Jung Lee's head bent to his work as he put different ingredients into a bowl, grinding them up.

"Can do. Tribe leader, going to need some of your people and mages. Also, we should activate the ono's shield now so that more spores don't make it into the city," Jekoni said.

The tribe leader nodded, his scarred features tight. This man, who had been a warrior in the past, once again emerged. His battle was not on the dunes of the Heval plains or the grasslands. Now he was fighting for his city, his family, and the tribes that looked to him for their governing.

Time didn't have any bearing on Jung Lee as he worked at his table.

A shield appeared around Ossai, keeping people in and blocking any more spores from entering. A number of guards on the wall looked at Jung Lee nervously as he ground up different ingredients, boiled them, and turned them into pastes and powders, putting them through different instruments with quiet precision.

They had lived to fight off enemies of all kinds—people and creatures—and could stare down an army easily. Facing this infection, they were scared. There was nothing to fight: all of their hopes were in Jung Lee.

Mages were guided by Jekoni to create rain within the shielded city. This water was then boiled, destroying any of the spores that were on the buildings or in the air to slow the progression of the infection. Wells were also brought to a boil. Jekoni sensed infected tribe members and had them picked out to help with the wall defenses. Telling them they were infected would only create a panic.

Jekoni might be brash but he wasn't heartless.

Jung Lee opened a tap from one of his different glass purifiers. A glowing blue-green liquid filled a vial as big as Jung Lee's thumb, and with a wave of his hand, the heat of the solution was removed by the Fire Affinity spirit as he passed it to a guard.

"Give this to Jekoni," Jung Lee said.

The guard nodded and hurried off, another taking their place.

"Fill these vials—don't spill." Jung Lee brought out boxes of vials as he waved at the spout filled with blue-green glowing liquid.

Jung Lee moved to another part of the table, the guard now working as his assistant without complaint. Jung Lee waved his hand and a large cauldron appeared in front of him. He tossed in a large number of ingredients.

"Have those who sell potions come to me with the potions to stop infections, poisons, and status effects," Jung Lee told another guard.

They barked at four others before they rushed off. More guards took their places without getting in Jung Lee's way.

Jung Lee waved his hand. Water flowed from his hand as his Air and Water Affinities worked together, drawing it from the atmosphere.

He snapped his fingers on the other hand; blue flames shot out from his fingers and darted under the cauldron, raising the temperature. Water stopped falling into the cauldron as Jung Lee whisked his finger above the cauldron. A portion of the Water spirit darted into the cauldron, moving the ingredients around. The water changed color as the medicinal ingredients seeped into the mixture, giving off an aromatic fragrance.

A guard returned, panting. "Jekoni says to keep them coming, a bit strong but he can administer doses so that they're not wasted."

"Take the filled ones to him as soon as possible." Jung Lee waved to the other guard who filled vials quickly and carefully, not letting a drop go to waste.

"Yes sir." The guard, even though he was tired, took the full vials, placed them into his bag of holding and then raced off once again.

Jung Lee changed a few settings on the last glass apparatus that purified the potion and was being poured out into vials.

With a wave of his hand, water appeared in a ball. A flame heated it from underneath. The water raced through the different dirty apparatus, followed by an air stream to dry them out. Jung Lee was already mashing up more ingredients within his mortar and pestle.

Once again he refined the different ingredients, turning them into pastes, powders, and liquids. He placed them in different glass tubes to be strained, or in crucibles to be heated.

He turned back to the cauldron and looked at the purple liquid inside. The wind carried over the cauldron, allowing him to smell it.

"Good." He waved to a guard. "Take this to the ono, pass it through, and say that it's for Malsour and Dave. It will directly attack the spores but will need a wide dispersion," Jung Lee said.

The guard nodded. He took five others to carry the cauldron to the ono.

After ten minutes, another yellow solution was falling into vials smaller than the blue/green liquid-filled.

"Fill these up as well," Jung Lee said. More vials appeared in front of him, leaving two guards filling vials from different spouts on his alchemist table.

"I've brought the different people selling or making potions," a guard said. Behind him was a group of men and women, from merchants to potion makers.

"Good. Show me your different potions I requested," Jung Lee said. They all pulled out different potions quickly and without fuss.

"Cure—will remove the effects on those without controlled limbs. Protect against the spores for a limited time if exposed. Useless. Useless." Jung Lee examined the different potions, classifying each as *cure, prevention*, and *remove effect*—throwing in *useless* more often than not.

In a matter of minutes, he had highlighted which potions would work and which would not.

"Potion makers remain," Jung Lee said. The guards pushed the others away as Jung Lee worked on his interface quickly. He created three different potion formulas with the headings of Cure, Prevention, and Suppression.

"The cure will destroy the infection in advanced cases. Prevention will allow someone to walk within the spores without being affected for a time. Suppression will remove the status effects if applied quickly enough and will destroy spores that they directly interact with. Break up into three groups due to what potion you would be best at making. I will provide ingredients and tools as well as twenty gold for an hour of work. If you are fast enough, you will gain a bonus." Jung Lee waved his hand and alchemy tables appeared from his arm as the street was quickly covered in equipment.

The potion makers quickly broke into three groups as Jung Lee then removed ingredients listed on the different potion formula sheets.

"See that they have all they require." Jung Lee handed three hundred gold to the guard captain who had brought them to him.

The man nodded solemnly.

"I will be with Jekoni, looking over the infected," Jung Lee said.

"Yes sir." The guard bowed his head slightly.

Jung Lee seemed to float into the air, moving in a flash toward where Jekoni was.

He sent messages from his interface to the Stone Raiders' leadership and Dave. Now that he had created the three potions, they could be spread to Norkurn Mountain and a counterattack could be made against the Elsoom spores, so that they could be stopped.

Chapter 5: Chemical Warfare

Dave was once again back in his smithy. Already the different groups within Terra were armoring themselves up, readying to deal with the Elsoom spores.

Dave stood over a grand working, his hands moving across the soul gem surface. Within, someone might be able to see a thick purple liquid that had been so compacted it looked to be a crystal. Multiple seals were layered within the grand working. Dave let out a breath and held out the shell to the waiting dwarven shield bearer.

With a grunt, he took the grand working, depositing it into their bag of holding before he rushed off toward the teleport pad connected to Norkurn Mountain.

With Jung Lee's potions, the dwarves had gone into overdrive. All across Emerilia, potions were flooding into Terra and then Norkurn. They'd covered the entire city within the mountain in the purple potion that killed spores on contact. People were all being checked out for infection; the cure was passed around to those who showed any signs of infection.

The Terra smithy was filled with all manner of people who knew how to make grand workings, combining the soul gem container with the suppressing potion and powering the whole thing from Terra's power grid.

Dave wiped sweat from his face; seeing that there was no more potion to work with, he turned to his furnace and the bow within. He took a Stamina potion, swigging it back as he moved with a determined face to the furnace.

He took a few moments, looking at the faintly wavy design of the bow, restoring himself slightly. He stepped forward into the heat of the furnace.

Waves of heat rolled over him as he put his hands into the furnace, touching the bow with both of his hands. The metal and materials within started to move at a speed barely visible to the human eye.

In his time within the Weapons of Power vault, Dave had gained some inspiration and ideas.

In his hands, a black-bodied bow grew. Across the front of the bow were Mithril guards. They looked like flames spreading out from the grip where one would place their hand and notch an arrow.

These Mithril coverings lay over black ebony, metal that had been specially treated and engraved to make it elastic instead of brittle. It was not a standard bow but was made with the pulleys of a compound bow.

The pull weight on the bow was stronger than most Level 300s could apply. Runes glowed with a red light along the ebony body and the Mithril flames. As the runes finished, the bow seemed to cool, unaffected by the flames anymore.

Dave pulled the weapon from the furnace. Sweat soaked his clothes and his face as he took the bow to another table. He strung the compound bow, fusing the high-tensile metal and organic thread string.

He took a deep breath and cut his thumb open as he closed his eyes. He created a seal on the weapon with his blood. People looked over to Dave; they felt the deep rush of power as Dave poured out his Willpower into the weapon, changing it into a Weapon of Power.

The air around Dave vibrated as the seal across the weapon seemed to turn into flames, descending upon the weapon. The seal on the bow seemed to be absorbed into the weapon. A red aura covered the weapon before disappearing. The runes became more powerful and tyrannical, no longer lit with a red glow but rather looking as though they were made from dancing flames.

Dave panted, his legs shaky as he fought to stay on his feet.

A screen appeared in front of him.

Quest Completed: Dwarven Master Smith Level 8

You must craft 3 Weapons of Power, 20 weapons of SS quality, or 150 of S Quality with your Smithing Art (Currently 3/3, 0/20, 0/200)

Rewards: Unlock Level 9 quest

+10 to all stats (stacks with previous class stat increase) 800,000 Experience

Class: Dwarven Master Smith

Status: Level 8

Effects:
Allowed access to all Dwarven Mountains and smithies.
Allowed to take on smithing apprentices.
+80 to all stats
Access to special quests.

Quest: Dwarven Master Smith Level 9

You must craft 4 Weapons of Power, 30 weapons of SS quality, or 250 of S Quality with your Smithing Art (Currently 3/4, 0/30, 0/250)

Rewards:

Unlock Level 10 Quest

Stat Increase

Active Skill: Soul Manipulation

Level: Master Level 5

Effect: Tools you make to manipulate souls and their energy is 95% stronger. Able to use soul energy to fuel spells. 30% increase to soul energies reserves (can only be used for spells; does not act as extra Willpower points).

Cost: Dependent on creation.

Active Skill: Soul Smith

Level: Expert Level 9

Effect: 81% less soul energy necessary for crafting with soul smith.

Cost: Dependent on creation.

Active Skill: Builder

Level: Master Level 8

Effect: Speed and efficiency is doubled. Creations material cost is reduced by 40%.

Required: Tools

He looked at the weapon in his hand, holding it by the grip. There was a small wheel on the side of the weapon. With a flick of his thumb, the wheel rotated; different runes lit up as the different runes came into place.

"Dave, you best go get ready. The Stone Raiders are moving out in thirty minutes." Kol passed Dave a Stamina potion.

Dave drank the potion greedily. "Thanks," Dave said, his voice hoarse from all the energy he'd expended.

Kol nodded as Dave made to head to the roof, the bow disappearing into his bag of holding.

***

Party Zero were all gathered in the lobby on their floor of apartments. Dave joined them, looking tired as he stuffed a sandwich into his face and his hair still wet from the shower he'd just had.

Deia smiled to Dave in relief.

He opened his bag of holding and pulled out a bow.

Everyone took a sharp intake of breath as the weapon was revealed. Power seemed to roll off the compound bow.

As she took the bow, she felt her Fire Mana revolve faster and faster, seeping into the bow. The air around the bow shivered with the Mana flowing into it.

A screen flashed in front of her face.

Firecracker's Bow

Using multiple different techniques, spells, and runes, this bow was formed from metal. Within this Weapon of Power, one's Fire abilities are focused and greatly increased.

Quality: Weapon of Power

Abilities:

Fire Affinity spells are 15% stronger

Fire Affinity spells cost 10% less

Every arrow is imbued with Fire Affinity, increasing their attack potential by 5-20% depending on quality of the arrow

Grows in power through use

Soul Bound

Preset Fire Affinity spells to be cast with arrows. (Fiery Rain, Piercing Heavens, Fire Lance, Plasma Arrow)

Charge: 456,000/456,000

Durability: 937/937

Her eyes filled with complicated emotions.

"And you won't be using it today," Dave said, his voice firm.

She looked to him, finding cold eyes as she straightened her back for a fight.

"There is some kind of damn spore out there that can turn people into zombies and kill them. I'm not going to have you expose yourself to it just because you think you have a duty to come with us everywhere," Dave said.

Deia looked to the others. They didn't look as if they wanted to get involved but they were backing up Dave.

"Dave—" she started, her voice hot.

"Deia, if you go out there, we're going to be so scared for you that it'll distract us," Anna said in a firm voice.

Deia wanted to argue and rave. Just because she was pregnant, she wasn't useless.

"If it was just a physical enemy then we wouldn't be as scared for you. Here, with these spores..." Gurren, in his Devastator armor, shook his head.

Even Steve looked serious.

The hot anger building in Deia's stomach disappeared as she sighed. In one hand, she held Dave's bow to her; the other she rested on her large stomach. *I have to live for the both of us.*

She looked to the others and their expressions. They didn't want to argue with her, but they were going to see her and her baby safe.

"I'll stay within Norkun," Deia said.

Relief showed on everyone's faces as they looked to Dave.

"I still don't like it and I'm going to have shield bearers assigned to drag you back to Terra if something happens," Dave said.

Even with his firm gaze, Deia could sense the fear in his voice and manner.

"I'll stay to the rear. They're already a week late," Deia said, scolding her belly and the one inside.

Everyone seemed to take a relieved breath at Deia's words.

Even in the last stages of her pregnancy, she wouldn't let it hold her back much, still staying close to the front. Here she would truly be in the rear in Norkurn Mountain.

She gripped the bow tightly and checked her leather armor. With the baby, she'd had to take off her Abscondita chest plate, reducing its strength. Still, she had the sword Dave had made her on her hip, as well as different potions on her belt.

She pulled her old bow from her shoulder, pulling off the quiver of holding from the grip. She put the bow away and attached the quiver to her new bow. She pulled on the string and her eyebrows rose. The pull on the bow was impressive and even with the Mithril and ebony construction, she could sense the flexibility in the altered ebony.

"Well, let's go kill some damn spores," Lox said.

Party Zero jumped into one of the descending lifts. All of the Stone Raiders were flowing down out of their homes, training areas, and wherever they found themselves, gathering in the massive cleared area around the Stone Raiders' towers.

There were a number of other people there, from the elven Fire mages of Asha-moor to the potion swigging forces of the Egas Nation. There were few fighters; most of those roles were taken up by the Stone Raiders and other player-ran guilds: they could come back—POE's couldn't. The Fire mages and potion drinkers could stave off the spores as well as counteract the Elsoom spores directly.

Josh and the different leaders spread out to their different groups. Once everyone was ready, Josh stood in front of them all. "Let's raid!"

Cheers rose from the players as the POEs grunted in agreement.

Today they would beat the first true group from the event Of Myths and Legends to spawn into Emerilia—or die trying.

Chapter 6: Eradication

"Load tubes one through fifty-three!" an artillery commander yelled out within Norkurn Mountain. There were many layers to dwarven mountains, the exterior of which was the natural mountain; the armored walls were strengthened and compacted stone as well as metal in critical areas. Then there were the defensive runes. Floors and floors where dwarves could stand to repel attacks from the sky and ground. Then there were chambers that passed through these. In these areas, massive gears started to churn.

Grand workings with purple-looking crystals were loaded into massive chambers. Metal plates were locked and sealed behind them.

"Loaded!" gun commanders yelled back.

"Engage Fire runes!" the artillery commander said to his assistant. Runes started to glow, heating the air until it shimmered.

These were meant to kill any spores that tried to enter the mountain.

"Open covers!"

Massive gears shifted as the mountainside seemed to shake at three dozen different locations. Dirt, rocks, and pebbles fell down as holes appeared on the Norkurn mountainside. These holes had not been seen in centuries. To many, these holes represented disaster.

"Run the guns!" The commander's voice was followed by huge gears moving the massive artillery assemblies out of the inner areas of the mountain.

From the outside, these rune-covered artillery cannons looked like some great sea beast rising from the depths, and each gun shone with cold light.

The moving gears finally came to a stop. Locking noises reverberated through the mountain as each gun settled into a firing location.

"Check elevation and traverse onto target!"

The cannons shook once again as wheels were turned. Magical Circuits and gears turned these small wheels, changing into massive movements that were capable of shifting the enormous guns. No other race would have been able to create these weapons and the incorporated systems other than the dwarves. Not even the Aleph had the industrial background to make these massive weapons.

"Gun one on target!"

"Gun seventeen on target!" Guns were called out as on target until silence descended.

"One suppression round followed by rain round! Confirm!" the artillery commander called out. His words were repeated back to him without fail.

"Ready guns!" The commander waited for a moment before he took a deep breath. "Fire at will!"

Runes along the lengths of fifty-three guns glowed from their base to the tip of their barrel. As soon as they did, the guns recoiled as the grand working rounds contained within were spat out into the sky.

The entire mountain shook with the shock waves of the passage of the grand working rounds. The mountain was covered in dust from rocks and loose material being thrown violently into the air.

As the guns recoiled, the chambers were opened and new rounds were inserted before the guns ran out again. The process took less than two minutes before elevation changes were called out from observation rooms where dwarves with massive telescopes stood.

The guns' wheels were adjusted onto target before they once again glowed with runes and a new round was expelled out into the world.

The grand working rounds tore through the sky, reaching different distances over the forest where the Elsoom spores seemed to originate from. Anything alive in the forest was dead or dying under the brown murky air that indicated where the spores were thickest. These grand workings exploded above the forest, turning the sky purple.

The second volley of rounds went much higher than the first ones. As their grand workings activated, thick black clouds formed where they passed.

These clouds hung above the purple haze that was slowly covering the murky brown forest. Lightning flashed between the converging clouds, sending the forest into shade as rain started to fall from the heavens.

The murky brown spore cloud was pushed down as the purple suppressing potion descended under the heavy rainfall.

The thick spore cloud quickly began to thin away under the rain and potion's effects.

"Check guns! Prepare Fire shells!" the artillery commander called out.

***

"Seems like that potion of yours worked," Lox said to Jung Lee, who had been added to Party Zero.

"I hope that it will be enough for the coming fight," Jung Lee said.

"Even with the potion killing off the airborne spores, the creatures that have been deeply infected will be walking incubators for the spores. If they bite a person, they'll be able to directly inject a powerful strain that will take only a few hours to turn a living creature," Jekoni said.

All attention was then focused on the different interfaces that were showing feeds from Aleph automaton scouts. They had been moving through the forest for a couple of hours now. With the spores gone, they were able to see much more clearly as they moved deeper into the forest.

Creatures covered in growths leapt out from the shadows here and there, though the scouts were hidden well, with only a few being discovered accidentally.

"That's gross." Steve looked at the diseased creatures.

The scouts kept moving onward. The diseased creatures were spread out, but they seemed to be all facing away from one direction.

Trees and undergrowth were in various states of decay, with brown and purple mushrooms growing on them. Under the suppression potion-infused rain, these mushrooms looked as if they were melting.

The spore cloud that had been greatly dispersed was stronger the deeper the scouts went, with thin floating threads fighting against the suppressing potion. These threads became thicker and thicker until they created a wall-like fog that blocked out the light of day entirely.

The scouts moved in, switching to their arcane sight.

There was a ring of massive one-meter-wide and three-meter-tall mushrooms.

Ten meters past them, there was another ring, these mushrooms double the size. In the center, a mushroom, five meters wide and twenty-five meters tall, dominated the nearby landscape.

Spores drifted from the massive Elsoom central stalk, and the two surrounding rings pushed out more and more spores, creating a fog so thick that it looked like soup.

Through the mountain range, guns could be heard moving as they locked onto their target. Moments later, the mountain rumbled as the massive artillery cannons fired.

Spores that had been lazily floating around now surged upward, creating a solid murky brown dome.

Aerial drones showed the dome that formed around the Elsoom spores. The leaking spores condensed rapidly into a solid dome-like structure.

The grand working Fire spells slammed into the brown dome with flashes of rolling heat. Anything caught in the vicinity was incinerated until there were not even ashes left.

The brown dome simply seemed to absorb the explosions, deforming slightly with the impacts before snapping back into position. The dome slowly shrunk under the continued barrage but even after five continuous volleys, it was only reduced by ten or so meters.

"The defensive power of these Elsoom spores is incredible. They might not be sentient, but they'll do anything to survive," Jekoni said.

Those hearing nodded as their stomachs churned with nerves.

"Hope you're all fine with a bit of rain!" Josh said over the event group chat that had been pulled together.

The massive gates leading to the outside world started to open, revealing the trading town that bordered Norkurn where people usually gathered to trade with the dwarves. Beyond that was a large, untouched forest.

The Elsoom spores were located in this forest directly between the city Ossai and Norkurn Dwarven Mountain.

It was clear that the grand workings were weakening the spore cloud, but they weren't having any clear sign of victory. It was time for the event group to get to work.

Everyone downed yellow potions that would suppress the effects of the poison in their bodies as they started forward, picking up speed as they raced through the empty town beyond Norkurn's gates.

Infused rain poured down and lightning flashed overhead as they flew past the empty buildings. Everyone had been quickly evacuated and checked out till there was not a soul left in the town.

Jung Lee followed with Party Zero as Fire mages created Fire-imbued Mana barriers. These would kill any spores they came into contact with. However, they only slightly warmed up the rain that fell on the event group.

This was the event that they had all been waiting for. Fears, anxiety, excitement—all of these emotions and more flashed over these people's faces as they ran toward an uncertain future.

Dave, Anna, Induca, Suzy, and Malsour rode creations they had made from their Mana and the materials around them. Jekoni floated behind Jung Lee, who was running with Steve, Lox, and Gurren.

All around them were warriors following hot on their heels, racing under the dark skies as rain continued to fall down. Thunder rolled through the clouds as they all watched their status effect timers slowly tick down, reminding them that they had thirty minutes before they needed to drink another potion. However, if they were to come into contact with the spores, the suppression effect's duration would decrease faster and faster.

As they entered the forest, the outer reaches appeared healthy but the deeper they got, the worse it looked.

"Creatures!" Anna called out.

As they passed from the healthy part of the forest to where the trees showed decay, creatures started to appear from the ground or anywhere they had found places to hide.

Dave combined his twin rods together into a two-handed claymore. "Looks like I can work on my weapons master class!" Dave's feet touched down as he continued forward alongside the others on the ground.

They cut through the oncoming creatures. Their level was nothing compared to Party Zero, who were able to kill them in one or two hits.

Some bloated-looking creatures exploded, only to have Induca focus her flames on the area so that none of the spores made it into the air.

The party continued forward, their pace only barely slowing.

They passed the decaying part of the forest and entered what looked to be desolate wasteland. Here the living creatures and plant life had been consumed by the spores. When the suppressing purple potion had coated the area, the spores had been killed off, leaving behind this barren land.

In the distance, Dave could see the brown mass that was slowly being burned away by the suppressing potion as well as hammered by constant Fire grand working shells from the dwarves.

"Well, looks as good a place as any to counterattack!" Kim emerged from the forest, others around her. "Mages, prepare artillery spells to disrupt that spore shield! If we break it, then the dwarven artillery can take it down. All the experience, none of the dying!" Kim yelled over the group chat.

Mages grouped together; spell formations appeared around them and locked together like gears in a grand machine. Power surged from the mages into the spell formation before various spells were unleashed on the spores.

Pillars of Affinity-colored light appeared above the spore shield or from the spell formations.

More and more mages grouped together, increasing the power of their spells.

The dome recoiled with the hits. The spores that made it up seemed to move faster and faster in rage.

"Melee, watch for creatures in the underbrush! Half to ranged!" Dwayne yelled.

"Ranged attackers, ready yourselves!" Josh called out. Bows were pulled out and arrows notched while destruction staffs and bolt throwers were angled at the murky brown dome.

Dave's claymore changed to a bow. He pulled back on the string and a bright glowing gray arrow formed in his hands.

Jung Lee looked over at the arrow in interest.

"What, you didn't think you were the only one with all the Affinities?" Dave grinned in the downpour.

"Release!" Josh barked.

Hundreds of arrows whistled through the air as destruction staffs let out continuous streams of Affinity Mana at the dome.

In front of Induca's hands, a plasma cannon formed from sheets of different-colored fire. As the plasma round was released, the rain was parted and the ground for ten meters on either side was baked dry while the ground under the round cracked under the heat.

Malsour unleashed curses on the dome, greatly restraining the speed of the spores and making them more vulnerable to attacks.

Anna's blade hummed as the clouds moved with her direction; the rain lessened around the edges of the forest and focused on the dome while the air currents turned the raindrops into bullets.

Suzy had her forces spread out, looking for spore-infected beasts. Lu Lu was on her shoulder, her little head looking around in curiosity.

Steve, Gurren, and Lox fired their ranged attacks while keeping an eye out for anything that made it through the fighters.

The spore dome seemed to grow a limb that smashed at the incoming arrows. Dave's arrow, which had been hiding among them, cut through the spores and disappeared into the dome.

The dome shuddered for a bit before retreating a meter.

Dave was about to release an arrow when Jung Lee raised his right forefinger, his right hand resting on the hilt of his sword.

Around his arm, waves of light, shadow, water, fire, green vines and air all spun together faster and faster before conglomerating around his fist. It turned into a small silver-looking marble.

The Affinity streams died off, flowing into the marble. As the last stream reached the marble, it shot off from his hand. It was silent and unremarkable but Dave sensed a powerful concentration of magic within the silver marble.

It quickly disappeared.

Dave barely saw it as it entered the dome. The five-hundred-meter-wide dome shuddered and compressed inward by fifteen meters, more than even the dwarves' massive Mana artillery cannons had been able to accomplish.

"Incoming!" Dwayne yelled.

Weapon kits were changed out as melee types focused on the infected creatures that were now coming out of the corrupted and dying forest. These creatures only had faint traces of what they were before. Most of them were bloated, as if a balloon with too much air within them, ready to pop at any moment.

With every breath, the creatures released clouds of spores into the air. Their open wounds had wisps of smoke where the suppressing potion-filled rain touched them. There was a wild light to their eyes as they rushed to meet those who attacked the grove of Elsoom spores.

"Fire mages, take out the creatures!" Kim yelled.

Flames rushed out of mage formations. The air became hot and muggy as the rain evaporated along this line of fire that reached out to cleanse these creatures.

Here and there, flames grew as a creature exploded and released spores into the air. Creatures made it through the wall of flames to be greeted by the melee fighters.

"I'll stay here and protect the party. Gurren, Steve—go and help the other members of the group," Lox commanded. His body glowed red as he'd activated his Fire Affinity. Rain sizzled off his Devastator armor as the other two ran off. With their armored bodies, as much as creatures wanted to hack and bite them, they wouldn't be able to get the armored giants.

Lox kicked a massive snake that exploded like a bag of overripe garbage. His sword cut through a gorilla, cauterizing the wound before the creature fell.

Jung Lee simply waved his hand as the creatures were turned to ashes and floated away.

More and more creatures piled in, rushing the wall of fire around the group. They reached the fighters who were in a panicked melee and covered the mages and ranged attackers who were unleashing their attacks on the Elsoom spore grove and its brown dome.

Dave disregarded the creatures. Although a single bite or scratch from them would turn a person into an Elsoom spore zombie, they needed to destroy the root cause, not just the offshoots.

Dave drew and released an arrow, unleashing it into the brown dome, and as the first landed, he made another. The spores were trying to fight off the incoming attacks, forming limbs to bat away the projectiles to no avail.

The dwarven artillery fell on the dome, destroying any limbs that their Fire rune-imbued shells touched.

The Elsoom spores were a hellish existence if left unchecked but they weren't sentient, only incredibly aggressive to the point of killing anything else that was around them.

The fighting with the creatures became more savage as more and more made it through. People were pulled back and some mages had to lend support instead of firing spells at the spore dome.

Finally, from the dome, a fleshy-looking surface appeared. The outer ring of Elsoom spores had been exposed!

Seeing that their attacks were working, the ranged attackers and mages increased the rate at which they fired.

The dome continued to move inward, the Elsoom mushrooms being exposed by inches.

One of the Elsoom stalks erupted in flames as its hit points reached zero. The dome convulsed, revealing more of the Elsoom grove.

The actual Elsoom fungi weren't that strong, going down with just a few hits, and the dome shrank inward at an incredible speed. It wasn't long before the inner ring of Elsoom stalks could be seen.

"Focus on creatures!" Josh called out. The creatures were doing anything to attack the event group, and people were being pulled away as melee types stowed their ranged weapons and joined the fray.

The creatures were met with a wall of fire, weapons, and spells.

The spore dome was incredibly powerful to resist such firepower; when these same spells were unleashed on the advancing creatures, only craters were left in their wake, with no sign of the creatures that had been there just moments before.

"Switch back to the dome!" Kim called after a few short minutes of pushing back the creatures.

The melee types got into a rhythm of dealing with the infected beasts while Fire mages moved alongside, mobile flame throwers to purify the air and corpses of the dead.

Slowly the second ring of Elsoom spores started to be worn away under the explosive thunderclaps of the dwarven artillery and spells.

As the last of the inner Elsoom mushrooms fell, a cheer rose from the throats of the event group. People were downing Mana and Stamina potions before throwing themselves back into battle.

The cheers died down as the dome contracted rapidly by itself. It swarmed over the massive Elsoom stalk that had rested in the middle of the grove. A magical formation started to form around it.

Dave pulled his bow apart. The conjuration faded to dust as he slammed his fists together, holding the rods. Gray runes lit across his body and gray smoke streamed past him, rushing toward his fists as if rapids gathering toward a waterfall.

A magical formation made of overlapping magical circles formed in front of his hands, varying sizes before forming a final circle the size of his fist. Mana surged through these rotating spell formations, and into the growing one around the central Elsoom spore.

The spell formations around the spore paused before a faint cracking noise could be heard. The formations exploded and wild Mana surged outward, tearing up loose dirt and rocks as the wave front of an explosion charged toward the teams.

"Mana shields!" Josh called out.

Stone Raiders all turned their amulets or armbands that were emblazoned with the Stone Raiders' emblem. Charged vault soul gems within their bags of holding fed power into these amulets, working together to create a massive Mana shield.

The wave front slammed into the shield. Unlike a barrier, shields used more power and stopped anything coming through. The wind howled as infected creatures were slammed into the shield, turning into a bag of exploding spores.

Shock registered on the faces of many. Dave's face was solemn as he continued to channel a stream of gray smoke into the spell formations, which spat out a gleaming silver thread. Dave opened a hole through the shield, allowing the thread to shoot out as a gray ray of light, directly into the enormous mushroom.

Jung Lee looked to Dave as the light stopped and the spell formations unraveled.

Dave hooked his rods into his waistband as the blast wave of the Elsoom spores' backfiring spell passed.

The dead ground around the spores had been swept clean.

The battlefield seemed unnaturally quiet after the passing of the wave front.

Moments later, rain fell to the ground all at once.

Screens appeared in front of everyone.

Event: Of Myths and Legends

You have defeated a glade of: Elsoom Spores.

Objectives:

Stop the spread of the spores and infected.

Defeat the Elsoom Spores

Remove the infection

Rewards:

250,000 Experience

Resistance to all poisons increase by 10%

Zolun Tribes now view you as: Ally

Event Bonus

You are part of the first group to defeat a spawned-in group of creatures from the Event: Of Myths and Legends.

You gain +10% experience for the next week.

(Gain additional 25,000 EXP)

Dave nodded and opened up his weapons master class quest.

Quest: Weapons Master Level 4

One handed and shield 251/1000

Two handed 84/1000

Dual wielding 12/1000

Archery 498/1000

Rewards: Unlock Level 5 Quest

Increase to stats

Passive skills from other weapons increase from 25% when not equipped to 50%

"Well, got a long way to go until I get the next level in the class but the passives are going to be one hell of a bonus," Dave muttered to himself.

"Okay, let's make sure that none of the creatures escape here and infect anyone else." Josh sounded tired as the rain from above started to thin out and shafts of light broke through the clouds.

"Well, that's the first round done," Suzy said.

"I somehow doubt it's going to be as easy every single time," Induca said.

"I feel like ice cream. Anyone else?" Steve asked.

"You still don't have a mouth!" Lox said. The sound of metal on metal sounded out as Lox clipped Steve's head.

"A man can dream!" Steve said, another metal smack ringing out.

"You're not even a man!" Gurren said.

"Suzy!" Steve complained, pouting as he held his arms over his head to defend against any more smacks.

"You're a big boy now. Not my fault that they both got armor as strong as your body," Suzy said with a cool, indifferent smile on her face.

Lu Lu preened herself on Suzy's shoulder. She had shot out a few lightning strikes here and there but she was only a low-leveled creature, unable to affect the battle much. Still, with Suzy sharing experience and the small attacks she'd landed, she'd been able to gain some levels and become more powerful.

Chapter 7: New Arrival

Denur's eyes thinned as she dismissed a message from one of her granddaughters who lived outside the Densaou Ring of Fire.

A marker had appeared at the mountain that she called home, between Northwood and the Great Ashal forest.

She opened her interface to send a message to Deia.

***

Deia finished reading Denur's message. She quickly stood from where she had been sitting while reading a book in her room and made for the door. It didn't take long for her to reach the elevators and then take one upward to where the guild leaders lived.

She sent a message to all of them to gather.

By the time she made it to the top floor, the leaders were all there waiting for her.

"The next spawn marker has been found," Deia said in response to their curious looks.

"Where?" Lucy asked.

"In the mountain between the Ashal great forest and the Northwood forest on Ashal." Deia winced slightly at a painful twitch in her lower stomach.

"We'll get the Aleph to scout the area, see what's going on. I think that there is a dragon also there. I hope that it won't inter-fere," Josh said.

"The dragon won't. She's heading for the Densaou Ring." Deia's voice came through clenched teeth as she leaned against the wall heavily.

"You okay?" Cassie looked at Deia's pale face.

"Little guy is just a bit feisty today," Deia said with a pained smile. She frowned as another bout of pain passed through her body. She gritted her teeth together as her legs trembled.

"I think that we should get you in to see Jules." Kim looked at Deia.

"I think that you might be right." Deia let out a hissing breath as the wave of pain dissipated.

Lucy pulled out her magic carpet, getting Deia on it as she and Kim took Deia to see Jules.

The others got to work to check out the conditions of the new spawn marker.

Deia was in front of Jules just a few minutes later.

"Okay, well, the good news is that you're going to have a baby. Bad news—it's going to hurt like almighty hell." Jules looked to Deia.

Deia let out a grunt. She had been in pain before, but with this there was nothing that she could do but endure it. With Jules and all of the healers who were milling around, Deia felt safe.

Her contractions kept coming; after some time, she started to get used to it.

Dave burst into the room, his face pale and scared for Deia. As his eyes locked on Deia, he seemed to teleport across the room, holding her hand in his as he moved her hair out of her face.

Deia relaxed slightly. "Ready to be a dad?" She closed her eyes as a contraction passed.

"With you, definitely." Dave's pale skin regained some color as a brilliant smile spread across his face. He kissed her forehead, his eyes only for her and a massive goofy smile on his face.

Deia couldn't help but feel her heart melt at the look Dave gave her. "You're going to be a great dad," Deia whispered.

Dave's eyes went a bit misty as he cleared his throat. "And you're going to be an amazing mom." Dave sat on the bed and looked at her. A look crossed his face. "I'll tell your mom and dad." Dave opened up his interface as there was a knock at the door to the room.

Deia looked over. Her eyes misted up as all of Party Zero stood in the doorway.

From goofy to reserved smiles, all of them were looking at her and Dave. Deia could feel the love and care that they shared toward her.

She wiped her eyes with her free hand as they all poured into the room.

"Heard we're getting a new addition to the party soon enough!" Suzy said.

There was a flash of light, drawing the healers' eyes as a gnome appeared.

"I'm in the right place, right?" Bob looked around wildly before his eyes landed on Deia. His face showed unreserved joy as he ran to her side.

Deia could only laugh, tears in her eyes at his antics.

Dave closed his interface before he frowned. "Kol, will you get out of the damned hallway and get in here!" Dave yelled.

Thankfully, the room was large; with healers' magic and healing potions, hospital beds were rarely filled, allowing them to take over the large room.

A somewhat embarrassed Kol stepped into the room and scratched his head awkwardly.

"Can't have Grandfather Kol and Bob missing out on this." Deia looked to Dave and squeezed his hand.

Kol and Bob had stunned looks on their faces, looking to each other and then Deia and Dave.

"Seems we've got most of her aunts and uncles here too," Dave said softly. Slowly Deia and Dave looked to Party Zero.

Suzy and Anna wiped their eyes as the others smiled. There were a number of misty eyes among the group.

"I'm gonna be the best friggin' uncle ever!" Steve declared, a wild smile on his face as he fist pumped and jammed his hand into the ceiling.

The room burst into laughter as Steve looked at his stuck hand.

Jules, who stood in the corner of the room, had her arms crossed. Her forefinger tapped against her arm as her foot tapped on the floor.

"Sorry." Steve carefully pulled his hand out of the ceiling as dust and debris rained down from the hole.

Anna created a tornado that made sure none of the dust and debris spread while Malsour used the materials to fix the roof.

Jules sighed as her severe expression softened. "Okay, let's try to keep it to two or three people in here at a time. The room isn't that big."

Party Zero figured out who was staying and not moving to the waiting room down the hall.

Deia gasped at a contraction but now the thread of fear that had been growing in the back of her mind dimmed as she looked at those faces and the pure love and caring that radiated out of them.

***

"What?" Josh stood so fast his seat fell backward.

"Deia is having her baby right now," Cassie said with a glowing grin as she stood at the entrance to his office.

"Well, what are we standing here for!" Josh blurred until he was next to Cassie, but as they started running for a lift to take them to the medical facilities, they passed Esa.

"What's wrong?" Josh asked, looking at her fully armed and armored.

"We just had a group of fifty humans all hiding their faces and with powerful-ass auras show up! There's also an elf and a baby with them," Esa said.

Josh frowned before his eyebrows rose in shock. "What's their last names?"

"Dracul," Esa said, confused as to why it was important.

"They must be Deia's mom, dad, and family," Josh said in a low hiss.

Esa's head shot up violently. "You mean the drag—"

Josh cleared his throat forcefully. Esa knew about Emerilia, the dragons, and all the secrets of Emerilia and Party Zero, just like Josh.

Esa closed her mouth, wincing as she stopped herself from saying anything more.

"Her father's name is Oson'Mal; he should be the elf. If that's right, let them pass. We do not want to annoy them," Josh said, his voice grave.

Esa nodded and opened her interface to enter into a private party chat with the guarding force at the teleport pad where the Draculs had come through.

They took the elevators down to the medical facilities.

Dwayne and Lucy met up with them. Kim was already in the large waiting room. Party Zero, Bob, and Kol were already there.

Josh looked at Bob; he still couldn't get a read on Bob's aura, but from what he'd seen, the gnome was one of the most powerful creatures in Emerilia.

Bob saw the leaders of the Stone Raiders appear, and nodded to them as he continued his talk with Kol. The two normally reserved men had deep smiles on their faces.

Party Zero greeted them, telling them that Deia was fine, and Dave was with them as well as Anna, Suzy, and Steve.

Lu Lu was on Induca's shoulders. Her cute head bobbed around and she let out interested rumblings as she looked at everyone there. She let out a confused squawk at the sound of tens of feet tearing up the hallway.

"I'm guessing that might be related to you," Josh said to Induca and Malsour.

"Probably." Malsour sighed while Induca laughed and scratched behind Lu Lu's head.

A woman wearing deep-red leather pants and shirt entered the room. Her deep red hair was pulled back in a braid that came down her left shoulder.

Beside her there was an early thirties-looking wood elf with tanned skin and brown hair. He wore a kind smile and held a baby in his arms.

The two of them looked like a couple who had matured beautifully together.

Even with her kind smile, Josh felt the hairs on the back of his head rise in shock. He knew that Deia's mother was actually the goddess Fire, but hearing that and seeing her were two vastly different things.

Behind her were fifty or so people, with varying ages from teenagers to late twenties.

Behind Fire, there was a woman with similar features to Deia and Fire, and by the other people in the group's reactions it was easy to see that she was deeply respected by them.

Denur! She must be!

There was a heavy feeling in the air as Bob and Kol moved to greet the new arrivals.

"Looks like all the Draculs and Osons made it out today," Bob said with a kind smile.

"How—" Fire asked, her voice powerful and dominating with a hint of fear in it.

Bob cut off her words with a wave. "She's just fine. Healers are there, as well as friends. We can't all cram in there, but I think they'll make an exception for Deia's mom and dad." Bob smiled.

Fire nodded and strode forward, moving to the door.

Denur moved to Induca and Malsour, greeting them. The other Draculs talked among themselves and introduced themselves to all the others.

"Denur, this is Josh, the leader of the Stone Raiders, and his girlfriend Cassie." Malsour waved to Josh and Cassie, who stood next to them.

Denur's eyes narrowed slightly as she extended her hand out. By her look, she seemed to be studying and evaluating Josh.

"Lady Denur." Josh shook her hand.

"I have heard good things about your Stone Raiders," Denur said, her expression unreadable.

"Thanks." Josh smiled.

Denur looked to Malsour and Induca, unsaid words passing between them.

"Later, I think that it might be a good idea if we are to have a meeting and talk about the future," Denur finally said.

Josh's eyes went wide as Cassie made a noise of surprise.

A small smile spread on Denur's face at Cassie's note of surprise.

Cassie turned red in embarrassment.

"Though that is something for later. Today, I hope we can just celebrate a new arrival," Denur said.

"Agreed." Josh's face softened as he smiled.

A cry came out of Deia's room.

"Looks like it will be sooner rather than later," Induca said as everyone went silent and looked to the room.

"Yeah," Josh said as his heart, which seemed to have been wrapped in ice after that scream, calmed down as he let out a breath.

***

Koza was looking at a massive interface screen. He was the Aleph council member in charge of security and the Aleph military.

Here they were controlling Aleph scout automatons all over Emerilia. There were automatons watching bandits and kings; others were searching different dungeons, though the ones that everyone was focused on were moving through a sheet of water that fell from the massive mountain located between Northwood and the Great Ashal forest on the Ashal continent.

The dragon who had lived on the mountain seemed to have left. The entrance to its lair was higher up in the mountain. This entrance was for something else.

The automatons passed through the waterfall, finding a cave behind it.

As they continued forward, the cave revealed goblins and hobgoblins, as well as tamed Earth and rock trolls. The tunnel system was complex as it moved deeper and deeper.

The automatons moved forward slowly, each operated by a different controller so that there was less chance of the inhabitants noticing that there were invisible eyes watching their every move.

Slowly they made it through the tunnels, which started to open up more and more.

They reached a number of small living areas that held around fifty or so hobgoblins and goblins. Behind the goblins, tunnels led deeper into the mountain.

These were all mapped out as automatons continued forward.

They passed through larger and more well-maintained tunnels before they came out into a massive underground area. A small lake ran through the open cavern; crops grew on either side. Houses and huts covered the ground, with none of the constructs over a floor high. All of them looked shabby and poorly made.

Glowing moss on the ceiling gave off a constant shimmering glow. The goblins and trolls were used to low-light areas and walked around without trouble, talking in their guttural language, fighting here and there and moving around the open cavern.

The automatons moved through the area.

"What's that?" Koza pointed to a table where a goblin was cutting up beasts in a number of ways with a crude and dirty hatchet.

A controller moved in close to look at the different beasts they were cutting up.

"That's a silver headed ram, and an ebony rhino," one of the Aleph observers said, referencing their Librarian necklace.

Koza shook his head. One couldn't see the levels and names of people through the Aleph automatons, so they were having to guess.

Being on Ashal, these goblins and trolls weren't normal. Seeing that they were actually eating such powerful and strong beasts as the silver headed ram and ebony plated rhino indicated that they were actually powerful fighters.

"Continue on." Koza hid his inner frustrations at the new information; fighting through these caves would be a hellish task.

"I've got something!" a controller called out, and Koza moved to check the controller's share of the interface.

"The hell is that?" Koza muttered.

He was looking at four different pillars that were arranged around a central pillar, all of which were engraved with runes. Between each of the pillars was a simple screen.

Spawn Point

Days Hours Minutes Seconds

15   7   46   21

Koza stopped leaning on the controller's chair. "Looks like we found the spawn point," Koza said simply.

Koza frowned as a goblin hit one of the columns around the spawn point. A flash of lightning jumped from the pillar, striking the goblin, and turned them to dust.

The goblin had died without a noise.

"Sir, I've got something else here," another controller said in a puzzled voice.

Koza moved to see their shared feed. "A portal?" Koza looked at the portal that was in the middle of the cavern on an elevated platform. It was in a large courtyard of the only stone building in the cavern. Unlike the rest of the underground city, this building had straight edges and signs that it was made by someone who knew how to build a proper structure.

The spawn point marker stood in front of the portal. Koza's hand tapped on the hilt of his sword, lost to deep thoughts. *I have a feeling that this spawn location isn't going to be too simple.*

***

"One more push—nearly there!" Jules yelled.

Spell formations glowed all over the room. Deia, who could control flame as if it was but another limb, was unintentionally creating different spells in the room. The heat in the room had already soared as Denur and Fire did their best to contain it all from outside.

Dave was focusing on tearing her spell formations apart from inside lest she create a flame storm or a fuel air bomb.

The healers were frightened of the spell formations and increasing heat. Jules, however, didn't seem scared in the slightest as she focused on the little baby in her hands.

Deia let out a grunting scream; her hand crushed into Dave's. He'd had to reinforce it with Mana so that she didn't turn it into dust.

There was a sound of crying. A healer used a Water spell, cleaning the little girl Jules was looking over. Her fingers glowed as she studied the little girl struggling weakly in her arms.

Deia's breathing was fast and heavy. The spell formations faded away as Dave let out a sigh of relief.

Deia was passed a healing potion that she took with both hands, her eyes locked on the crying little girl in Jules's hands.

Dave numbly moved forward as Jules opened her eyes.

"She's a healthy baby girl," Jules said with a smile to Dave and Deia.

Dave was passed a blanket. He held it as Jules passed him the little girl—his baby girl. He carefully wrapped the blanket around the crying little one, finding water dripping on her forehead. He felt a wetness on his cheeks as he looked down at his daughter.

Her eyes were forced shut and she was crying out about her injustices to everyone.

Dave rubbed his finger against her cheek gently. She had stolen his heart so much that his chest hurt as he laughed and cried.

"Let's go see your mommy." Dave gently touched his daughter's slightly peaked ears. He looked to Deia, whose tired face was filled with an unreadable mix of emotions.

Deia held out her hands; Dave slowly and gently placed his daughter in Deia's arms.

She held her in the crook of her arm, while Dave stood at Deia's shoulder, looking down on her and their daughter.

His hand rested on Deia's back as she leaned back into it.

Time seemed to stand still as the healers checked various things before leaving the room.

"Let us know when you're ready and we can let the others come in in small groups," Jules said in a soft voice.

Dave and Deia looked to Jules's kind smiling face.

"Thank you, Jules," Deia said.

Dave nodded, his eyes conveying his thanks as Jules's smile widened.

"Just let me know if you three need anything," she said in a soft voice. She turned and left Dave, Deia, and their baby girl alone in the room.

Dave sat down on the bed next to Deia. She leaned into him as he kissed the top of her head, both of them looking at their daughter.

"Next time, try to not blow up the damn room," Dave muttered.

"Next time? How many kids were you planning on us having?" Deia's eyes narrowed as she gave a saucy smile.

"Enough." Dave grinned.

Deia snorted and shook her head. "You push a watermelon out from between your legs next time."

Dave smiled at the love in her voice as she looked down at their daughter, and knew that she believed all the pain had been worth it.

The door opened as Mal put his head through it. "You fine with a few visitors?"

Dave looked to Deia for a second before he looked back. "Get in here, Grandad," Dave said.

Oson'Mal, Fire, Bob, Kol, and all of Party Zero moved into the room, standing around the bed as they looked at the little girl in Deia's arms.

Fire held up Desmond and tilted him so that he could see Dave, Deia, and their daughter.

"That's your niece, Desmond. You are going to have to look after her," Fire said.

Dave smiled, looking from Fire to the wide-eyed Desmond.

He looked at the people around the bed, and sensed those who waited in the hall to see the newest arrival. He cleared his tight throat and squeezed Deia to him.

He had come here as a man trying to escape his life. He'd found a secret, a purpose, and he'd made a family from friends.

The path forward was a hard one; there would be trials and tribulations, but he would walk it beside his friends and family, so that Desmond, his daughter, and Emerilia's children could make their own destiny, instead of being entertainment for the Jukal Empire.

Chapter 8: Unexpected Change

It had been three days since Dave and Deia had brought their daughter into the world. Bob was in a conference room looking at the different people sitting at the table with him.

There was the Stone Raiders' leadership; Alkao and some advisers from Devil's Crater; Hamdir, the leader of the Aleph Council; and Koza, the leader of the security seat on the Aleph Council. Three dwarven master smiths and one dwarven war council leader. There were orcs and gnomes, humans and Beast Kin, demons and elves, with every race in between. Here every leader from the embassies with Terra sat, listening to a messenger from the Markolm continent and elven nation.

People frowned as the high elf finished talking. High elves liked to talk but his message was short and simple.

Someone had killed their first elder in cold blood. Anger and fear filled the hearts of the normally peaceful people, looking to find the killers and deal with them. With each day Markolm was becoming more violent.

Bob let out a noisy breath.

"Looks like they're coming back to their homeland," Bob said to Kol, one of the three dwarven master smiths.

"What do you mean?" Josh asked from across the table as the conversations died down.

"Markolm was not the elven continent at first. It started off as Light's continent.

"She took plots of land from all over Emerilia, making the four different areas on the continent. She made the entire place somewhere people could pilgrimage to, in order to worship her. It was the original Per'Ush island. It floated around Emerilia so people could see it and devote their power to the Lady of Light.

"It was the home of the angels. With their devotions, the Lady of Light was more popular than ever—she was one of the strongest gods in the Pantheon.

"Things might have been great, but as good things rise, so must they fall. When the demons disappeared, the angels were more aggressive in how they got people to devote themselves to the Lady of Light. In their eyes, there was only one goddess. As many believed in other gods and goddesses, there would only be conflict.

"As Markolm floated over the lands, the angels would descend day and night, purging anything and anyone that was devoted to the other gods. The battles with the mage's college and guild were spectacular. They did so much damage to Markolm that Light had to overdraft her power from her divine well.

"She was readying her counterattack when the angels were imprisoned. The Lady of Light had a terrible reputation. With the angels being banished, she didn't have the power to keep Markolm suspended and also fight off the other gods who, seeing her in weakness, were gathering their forces. Markolm descended into the seas as the fanatics fought against the other members of the Pantheon who were getting retribution for the killing of their Creatures of Power, champions, or simply to try to wrestle control of her divine well away from her. The fanatics were cleared from the continent, and more issues came up, with people leaving to deal with other problems in Emerilia.

"Markolm didn't have dungeons or many resources. The land was burned and Mana-deficient from the battles waged on it. However, the elves who were being persecuted across Emerilia needed a place to retreat to. They moved to Markolm, a place where they could defend themselves. They created a free elven society, rescued elves from slavery and restored Markolm. They brought life back to the land with their magic, and used the different weapons and items from the various churches and halls in Markolm to improve themselves. Dungeons grew on the continent. Portals happened and Markolm grew into what it is today. From what you've said, it seems that Khanundra thinks that Markolm hasn't changed at all. She sees the elves as mere subjects to be monopolized in order to increase her lady's power. It doesn't matter that you're not the same fanatics. To her, all should bow before her lady, or in her mind, the true and proper goddess," Bob finished.

The elves, dwarves, Aleph, and Devil's Crater faction nodded, many of whom still had records from that dark time. Others around the table frowned, learning this history for the first time.

With so many conflicts, kingdoms rose and fell quite a bit in previous centuries. Ashal might now be regarded as a constant war zone between different groups. In the past, all of Emerilia had been like Ashal.

History was hard to record if it was constantly destroyed in wars. The older races had collections and libraries that held information on things that the younger nations never remembered.

The smarter representatives paid attention to who was nodding. These people were some of the strongest in Emerilia, and were dragons sitting on a deep ocean. There were hidden depths behind them. People are people, whatever their forms, they knew without a doubt, angering them would be the height of idiocy.

Many of these eyes lingered on the three humans who wore identical cloaks with blue, green, and black inner layers.

Their levels were hidden and their last names were all Dracul. None had heard of a Dracul clan with enough power to stand at a table of people who could get nations to move. However, the faint feeling of power and their knowledge on Markolm raised the others' interest in this trio.

Josh's face was unreadable with this information. Slowly he sighed and looked to the envoy.

"We are not yet strong enough to contend with someone like Khanundra," Josh said bluntly. "However, when we are strong enough, we will help you free yourselves of her and her goddess's influence. In the meantime, we will do all we can to aid you."

Just a year ago, this kind of declaration might have been laughed at, but now the Stone Raiders stood at the peak of player guilds of all time. Terra was a hub of commerce; their people were strong, inventive and loyal. When they made a promise, they kept it, no matter what. One would only need to look at the people of Devil's Crater or Aleph. These two groups had been incredibly weak when they returned to Emerilia. The Stone Raiders had sacrificed a lot in the name of their alliance. Now Devil's Crater was an adventurer's dream; they had one of the strongest militaries in Emerilia. Their DCA soldiers' strength was equal to the leading elites of an Ashal military.

The Aleph produced goods faster than the dwarves and were closely connected to the Mirror of Communication schools, as well as the mage's college and dwarves. They had become an economic superpower with their factories and underground greenhouses.

The high elf messenger bowed his head. "Thank you." Their words were simple, but a high elf doing more than simply tilting their head showed their respect toward the other party.

Josh returned the gesture before he looked to the table while the messenger sat down. In this, they would also be acting as a secret envoy to the people of Markolm. They might not be able to act out in the open but they would help where possible. Every race and group was threatened by this event.

"We have twelve more days until that spawn point opens under Goblin Mountain," Josh said. Someone had come up with the nickname and it stuck. The number of goblins inside was massive, making it one of the biggest goblin settlements in known history.

"Now we know what we're looking for with the spawn points. Though, with the spawn point being right next to a portal, we're not sure what's going to happen," Josh continued on as Bob zoned him out, going over the information they had.

Some inhospitable worlds were used to seal up creatures. It would only be possible to reach them with a portal. The angels were sent to one of these worlds.

"So, right now it looks like it's once every three weeks one of these spawn points open up. We've got to keep an eye out for more of them. This is just the first couple of waves. We've shown ourselves and the people of Emerilia what we can do when we work together. In the future, our abilities will only grow," Josh said, drawing the meeting to a close.

***

Captain Adams looked at the latest feed from Emerilia. She knew that the event Of Myths and Legends was starting on Emerilia.

It was supposed to be a baptism by fire that could change Emerilia forever.

The feed had been sped up, as it showed a brown cloud spread out over a forest, rapidly destroying it. As clouds then covered the skies, she switched to heat sensors and watched as powerful artillery shells slammed into a dome of organic matter, burning it away slowly.

Each of those strikes has a tenth of the explosive power of our interceptor missiles.

Even these massively powerful weapons weren't that strong in the face of the creatures on Emerilia. As we continue to monitor their situation, we can see that every day, all the people on Emerilia were fighting for their lives, with opponents who were just as smart and, some are much more powerful to boot.

Electronic signatures overlaid the heat signatures as mushroom-like items were revealed, and then finally a massive electrical disturbance distorted the image. The distortions flickered and died off before being replaced with roiling brown clouds. As the clouds broke up, a barren wasteland was revealed below.

She paused the video, taking images from before the brown clouds started to spread out to after when the clouds cleared.

The destruction left behind was incredible. The landscape had been completely changed within a day.

"That was just their first battle. What are the others going to be like?" Adams said to herself.

She closed her different screens and looked out her window. It was a feed from outside the asteroid she was now stationed on. Shipyard three was the newest shipyard they had and one that was wholly devoted to using just methods from Emerilia to make vessels.

With a sigh, she got up from her desk and moved to the door.

She left her office, nodding and smiling to people she passed. As the first captain to not only take a ship past the Deq'ual system, but to also bring them back information, pictures, video and sensor logs from within Jukal systems, she had become something of a hero.

Now there were five other ships that had taken up the mission of plotting out the Jukal Empire and its influence.

They had changed a lot from when Bob got his information. However, the major systems and routes were all the same.

There were more people in the military than ever before. Ships were being worked on every day. New habitats were being set up and people who had been put into cryo due to overpopulation were being woken up.

The active population was quickly growing. People were having more children and a sense of hope filled the air.

As she stepped through a series of air locks looking into the central hub of the facility, she activated her Mana shield. Edwards had taken the technology and nanites that made up the Jukal interface and reverse engineered it so that it was wholly his design, and there was no chance of the Jukal getting into it or somehow having a kill switch in it.

The new hub didn't need to rotate as gravity runes kept everything secured.

It looked as if there were a series of crystals glowing inside the asteroid. All of the facilities within the asteroid were made from soul gem constructs. With powerful AIs, combined with massive power plants and the information that Dave had given them, they had been able to make the shipyard habitable in a matter of weeks instead of months.

The soul gem constructs were still turning the inside of the asteroid into a habitable area and a place to work. The first ships had been started. These were basically soul gems that were held in one position as they followed their instructions and grew from crystals into superstructures. Once this structure was completed, then armor could be mounted to the exterior. The soul gem construct could make a non-slip surface and also appear in any color instead of just looking like a glass container with motes of light slowly moving around. As long as they were supplied with power, these soul gem constructs would continue to grow to completion. They also had the ability to hold charge over a long period of time to be used in an emergency, as well as self-repair functions.

They were an amazing construction material, though programming was a pain in the ass that required multiple AI and human controllers to get all the runes right.

Adams moved from the air lock, leaving through an incomplete hallway where the soul gem was just touching in the middle, with the rest slowly growing to seal the space up. With the yard still in construction, there were multiple areas where there wasn't any atmosphere.

The people in Deq'ual were taught from a young age about how to live in space, and the dangers that were a part of where they lived.

It would be strange going to a planet with wide open spaces as big as this without a helmet. Adams shivered a bit, remembering decompression videos as she thought of wide open areas.

She moved through the different areas; some didn't even have gravity yet, but that was easily handled by Adams. Finally, she reached a workroom out of the way and buried deep in the asteroid walls.

Server banks covered the walls as Edwards was having a quiet conversation with an AI hologram that floated above his desk.

The AI looked to Adams, drawing Edwards's attention to her.

"Hello, Admiral Adams. What can I do for you today?" Edwards asked.

"I'm just seeing how everything is going with the magical coding for the soul gem constructs." Adams looked to the AI with a frown. "Is that a new AI?"

Edwards's annoyed look turned into a brilliant smile as he moved to the side so that the AI was visible.

"This is Shard," Edwards said with a flourish. "AI to the Aleph people on Emerilia."

Adams's face was a picture of shock as she looked at the dwarf/elf face that seemed to hold a gentle but aged quality to it.

"Hello, Admiral Adams. It is good to meet you," Shard said with a kind smile.

"You two—how is this possible?" Adams asked.

"I am running through a Mirror of Communication so that Edwards and I can work on different projects without him having to visit me within the Mirror of Communication," Shard said.

"He's been helping me out with the soul gem construct magical coding. That's a mouthful, even for me!" Edwards chuckled.

"The new class of ship that you are building is extremely complicated and the requirements needed for the ships are large. However, if we can complete this prototype, then we can start to grow these ships instead of making material and soul gem construction hybrids." Shard looked to Edwards. "Though we will need to agree to share the plans once completed."

"What do you want these plans for?" Adams asked.

"So we can build ships as well. By we, I mean the Aleph and Dave," Shard said.

"You want to build ships—how?" Adams asked.

"Dave has taken over a moon. He's got drills and other machinery hollowing it out and building a number of facilities. He also has built a shipyard for his different prototypes deep within Emerilia. He has plans to construct several more shipyards. We're not planning on just letting the Jukal know that we know about their system and not have a way to fight back," Shard said in an amused tone.

"What kind of ships are you building?" Adams asked.

"Arks and destroyers," Shard said. Two holograms appeared in front of him, rotating slightly.

Adams looked at the two vastly different ships. One was a purebred warship. It was sleek and orderly, with weapons emplacements and missile tubes. The other was massive with bands of weapons and armaments that rotated around it. Each ship was covered in glowing runic lettering. These ships were not borne of technology; they were vessels powered by magic and Mana.

"I am translating all of the necessary requirements into magical coding, which is part of the reason that I needed to be physically here. I am limited in my processing ability. Being here, I can run thousands of times faster with all of these servers linked to me," Shard said.

Adams looked around at the different banks that were quietly humming in the room. "How long will it take for you to get the coding ready for our ships here?"

"About a week—maybe two, depending on changes," Shard said.

"Tell her how long it will take for you to do the coding for the destroyer-class warships." Edwards crossed his arms and looked at Adams.

"Approximately two months, at least," Shard said.

Adams was once again left in a state of shock at his words.

"A destroyer is seven hundred meters long and four hundred meters wide. Its systems are much more complicated and as I go, I will be running sub-processes to maximize the potential of the ship. You, however, already have a plan of different ships and I am simply changing it over and adding some modifications. I have a number of different, highly complicated, and specialized systems to combine together. Every project that Dave, the people in his class, and the people who work for him have come up with magical coding is stored within my mind. I can use these and put them together into something that I can't predict the effectiveness of. As better and cleaner magical coding is found and added to my memory, I can push updates out to the different ships so that they are always at the best possible condition." Shard smiled.

A warship with internals that can be changed and updated as if it were software. This thought ran through Adams's mind, her face blank. It was highly complicated but the possibilities... With time, these ships wouldn't ever become obsolete but instead become stronger and stronger, no different from brand-new ships built even a dozen years later.

"Holy shit," Adams muttered to herself.

***

Lucy smiled to the Stone Raiders and other traders and customers who flocked to Verlun's Stone Raiders' Guild Hall.

Since the fight with Lord Esamael, Verlun had turned into a trading hub, with the Stone Raiders' Guild Hall becoming a pillar for the city's trade and commerce.

Now, massive fifty-foot walls surrounded the growing complexes of stores of all kinds. The ono here was constantly in use, moving people to Terra. The teleport pad had been moved to Terra so that the city could connect to more onos. The network of onos and teleport pads was massive, connecting nearly all of Emerilia.

Lucy's pace picked up as she entered the guild hall. She quickly rushed up the stairs until she was within Florence's office. As she entered, her calm face turned into a frown. "What was it that you wanted me to rush over here for?" Lucy asked Florence, who stood in her office.

"Well, someone wanted to talk to you," Florence said.

"Who?" Lucy asked.

"Me!" an excited voice said. A woman wearing airy white clothes appeared in Florence's chair.

"Lucy Vernia, I am Venfik, friend of the Lady of Air." Venfik, an older, refined-looking elf with the vitality of a man much younger, smiled kindly as he waved to the child-like woman in Florence's seat.

"Lady of Air," Lucy said, as if tasting the words, looking at the two people in front of her. She felt that they were strong, but they hid their strength well.

"That's me, but you can call me Air. I think we're going to become *great* friends!" Air said.

"Very well. For what did you wish to meet me for?" Lucy asked.

"Most people get all frazzled about meeting me, bowing and that stuff." Air waved her hand, as if dismissing it. "Seems you really are a cool cucumber." Air winked and giggled a little bit.

"Air," Venfik said, in a tone of a man with endless patience.

"What?" Air looked to Venfik.

He gave her a look, turning his head to look at Lucy and then back.

"Well, I was going to get there eventually," Air muttered as she pouted slightly. Her face quickly brightened as she smiled to Lucy. "Be my champion."

Those three words made Lucy's eyes go dull but she didn't move a muscle.

Florence's eyes went wide, looking around the room.

"Why?" Lucy asked.

"Huh, most just take the damn power-up. Well, why, why indeed? I like Emerilia, don't really want to see it destroyed. If you become my champion then you'll get access to information networks across nations, from the highest seats in power. This means you can find out where these spawn points are going to be faster, also access to a ton of information on the different kinds of creatures and the like. Though I bet Fire has all that stuff, so that's not really all that big of a plus. Hmm, well, I kind of want you to convince Fire, Water, and Neuty to let me join in on the plans. I've already started to unite Ashal and I'm getting bored! I want to be a part of messing with Earth, Dark, and Light." Air nodded with a proud smile on her face.

It reminded Lucy of a child who had been praised for spelling out a word. Lucy's gaze moved to Venfik. The old elf smiled kindly; he acted as if he was a fatherly figure to the childish Air.

Increased access to more spies was a big bonus, but she had information networks already. Also, vouching for her to the other gods and goddess who were supporting the Stone Raiders and the people of Emerilia was asking a lot.

"I barely know you, why would I put in a good word for you with the others?" Lucy crossed her arms.

Some of the childishness seemed to fall away for a split second, morphing into a calculating look, and then her playful smile returned so fast that Lucy didn't know whether she had really seen the expression on Air's face.

"Good, then we can work closely together and we can start to change the outcome of this event!" Air said.

"What?" Venfik, Lucy, and Florence said at the same time.

"There is little for me to do within Emerilia right now. All of the alliances and treaties that I have backed have been confirmed and they are becoming stronger with time. My other champions are looking after all of the details now. I can help you in dealing with the different people who have allied themselves with the Stone Raiders to see that they do not let their support waver. If they are being attacked but there is a bigger threat, it will be hard to get them to move the forces that they hold in Terra to help rather than look to their own people. I can help to get past these stumbling blocks and others. Also, I know that there is some group behind Neuty. I want to find out more information on them and what they're doing," Air said.

Lucy felt her eyebrow rise. Air might act childish, but behind it all she had a sharp mind that allowed her to influence Emerilia from the shadows.

"Also, I think we should be able to find out where the other members of the Affinities Pantheon live in case we ever need to pay them a visit."

The offer was amazing, but still Lucy was hesitant. "I will need to talk to others before I can reach a decision."

"Fine, fine—just don't take too long. I'm really bored." Air stretched out the last word as Venfik sighed slightly, wrinkles appearing on his forehead.

Lucy didn't know whether to smile or frown as Air sent her contact details to Lucy.

A champion of the Lady of Air. She might be a little odd, but she's kind of fun. I hope that I can trust her in the future.

Chapter 9: Hope for the Future

Dave closed the door behind Induca and Suzy. He felt drained with the events of the last couple of days. He moved through the apartment he and Deia lived in. He was about to make it into his and Deia's room when little Koi started to cry.

"I feel like this is going to be a common thing," Dave muttered. The corners of his mouth pulled upward into a smile. He turned toward Koi's crib. Dave and Deia had settled on the name before they left the hospital.

"Hey there little one, what's wrong?" Dave gently picked her up. He held her up and smelled her bottom. "Phew, okay, stinker!" Dave's eyes watered a bit as he carried Koi over to the changing table.

He got off the nasty diaper and replaced it. Dave found out that Emerilians were still using cloth wrappings for diapers. He'd taken patents off the Internet, got a factory working, and the Exdar's Traders were now selling baby diapers by the ton across Emerilia.

He'd also made baby wipes and all other kinds of items to look after Koi with.

He quickly cleaned her up and placed on a new diaper.

Koi's cries had fallen away as she played with the rack of items above her head.

Dave shook his head as he got her little one-piece sleeping clothes back on. He grabbed a bottle of prepared milk, checking it was the right temperature. He picked up Koi and held the bottle up to her lips. Her covered hands half-held the bottle while she clamped down on the end of the milk bottle and started to drink.

Dave smiled as she finished off downing the milk. Dave put the milk away; gathering Koi up, he patted and burped her, bouncing her slightly.

She burped, her movements slowing down as her eyes started to close. Dave cleaned up her face, humming slightly as Koi slowly fell asleep.

He laid Koi down in her bed, wrapping her up like a small burrito so only her head was visible. She looked so peaceful as she laid there.

Dave yawned, smiling as he left the room and headed to his own.

Deia was passed out in bed. She'd had it even harder in the last couple of days. She'd been on Health potions and the like.

In the space of just a few moments of Jules's attention, it was as if she had never had a child.

Dave threw off his clothes and got into bed.

"How is she?" Deia asked faintly, not opening her eyes as her arms moved around Dave. Now without her belly, she once again could fully cuddle Dave.

"She's fine, put her to bed." Dave's arm curled around Deia, his fingers drawing over her lower back.

Deia let out a happy noise, moving slightly to kiss Dave before settling her head on his shoulder.

Dave quickly fell asleep, cuddling his woman to him as his daughter peacefully slept in the other room.

***

Malsour looked at the laboratory that Steve, Dave, Bob, and he worked in most of the time.

He looked at the fusion reactor, the Mana wells, the teleportation array, different machines and coding plates laid across the room, from parts that could make up a surface-to-space missile, to dwarven artillery cannons and plans of the plasma cannons that Deia and Induca wielded. There were locked and secured orbs that Dave had made.

Here was where they made the weapons and devices that could save Emerilia in the future.

He moved to a new area at the back of Pandora's box. He passed through a nondescript doorway and entered a room with two different portals, and three onos. The onos connected to the seeder buried under Cliff-Hill, shipyard one, and shipyard two, which had just been started. There were automated carts moving materials that had been mined from shipyard two to one in order to be refined down.

The portals connected to moonbase one and the *Datskun*.

Pandora's box acted as a hub between all the various secret locations within and beyond Emerilia.

Malsour passed through the portal connected to the moonbase. The open area from before had changed greatly.

Along one wall, there were all manner of automated industrial machines that looked to growing the moonbase and increasing the number of automatons within it. There were also growing areas and storage tanks that created solutions that Bob would need to grow the players' bodies and store them.

The middle of the room was filled with pods cocooned in all manner of machines and tubes. The opposite wall looked bare, with simple empty racks and connection ports. The middle area was supposed to grow the bodies of the players while the left side was supposed to hold all of the grown bodies.

Malsour's senses spread out as he dropped his Mana shield. Bob had finally got the mix of air within the area to a breathable state.

Everything was lit with a soft light that came from parts of the soul gem constructs that made up nearly everything within the moonbase.

The moonbase had grown to three times its original size since they had first arrived and it was still increasing in size. Missile stocks had been brought up from shipyard one and launchers were being made, waiting to be installed.

The miners and repair bots were happily excavating all that they could; given enough time, they would hollow the entire moon.

Malsour looked to where Bob was working at a desk with all manner of interfaces around him and a pod in front of him with connections and ports that looked identical to the ones that were within the middle area of the base.

Malsour walked over to where Bob was.

Bob pressed a button as a sudden light filled the pod next to him.

"How is everything going?" Malsour asked.

"Slowly. It takes a lot of time to synthesize the information from the player's DNA. It sounds easy to just grow a body from someone's DNA map, but it isn't. I'm able to make organs, muscles, tendons and all the rest, but putting it all together is complicated as hell." Bob sighed.

"What about linking the minds together and imprinting the player's brain into their body?" Malsour asked.

"Well, that's actually kind of easy, seeing as I was the one to come up with that tech," Bob said with a little pride.

"You built the process of taking the memories and thoughts from one brain to another?" Malsour asked.

"Yes, I was one of the chief engineers on the animation machine, what is called the Altars of Rebirth. So I know how to do the imprinting. Growing the body—that's just a pain in the ass. Trying out different layering methods but I keep on making bodies that have odd and different dimensions. I've got to refine down the growing chambers' coding ever further to get the kind of in-depth and controlled results that I want." Bob said the last part more to himself than to Malsour.

"Well, hope it goes well. I'm going to check on some of the other projects," Malsour said. He wasn't a biologist; if someone needed to make a mechanical system, he could create it from plans or even an idea of what it was supposed to do. However, machines that were supposed to make bodies were way out of his league. Also, Bob had his own AI to translate his plans into magical coding.

"Thanks. Good luck with the launchers," Bob said.

Malsour pulled out a silver surfboard and threw it down. Pillars grew underneath as he stepped onto it. He surged forward, as the pillars formed a moving base under the surfboard. He quickly left the developed areas of the base.

There were refineries constantly working; a single massive refinery was being built as well. A second fusion reactor was also being assembled.

Factories were constantly making more machines or other components.

There was a storage area where automated carts were dropping off finished products and unrefined materials from the mining drills. Others were picking up parts and automatons, shipping them to the expanding areas of the base while still others were taking the refined materials and heading to the portals.

Automated miners spread out in all directions, mining out ore-rich areas within the moon and expanding the facilities. Already, a third shipyard was being built, as well as massive factories. The moonbase was meant to be a fallback position if they ever needed it. As such, it was also making all the kinds of machines and things that they would need to fight anyone who came looking for them.

Resources were at a premium. Thankfully, with Dave, Shard, Steve, and Jeeves all working on coding up a soul gem construct for the destroyer-class warships, they were going to be able to save a lot of resources. The battleships that were in shipyard one were still under development, but shipyard two and three would hopefully be growing their ships by the time that they were done.

Malsour passed rollers that were smoothing out armor plates and engravers that placed magical code within the metal sheets, then silver that was injected into these carved runes.

The more complex factories were still on Emerilia, but it was their hope that soon they would be building the more complex factories in the moonbase.

Malsour rode past massive formed metal pieces with coding covering them and multiple rings of runes underneath. These were being slowly worked on by repair bots; they didn't have factories big enough to work on these pieces.

He continued forward until he got to a number of massive storage crates.

The surfboard slowed down as he stepped off without pausing. His control over Dark materials had reached such a degree of control he could use it without thought. With a flick of his hand, the massive chests opened. He looked inside, a cold smile spreading across his face.

There were a half-dozen metal tubes with four banks of coded sheets along each side.

Malsour waved his hands as the soul gem construct above him grew into two hands and descended toward the chest. It reached inside and pulled out one of the metal tubes. It had looked only about a meter in length when it was inside the crate. Once it was free, it grew until it was nearly ten meters in length.

The soul gem hands held the massive tube carefully.

"Looks like they're finally ready." Malsour smiled as he looked over the tubes and its coded plates.

The plates were held in metal braces that ran the length of the tube and inserted into the actual tube. Inside the tube, there were thick ebony lines where the coded banks were attached. Titanium and aluminum plates were flush with these ebony bands and covered in heat-absorbing runes.

At one end, the tube was open; the other was closed by a sliding hatch. In the middle of the tube, there was another hatch that could seal the tube completely.

A missile would be placed into the tube, the rear hatch sealing. Then it would be accelerated by the banks of coded plates, which transmitted their force through the ebony strip.

The middle hatch would snap open and the missile would erupt out of the tube before its magically coded engines would fire, increasing its speed as it charged toward its target.

Malsour finished inspecting the tube and the soul gem-created arms put the tube back as Malsour moved to another group of chests. He opened these, looking inside at the racks filled with missiles.

They looked like cigars that had one end cut.

There was no visible engine as the original idea of taking the destruction staff coding and adapting it to produce more thrust gave way to Dave putting in proper gravity engines that could push the missile away from the ground or firing platform and then pull itself toward its target. It was much faster and the energy requirements were actually less with Dave's knowledge for gravitational anomalies combined with his knowledge on space and time.

The main body held a grand working. These varied from pure destructive wild Mana that was more powerful than most nukes and cleaner as it was a pure energy weapon.

Then there were gravity distortion workings that would create multiple twists and warps in space, like hundreds of portals connecting to one spot. These gravity fluctuations were supposed to be extremely powerful but they hadn't tested them out as they didn't want to alert the Jukal.

They were some damned scary weapons.

Malsour raised the ground under the crates and stepped onto his following surfboard. He whistled as he took off through the base again, a dozen or so crates following him.

*****

Josh looked to the woman across from him. She looked like a mid- to late-twenties woman, all of her curves in the right places and a cloak that made someone want to see the body underneath.

However, Josh wasn't thinking about this at all.

This beautiful woman was unreadable; even though she looked young, she had an ancient air to her. This woman was in fact the mother of dragons, Denur.

Cold sweat slowly fell down Josh's back as he gave her a strained smile.

She had been simply studying him for the last few minutes, not saying a word.

"My family and I will not be able to help you with every issue and there are a number who will not lend their help unless absolutely necessary, as they have children and other commitments," Denur said.

"Do you have an idea of the number of your family who would be interested in helping out the Stone Raiders' alliance with this event?" Josh asked hesitantly.

"No more than twenty and that number is liable to change. Also, with joining this alliance, we expect that others will aid us as we have aided them," Denur said.

Josh nodded, his face grave. "Of course." His heart trembled. For the dragons to ask for help in case of attack brought home just how strong the creatures and races that might come through the event's spawn points might be.

"Good. Our strengths lay in aerial battles and those out in the open. Fighting in tunnels and underground areas would merely weaken our attacks and make it harder for us to use our full strength," Denur said.

"Understandable. It is my aim to use everyone in situations that they are the most effective. It was the reason that we left the dwarves in Norkurn instead of have them fight beside us. If they had been with us, then we could have held the beasts off easier. But while most of us can come back from the dead, they can't," Josh said. "I plan to have the Stone Raiders and any other player guilds go into the most dangerous situations because we can die and come back. The people of Emerilia can't."

Denur nodded, her face remaining expressionless. "I will give you my contact information. If you have any questions, ask Malsour and Induca." Denur stood.

Josh rose too.

"Let's hope that we can save Emerilia," she said with a small smile, her eyes sad before she moved to the door.

Chapter 10: Ready Wave Two!

"Okay, so we know where the next spawn point is—the issue we have is getting there," Lucy said to the combined Stone Raiders and the leaders of the Terra Alliance.

A map appeared in the middle of the room, showing Ashal.

"To the north of Goblin Mountain, there's grasslands and forest until the northern coast. To the west, there's the Great Ashal forest and the Densaou Ring of Fire. To the south, open plains and grasslands and the edge of the Great Ashal forest. To the east, there's the Northwood and then Devil's Crater. The closest place we can move from is the outpost in Northwood at the Six Affinities Temple. From there, we can move to Goblin Mountain. If this was nearly any other continent, then we could dispatch a small and quick party to cross the area, reach Goblin Mountain, throw down a drop pad and then we could put an ono in at the base of the mountain. If we send a small party, it's more likely that they'll be eaten up by the Ashal wilderness." Lucy looked around the room. The different leaders nodded their heads; these people who had been sent by their respective leaders were not dull and knew the realities of fighting on all of the continents. "What we're going to have to do is what we did with the outpost at the Six Affinities Temple. We're going to have to move a large force that is well versed in moving through this kind of terrain and with enough power to fight off Ashal's beasts, moving through the wilderness to the mountain before establishing an outpost and placing an ono there."

"How long is that going to take?" one of the ambassadors asked with a serious face.

"Seven days by air, twelve if we send them by ground," Lucy said. "Once they are at the location they can put down a drop pad and we can insert an Ono in and move the rest of our force over in a day."

Murmurs broke through the crowd. If they wanted to get an ono there before the spawn point was activated, then they would have to fly it and it would only be a day earlier at the max.

A laughing voice sounded in Lucy's ear.

"I can get it there within a day if you want my help," Air's voice sounded out. However no one in the room seemed to hear it other than Lucy.

Lucy stopped herself from looking around wildly. She slowly glanced around the room as if she were looking at the leaders before her eyes fell on an aide to one of the ambassadors. Her face and body were plain and easy to overlook but those eyes flashed with interest as Air smiled. To her side, there was an elven-looking servant with a water canter ready to fill up the ambassador's water. He had an apologetic look on his face.

"Are you sure?" Lucy didn't even move her lips, the words only audible to her.

"I guarantee it," Air said.

Lucy took a deep breath.

"There is another option," she said. The room became silent in a matter of seconds.

"We have a silent ally who might be able to drop it off in a few days. If they can do that, then we can start building a defensive structure almost immediately. However, even if this works out, then we're going to have to deploy a large force to protect those who are building the defensive structure." Lucy sat back down.

Dwayne took over the meeting, talking about the strategy of what they would do once they had an ono down in the area.

Lucy looked to Venfik and Air, who smiled slightly before leaving the room.

Just who the hell did I ally myself with?

***

Fire, Water, and Bob were in Fire's office.

Bob looked over Water with an approving look. "Seems that you haven't been sitting back in your time here."

"With the mage's college's resources, I have been able to learn quite a bit." Water smiled at Fire.

Fire smiled at his praise. Seeing his strength grow made her slightly nervous still; it was a knee-jerk reaction of fighting each other for so long. Now that they were on the same side, it was still hard for her to believe sometimes.

"I keep on hearing that Jelanos is having trouble trying to confuse your different teachers and helpers who keep on praising your control over the Water Affinity." Fire snorted.

Water let out a rich, deep laugh. "They are amazing teachers. With their help and knowledge, I have been able to increase my abilities quickly," Water admitted.

"Good. We're probably going to need it soon enough. Dark has gone quiet, which, knowing that arse, doesn't mean good things. Earth is in Ashal, creating creatures and sending what aid he can spare to the people who follow him. If he wasn't such a blockhead focused on gaining more power and people to control, then he wouldn't be so bad," Bob complained.

Fire and Water both had solemn expectations. Earth rated how strong he was by the amount of land that was under his creatures', or those who gave devotions to him, control. When he had supported Dark at Boran-al's Citadel, it was because Dark said that he would clear the land of all people who didn't follow him. However, if the land was cleared of people, then nature would once again start taking over, bringing it into Earth's domain.

He'd attacked the elves in Kufo'tel because he knew of the number of Fire mages and others who weren't giving him devotions but still living in his forests. He governed his land like a king: if those within it gave him their devotions, he would lend them his strength to continue to control his land.

"Light, however, is not being quiet—well, at least her true champion Khanundra has been moving through Markolm. She's been meeting with the various leaders on Light's continent, killing those who don't agree to follow the Lady of Light or accepting their devotions and demanding more from them and their people. Markolm is becoming a darker place. People want to flee but their prejudices with having their own elven nation after being persecuted for so long is holding them back," Bob continued.

"It seems that Air has been out there spreading the goodwill." Fire looked to Water. As he'd been so focused on training, he got most of his information through his mer-people rather than Bob and Fire's own networks. "She has settled the conflicts within the Ashal continent, as well as a number of disputes across Emerilia. We've been so focused on other things that we haven't really noticed. Seems that she was serious when she wanted to join us. It also appears that she has moved into Terra. She's hiding out there but she wants to take Lucy as her champion and give her access to her information networks. She is also helping out the alliance by easing over tensions and getting the ambassadors and military forces to work together."

The room was quiet for a bit, with everyone in their own thoughts.

"It is always best to not underestimate Air. She might be the Affinity for Air, but her passion is for secrets, to create motion and get the world to move and change. Although she would never go with Light and Dark who are interested in changing the world so everyone obeys them, or Earth because he wants to rule Emerilia like some kind of medieval king, she does make a suitable ally for us," Water said.

"She is one of the smartest people I know of. Even I don't know the full extent of what she can do and has done on Emerilia," Bob said.

"So now we have to figure out if we trust her to have Emerilia's best interests in heart or if she's playing a prank," Fire said.

"Well, she has never directly got anyone hurt because of her actions other than that time with the demons. How was she to know that the Dark Lord would start killing them from the inside and send all of his beasts to kill them, actually aiding Light?" Water said.

Bob and Fire both winced.

After the demons had been nearly wiped out, Air still seemed to act a bit childish, but that innocence and playfulness from before was reduced. She understood that her actions had consequences; as such, she thought out her every action completely before she carried it out.

Afterward, she might have messed with different people here and there, but there had been very few times when someone died.

Those who did die were usually the ones stirring up problems for others. Much like Esamael.

She had let Esamael run free, gain his supporters so that she could find out the extent of his network; with Lady Merguine and King Sigaird and the Stone Raiders, she had made it so that they got the information that they needed.

The Stone Raiders blunted the attack by Esamael and took out his army, and then Sigaird and Merguine—with the information from the Lady of Air—had been able to wipe out all of the dissenting forces within the kingdom and finally unite all of Gudalo into a republic.

This was Lady of Air's way. Fire knew of a number of times that she had overturned plans made by the other members of the Affinities Pantheon.

"I feel like we should watch her closely. If she proves herself—well, we need allies," Water said.

Bob and Fire looked to each other before nodding.

"Fine, we'll wait and watch," Bob said.

***

Two days after the meeting with the Stone Raiders and their allies, a drop pad appeared in front of Goblin Mountain.

Lucy let out a sigh of relief as she closed the message screen. A faint breeze was carried through her office.

"Well, looks like everything went well. When you going to put an ono there and make up an outpost?" Air's voice carried through the office, making Lucy jump slightly.

"Air, what did we say about sneaking up on people?" Venfik reprimanded as he glided through Lucy's open balcony door.

"What? I've been stuck mediating between the Opheir kingdom and the Gudalo republic about some ancient damned trade agreement they had for the last two days!" Air stomped her feet.

In her mind, Lucy wasn't able to connect or overlay the Lady of Air with the woman who stood in her office, being chided by her elven aide who acted more like a parent who still attempted to teach his recalcitrant child some manners—and continued to fail.

"If everything goes well, we'll get an ono ready, then we'll have the elven rangers and DCA ground and air forces spread out, followed by the dwarves. We'll get the engineers and Dark mages from the various groups to get working on the camp, holding mounted forces in reserve. The dwarves will hold the camp as it grows and the elves will watch the forest, with the DCA patrolling the skies.

"If they come into anything, the elves and DCA will kill or slow down any threats. If it's a big threat, then the DCA aerial forces will assist. If they aren't enough, then the mounted forces will be called in to support," Lucy said.

"Cool! So when we have the place, what will we do?" Air slumped down onto Lucy's couch.

"Were you listening at all when you were in the meeting?" Lucy asked.

"About ten percent." Air shrugged.

"Once we have the place secured, then we're going to hold it. We're not going down into the mountain—that would just be a mess. Whatever spawns inside the mountain—hopefully they don't have the best relationship with the goblins—the two of them fight it out; then, if they're weakened, we can move in and clear it up," Lucy said.

"Smart—let your enemy do the work for you." Air nodded. "Well, I'm going to get a pina colada in Heval. Have fun with work!" Air jumped to her feet and moved to the balcony.

Lucy sighed and sat back down at her desk.

"Oh, and the next spawn point has been found. In the orcish swamps. Looks like it's got," Air cocked her head to the side in thought, "about seventeen days before it opens. Seems they're opening up faster." Air's smile became faint as her playful tone fell away for a moment. She turned and took off into the air in a rush. There was only a light breeze even as she passed through at speeds that should have shattered the air.

Venfik gave Lucy a piece of paper, bowing slightly to Lucy before he, too, sped up into the sky.

Lucy opened the paper. It disintegrated in her hands but a way point appeared on her map while a new screen appeared.

Event: Of Myths and Legends

The Lady of Air has given you a location of a spawn point.

Objectives:

Defeat the creatures that exit the spawn point

Failure:

Emerilia becomes overrun

Allow more than 80% of Emerilia's population to die.

Rewards:

Experience

Unknown

A second screen appeared after the first.

Spawn Point (Orcish Swamplands)

Days	Hours	Minutes	Seconds
17	8	51	38

She pushed the timer away and opened up the timer for the Goblin Mountain. Once everyone had seen it, it was accessible in the Event tab.

Spawn Point (Goblin Mountain)

Days	Hours	Minutes	Seconds
9	2	44	18

"Eight days between the two." Lucy rubbed her forehead, a headache brewing as she moved to the tab with the information on the orcish swamplands and then shared it with the rest of the Stone Raiders' leadership.

***

Malsour stepped out of the teleport array and found Dave.

"There you are!" Dave said.

"What did I miss?" Malsour looked sideways at Dave.

"We're going to Goblin Mountain in a few hours. What have you been up to?" Dave asked.

"One big exit formation laid then I was putting in missile tubes. Had to get to the moon's surface, make doors from the surface material and then lay them in. I put in Light runes on the ends of the tubes so that they can cut through the rock no matter what," Malsour said.

"Huh, makes sense." Dave nodded.

"So, what's this about Goblin Mountain? Thought it would take a few more days before we were able to get anything outside it. Thought that it was going to be really close, actually," Malsour said.

"Well, seems that the Lady Air was willing to give a helping hand." Dave turned and moved for the exit. "Though right now we need to get you headed over there. You're the strongest Dark mage we've got and you were in charge of making the other outpost at the Six Affinities Temple. As such, you've been picked to head up this job."

"How many people have I got and what kind of resources?" Malsour asked.

"Well, I just got you a Mana well and some clean soul gem constructs that will clean a designated area and create a pad underneath. You just need to worry about the damned walls. Also, figure out what settings you want to have in the soul gem constructs. Be easier to program in the magical coding for Mana shields and barriers than doing it into the surface of the walls," Dave said.

"Makes sense. Can I see the Mana well?"

Dave threw him a pouch of holding that could be folded out to pick up and drop larger items.

Malsour pulled out the soul gem-covered Mana well. With a flick of his hand, his surfboard came out, creating a hand to hold it.

The Mana well was only two feet along each side, but the soul gem was about five meters wide in every direction and packed with power. With the power buildup, it would make the soul gem grow faster.

Malsour also saw a number of vault soul gems were in the bag to speed up the growth.

He accessed the soul gem construct and checked the settings. It had the basics within it and connected to his interface. Basically, it was drag and drop. They would make different structures from pre-set items, or things that they coded in, on their interface. Then once they accepted it, there was a certain amount of power required and a timer that would say when everything would be completed.

With more power, the timer went down; with less items or less complicated items being made, then the timer would also go down.

It was like a city building but with less necessary resources and messing around.

Malsour followed Dave as he continued to play with the settings. "How many people are we taking, and how many people are supposed to be based there?"

"About a hundred thousand are going with us. There should be around fifty thousand based there. We've got fifteen thousand in three dwarven warclans, then fifty thousand DCA, with half of them being aerial and half ground forces. The rest is made up of players, supporting groups like the mage's and adventurer's guild," Dave said.

Malsour tapped his chin in thought. "I'll make it double the size of the outpost at the Six Affinities Temple, but then I'll make the walls taller so that more people can fire from them at any time. Also make sure that it's on a rise so that the dwarven artillery has maximum range. Also emplacements along the top of the walls for their guns as well." Malsour dissolved into talking to himself as Dave led him into Terra, and then to an area where there were thousands of soldiers preparing themselves.

Up front were the Stone Raiders, followed by the dwarves, and then the scouting DCA and elven forces. Finally there were the engineers as well as Dark and Earth mages. The mounted fighters were all waiting off to the side, ready to move in but not blocking up the routes for those who would be going first.

"Oh, Shard told me that we should be getting the second section turning and attached within a short while," Dave said.

Malsour looked up from his increasingly complex blueprint on his interface. "That soon? It will be good to see. The third section should come along even faster than the second."

"And we've already gained permission for the fourth and fifth section," Dave said with a proud smile.

"It would be five kilometers long by that time," Malsour said in a somewhat stunned voice.

"Yeah, be bigger than most major cities in all of Emerilia. Though we have more traffic moving through Terra than any other city in the world. We've got jobs and opportunities—people are always looking for those things," Dave said.

Malsour nodded as a whistle cut through the air, making those with good hearing wince as conversations died down.

"The ono has been placed. Moving out in one minute!" Josh said to the event group assembled to tackle Goblin Mountain.

People checked their gear one more time as Dave and Malsour moved quickly to the front of the groups to where the Stone Raiders waited. Among them was Party Zero.

"What are you doing here, Deia?" Malsour asked with a stunned voice.

"Mom is looking after little Koi. It's been awhile since I got to be on the front with everyone. I need to see that my skills haven't become rusty," Deia said.

Malsour nodded. It made sense. Deia was the leader of Party Zero, but it had been months since she had been really in the thick of a battle or that she had been able to unleash her true strength. She had refined her spells and abilities in those few months but there was no telling what she would be able to do now.

Malsour looked at the members of Party Zero. By now they were all veterans of tens of battles. They knew what was coming; still, it didn't stop them from having that nervous edge that came with a new adventure that had the possibility for leaving people wounded, or worse.

Jung Lee had formally joined Party Zero. Jekoni floated beside him, looking at the assembled forces with interest.

The teleport pad flared to life; the wall behind it was replaced by a grass plain with a massive mountain standing over it all.

"Move out!" Josh yelled. The Stone Raiders lurched forward. The other groups followed closely behind as they left Terra and came to the base of Goblin Mountain.

Malsour's senses extended outward as soon as he was through the portal.

"These locations look decent," Dave said. Markers appeared in Party Zero's shared map.

Malsour looked to them all, checking them against what he had sensed and could see. "This position." Malsour picked a location.

"Okay, you two get started and be ready for those coming behind us. I'm passing it up to Josh," Deia said.

Malsour and Dave nodded. Malsour waved for Steve to join them as they ran for a single glowing marker.

In the quiet meadow, the creatures that had been enjoying the midday sun were suddenly startled as the shiny rock with odd characters all over that had appeared out of nowhere flared to life, and then began pouring out people from all kinds of races.

They started to move for one position as the creatures fled, stunned by the sudden events. However, these were creatures that lived on the Ashal continent. If they didn't know how to run away, or when to fight, then they wouldn't have survived to this point.

Just minutes after the people started spreading out into the meadow, the ground shook as a shining material with motes of light contained within it spread out from a large sphere of the same material. It spread out like a snowball melting in the summer light, revealing a box that still had a thin layer of the glowing material covering it.

The wild animals in the meadow weren't the only ones to notice this growing material, or the way the earth shook just before massive metal pillars shot out of the ground as if they were sea monsters rising from the depths of the sea.

A group of scavenging goblins made to attack the feeble creatures in front of them. As they raced forward, yelling their war cries, a dozen arrows cut off their cries. Shadows flitted outward as people coming out of the glowing rock spread in all directions. Most had pointy ears, beast-like features, or wings on their backs. This was the DCA and elven forces!

The Terra Alliance had staked their claim to the plot of land outside of Goblin Mountain and they had brought a force capable of defending it.

Chapter 11: Enemy Territory

The Stone Raiders' scouts had gone off with the DCA and elven forces, led by Josh.

Esa, Dwayne, and Kim were working with the dwarves to secure their lines.

The four dwarven warclans each faced a different direction, creating a rounded-out square with interlinked shields planted into the ground. Dwarven artillery was being brought to bear, the artillery commanders and their crews securing the artillery to the already two-hundred-meter-wide soul gem sheet that covered the ground.

Among the dwarven lines, there were the Stone Raiders as well as members from the Fellox and Portal Purge guilds.

The dwarves made up the front lines simply because they were more coordinated than even the Stone Raiders. If they had allies in front of them, then their ability to fight would be greatly reduced.

So the players took secondary positions, ready to aid as needed.

Dave and Steve were finishing up with the commands for the soul gem construct as well as placing soul gems around the Mana well in slots that drained the power into the soul gem construct.

Malsour and Jung Lee were with the engineers and mages with a Dark or Earth Affinity.

The Earth mages moved out. Their job was to level out the forested areas a bit more, as well as collapse any tunnels that were underneath it.

The Dark mages were all bringing threads of stone and metal from the bedrock below; these would hook into the soul gem construct and be the basis of the walls.

"Done!" Dave said after he'd checked the plans for the fifth time. He accepted them and the soul gem construct stopped just growing outward wildly; one-foot-wide lengths shot out in four directions.

They reached out five hundred meters in every direction before spreading outward to either side until they reached the other edges of the extended soul gem lengths. Once they met, they spread out ten meters and then started growing upward, creating the basis of the wall.

"Good here," Steve said. He'd been working on the overall magical coding as well as checking the structural strength of everything.

"Well, now you can help me with feeding this thing power." Dave pulled out more and more vault soul gems, draining them.

An automated cart came through the still open ono. A repair bot picked up the empty soul gems before racing back to Terra. It would charge them off of Terra's power grid and bring them back.

Dave continued to dump more soul gems in the power intakes. The soul gem construct continued to grow at a rapid rate.

Finally, the threads from the bedrock had secured themselves to the Mana well and the foundations of the soul gem inner layer for the walls. They started breaking through the ground and wrapping around the growing soul gem walls. The glass-like walls became much thicker and imposing as they were covered in layers of stone, metal, and sand. These layers were the best to protect the walls.

With the number of Dark mages and various engineers, the soul gem constructs were only just capable of growing faster.

The automated cart and repair bot reappeared with charged soul gems. It came with an extra Aleph repair bot. This one pulled off the soul gems, placing them into the right place while another gathered up the used soul gems.

Dave and Steve dropped off their remaining soul gems for the repair bot.

"Time to golf! Sorry, erm, defend this outpost? Is it an outpost? Kind of more like a castle." Steve looked to Dave.

"How was it that you're the personality of one of the most complicated rune creations in all of Emerilia?" Dave asked.

"'Cause I like turtles?" Steve shrugged as if he, too, was confused.

"Oh God." Dave didn't know whether to laugh or cry as he shook his head.

***

"Goblins are on the move," one of the DCA forward scouts said over the brigade chat.

"Force strength?" Kala looked over the preparations that her people had made. With the aid of Earth magic and some devious know-how, they were creating ambush positions and traps.

"About three hundred," the scout said. There was none of the panicked uneasiness from a few months back. Kala quietly praised the scout in her thoughts.

"Malkur, would it be possible to break up those forces before they reach our lines?" Kala asked.

"We can do that," Malkur agreed.

"Very good. Have your people ready themselves. Doi'Kun, your elven forces—are they in position to harass the goblins? Need you to aggro them and pull them into smaller bands. Then get your people to kite them to different ambush locations," Kala said.

"We are ready," Doi'Kun said.

"Good. Malkur, go and say hello," Kala said.

DCA aerial forces rose up into the sky, gaining altitude.

Kala looked to her preparations, checking with her different leaders when the first Mana bombs started to shake the ground with their impacts.

"Kiting the groups," Doi'Kun said as explosions continued to rock the ground.

Kala looked to her map. The charging and ramshackle mess of a formation that the goblins had adopted had completely fallen apart. They were now racing at the targets that they could see.

"We've got pockets that our Mana bombs didn't work in," Malkur reported.

"They probably have shamans," Kala said.

"I will have my rangers target them first," Doi'Kun said.

The mass of creatures had been thinned out and they rushed outward in multiple directions. The elven rangers were at home in nature; their bows and spells kept the goblins focused on them, using their anger to drive them apart and into isolation.

Clumps of rangers hiding in camouflaged positions seemed to appear from the ground as they unleashed barrages of arrows at the shamans, taking them out before they rushed off into the forest. The kiting groups had to work harder to keep the goblins focused on them.

The DCA aerial forces swooped in, unleashing Mana bombs and bolts on the smaller goblin groups.

The goblins were once again broken up.

Hidden elven rangers appeared in the midst of this destruction, aggroing smaller and smaller groups.

Using the confusion of the explosions and the goblins' fiery tempers, in a short period of time, the goblins' three hundred was reduced to two hundred and all in groups of no more than eight.

"Customers coming in," Kala said to the group that she was in command of. She was on a slight rise with bushes, looking down on a muddy and bare stone gully.

The elves flashed through, their arrows whizzing through the air. The slightly rough terrain didn't slow them in the slightest.

With their ability to read the land, they were able to easily avoid the various traps.

They led the goblins by the nose, just barely missing the traps so that the goblins didn't realize that there were any traps.

The goblins entered the gully, grunting and panting as their pace slowed and they started the arduous climb up the sloped gully.

Kala waited until they were all within the gully. "Fire!"

The DCA stepped out of the bushes on either side of the gully as an explosion went off at either ends of the gully. Rocks, debris, and the explosion killed a few and stunned the others. The DCA didn't give them time to recover as the gully lit up with the destructive light of hundreds of Mana bolts.

"Hold!" Kala called. The bolts stopped firing, leaving behind a gory scene with the gully turned to mostly glass. "You've got thirty seconds to loot then we're off to the next position!"

The DCA rushed in, taking the loot from the floating tombstones above the goblins. This was given to the officers, who stored it in a loot bag.

"Let's go," Kala said.

The DCA faded into the overgrown meadow, not making a sound. Explosions reverberated through the forest as well as the screams of goblins and the occasional clash of metal on metal.

None of the goblins made it through the rough forest beyond their mountain. The DCA was rarely seen and the elven rangers seemed untouchable with their agility and mastery with the bow.

As the forest once again fell into silence, the tigers within it prepared for more prey. New ambush locations and traps were added while wounds were checked and wounded were sent back to the camp. They hadn't lost anyone but they had received fifteen wounded, ten of which needed healers' attention.

The training for last couple of months had turned the DCA into hunters and warriors capable of working independently and effectively. Even the elves who had seen warriors and soldiers from all over Emerilia for hundreds of years gave nods of respect to the members of the Devil's Crater Army.

***

The walls were coming up faster and faster. The DCA and elves had been able to repel five different attacks, each of them bigger than the last. Shamans and hobgoblins were coming out in considerable numbers in the latest groups.

Goblin Mountain had truly earned its name. There must have been thousands of the creatures hidden within it and the surrounding tunnels that connected to it.

The walls had already reached thirty meters into the air; they'd be completed in a number of hours.

Artillery cannons rumbled as the powering soul gems were ejected and new ones slotted into place. Wild Mana arched through the air, landing beyond Deia's eyesight. Plumes of dirt were thrown up in the air with their impacts.

The goblin shamans were making it harder and harder for magical spells to work in their area. The dwarves were instead exploding their rounds in the air above the goblins. That way, the spells weren't weakened by the shamans.

The concussive blasts were enough to mess up the shamans and their chants for the DCA aerial forces to target the shamans.

Elves moved around and peppered them with arrows from a distance.

Each of the shamans had personal guards willing to die for the shaman they protected. Some even threw themselves into the way of arrows so that it wouldn't get the shamans.

The fighting was heating up with the Goblins actually using some rudimentary tactics.

They goblins were harder to split apart, making the ambushes harder to win. Add in the fact that these goblins had much deeper Vitality than other goblins, they were not an easy foe, let alone a one hit kill.

Trumpets bellowed out from the mountain. The goblin forces paused their attacks before they rushed toward the mountain.

Deia frowned as she looked at her map.

"Looks like they're regrouping," Anna said from Deia's side.

"Which means they're going to be a real pain in the ass later." Deia sighed.

The goblins weren't too hard to deal with, but their strength was not in their tactics or the way they fought. It was in their numbers. Goblins grew like an infestation. Many of them might die young but there was so many of them being born every day that their numbers always swelled.

They were one of the few races that were considered an adult of their race in as little as three months. Their instincts were more like animals' than sentients'. It was one of the things that made them so vicious and such an annoying enemy. In three months, they knew how to fight, could communicate as little as a goblin could, and also knew their position within their tribes.

With all of the goblins returning, they would now be able to pass on information on the DCA and elven forces waiting in ambush. They could also gather a much larger goblin army to attack.

"Looks like we'll just have to wait and see. At least this way then hopefully the goblins and whatever spawns can destroy one another," Lox said.

"Goblin prejudice," Steve chimed in.

"Oversized rodents," Gurren spat.

"We all know that you just spat on yourself in your dimensional bag," Steve said.

"I'm going to check on the rest of the guild," Gurren said.

"Is it in your eyes? Don't step on anyone!" Steve yelled as Gurren walked away. Steve turned to the others, holding his hand up as if sharing a secret with them all. "Always imagined myself as a giant, you know—fo fie fe fum, rawr, crash big feet and crushing my enemies beneath my feet."

"Are you thinking of a giant or Godzilla?" Suzy asked.

"Is there a difference?" Steve asked, actually puzzled.

"I blame it on too much television," Anna said to Deia.

"And who was the one that uploaded all of that television?" Deia shot back.

Anna closed her mouth and looked to Steve. "Well, he didn't turn out too bad," Anna said as Steve made sound effects and stomped on the ground as if he were some giant.

The surrounding dwarves were looking from Steve to their fellows with confused looks.

"Maybe you should hit yourself a few times with a heavy mace and you might actually believe it," Deia said.

A small smile rose on Anna's lips.

"Shake in your boots and fear the power of Party Zero, *neouw* bash." Steve swung his hands out.

"That's King Kong," Suzy said in a pained voice as she held her head with her hand.

Lu Lu cooed at Suzy, licking her hand.

Induca patted Suzy's shoulders in comfort. "At least you've got one contracted creature that isn't a complete idiot."

"Wonder if I could add that to my titles. Ohh—you know what's a good song!" Out of nowhere, an electronic keyboard started to play.

"we can dance if we wanna, we can dance all the time. But if your friends don't dance well they ain't mates of mine!

"Oh God, he's singing!" Lox turned and ran away.

"Weak dance but it works!" Steve ran after Lox. "Come on, little cha cha!" Steve yelled, following Lox, the sounds of "Safety Dance" becoming quieter as Steve chased Lox around the growing castle.

"I...I created a monster," Anna admitted, her head dropping to her chest in defeat.

"Yes, yes you did," Deia said. It was her turn to pat Anna's back as she let out some choked laughter.

Eventually they once again faced outward, waiting for the goblins to attack.

After a few minutes, Lox was still being chased by Steve, who was now singing "Down Under."

Even the stony-faced shield bearers had trouble controlling their expressions as their beards quivered in amusement. Party Zero hung their heads in shame, deaf to Lox's cries and damnation against Suzy for not controlling Steve and Anna for his upbringing.

*****

Lox and Gurren glanced over at the castle walls. They had finally been completed after ten hours. They were stronger and larger than the walls at the Six Affinities Temple outpost. Barracks were being built into the central areas of the castle, with dwarven artillery resting on top.

After their retreat, the goblins had not left their mountain once.

The DCA and elves had brought most of their forces back to the castle. The land between the mountain and the castle was filled with pre-planned ambush positions as well as thousands of traps.

Aerial forces and elven rangers moved around the mountain, mapping it out as the DCA ground forces waited, ready to make any goblins that left the mountain pause so that the DCA and elven rangers could be roused and sent to attack the oncoming force.

Still, nothing had happened.

Dave and Deia had returned to Terra in order to see little Koi. Being away from their baby was hard on them but it brought them relief to know that if Deia fell in battle, then their baby would be safe and Deia could respawn without difficulties.

Suzy had also returned to deal with managing the Grahslagg Corporation. Anna was meeting with Kala and Malkur; Steve had finally stopped singing and was helping Malsour out.

Jung Lee was getting lessons from Malsour on his manipulation of materials with the Dark Affinity. Induca was teaching him about Fire Affinity.

It was easy for Jung Lee to call on both of the Free Affinity spirits that rested within his body. However, his fine control wasn't the best. Jekoni was also helping out, as well as being pestered by the mage's guild members.

They'd figured out who he was and were asking him all kinds of questions and following Jung Lee around, saying that they wished to protect the two of them from any harm. Jekoni was a revered archmage of the mage's college, while Jung Lee was a phenomena that they couldn't understand.

"How long do you think before the goblins come?" Gurren asked.

The barrier of leader and shield bearer had been erased long ago; still, Gurren showed a deference to Lox when they were fighting. It made them a good team. There couldn't be two leaders on a line when they were fighting beside each other.

Even Steve, with all of his quirks, acknowledged Lox as the leader of the melee fighters in Party Zero.

Lox puffed on his pipe. Both of them were out of their armor. A fragrant smoke filled the air as Goblin Mountain was clearly visible less than two kilometers away.

"Goblins get smarter the more of them that there are. There's more possibility for a smart one to climb the ranks to alpha and push the others down.

"I think that it will be a few days at least, or they might even wait for us to attack. We're annoying out here but unless we attack them, then we're at a stalemate.

"If we were fighting in a dwarven mountain, it would be much easier to flush them out. As it stands, this is their mountain. We know the kinds of tricks that one can place in their own mountain if they desire to hold it." Lox gave Gurren a sideways look.

Gurren grunted in agreement. "Thankfully for us, we're fine with staying out here. Whatever comes through that spawn point is probably going to be attacked by the goblins. They love their territory and within their mountain, they should be incredibly strong. However, if whatever creatures come through the spawn point are anything as strong as the Elsoom spores, then the goblins will probably hurt them and then be defeated. In that situation, it will then come to us to clear them out. If the goblins kill the creatures that exit the spawn point, then leaving Goblin Mountain alone would be the best plan. We would just waste lives and resources to kill off the goblins that have done little to harm anyone else. They're far from civilization and not an immediate threat. We need our strength for the other creatures in the event."

"Well said." Lox nodded slowly. "However, I do not think that the goblins will be able to hold back whatever exits this spawn point."

"I, too, get that feeling," Gurren said.

They descended into silence as the afternoon turned to night. A faint smoke circled them from Lox's pipe as it glowed with embers.

***

Deia finished feeding Koi, who was happily grasping at the air, trying to pull on her mother's ears and braided hair.

"You're going to make your mother go bald if you keep pulling out all of my hair," Deia admonished the cute little girl, who seemed to increase her attempts as a rich laughter filled the room.

Opposite Deia was Fire, with her own boy Desmond.

"Not too loud or else you'll wake the other babies." Deia looked to Dave and Mal, who were slumped in comfortable seats, fast asleep.

Deia and Fire both gave their respective partners loving looks. Deia burped Koi; even with the meal and burping, Koi was still active.

"Well, you can play with your toys instead of my hair." Deia put Koi on the ground underneath a playset with all manner of objects dangling from it.

Koi let out happy noises, kicking her legs oddly as she grabbed the different hanging items.

"Seems my granddaughter is much more active than her uncle," Fire said softly as she wrapped up the tired Desmond in a blanket, slowly rocking him as she took him to a nearby crib.

"Are you sure you're fine with looking after them both?" Deia asked as Fire returned to the couch.

"I can't do much right now, just try to organize people and things so that Emerilia doesn't fall into chaos. Also, I have a number of helpers." Fire smiled and waved at the center of the volcano where the Dracul clan lived. "They're more than happy to look after Desmond and Koi as if they were their own children. We live for a very long time. Settling down is something that not many are willing to do in our family, making the young more precious than riches and power."

Deia smiled; after a moment, she sighed. "I wish that we could just stay like this, no damn Jukal, no event—just be left alone."

"I know, I know," Fire said comfortingly.

A notification made Dave wake from his slumber as Deia looked at her messages. It had been seven days since they had started building outside of Goblin Mountain. The castle had been finished four days ago. Since then, they had been just observing the mountain for any movements. It looked as if there was finally some. She looked at the short video contained in the message.

It showed goblins, trolls, hobgoblins, and shamans all gathering in the cavern as they started to give offerings to the portal as if it were some almighty holy relic.

This was a ritual by the shamans. The offerings would be burnt away as an offering in order to increase the strength of those going into battle.

There were thousands of creatures packed into the goblins' city. The video cut to a group of hobgoblins. All of them wore vastly different clothes and had a pair of guards at their back.

These must be different goblin tribe leaders.

One of the hobgoblins was talking; all of the other tribe leaders were faintly red as they watched him with heat in their eyes. As he finished, the tribe leaders were swept up in his words; their weapons came free of their sheaths as they waved them in the air.

The shot changed to the city.

The entire Goblin Mountain was cheering: a green and brown mass of goblins—with specks of gray for the rock trolls—waved their weapons about, excited for the oncoming battle.

"Looks like we will be returning to Goblin Mountain." Deia looked to Dave. They hadn't spent as much time with Koi as they would have liked but they were fighting for her future. They knew what was to come and they wouldn't shirk their responsibilities. Nor would they bring Koi close to the danger that they would need to deal with.

"I will look after the little one," Fire said, reassuring Deia as she picked up Koi.

Koi complained about being taken away from her toys, her face screwed up as she began to cry.

Deia's eyes were wet as she kissed Koi's head. Dave hugged them both, kissing the top of Koi's head, too.

Mal, who'd woken up from Koi's crying, rose from his seat, sensing something was amiss.

Deia handed Koi over to Fire with a shaky breath.

"Look after yourselves and defeat that goblin army and whatever comes through that spawn point," Fire said.

Oson'Mal nodded as well, his face filled with complex emotions. With their ability to respawn, he wasn't scared of them dying, but still there was a part of his mind that continued to fear losing them as they went off to these battles.

"We'll see you soon," Dave said.

In a flash, they disappeared from Fire's apartment, using a modified magical circle that Dave had given Fire plans for.

Deia took a deep breath as they stood in Pandora's box. She got her emotions under control as her face hardened.

"It's hard to leave her behind but we have to." Dave held her hand, his face filled with understanding.

"I'm her mother and she's been born for only a few weeks and I've been gone for nearly a third of that time," Deia complained.

"You're a great mother and we'll have plenty of time to spend with her after all of this," Dave reassured her, bringing her into a hug.

Deia hugged him back, her fears and worries slowly lessening. After a few moments, they released each other.

"Now's not the time to get sappy. We've got a goblin army to fight!" Dave said, trying to channel his inner excited gamer.

Deia gave a weak smile and nodded. "Let's go and see what these goblins can do."

They walked hand-in-hand out of Pandora's box.

Chapter 12: An Army Rises

Induca looked at the timer that was slowly rolling downward in her Event tab.

Spawn Point (Goblin Mountain)

Days Hours Minutes Seconds

0   7   15   49

The goblin army had gathered all of their considerable strength, filling the mountain and the tunnels through it. For nearly two and a half days, they had been giving resources and material offerings to the portal.

They had burned the different resources within massive fires, shamans throughout the mountain working as one, chanting together and burning the materials in sacrifice. Light surrounded the goblins, making them stronger.

As the ceremony came to the end, the hobgoblin who ruled under the mountain waved a crude hammer in the direction of the castle.

That had been just a few minutes ago.

Induca looked to the feeds that showed the outside of the mountain from the Aleph automaton scouts.

The goblins, their slave trolls, and their hobgoblin elites rushed out from under the mountain. They grouped together in tribes but there was no tactics to their movements and they weren't part of a formation.

Imbued with the power of the ritual and with such a massive army around them, the members of the army grew bold as they let out their warbling war cries.

"Artillery, fire!" The dwarven artillery commander's voice rang out.

Dwarven artillery pieces rocked backward as artillery spells shot from their barrels and Mana clouds created a halo around the end of the gun's barrel.

These were the newest dwarven artillery, the kind that could use grand workings as shells and were made from heat-resistant materials and heat sinks that recycled the heat into charging the internal soul gems.

A few seconds after the first artillery spell had left the barrel, a second was released. The artillery pieces bellowed, filling the skies with the glow of multiplying artillery spells.

The first shells didn't detonate as their shamans' range had increased with them working together. The second didn't work either, but the third did. The explosions created miniature suns in the sky for just a few seconds.

The dwarves adjusted their following shells to the effective height of the third volley of spells.

Under the vicious pressure waves and debris that was tossed up, a number of the goblins died, but it was nothing like the effects would have been if the rounds were allowed to land.

"We could hit them harder and hurt them more, but instead we're going to just try to slow down their attempts to leave the mountain. This feels strange," Induca said.

"I know what you mean. We could use a massive fuel air bomb spell on them and decimate them but instead we're standing here, hoping that we don't kill too many of them in seven hours so that they will turn around and kill whatever comes out of the spawn point," Deia said.

"Bit of a strange conversation," Suzy commented.

Deia and Induca shrugged and continued to look at the advancing army.

The aerial forces were now harassing the goblins, trying to divert them and pull them away from the main body.

Some followed, but the army coming out of the mountain exceeded one hundred and fifty thousand. Just that number alone was enough to raise eyebrows. To have that many goblins in one location without them fighting all the time spoke of the power of the goblin tribe leaders and the harshness of Ashal, where goblins would work together against the creatures of the continent.

The front of the army started to enter the various traps, from quicksand to quagmires and entangling vines or Stamina-burning hexes. These were all curses and area of effect traps that would slow down or weaken an opponent. Nearly five kilometers of ground had been filled with these traps.

The goblin momentum fell as they slugged through the traps.

The DCA ground forces and elves tried to kite groups away, to take them on a journey. The elves focused on the shamans, trying to take them out with their arrows. It worked in limited degrees.

Induca let out a bored sigh and leaned against the parapet.

Commanders went around telling people to relax; it seemed that the plan to slow down the goblin army was working. Goblins were territorial; if there was someone in their land, they'd attack. But if one appeared within their home, they would go crazy.

Using this logic, the alliance was slowing down the goblins instead of killing them. Killing them would be a waste of resources and they would be weakening the power they could use to fight whatever came out of the spawn point.

Four hours slowly passed, with wounded being brought in occasionally. The goblins were in disarray. A number of them were being taken on a trip by the elves and the DCA.

They were angry, tired, and their Stamina was at an all time low. With the shamans blessing that they had received, they were restoring their lost Stamina much faster than they would have done by themselves.

"They've passed through the last of the traps and are on their way to us," Deia said, listening to the party leader channel.

"Nearly two hours to go and nothing lays in their way before they reach us," Anna said.

"It seems that Kim has a plan for how to deal with the goblins if they get closer," Deia said.

"How?" Dave asked.

"Turn the ground to mud," Deia said.

"Muddy goblins. Maybe they'll smell better—couldn't be worse," Steve said.

"Still don't have a nose," Lox muttered.

Under Kim's control, the Earth and Water mages went to work, turning the land in front of the goblin army into a soupy, swampy mess.

It was hard to tell from just looking at it, but as soon as someone stepped onto the muddy area, they would get stuck up to their waist in the soupy and sticky mess.

"This could be funny," Gurren said quietly.

Induca smiled slightly as the goblins yelled their war cries. The people within the castle looked slightly interested but not overly.

The goblin's war cries died somewhat as they dejectedly rushed forward.

"They're like children who get ignored," Jung Lee said.

The goblin army ran forward and collapsed forward like someone running at massive waves and having their feet swept away.

The goblins' war cries had a confused note to it as the ground gave way and they tumbled into the mud that lay underneath the thin ground. Goblins cursed and yelled at one another as the ones behind them started accidentally stepping over them, only to also fall into the mud as well.

Induca chuckled and shook her head at the angered goblins and blank-faced, confused trolls.

***

"Huh, looks like they've fallen into a mud fight." Lox yawned before he put down a card on the makeshift table he, Gurren, Dave, and Deia sat at. Malsour was taking a nap on top of the battlements while Suzy and Induca were talking to Anna about what she should do with her hair and how she should expand her wardrobe a bit more, as well as different clothes she should get when going on a date with Alkao.

Steve looked up from sharpening his axe. "That doesn't look like mud. It looks like the goblins are throwing other goblins." Steve stood. "Hey, that's my move, you bastards! Stop throwing the halflings!"

Dave, Lox, and Gurren looked to one another before looking to their cards.

"It's not fair! I wanted to be the master halfling thrower!" Steve complained.

Suddenly the air distorted and Steve was thrown over the wall, falling down the inner castle wall.

Dave coughed and put a card down as there was a loud metal on stone impact.

"I'm okay!" Steve yelled back up.

"Seems like these floors are getting slippery," Lox commented.

"Very slippery. One might fall once or twice on them," Gurren agreed.

"Dave," Deia said with a low voice, looking to her husband, who looked like a paragon of virtue.

"Those falls are dangerous," Dave said.

"Yes, I hope that they don't happen again," Deia said.

Dave smiled awkwardly under Deia's narrowed eyes.

"Steve was right. The goblins are throwing one another across the mud," Induca said.

"Most progress they've made so far," Anna mumbled.

"I've got to see this." Dave held his cards to his chest and moved to the wall.

Indeed, the larger goblins were throwing the smaller goblins at one another as they brawled with each other.

"We've got another ten minutes before the spawn point opens," Suzy said.

"We'll finish up this hand and get armored up," Lox said.

"Sure you're ready for it?" Dave smiled.

"I'm sure." Lox's eyes narrowed in challenge.

***

In the last twenty minutes before the spawn point opened, the goblin army seemed to be doing their best at goblin shot put. They threw one another forward; it seemed that they had gotten over their grudges now.

People were even placing bets on how far the goblins would go. It felt more like they were out at a picnic than watching a vicious army that was trying to attack them.

Everyone readied themselves and moved to the walls.

Malsour watched the feed from an Aleph automaton scout that was watching the spawn point. "The portal is activating!"

Dave opened his interface as well, switching to a feed that showed the portal. Mana covered it as a whirring noise could be heard.

Goblins that had remained within the village looked at the portal with interest.

As the spawn point hit zero, the portal activated and the ground began to shake.

"What's going on?" Suzy yelled as the entire castle shook.

Malsour's senses picked up something odd. His eyes thinned as he focused on the different oddities. "There're castles rising from the ground!"

"What?" Dave yelled.

"That only happens when a species from beyond the portals makes it into Emerilia and only in certain locations," Induca yelled back.

"Most of them have to make their own positions or they have to take over positions from the Emerilians. Only the stronger, more powerful races will actually have a castle system rise out of the ground around the exiting portal."

Malsour focused on the portal, which had debris from the massive ceiling above falling down around it. A Mana barrier stopped anything from landing within twenty meters of the portal.

A line of spears came through the portal first. They were thrust forward and then pulled back, their actions no less refined than the dwarven warclans.

The spear line advanced before purple and green shields appeared. The creatures behind the shields and spears made Malsour suck in a cold breath of air.

They looked like lizards and were six foot tall and four wide. Their bodies were squat and powerful, and they had two arms, two large legs, and clawed feet. They had two long necks, with heads that bore a similarity to a vulture's. Each head flickered back and forth, looking for threats.

All of them wore identical green and purple armor. The first group out slowed their pace.

A second group came out behind them and moved through openings in the first, reinforcing them. More and more came out of the portal as they formed a circle around the portal.

The goblins made aggressive noises. They might respect the portal but they didn't want anything or anyone in their city.

These lizards didn't care. They spread out, looking at the goblins with little interest. It was as if they detested the goblins' very existence—as if not worthy of their interest.

"They're Nalheim warriors," Malsour said.

Event: Of Myths and Legends

You have figured out a race that have spawned in!

The Nalheim have once again returned to Emerilia. They aggressively attack anything near portals trying to forge their way through and establish colonies within Emerilia

Objectives:

Defeat the creatures that exit the spawn point

Failure:

Emerilia becomes overrun

Allow more than 80% of Emerilia's population to die.

Rewards:

Experience

Unknown

"I thought that they were wiped out," Induca said.

"So did I," Anna said.

A horde of green lizard-looking creatures that had eight limbs and were ten feet long and five high walked out of the portal. On their backs there was a Nalheim warrior.

"Kill them." One of the Nalheim waved their hand.

The amassed ground-based Nalheim moved forward as one.

Goblins charged forward.

Spears flashed and green blood colored the ground as the goblins were cut down mercilessly.

Anything living that got in the Nalheim's way was cut down without a hint of regret.

More and more mounted Nalheims and their dismounted brethren swarmed through the portal, their numbers rapidly rising.

"Nalheim?" Deia asked.

"They have one powerful body but two heads that can work together so well that it's as if they're one single entity.

"One works the spear; the other uses the shield, never leaving holes in their defense. They're strong creatures but many of them die before they mature and their birth rates are low. While there are a number of them that fight dismounted, their skills lay in their mastery of beast taming. They ride war lizards like what you're seeing, as well as sky screams, and their generals ride atop golden gryphons," Malsour informed those who were around him.

Suddenly, horns started to blare from the mountain.

The goblins looked to the mountain; their yattering and grunting fell away. Their eyes glowed red as they started to throw the smallest members out toward Goblin Mountain.

The goblins still on the mud lake's shore yelled and charged toward the mountain.

"Reduce the water in the trap," Kim said to the mages.

Fire mages increased the temperature while the Water mages pulled out the water and Earth mages firmed up the ground. The goblins started to move faster and faster, headed toward their mountain and ignoring the castle they had been intent on attacking beforehand.

Malsour looked to his map. Already the elves and DCA who were in the field started to lead those they had taken on a ride back to the mountain.

Others were scouting out the new castles that had appeared. They expanded outward from the mountain: each of them two kilometers away from the mountain, each of them arrayed around like the points of a compass. Five kilometers past the first castles, there were secondary castles.

"Emergency leader meeting." Josh pointed out a marker on the largest building within the castle that extended above the defensive walls.

Leaders rushed toward the building. They had to figure out what to do with this new threat.

***

"These castles look like the kind that you would find if you went through a portal. Each castle that you can control, the more land comes under your control. Once you control them, you can fix up the walls and add defensive Weapons of War. Assaulting them is a pain in the ass. If we can get control of them, then we will have a defensive wall around the mountain." Kim, the leader from Portal Purge, pointed to the map in the middle of the command post.

"The DCA scouts report that when they entered the castles, they started to see a progress bar above their screens that showed that would allow them to capture the various castles," Malkur said. Kala was leading the forces that were in the field while Malkur's forces were ready to support at any moment.

Everyone looked to Josh.

"I propose that we take command of these different castles. If we can get artillery on them, then we can hopefully block the Nalheim from advancing out of the mountain," Josh said.

The different leaders of the various races nodded.

"Malkur, get your DCA aerial forces to take your ground forces to the nearest castles. I want them to get a drop pad in every location. Once we have those drop pads down, we can put onos into every single one. As soon as they're down, we'll push people through so that we can get in there and capture these castles faster.

"We'll split our forces into five: one to stay here and the others to move to the other four locations nearest the mountain. We'll bring more through the onos at those other locations and move some of our forces here through our ono here and through Terra to the other castles. With the onos, we will be able to mutually support one another. We can move our forces from castles that aren't under heavy attack to those that are, boosting our numbers."

The cost of those onos was a heavy one, but if they could capture them all and make a defensive grid around Goblin Mountain and pin the Nalheim down, then they could stop them from spreading across Emerilia.

Problem is that we've got even more creatures coming through a spawn point in the orc swamps in the Gudalo republic.

With his orders, people started to move.

"I want each of those castles checked and reinforced. See if Malsour can take a look at that," Josh said to Lucy, standing by his side.

She nodded and opened up a private chat on her interface.

Josh's heart raced as energy built within him. He'd encountered another strong enemy as well as an exciting situation. Here it wasn't just a battle; it was a conquest. He would have to take and hold the castles to keep them from the Nalheim.

Pitting his forces against the Nalheim made him feel alive! A smile spread across his face.

He and the Stone Raiders could die; the POE forces that backed him up could be hurt. But playing on this knife's edge where victory and loss could go any way with just a small victory or a small mess-up—this was a gamer's dream!

Chapter 13: Conquest

As soon as a drop pad was placed, an ono would appear within the newly arrived castles in a flash of light. The DCA forces would wait before people started to come through the onos to continue capturing the castles.

Other aerial DCA groups raced toward the other castles, the ones that were directly around Goblin Mountain. Smaller groups headed for the second group of castles.

Party Zero had been called on to check the castles. They stepped out of the ono and into one of the new castles.

In the center, there was a circular building with multiple arrow slits and four massive doors to enter it. This rose two floors from the ground, with a wall framing it and positions for people to stand and fight anyone who made it inside the castle's main walls.

Extending from the center of this circular building was a square tower that extended ten more floors above the circular keep. While the circular building was fifty meters in diameter, the tower was twenty-five meters by twenty-five meters.

At the last four floors, there were landing areas for flying beasts as well as casting positions for mages or artillery. The top of the tower also had a raised wall around it, like the circular building below. Archers, mages, or other ranged people and weapons could be located on this rooftop.

Around the circular main building, there was a cobblestone area that extended fifty meters before it reached the inside of the massive main walls.

These were seventy-five-meter-tall monstrosities. They were laid out in a pentagram with massive fifteen-meter diameter towers on each corner. The walls were a meter thick, made of fused stone with a five-meter-wide passageway inside and an internal wall also made of a meter-thick fused stone.

Casting balconies were on the upper levels; arrow slits covered the second-story walls and up. From the towers, one could hit targets in the distance as well as those who were directly assaulting the walls.

The castles had an ancient and untouched aura to them. As if monoliths from a lost time. There was also a strength and sturdiness to every wall and door within those walls.

The castle could take a number of hits before its walls would be destroyed and an army could make its way inside that's for sure, Dave and Malsour used their sensing abilities to look through the castle to search out points of weakness and their strong points. "We're going to need to engrave those walls with defensive runes, or we're going to have to get the soul gem construct to do it," Dave commented.

"We're also going to need to place Mana barrier runes or constructs on those walls, the keep, and tower. Interlinking them together for mutual defense would be for the best," Malsour said.

"The ground also needs to be firmed up and we're going to need to flatten the area around the castle so that people have clear lines of sight. There's rock outcroppings everywhere and some trees in the way to the west that are going to give an advancing army some cover from us," Dave said.

Next to them, dwarven engineers jotted down everything that they said.

Steve was listening with half an ear as he worked with a soul gem-covered Mana well in his hand.

Dave and Malsour opened their eyes and nodded to each other. They hadn't found anything else that would need their immediate attention.

"I wish that we had more Mana wells to properly solve the power issues here," Malsour said.

"I know what you mean but we've only got a limited amount and we're already eating into our reserves. I've only got a limited number of factories and I need to personally sit down and work on each of them to make sure that they work. I'll try to step more of them up later."

"You've done a lot. These Mana wells and soul gem constructs are a great help. We'll just have to keep juicing them up with soul gems to grow the soul gem construct, then we can get the Mana well to charge up the soul gem." Malsour clapped Dave on the shoulder.

Dave nodded but it was clear that he wished he could do more.

Malsour turned to Steve. "You done with that well yet?"

"Just inputting the different things," Steve said.

Now that they had made the defenses for the castle that they had personally built, they had more templates with which to work with. Steve was just in the process of compiling them together.

"Done." Steve moved to the center of the castle, directly underneath the tower, and put the Mana well and soul gem construct down.

The soul gem rapidly grew outward. The Mana well rose to chest height as it glowed fiercely. The runes across its surface glowed with power as the soul gem grew out from its stand at a rapid rate, covering the stones under a layer of soul gem.

An automated repair bot and cart started to place soul gems into nooks around the Mana well, visibly increasing the rate at which the soul gem construct spread out across the room.

"Remember those settings—we'll probably have to do the same with the next one," Dave said.

Party Zero moved to the ono again, stepping through the side opposite to where people were flooding out of Terra and into the eastern castle.

Deia led them to another teleport pad, where a line of soldiers moved through the teleport pad and into the northern castle.

The soldiers parted, allowing Party Zero to go ahead of them.

Once again they entered the teleport pad and exited the pre-placed ono.

They moved to the center of the tower, Dave and Malsour swarmed by engineers and mages as they listened to the issues that the two listed off. An automated cart and repair bot was already waiting with charged soul gems.

Steve uploaded the same template from the last castle into the soul gem construct/Mana well. The castle and its walls were identical to the eastern castle's.

Steve once again placed the Mana well and soul gem construct as the automated cart and repair bot went to work, stuffing the charging ports in the soul gem construct with powered soul gems.

They did the same with the western and southern castles.

They got two more of the secondary castles before they ran out of Mana well and soul gem constructs.

Instead, they had to just use the soul gem constructs. With the second line of castles, they ordered more of the forests to be cut back so that they could see threats not only from the mountain but the Ashal wilderness.

Once they had finished with all of the secondary castles, Dave, Malsour, and Steve retreated to Pandora's box.

The Mana wells, soul gem constructs, and rechargeable soul gems had proved their worth. The problem was that they needed more of them. The three of them went to work on putting more factories for all of these different items online.

***

Not everything was as peaceful as the improving of the newly emerged castles.

Deia watched the feed from Goblin Mountain and the different Aleph scouts dotted around it.

The goblins quickly escaped the mud pit as the event group at the castle they had built to the southeast made it possible for them to climb out of the mud pit trap. The goblins didn't seem to notice in their rage as they charged toward their homes. They didn't even notice how few traps they ran into or how the dwarven artillery was suspiciously silent.

The Nalheim's forces were growing by the second. As it became clear that the goblins within their mountain city weren't able to put up much of a fight, the dismounted Nalheim and those riding atop their war lizards broke into groups of six and started to rampage through the mountain city. Although the dismounted were systematic in their methods and killings, the war lizards were brutal and ferocious.

They would use their tusks, teeth, and claws to kill anything that wasn't Nalheim. They would crash through buildings, their shield-like faces easily taking the impact. Spears and arrows simply bounced off their armored heads. Their hides were exceptionally tough, even when a goblin was lucky enough to hit them from the side.

The Nalheim riding them could guide them with just squawks from their beaks and squeezing their legs. They were master riders: they could stand upright, their shield slamming away incoming arrows and spears while their own spear darted forward to unleash a ripple of yellow-green energy that cut through the goblins' soft skin.

There were thousands of the war lizard riders and even more of the dismounted. They were quickly destroying those who stood in their path while more continued to flow out of the portal in never ending waves.

Although the goblin army had not been able to get to the castle outside of the mountain in seven hours, now that their path was unobstructed, they were racing back in record speed.

Although the castle was within what they considered their borders, the city was their home. If someone attacked their home instead of just being in their territory, they'd fight those attacking their seat of power.

They made it back to their city within twenty minutes after the horns went off.

They charged into their mountain, rushing to meet the Nalheim.

The Nalheim didn't show any sense of being shocked; instead, they looked excited as more goblins and their slave trolls appeared. With the rush of incoming reinforcements, a good number of the unprepared Nalheim were simply overwhelmed with numbers and cut down.

The goblins surged around the groups of Nalheim. The goblins paid a heavy price to take out a single Nalheim but they were able to cut them down.

The Nalheim were limited in the number that could leave the portal at one time, while the goblins had already organized themselves and were ready for battle.

The war lizards and their masters killed hundreds of goblins and their trolls but they, too, were suppressed. Without the spells from their spears, the riders had to resort to using their shields and spears. Their ability with the dual weapons was amazing; a clear line separated their ability from the ability of the dismounted.

The arrival of the goblins forced the Nalheim to pull back and into a defensive grouping. Their losses were considerable as they had to try to separate themselves from the fighting and into the formation.

The goblins didn't slow down or give them room to breathe as their stronger hobgoblins and trolls were devoted to the task of fighting the Nalheim.

Green goblin blood and orange Nalheim blood covered the ground. Corpses were scattered around, some disintegrating, leaving behind the floating tombstones of the dead creatures.

The war lizard-mounted Nalheim rushed out of the formation, leaving bloody carnage in their wake. Some were pulled to the ground to their deaths and not even the war lizards could stand up to all of the hits from the goblin army.

They returned to the formation after their charge, missing some of their people and a few war lizards, covered in wounds as well as their and their enemies' blood.

Deia shivered as she saw the excitement and warbling cries of the Nalheim. They seemed *excited* by the fighting.

There was a break in the lines of war lizards and dismounted Nalheim from the portal.

A massive bird shot through the portal; it let out a scream that paralyzed the weaker members of the goblin army. This was a Nalheim-mounted sky scream. A dozen more followed, with dismounted and war lizards coming through after them.

The sky screams looked like a tie-dye shirt made from purple, pink, and white. They had massive wings made of skin; where the wings bent back, there were sharpened talons. Their heads were shaped into a point and looked to be hardened like the war lizards'. Large sharpened claws tipped their two feet; they looked as sharp as a saber and were nearly thirty centimeters long.

They were large enough to hold a Nalheim comfortably in a riding harness. These Nalheim looked down on the battle with mild interest, like savage predators looking at an easy meal. They jabbed their spears forward, their spells falling apart under the shamans' magical suppression ability.

The sky screams lived up to their names as they turned and dove in the large cavern, picking up speed as the goblin army in their path tried to recover from the stunning effect of their scream.

The sky scream's head was like a spearhead. They used their faces to plow through the army, their claws low and spread out to catch as many people as possible with their blades.

Others pecked their heads as they flew past the goblin army, piercing armor and bodies with ease.

However strong and powerful these sky screams were, it wasn't all in their favor. Here and there, a goblin in the path of the scream attack recovered and was able to stab the sky scream. Goblin archers unleashed their arrows, holing the sky screams' skin wings and making them screech in pain.

Two of the sky screams fell, depositing their riders into the middle of the army. Ten of them flapped their wings to gain altitude and did their best to avoid getting hit with arrows.

The two mounted Nalheim who had landed within the goblin army were making a mound of dead around them. They were bleeding in various places but still they continued to fight, their spears lashing out to take a life as their shield defended. Their heads were pointed in opposite directions, allowing them to fight in three hundred and sixty degrees.

The Nalheim were trained in fighting with their spears and shields, but the goblins pushed in so close that the Nalheim weren't able to use the length of their spears to full effect. And there were too many goblins for the Nalheim to deal with. They took down nearly forty members of the goblin army before they succumbed to their wounds and the goblin army poured in on them.

The sky screams were pushed back into the skies and needed to fly constantly lest the shamans fire Mana bolts at them, or they get caught by spears and arrows.

The dismounted Nalheim were holding, but their losses were still being recovered and they were still losing more even as reinforcements came in.

The war lizards cut down tens of goblins with every charge, but lost a handful of their own every time.

Sky screams unleashed their attacks as they passed. Although the Nalheim were unaffected, the goblin army was left in a state of paralyzed pain for a few seconds.

The dismounted Nalheim and war lizards used this to kill hundreds of the goblin army in a short time period. Wherever the sky screams left stunned groups of the goblin army, the Nalheim on the ground quickly advanced, killing the paralyzed members of the goblin army.

As time went on, Nalheim continued to die, but at a much slower rate while they were cutting swathes through the goblin army.

The goblin city was burning in the destruction. The shamans guided the fires at the Nalheim. They attacked with their spears and their distorting magical attacks actually weakened the fires.

The shamans pooled the fires together; they compressed and condensed into snakes of fire before they charged forward.

They were harder to defeat and opened up the Nalheim formation. The Nalheim were slow at moving on their own feet but not with their weapons. As they tried to replace the losses, some of the goblin army made it inside, turning these contested areas into chaos.

They fought a pitched battle. The war lizards and sky screams stunned the goblin army that had made it through enough so that the dismounted and lizards could push back and the dismounted could once again form their fighting walls.

Smoke filled the cavern, as did the sounds of battle.

The city was filled with vicious fighting, the Nalheim holding their ground as they were reinforced. When they deemed they had enough people, they started to move forward. The new reinforcements moved forward with them and filled in any gaps that they had in their lines. Their advance was slow as their numbers built up around the portal.

Nalheim wouldn't switch out with one another; they would fight to the bitter end. Only when one died would another take their place.

"It is not going to be a good time fighting these guys," Anna said.

"The Nalheim religion says that to die in battle is the best way to die. They also believe that the more creatures that they destroy and kill, the more honors they will bring to themselves and their people. Once they are engaged in a fight, they will fight to the bitter end, never healing themselves unless the battle has ended. It's why the dismounted Nalheim will fight until they die, not even thinking of seeking out the aide of a healer. They don't even have healers as their natural regenerative abilities are enough once they are out of battle," Induca said.

Deia looked at the wounds on a Nalheim. It was a deep cut that had opened up their forearm. The Nalheim never paused and instead kept going through the pain. In front of her eyes, the wound stopped bleeding and started to seal back together, a layer of fresh green scales on its arm.

Deia shook her head and let out a sigh.

The goblin army was killing off a great number of the Nalheim, but they were trading at a rate of ten goblins to one Nalheim at least.

The Nalheim were advancing but still there wasn't that many of them that one could fight at one time. The sky scream riders fell down occasionally from ranged attacks and the lizard riders and dismounted also fell under the ranged attacks but in close, it became much harder to kill them.

It had been a few hours since the Nalheim had entered Goblin Mountain. There were now sixty or so thousand of them and their numbers were growing. Half of their forces were dismounted; a third rode lizards and the remainder were on sky screams.

The goblin army had called on more forces from all of the interconnected cities and tunnels. There were nearly four hundred thousand goblins at their disposal; however, they were getting ground down by the Nalheim's attacks.

Deia closed her interface and looked out from the castle that the event group had created. It had earned the name citadel due to its massive size compared to the other castles and the fact that it was the headquarters to all of the other castles.

The others were labeled North, East, South and West. The inner ones had an added one so the north inner castle was North One, while the outer was North Two.

Nighttime was coming. The castles glowed from the soul gem constructs covering the castles from the floors to the walls. Strips of soul gem ran from the main soul gem construct and to the walls, where they ran along the exterior walls covering them in defensive runes before moving to the five towers that connected the different walls. In these towers, Mana barrier anchor points were created. Others were made over the inner circular building and around the tower.

With all of these working together, the castles could create powerful barriers that would cover the entire castle from incoming attacks.

If the Nalheim continued to push more of their forces through the portal, then they could take Goblin Mountain and subdue the goblin army. If they didn't, then the goblin army would be severely wounded and weakened but they would kill off the Nalheim that had exited the portal.

***

"Lo'kal, why did you call this meeting?" One of the Jukal advisers to the emperor looked to Bob in his gnome form pacing up and down a room as he appeared.

Bob didn't know how long he had been waiting for, but he knew it had been a few hours. All of the advisers and people who thought that they were important loved to make him wait.

He had been a man of position and power, though with time his power had diminished and his clan had stopped caring about their family member who was practically imprisoned on a planet of his own making, looking after his own creations.

The adviser's bored and morose tone made it clear that he thought of this meeting with Bob as nothing more than a chore that he would much rather be finished with.

"Why was I not informed that in the event, that portals would be used in order to access other planets for creatures for the Emer-ilians and players to fight?" Bob demanded.

"The plan was put into place by you; we just added a few things to it. The planet that the Nalheim race live on has gained the atten-tion of the Freaou race. They've paid their dues and taxes—proven their loyalty—and so it was deemed that they would be allowed another planet. Nalheim is the planet that they were approved for. With this event, the Nalheim will either be wiped out or have such low numbers that our own Jukal fleet won't have to deal with many and we can save on sending out more ships to the planet," the ad-viser said, as if he were explaining it to a child he knew wouldn't understand it.

"I'm the one who made the event but I wasn't told about this!" Bob yelled.

The Jukal looked to him with a bored expression. "I have made a note of your frustration. Is there anything else?" The adviser let out a tired breath and rolled its eyes at Bob, still in his gnome body.

Bob let out a hot breath through his nostrils. "No." With a wave of his hand, he left the Mirror of Communication conference room and returned to his ship, the *Datskun*.

Within the conference room, the Jukal adviser frowned. He had never had anyone be so rude to him or leave before him. He was one of the most powerful people in the Jukal Empire; everyone had shown their subservience to him, day in and day out. He waved his hand, happy to be done with Bob.

Bob tapped his fingers on the command chair of the *Datskun*. He felt the new power that thrummed through her. He'd built and installed all of her old fusion reactors. He hooked them up to factories, using the excess power to build different parts to either bring the *Datskun* fully online, or for the various secret installations across Emerilia and the moon.

He looked to the second moon, where three ships were coming in from out of system. Every three months, like clockwork, the Jukal sent three ships to replace the three that floated around the second moon.

They would take control of the moon and the military facilities within it: the legions of drones that were ready to be called on at a moment's notice and the orbital satellite network.

Everything was looked after by AIs but the second moon acted as a command center for it all. A hard line connection to Emerilia if the long-range kill switch that Bob had, or the empire, didn't work.

Bob sighed as he looked at that revolving marble from *Datskun*'s main screen. He watched Emerilia, the planet he had terraformed and brought a race back from the edge of extermination on.

"I'm not going to give up without a fight," Bob growled. He stood from his chair and headed toward the cargo bay, where a portal to Pandora's box was constantly open.

***

The Nalheim stopped coming through the portal when their numbers reached one hundred and fifty thousand.

Five generals, all riding atop golden gryphons, marched out at a leisurely pace, as if the war that was happening around them were some mildly interesting parlor tricks.

The goblins were forcibly suppressed with the powerful auras of the five generals.

As the generals arrived, all of the Nalheim attacked. The four hundred thousand goblin army had been reduced to two hundred and fifty thousand. Tombstones and bodies lay across the goblin city; the fires had long ago burnt anything standing within the cavern.

The smoke and the limited light of the cavern made it hard to see but the Nalheim and different creatures in the goblin army remained unaffected with the limited light.

The goblins were tired and enraged from trying to fight those in the citadel and now the creatures that were pouring out of their portal and had ruined their homes. All of the goblins in the surrounding areas had come to fight. All of them piled in. The goblin army was tired but they were still fighting strong.

However, the Nalheim were simply better trained, with better abilities and gear. Their weapons were all made from sharpened steel, while the goblins' weapons were largely rusted and blunt. Most of the trolls were simply using tree limbs or stalactites as clubs.

For every Nalheim that went down, ten to eleven of the goblins fell. That number only increased as the goblin army became tired.

Throughout the night, they fought a bloody and desperate battle.

As the dawn started to appear in the sky, the sky slowly became lighter and the goblin army started to break. At first it was a few of them rushing off, too tired and scared from the repeated slaughter. Goblins were territorial, but they were also cowards in most situations. If they had an escape route, they would take it.

When the Nalheim reduced the goblin numbers so they were less than their own, nearly one hundred and twenty thousand on either side, the first few started to flee. Some of them were cut down by the more loyal supporters.

The goblin army held on for another hour. The Nalheim saw that the goblins were weakening; they changed their formation to try to envelop them and cut them off from an escape route.

Some more tried to escape, tribe leaders leading their people away. Tribes started to fight with one another, turning the battlefield into chaos of people trying to fight the Nalheim, then the goblins fighting one another and others running away as fast as possible.

Within forty minutes, the goblin army was no more, with either all of them fleeing or being killed off.

The Nalheim went through the cavern. Their spears made sure there was nothing left alive within the underground city's ruins.

"Seems that the battle will soon be upon us," Jung Lee said.

"Wow, I'm like centuries old and that still sounded dumb as hell," Jekoni said.

"You've been spending time around Steve, I see." Jung Lee looked to Jekoni's floating body.

"I have to say that it's good to relax once in a while—no students, no body, no..." Jekoni's hat flopped onto his face. "No thankful hat." Jekoni stared at the top of the hat in his face, his eyes crossing over.

Jung Lee smiled. It was good to see Jekoni unwinding a bit. "Only took the possible end of the world," Jung Lee muttered to himself.

"What was that?" Jekoni flicked his head back and his hat returned back to flopping backward.

"Just talking to myself, dear friend," Jung Lee said. "What do you think they will do?"

"Probably recover from their wounds then start moving out of Goblin Mountain. Past that, haven't got a clue," Jekoni said.

Jung Lee nodded. His eyes passed over the ground. Without conscious thought, the air distorted in front of him so that he could see the different DCA groups that covered the ground around the mountain. Since the goblin army pulled back to their mountain, the ground forces had sowed the ground around Goblin Mountain with traps.

Without needing to have roads between the castles, it meant that the DCA soldiers could put down as many traps as possible.

Mages and engineers from other races joined together, creating a sea of deadly areas. The different races and groups all brought in new ideas, evolving and changing the traps as they went. What worked for one section of traps wouldn't work for another.

Jekoni watched one of the dismounted pass through the portal.

They returned moments later. Behind them, more Nalheim started to flow from the portal. These fresh troops didn't stop within the goblin city; instead, they headed right for the nearest tunnels. The sky screams walked through the small tunnels, looking awkward in the small confines.

Behind fifteen thousand troops, ten thousand lizards, and five thousand sky screams, golden gryphons marched proudly. The generals on their backs looked uninterested with anything going on around them.

Jung Lee looked out at the meadow. The ground rumbled and fell downward suddenly in an area.

The traps hadn't been laid to just hurt those who stepped on them. They were also aimed at collapsing the tunnels that lay beneath the meadow and those that might pass through them.

Quickly, the Nalheim found out that the tunnels were largely trapped. Annoyed, they started to return to the goblin city, only to find that they had passed under other traps, which now collapsed the other side of the tunnel and pinned forces between rubble.

Fire bloomed within these enclosed areas. The ground heated up and melted down on top of the Nalheim.

"Smells kind of like chicken," Jung Lee said as the Nalheim trapped in the tunnels were roasted by the heat-traps. He had little mercy for those who wished to take over his world and sow destruction in their wake.

Thousands of Nalheim died that night. Only ragtag groups made it back to the goblin city as more and more fighting forces continued to exit the portal.

Only one tunnel passage hadn't been trapped: the one that exited the mountain the quickest and faced the citadel.

"How's it going?" Dave stepped up beside Jung Lee, holding out a warm cup of Xer.

"Looks like my night was better than yours," Jung Lee said. Dave looked tired; he could go a few days without it affecting him much, but Dave looked as if he'd exhausted not only his mind but his body.

"Spent the night making factories to make Mana wells and soul gem constructs," Dave said.

Jung Lee nodded. The two items had proved their abilities to everyone. To be able to grow defensive runes into a castle within just a few hours, if given sufficient power—it was unlike anything Jung Lee had seen before.

"The Nalheim won. They started to try to explore the tunnels around Goblin Mountain. They found the traps within the tunnels. Entire brigades of thirty thousand were trapped in those tunnels when heat and curse traps were activated, burning them alive or draining the very life from them. Some of the forces made it out of the traps. Let the other brigades know. Now the generals are all together and talking with one another. Been that way for like four hours," Jung Lee said.

"Well, that shows they're really good at making plans," Dave said.

"Once they're fighting, they're a powerful force, but yeah, they don't like making decisions quickly," Jung Lee said.

"Well, I'm going to get breakfast and a nap if I can swing it. Let me know if they figure their shit out. Interested to see how effective the traps that the DCA put out are going to be." Dave turned to leave.

"Will do." Jung Lee didn't need to eat much. The Free Affinity spirits fueled his body. If he wanted to join for a meal, he'd let the others know, but now they just assumed that he wasn't really interested in eating. He ate once every couple of days and was fine.

Anna came up and started to teach him about general Mana manipulation as well as the different Affinities and their abilities.

Jekoni added in a few pointers while Jung Lee soaked it up. He'd mostly taken the path of the fighter. His only tie to the mage's college and guild was the fact that he was always searching to advance his knowledge of potion making, which was an area of study within the mage's college.

The midday sun had just crossed over, indicating the coming afternoon, when Jung Lee looked to the screen on his interface that showed the Nalheim generals.

They spread out, yelling their orders as Nalheim brigades—or what was left of them—moved forward toward the only tunnel that hadn't collapsed.

"Seems that the Nalheim's conquest of Emerilia has started in earnest," Jekoni said in a somber voice.

"Artillery crews to your guns!" A dwarven voice rang out across the citadel.

In all of the first ring castles, dwarven artillery units moved to their weapons, checking that they were ready for action; safeties were removed and ammunition storage crates were opened. Soldiers from various races moved to the battlements. They weren't as hurried as the dwarves but they were still prompt in their response.

DCA aerial forces checked their flight gear, armor and their wings, stretching and readying themselves for the coming battle.

Mages grouped together, figuring out who would lead their artillery spells and circulating their Mana so that it was ready to use within a moment's notice.

Jung Lee felt as if his body had woken up. Purpose was etched into the faces and hearts of every person there. They were all here for one thing, one reason: to defend their homes and drive back the invaders. They would succeed or die trying.

***

Dwayne stood on the highest building within the citadel. He used a magical telescope to see the entrance to the mountain that the Nalheim would be exiting from.

As they tried to enter other tunnels, they were once again trapped and killed off.

The Terra Alliance had killed off more of the Nalheim with their traps so far than the entire goblin army had.

Dwayne looked around the citadel. Unlike the castles that had risen from the ground, the citadel was made from black stone and soul gems; the castles were made from gray fused stone and were lit by the growing soul gem constructs within their walls.

The soul gem constructs had formed the shielding and reinforcing runes and paused in their efforts, storing up the power that they were supplied. It wouldn't be smart to have them continue building and then have no actual power left to power the defensive runes when the Nalheim reached the various castles' walls.

Dwayne opened up his interface and moved to the Event tab. There was just one timer remaining.

Spawn Point (Orcish Swamplands)

Days Hours Minutes Seconds
5   17   31   34

He sighed at those numbers. As he glanced to his interface screen, another thirty thousand-strong brigade had moved out of the portal and another followed on its heels.

The original nearly two hundred thousand Nalheim had been cut down to eighty thousand with fighting the goblin army.

Three hundred thousand had then poured out of the portals in thirty thousand units; they'd entered the various goblin tunnels. More and more came out of the portal and died in those tunnels, following their fellow brigades. The three hundred thousand swelled to six hundred thousand moving into that massive network of tunnels. The eighty thousand had started out when people started making it back to the goblin city, saying that the tunnels were death traps.

Nearly seven hundred thousand was reduced to just under three hundred thousand, but every minute, more Nalheim came through that portal. Now they were finally marching out of the mountain; they had returned to five hundred thousand in strength.

Dwayne felt his heart clench at those numbers. The Demon Horde led by the Dark Lord had been nearly ten million strong when it started out, though the DCA had time to wear them down on their travel across Ashal. They were tired, without proper leadership and just a fraction of their original force when they made it to Devil's Crater.

"These Nalheim don't care for losses, much like the demons, but they're smarter. They work together—they have clear and effective tactics. They also have a constant flow of fresh soldiers coming in," Dwayne muttered to himself.

"What you doing up here muttering to yourself for?" Esa walked across the roof.

Dwarves were checking their artillery cannons. They were already set and ready. With just a command, they would unleash hell down upon the Nalheim when they surfaced.

"We've got to control all of these castles or it's going to turn into one hell of a shit show," Dwayne said.

Esa nodded. "Yes, though it seems that there's more to these castles than meets the eye."

"What do you mean?" Dwayne looked to Esa.

"Well, it seems that the people who took over the various castles noticed that they were getting points once they took the castles.

"They've turned control over to the leaders within the Terra Alliance, who then went to Party Zero with questions. Seems that we're gaining conquest points. The longer that we hold the castles, the more conquest points we gain. These points can be used to upgrade the castle's walls, the actual inner buildings as well. They can be used to create magical circles within the castle to increase one's fighting ability, or to build Weapons of War within the castle. Also, the castles can expand. There are major upgrades that would add in a second exterior wall while elevating the castle." Esa smiled.

"Are they pre-planned upgrades or can we pick them?" Dwayne asked.

"Bit of both. The longer we hold, then the larger changes will happen by themselves, like the additional walls. Though for weapons, Magical Circuits, and upgrading what we have already—that kind of stuff—we have to spend conquest points on," Esa said.

"How much of a boost are the magical circles?"

"Well, Dave thinks that they're similar to the kinds of magical circles that are within every major city and town that empowers the city guards to make them stronger," Esa said. "He said that he could do it, but he's doing so many things at the moment that it would be better to just buy it from the castle upgrade list. Would increase our fighting strength—would also make it so that mages and such would be stronger in their spells."

"Has Josh been told this?"

"Yeah, though he said that you and Kim should be the ones to decide what to do with the castles. He's busy dealing with getting everyone organized as the head of the Terra Alliance with Cassie and Lucy's help." Esa looked to Goblin Mountain. "Good thing is that because we control all of the castles, we're earning conquest points really fast. The longer we can hold them, the stronger they'll get. Also, while the overall size upgrades will happen after the same amount of time, we can use the points from the secondary castles on the first castles. It's not like the conquest points can only be used on the castle that they were earned from—they all enter into a pot. One second, I'll give you admin rights."

Esa opened up her interface and quickly moved through a few screens before a screen appeared in front of Dwayne's face.

Castle Conquest

You currently control (8/8) Castles

Earning: (8) conquest points per minute

Bonus: For controlling all of the Castles, you earn an additional (2) conquest points per minute.

Total points: 30,067

Rights: Administrative (Can spend conquest points to upgrade castle infrastructure and repair castles. Can also delete Castle infrastructure)

Eight more screens appeared below.

Southern Castle 1

Status: Under Control by Terra Alliance

Earn: 1 conquest point per minute

Evolution: 1 (Second evolution 10%). Can increase evolution to Level 2 by paying (90,000) Conquest points.

Upgrades: Soul gem construct defenses (player modifications do not count toward or against conquest points)

Southern Castle 2

Status: Under Control by Terra Alliance

Earn: 1 conquest point per minute

Evolution: 1 (Second evolution 10%). Can increase evolution to Level 2 by paying (90,000) Conquest points.

Upgrades: Soul gem construct defenses (player modifications do not count toward or against conquest points)

Eastern Castle 1

Status: Under Control by Terra Alliance

Earn: 1 conquest point per minute

Evolution: 1 (Second evolution 10%). Can increase evolution to Level 2 by paying (90,000) Conquest points.

Upgrades: Soul gem construct defenses (player modifications do not count toward or against conquest points)

Eastern Castle 2

Status: Under Control by Terra Alliance

Earn: 1 conquest point per minute

Evolution: 1 (Second evolution 10%). Can increase evolution to Level 2 by paying (90,000) Conquest points.

Upgrades: Soul gem construct defenses (player modifications do not count toward or against conquest points)

Northern Castle 1

Status: Under Control by Terra Alliance

Earn: 1 conquest point per minute

Evolution: 1 (Second evolution 10%). Can increase evolution to Level 2 by paying (90,000) Conquest points.

Upgrades: Soul gem construct defenses (player modifications do not count toward or against conquest points)

Northern Castle 2

Status: Under Control by Terra Alliance

Earn: 1 conquest point per minute

Evolution: 1 (Second evolution 10%). Can increase evolution to Level 2 by paying (90,000) Conquest points.

Upgrades: Soul gem construct defenses (player modifications do not count toward or against conquest points)

Western Castle 1

Status: Under Control by Terra Alliance

Earn: 1 conquest point per minute

Evolution: 1 (Second evolution 10%). Can increase evolution to Level 2 by paying (90,000) Conquest points.

Upgrades: Soul gem construct defenses (player modifications do not count toward or against conquest points)

Western Castle 2

Status: Under Control by Terra Alliance

Earn: 1 conquest point per minute

Evolution: 1 (Second evolution 10%). Can increase evolution to Level 2 by paying (90,000) Conquest points.

Upgrades: Soul gem construct defenses (player modifications do not count toward or against conquest points)

Castle Conquest

For controlling 4 conquest castles, you gain an extra conquest point (1) per minute

Castle Conquest

For controlling 8 conquest castles, you gain an extra conquest point (1) per minute

A new tab opened up in his quest log, next to his Administrator tab for Terra.

"Damn." Dwayne looked back to the different castles.

"Each day, the progression bar moves up by five percent. We're not sure what's going to happen at the second evolution, but in eighteen more days we can find out. Or if we have enough points, we can pay to upgrade one of the castles and find out," Esa said. "With every time that the castle evolves, we will earn one more conquest point per minute. Also, with upgrades, there are the ones that we do ourselves, which are listed but they don't cost any conquest points. They won't be affected by upgrades that we do apply but we can alter the different upgrades or items that are added to the castles, like we've done with the soul gem constructs."

"It says that as administrators we can repair the castles?" Dwayne asked.

"Someone broke a part of a wall, decreasing the hit points. We rebuilt it ourselves and we didn't spend points; we broke it again and then used conquest points. It's about one conquest point for one hundred hit points of Health, but the more damage, the longer it will take to repair the wall. If we're in the middle of a battle and don't have the time to have our own people repair it, then it allows us a second way to fix our defenses," Esa said.

"If the Nalheim take one of our castles, what will happen?" Dwayne asked.

"Then the evolution progression will drop down to the nearest level. So, say, if a castle is at Level 3 but is at 25% progression to Level 4, then it will start at Level 3 with zero percent level progression. They will also start to earn conquest points from that castle. We will lose the bonus for controlling all of the castles and stop earning conquest points from the castles.

"Also, any and all infrastructure we've built up for the castle will become theirs to do with as they wish. So if there are bolt throwers there that aren't destroyed, those become their bolt throwers," Esa said. "Also, I think that they will get a bonus from taking an owned castle from us."

"Targets out in the open!" the artillery commander yelled. "Fire shells, elevate trajectory for first three rounds. If they have a way to annul our magic, I want to know about it and hit them with something!"

Dwayne looked through the castles' different tabs. With his points, he could buy bolt throwers and some Magical Circuit traps around the castles. He could also buy catapults and a few sets of dwarven artillery and about six different types of grand workings.

He closed the tab. He was just looking to buy something when he didn't even know what would be the best for the situation. Holding onto his points and figuring out what to do with them later was the best plan.

Dwayne looked at the Aleph scout feeds. They showed the exit out of Goblin Mountain. Dismounted Nalheim were forming lines up as sky screams tore into the sky. War lizards moved around the dismounted Nalheim marching lines and charged forward in groups of five, looking to scout the area.

The artillery waited as the Nalheim continued to pour out of the mountain and into the early afternoon sunlight. Sky screams' cries filled the skies as they circled Goblin Mountain before they spread out and headed out in every direction.

"DCA aerial forces are ready," Malkur confirmed over the leadership chat.

"Dwarven artillery holding fire until they move out more."

"DCA ground forces working on more traps."

"Elven forces ready and waiting."

"Aerial support battalion ready."

"Citadel ready for action."

"Eastern Castle One Ready."

"Western Castle One Ready."

"Northern Castle One Ready."

"Southern Castle One Ready."

"Stone Raiders ready to reinforce," Esa said beside Dwayne. He didn't look back, his eyes focused on the sky screams in the skies and the advancing flood of Nalheim.

"Portal Purge Ready," Kim Soon-Ok said, looking out over her guild.

"Fellox Guild Ready," Gimel grunted. It was easy to hear the excitement boiling up within the two player guildmasters.

"Eastern Castle Two Ready."

"Western Castle Two Ready."

"Northern Castle Two Ready."

"Southern Castle Two Ready."

"Three brigades outside Goblin Mountain," a scout reported.

"Begin the attack." Josh's voice was solemn.

"Fire!" the dwarven artillery commander yelled and waved their hand forward.

Dwarven artillery fired down the line, creating a ripple of magical discharging halos. The inside of the citadel vibrated with the actions of the dwarven artillery.

The guns' barrels recoiled. Their projectiles howled through the sky as Mana halos dissipated around the barrels' muzzles.

The force of these massive weapons could be felt in Dwayne's chest and stomach with the massive pressures released. From nine different defensive locations, shells could be seen reaching into the heavens themselves.

Dwarves moved into action, checking their weapons, changing their elevations as observers called out corrections to each different gun crew. Once again the artillery cannons rumbled, spewing out new rounds.

Sky screams yelled at the incoming projectiles, unable to do anything against them except climb higher to get out of their range.

"To the skies!" Malkur yelled out. Wings unfurled as demons and Beast Kin rushed off the tallest buildings within the castles and citadel. They dropped down before flapping their powerful wings and rising up and into the air. They came together into fighting forces, quickly reaching a height above the dwarven artillery.

From the west, the Great Ashal forest shook as magical beasts let out their war cries and flapped their wings. The forest itself seemed to be rising as thousands of flying creatures rose from within that great and imposing forest.

On the backs of these powerful magical beasts stood elves and humans from multiple nations across Emerilia. They stood atop of their beasts that rose with powerful wing flaps.

Even the incredibly powerful magical beasts and creatures of the Ashal wilderness were silenced as the power of the Terra Alliance took to the skies, ready to defend their home.

Dwayne pulled up his telescope once again and looked to the Nalheim.

The dismounted and war lizards seemed to be pointing their spears at the sky angrily, but if one was to look closer, they could see the distorting light around the ends of their staffs. Their accuracy wasn't that good but with the massed release of distorting spells from their spears, they were able to defeat a number of the dwarven artillery spells before they reached their advancing lines.

Golden gryphons took to the skies. Their dominating roar made Dwayne feel his heart clench even at a few kilometers from these powerful beasts.

The dwarven artillery landed among the Nalheim war lizards and dismounted. They had lessened the number of incoming spells but there were nearly two hundred, coming in from nine different directions.

Purple Mana barriers flashed into existence, becoming lighter with the impacts of the artillery spells.

"Barrier busters for artillery batteries in the first layer of castles, Mana bombs for second layer!" the dwarven artillery commander barked. Settings were changed on the dwarven artillery with a number of movable bands that ran down the artillery cannons' length.

The Nalheim continued forward. Their spears lanced out at the artillery shells as they were bathed in destructive light. These Nalheim watched impassively as hell rained down upon them and continued to march forward.

Dwayne's respect for them rose, as he gritted his teeth together.

Wherever the Nalheim's barriers weren't—grass, shrubs, rocks, and dirt, all of it was torn apart under this heavy barrage. Dirt and debris was tossed into the air, creating impacts on the barriers and spraying dirt on the Nalheim soldiers.

Dirt was turned to glass and rocks cracked from the heat.

More of the Nalheim continued to pour out of the mountain as the barrier busters were fired.

In the skies, the sky screams charged toward the castles and citadel around Goblin Mountain, intent on killing those manning the dwarven artillery.

As they dove, the DCA was rising. From their hands, they fired Mana bolts, filling the skies with dazzling light. Around the sky screams, purple Mana barriers became visible, taking on the DCA's hits.

Lines of distortion were projected down by the sky screams' riders' spears, in turn lighting up the DCA's Mana barriers.

Light and distorting waves were exchanged at a faster and faster pace, personal and linked Mana barriers changing colors with the impacts.

Sky screams were hit with Mana bolts, being torn apart by the DCA, who were focusing on one attacker at a time. The Nalheim were fighting just one DCA soldier at a time.

As soon as a barrier went down, a sky scream was quick to follow.

The Nalheim, to their credit, continued to hurl their distorting attacks at the DCA, even as they plummeted toward their deaths.

The two aerial groups crossed one another.

The sky screams unleashed their stunning attack, sending many DCA soldiers tumbling, only to be cut apart by the sky screams' spear-like head or sword-like talons.

However, the DCA was not a weak force. Soldier for soldier, they were much stronger than the goblin army that the Nalheim had fought within Goblin Mountain.

Many were able to resist the attacks, looking after those who were affected and getting them away from the battle. Others unleashed their Mana bombs. They didn't have much range but they were able to easily destroy the sky screams' Mana barriers.

The skies filled with a furious melee; it was hard to tell where the Nalheim sky screams and Devil's Crater soldiers started and ended.

The Nalheim, who rode proudly on their sky screams, were master beast tamers and wielders of the spear and shield.

The DCA aerial forces had become masters with the sky and their own weapons. They didn't have to rely on a beast to move them around; they could do it themselves. They had been trained for months till their reactions were automatic. It was clear to see that the DCA soldiers had drastically increased their abilities.

More and more sky screams entered the fray as the Nalheim war lizards found the first traps. They were incinerated by a simple Fire trap here, a shadow erupted there, leaving nothing behind. Light projections so powerful that they cut through three lizards in a single second flashed into existence.

The barrier busters dropped from the skies. They looked like tumbling spheres. As soon as they were close to the ground, what looked like lightning shot off from these spheres. They struck the Mana barriers, making them fluctuate slightly before overloading.

The idea had been taken from Dave. The Mana barriers were made to take in power, not to reject it, no matter where it came from.

With this, the dwarves had made artillery spells that sent compressed and wild Mana out. This was not compacted like the Mana bombs but instead allowed to roam freely once it reached a certain height above their targets. The Mana ran free, taking the path of least resistance and flowing into the Mana barrier power supplies until they failed.

Mana barriers started to come apart across the fields.

Generals howled out orders as the Nalheim surged forward. They weren't fast but the war lizards easily outpaced them, finding the traps that the Terra Alliance had left behind.

The dwarven artillery didn't try to chase those making it into the trap-covered land. Instead, they switched out their shells, half with Mana barrier breakers and the rest with various destructive shells.

Their job was to hammer the almighty hell out of the Nalheim leaving the mountain. Those in the secondary area filled with traps were under the domain of the Aleph automatons, elven rangers, and DCA ground forces.

The first of the destructive artillery spells started to land among the barrier-less dismounted Nalheim soldiers.

The Nalheim's orderly lines were torn apart. The survivors continued forward while a great number of them were killed off by the spells, or heavily wounded and left on the battlefield.

The slightly marred land was turned into a devastated landscape of smoking craters and crying Nalheim.

Even the ones coming in behind them were stunned by the sight. Still, they pushed forward at their best speed.

The war lizards and their riders were constantly finding more traps in their way. Magical or force-based traps covered the seemingly peaceful ground, leaving hundreds of dead and dying over the ground.

Dwayne felt faint hope in his chest but it was a fleeting feeling. Through the Aleph automatons within Goblin Mountain, it was easy to see that there were plenty more Nalheim coming through the portal.

This was but the first exchange.

More and more sky screams entered the skies; even a few of the golden gryphon-riding generals headed into the melee.

The forces from the Great Ashal forest let out their cries. Many of the beasts held a number of people who stood from their seats, unleashing arrows, bolts, spells, and destruction staffs at the sky screams.

They cut through the fighting DCA and sky screams. The DCA disengaged from the sky screams, following the reinforcements. They had been just holding the Nalheim in place.

A number of them were carrying wounded and quickly descended toward the castles or citadel to seek out medical aid.

The gryphons didn't head toward the fighters; instead, they charged toward the wounded leaving.

The sky screams followed them down toward the castles, their riders hurling their distorting attacks at the retreating forces.

The telescope in Dwayne's hands was crushed in his hands.

"Prepare batteries! Archers, give our wounded cover! Mages, see if you can reinforce their barriers!" Dwayne's voice rang through the command chat.

The DCA hurtled toward the castles and safety. With the Nalheim focusing on the able-bodied, they were now alone. The DCA didn't panic; instead, they closed their wings, turning into darts as they cut through the skies.

The sky screams and gryphons also closed their wings, their eyes red seeing their prey so close. The Nalheim let out warbling war cries as their attacks came faster and faster.

Aleph bolt throwers were pulled onto target by members of the Terra Alliance. These bolts hurtled past the DCA aerial forces so close that the DCA soldiers could hear them.

Mages unleashed their spells into the skies, smashing into the oncoming Nalheim. As the Nalheim came lower, the archers added in their own blows.

The mounted Nalheim were now fighting off the different spells and incoming bolts and arrows, overwhelmed by it all as their charge turned into tumbling as sky screams and their riders were killed off.

The gryphons took a pounding; their golden feathers and bodies crashed through spell after spell. Their riders stood in their saddles like war gods as their every thrust cut through the skies.

From the citadel's battlements, a woman wreathed in the white rushing tempest of air rose up.

Dwayne felt a hungry look cover his face as he looked to the Nalheim. Adrenaline coursed through his veins.

"Looks like they've pissed off Anna," Esa said, her voice hungry and cold.

Dwayne looked to Esa and then back to the battlefield, the look of rightful and cold vengeance in their eyes. "Welcome to Emerilia," Dwayne said in a deep voice.

Anna rose about ten feet above the citadel's exterior walls. The wind around her was like a tornado, but there was no noise, no wind pulling at those near her. It showed her absolute control over the force of Air.

She drew her blade out to the side. A clear and clean hum came from it. The wind seemed to gather around it and slowed, as if soldiers seeing their general.

Anna started to move; the air moved with her, gathering, compressing, following their master's will. It flowed into orderly lines—there were no ebbs or peaks as the lines were clean, purposeful, and sharp.

Streams of wind gathered, adding their strength to Anna's.

Suddenly, she pointed her sword upward. The very wind cracked in her passing as she shot up faster than a bow from a string, surpassing the arrows that had been shot by the archers and the bolts that now filled the skies.

In her wake, these weren't thrown to the side but instead their speed increased greatly, as they, too, broke through the sky.

"Get behind me!" Anna rushed through the formation of DCA. They obeyed immediately, compacting themselves into a line, still darts heading toward the ground.

Anna's sword swung outward, a clear piercing noise that left one's ears deaf for a moment. A blade of wind fifty meters long spread out from where her sword passed. Her blade danced in the air as she continued forward, covering the DCA's retreat.

She had trained many of them; the Beast Kin had been her family when few would accept her. She accepted that she could not help all of them survive, but when she saw these wounded and their helpers being cut down, she wasn't able to sit by.

Her blade tore through barriers, sky screams, and Nalheim riders with ease.

A net made from cuts with her sword shimmered through the air. The white lines of cut air weakened as they were hit with the disrupting attacks of the Nalheim. But still it hit their flying formation like a hammer.

The Nalheim were trying to pull their beasts up and out of their dive, sensing the power of the woman in front of them.

"You want to leave?" Anna's cold and quiet voice seemed to resonate in everyone's ears as her sword flashed. Air blades appeared, faster than the Nalheim could react.

The gryphons flew toward Anna, a light in their eyes. They had found a challenger!

Anna's speed decreased once she cleared the last of the DCA aerial forces, before slowly falling back down toward the citadel. She would cover their retreat.

The sky screams tried to unleash their paralyzing ability, but the wind was changing constantly, not allowing the sound to transmit to Anna's ears.

She constantly wove attacks through the air and hurled them toward the oncoming Nalheim. Now that the surprise factor was gone, they were trying to find weaknesses within her attacks.

Dwayne watched as the threads of compressed white air slowed down, becoming less substantial as they reached Anna. She wasn't pulling as much air to herself as she was sending spell after spell into the oncoming Nalheim.

She continued to gather speed as she fell. A horde of Nalheim all in a diving formation now charged onward; under their concentrated attacks, the ones that had been trying to slow their descent and get away from her were now once again joining their fellows in hunting down Anna.

Her attacks continued to send more and more Nalheim to their deaths.

A golden gryphon finally reached her and its head slammed toward Anna. She held out a hand, a drill of air forming over it.

The gryphon cried out, startled as the drill became solid, spinning faster and faster, until it collided with the gryphon's face. Waves of visible force exploded outward in shock waves.

Anna's raised sword smashed the spear of the general on top of the gryphon away.

The sound of metal hitting metal was almost explosive as people covered their ears.

The general's blow might have been blocked but he wasn't done.

The gryphon had a large gash on the side of its face underneath its eye, where blood flowed freely. It had been able to save itself from dying at the last moment but not without injury. It let out an angered screech, its front paws trying to claw through Anna.

Anna nimbly danced out of the way of the gryphon's claws and beak while she and the general traded blows.

Their movements were so fast that most people only heard the weapons hitting one another. Dwayne could see that the Nalheim was using all of its considerable skill and its two heads and weapons to attack Anna, who was fending off it and its beast.

Anna suddenly shot upward again, past the Nalheim; it dodged to the side, receiving a nasty cut on its side.

The Nalheim could turn its head around but not its arms. Because it was standing up in the gryphon's saddle, it couldn't fight Anna as she shot past.

She sliced and jabbed forward. Her Air blade cut the general nearly in two as her thrust pierced through the gryphon's tough hide and into its insides. Anna sped toward the ground now. All of the DCA aerial forces had landed and were being seen to by healers.

As she got out from between the Nalheim and the Terra Alliance forces, the sky once again erupted into hell.

Spells that had been saved up as well as archers and those manning bolt throwers who hadn't been confident to use their spells when their allies were so close now unleashed their abilities.

There were nearly a thousand within the Nalheim group that had tried to hunt down the wounded.

Magical explosions tore through the skies as bolt throwers traced lines of bolts onto sky screams. Arrows cracked through the air with their force.

The Nalheim had nowhere to go.

Dwayne looked to Anna as she circled down and around, coming to stop with the rest of Party Zero, who stood on the exterior battlements, watching the Nalheim and their attempts to advance.

She looked as if she were breathing slightly heavy and there was sweat on her brow, but otherwise it didn't look as though she'd needed to exert any effort.

Dwayne's eyes looked to the gryphons and sky screams, as well as their riders.

They were powerful in hit-and-run attacks or when they were fighting against infantry out in the open or their opponents couldn't focus their ranged attacks on them.

With everyone walled up in the citadel and castles, they were able to focus their fire onto these aerial riders. Under that withering fire, not even the steely-eyed Nalheim were able to do much.

Chapter 14: A Time to Defend and A Time to Act

"Dave, what if something happens here?" Josh looked at Dave and the rest of Party Zero who all stood within the command post inside the citadel.

The Nalheim had been constantly engaged in aerial fights but they hadn't been able to make much progress on the ground.

The elves and DCA ground forces had even started to add in their own ranged hit-and-run attacks on the Nalheim.

They didn't fall into ambushes as they moved forward in one direction, no matter the terrain. The war lizards always rushed toward where the combat was like bloodhounds.

"You have more traps out there than I've ever seen anywhere!"

"It's kind of like an old man saying 'get off my lawn' but instead of using a shotgun, he used mines, and elves, and Devil's Crater soldiers, and more bombs he made in his barn when he was drinking *waay* too much moonshine," Steve interjected.

"Dude, not helping," Dave said.

"Okay, so we're holding them back and slowing them the hell down with all of the traps, but you want to go off to Gudalo and check out the spawn point in the orcish lands!" Josh said.

"If we can figure out how the spawn points work, maybe we can stop them, or figure out something to kill the things coming out before they get organized, maybe even learn something." Dave waved his arms.

Josh looked around the room before he looked to Dave, his eyes narrowed. "Okay, you make a good point." Josh rubbed his face and let out a deep breath. It was clear that running the Terra Alliance was not the easiest of jobs. "Just, I'll let you know if I think that the Nalheim are going to reach the castle walls. They haven't stopped coming out of that portal and I don't know when they will. If they can get to our castles, then hopefully we can push them back and hammer them at range. It's not as simple fighting this way once you know that it's real."

"I know, but it drives us harder to see that we can do our best by ourselves and those who call Emerilia home, whether they're players, people of Emerilia, or E-heads," Dave said.

***

"Why don't they pull back?" Malkur asked Kala as they stood on the battlements of the citadel. Malkur and his aerial forces had been replaced by Efri's people.

"I don't know. Maybe it's an honor thing, or the way that they evolved." Kala shrugged her massive shoulders. "One thing I know for sure—while they're slow about it, in two or three days, they're going to reach the citadel. That's when the real fight starts."

"The battle only comes to its conclusion when it reaches your walls. If it is the first time you're engaging your enemy, you've fucked up." Malkur smiled.

"Looks like all my wise words weren't wasted on you." Kala laughed.

"Just kept some of the gems." Malkur chuckled.

They fell into silence as they watched the fighting. It felt surreal; in any moment, they could be thrust into it and here they were just looking at it—hearing the explosions, seeing the artillery cannons firing and their impacts.

"What do you think is going to happen in the orc swamps in the Gudalo republic?" Malkur asked.

"The republic is already sending down their military from all of the races to be ready for anything that comes out the spawn point. We'll send some support there. Already there's a bunch of Dark and Earth mages going to make fortifications to hold back whatever is there or to launch an attack from. Unless they're much worse than the Nalheim threat, then we're going to stay here and fight off the Nalheim then go and help at the other spawn point. This is part of the Terra Alliance—we knew that we wouldn't be able to react to every single problem. This way we can respond to the worst ones so that the people of Emerilia survive, not just a kingdom here and there," Kala said.

Malkur nodded but it was hard; if the Nalheim were bad, then whatever was coming through the spawn point in Gudalo could be much worse.

With all of these spawn points dotted around and many that they probably didn't even know of yet, it was likely that they would get bogged down with so many cries for help from so many different people that they would have to make decisions that would allow a great number of people to die so that others could live. All of these decisions lay squarely on Josh's shoulders.

The people of Emerilia had become stronger, learning through the Mirrors of Communication. However, these creatures were not normal. Although the people of Emerilia might be able to put up a bit more of a fight, they could get away from danger much faster. If civilians could get out of the area, then the armies and warriors wouldn't have to worry about casualties incurred by their actions. These fights were not going to be easy but they were doing everything they could to survive.

***

Dave, Deia, Anna, Lox, and Gurren were all running through the orc swamps in the southwestern region of the newly formed Gudalo republic. The rest of Party Zero had been helping the Terra Alliance to build a large citadel like the one outside Goblin Mountain to hold the republic's army as they waited to see what would come out of the spawn point.

The five party members quickly entered the swamp. Even in midday, after about five minutes of running, they found themselves in fog. The farther they went, the denser it became.

"Halt." A deep guttural voice ground out through the fog.

Dave and the rest of Party Zero stopped, forming into a circle by reflex.

"Who goes there?" Deia asked.

"What is your purpose in coming to our swamp?" the voice asked. It seemed to come from all around them.

Dave pushed his senses out. His eyebrows rose in shock. He could only faintly sense the half-dozen creatures around the party.

"We wish to inspect the spawn point that is located in your swamp. We haven't been able to see one yet and want to know what it is capable of doing and how it works," Deia said.

When creatures in the event spawned, the spawn point had disappeared, both when the Elsoom spores spawned and when the portal had activated.

A shadow appeared in the fog, moving closer to the ground before the fog seemed to dissipate to reveal a seven-foot-tall orc. This orc was covered in muscles and scars. There were different paints on his skin to make it easier to hide in the forest. He didn't have much of a neck with those bulging muscles.

Even though his footfalls were light, the power that was wrapped up in this orc was not to be underestimated.

Rings pierced through his lower tusks; a tattoo ran from his neck down across his body. He wore only a simple loincloth and had a massive sword on his back.

"I am Ursk, leader of the White Smokes and owner of this territory." The orc crossed his truly massive arms.

"I am Oson'Deia, leader of Party Zero." Deia stepped forward from the group.

Ursk looked her over before his eyes flickered to the others in the party. "You wish to see the silver spawn point?" Ursk's eyes once again focused on Deia.

"That is correct," Deia said.

"Very well. If you defeat one of my people, then I will let you."

Another orc stepped out of the fog and stood behind Ursk.

Anna stepped forward as well.

Ursk nodded and moved to the side; Deia did the same.

The orc who had stepped up behind Ursk rushed forward.

Anna stood perfectly still, making no indication of moving. She looked rather bored as the orc closed in.

It punched forward, creating cannon balls of wind. Anna moved fluidly out of the way of these attacks, using the movements to get close to the orc. Her leg snapped out, hitting the orc in the gut and sending them flying. The fog was tossed around as the orc slammed through a tree.

Anna lowered her foot as the orc hit the ground.

Ursk looked from his fighter to Anna with a nod. "Very well, we will take you there."

Dave felt the others moving around them as a few went to check on the orc who had been kicked through a tree.

Ursk quickly guided them through the swamplands with ease.

Structures seemed to appear out of nowhere. These were wooden defenses, all of them pointed inward.

Dave looked over the different constructs which looked to be grown from the natural trees and other plants in the area.

They passed through a palisade and a row of spikes.

More orcs and gnomes were visible working on the different structures as well as moving in roving armed bands or just stopping and staring at the members of Party Zero who passed through, entering the center of these defenses.

Earth mage, Dave thought as the swampland that they were traveling through became solid ground as soon as Ursk put his foot down. The control he wielded was impressive as a path formed from his footsteps.

The swamp trees fell away after a few minutes and the fog cleared so that they could see better. They stepped out of the fog and into the sunlight once again, looking at the gleaming silver spawn point.

There were four pillars on the outside. All of them slowly turned; the central and larger pillar attached by poles and a metal plate beneath the smaller poles rotated its different runed bands at an even slower pace than the four pillars.

Dave didn't pay attention to the spawn point screen that showed the time slowly winding down. Instead, Dave and Malsour both moved to the spawn point, using all of their senses to gain more information on the machine in front of them.

Dave exercised his ability to cut the Jukal link as he moved up to the spawn point. "It's complex and made from Magical Circuits, though it's pretty much nothing more than a complex drop pad but with a timer built into it and a display ability."

"It's pretty simple. I think most of this was just made to make it look impressive," Malsour agreed.

"The range is pretty far—must be reaching the second moon where Bob stored all of the prisoners with the automated fighting drones."

"We might be able to shut them down, but as soon as we do, then the Jukal are going to know. There's communication protocols in here. They were probably made in order to make sure that nothing fails for this event, but they'd transmit as soon as there was an error," Malsour said.

"These defenses are pretty nasty too. Somehow it inverts the Mana—forcing it instead of acting on the outside world to act within whoever touches it," Dave said.

"That's pretty nasty. We can cast high-powered spells but having that Mana running rampant in our systems, it pretty much makes sure that anyone who attacks it is killed. The only other time I've seen systems like this is with the Altar of Rebirth and the portals."

"Well, this is just one more thing to figure out." Dave stepped back from the spawn point and looked at it all. It looked pleasing to the eye but it was a herald of death and destruction.

"I think that we might be able to figure out what kind of creatures that it would release," Malsour said.

"Oh?" Dave said. Knowing what was going to come through the spawn points would make it a lot easier to try to figure out how to defend against them.

"Drop pads can't move people and animate objects—well, they can but it's risky as hell. Only players can use them because there's a good chance that they'll die from the transition. The Jukal aren't going to send creatures over here for the event only to have them die upon arrival. Just looking after that takes up a lot of magical runes. If we can figure out how they're configured for the creatures being brought over, we can take that profile, compare it against the creatures in Emerilia's past and figure out what they are. However, if we have more things coming through a portal, we aren't going to be able to figure out what the hell they are beforehand as the spawn points are not only here to tell us about the event location but they act as teleportation anchors." Malsour looked to Dave.

"Okay, well, let's see if we can figure out what's supposed to be coming through this spawn point," Dave said. The two of them used their senses, examining the spawn point once again.

"Well, I guess we should leave them at it." Lox sat down on the ground. Ursk watched him closely in his Devastator armor.

Gurren followed suit as Deia and Anna pulled seats out from their bags of holding and started eating some food they'd brought along.

Ursk was slightly surprised at the relaxed attitude of the group.

He also sat down, watching Party Zero as Malsour and Dave muttered to each other and wandered around the spawn point. The others lazed around in the swamp.

***

For Josh, things weren't as relaxed.

He was with the military leaders of the Terra Alliance who had lent their forces. They were all under the command of Josh to ease the command structure. Josh had, in turn, turned over command over different groups to his different guild leaders.

Lucy was back in Terra, keeping everything running and looking after the guild. Florence had taken over the supply needs for the entire alliance while Jules led the healers.

Dwayne and Esa controlled different divisions of soldiers. Dwayne commanded those who were within the different castles, assigning a leader to each of the forces within them so he wasn't needed to okay every battle plan. Esa was in command of the Stone Raiders and other fast-moving POE groups as well as liaised with the other player guild leaders.

The player guild leaders had people within the castles and with the group that Esa directly controlled in Terra.

This was the quick reaction force. Taking from the dwarves, this group could use the teleport pad within Terra to move to any one of the castles in order to support them, swelling their numbers in a moment to repel any heavy attacks.

Kim commanded the different groups of mages and ranged attackers; like Dwayne, she had also designated leaders in every castle to deal with their own independent issues.

Malkur was leading the aerial fighting forces while the dwarven artillery were run by the dwarven artillery commanders but their orders were passed down by the various leaders, with the dwarven artillery commander managing the fire support requests.

Cassie was assisting Josh, who was in command of it all.

"So, we going to do it?" Jake, the strongest necromancer among the Stone Raiders, jumped from foot to foot in excitement.

Necromancers had pretty bad reputations, especially among the POEs. His avatar looked like a sickly pale teenager, though he constantly wore colorful clothes. Right now he wore a bright-orange shirt and a pink pair of slacks.

Where the hell did he find those clothes? Josh shook his head and sighed.

"Yes, we're going to use your plan." Josh looked to the dwarven artillery commander. "Load the animation grand working shells."

"Yes, sir." The commander opened his interface and he started to give out orders.

"All right, see to your people and be ready for the Nalheim to do anything," Josh said.

The different people nodded and disappeared.

Josh opened his eyes as he exited the Mirror of Communication and looked from the command post that he was in.

Having all of the leaders in one room was a terrible idea: if somehow the room was destroyed, then the command structure would take a severe blow. So they'd moved to using Mirrors of Communication to have their conferences.

A prompt appeared in his vision, asking whether he wanted to join Dwayne's private chat. Josh accepted.

"Josh, I've bought a rune to improve attack strength for the southern castle. It looks like the Nalheim are intending to attack that castle first. Also, we're up to 25% progression for the castles," Dwayne said.

"Sounds good. Hopefully that will boost the strength of Jake's grand workings."

"We can only hope. I've got people to see to. Talk later."

"Later." Josh cut the private chat. Josh stepped onto the balcony outside of the command post. From here, he was offered a view over the citadel's walls and across the battlefield around Goblin Mountain.

The ground outside of the mountain was a treacherous place. However, even with the mix of barrier busters and destructive rounds that the dwarven artillery dropped on the Nalheim, the Nalheim still made it past this hellish area and into the area that had been filled with traps.

There were too many Nalheim and they were protected by strong barriers. Although nearly half of those who exited the mountain were killed, with thousands pouring out of the mountain, they still had a massive fighting force.

Paths had been cleared out by the Nalheim charging constantly forward; thousands had died but it had worked.

The forces hidden in the meadows and patches of forest didn't just watch, either; they led lightning attacks on the Nalheim, hitting them with spells and ranged attacks before fading away once again.

It was estimated that nearly a hundred thousand Nalheim had come out of the portal every day. Today was the fifth day. Out of the half million who had made it to Emerilia, a hundred and fifty thousand had died.

All of the gryphon-mounted generals without fighting forces had rested on Goblin Mountain. They seemed to be waiting for something. Their force grew slowly but they were powerful combatants; three of them were enough to pressure even Anna.

Josh's eye moved from the gryphons and their golden bodies that reflected the sunlight.

Across the castles, the artillery seemed to quiet for a moment before they started up again. The roof atop the citadel's tallest building shook as artillery cannons once again fired.

Grand workings could either be used to power the dwarven artillery, just firing off Mana-based artillery spells, or they could be launched at the enemy. They were readied upon leaving the artillery cannon; when they detonated in the air or on the ground, then the grand working would unleash its hidden spell.

The shining grand working rounds traveled through the skies. They slammed into the ground and erupted into a green smoke.

The explosions from before had all died down as green smoke spread out across the battlefield, as if it were sentient.

The battlefield quieted down. Here and there, aerial creatures let out ferocious battle cries as they clashed. On the ground, the war lizards let out their roars as well, as if sensing that they had somehow gained the upper hand.

Even the generals on their gryphons seemed to look out at the castles in interest.

A deep groaning noise filled the battlefield as underneath that green smoke, things started to rise.

The Nalheim looked at the rising creatures for a moment.

The first stood on its feet. A Nalheim missing one head and a chunk of its right chest appeared. A green light filled its eyes, the signature of an undead!

Once rising, the undead Nalheim looked to its comrades and charged.

Five hundred thousand had left the portal but only three hundred and fifty thousand were left alive. These undead were not controlled by a necromancer, so they were at most half of their original strength. Most of them weren't complete, making them even weaker. However, only by destroying their brains would they die; this meant removing their limbs would make them weaker but it still wouldn't kill them.

More and more grand workings fell down across the ground, covering it in thick green smoke.

The Nalheim moved into formations; without the incoming artillery, they were able to coordinate better.

Josh looked inside the command post where interface screens dotted the walls, showing multiple feeds from across the battlefield. Many of the Nalheim had died over the space of the five days since they entered. However, with the game system, their bodies at most lasted several hours.

Still, this was enough to interrupt the Nalheim. If any of them died, then they would only join the ranks of the undead.

Dwarven artillery cannons paused in their fire. With none of the rolling explosions or rumblings of these massive guns, it was eerie as they heard the sounds of battle in the distance.

"Load Mana artillery shells and barrier busters!" the dwarven artillery commander called out.

The Nalheim were grouping together to try to fight off the massive number of Nalheim undead and their beasts. Sky screams with their necks torn out and holes in their bodies moved to attack the living sky screams in the skies.

The artillery fired once again, two guns moments after one another.

Josh watched them land.

The Nalheim had grouped together to fight the undead; it was too easy to be swarmed if one was by themselves.

These groups were perfect targets for the artillery.

Barrier busters went in, opening the barriers up as the second shell fired just moments after the first fell upon the barrier-less Nalheim.

The Nalheim who had been advancing were now stuck in a quagmire of fighting off their undead that kept them pinned in one place and having artillery rain down upon them.

"Sir, something is happening!" someone said within the command post.

Josh ran back inside, following everyone's eyes to a main display. "What the hell is that?" Josh yelled.

The creature squeezed through the portal, much like an octopus might move through a space smaller than it. It looked like a jellyfish with hardened scales along its top. Thin, almost whip-like orange and green tentacles seemed to move around aimlessly. The creature was clearly suspended in midair with some kind of magic or ability.

The Nalheim moved out of the way of the beast.

As soon as a path was made, the creature raced through the tunnels, expanding and contracting again so that it could fit. Its scales flashed with reflected light before it sped out of the mountain and into the sky above the entrance to Goblin Mountain.

A hellish scream made the very air around Goblin Mountain distort. It made the sky screams seem as if they were nothing but mewling babes. Josh felt his very bones rattle with that force.

Artillery spells in the sky were destroyed; trees were ripped up and thrown away from the mountain as dirt and debris created a dust wave that rushed outward, as if an explosion had just gone off.

The jellyfish-looking creature flicked its tentacles. Distortions appeared along the path of the tentacles, cutting five-meter gashes into the ground.

The generals on their gryphons who had looked down upon the battle with cold aloofness now bowed their heads toward this creature. Their gryphons likewise lowered themselves to the ground.

"All batteries fire!" the dwarven commander yelled out.

"Be ready for all attacks! Everyone to full readiness!" Josh yelled out, pulled from his reverie. He opened up a private chat to Party Zero. He didn't know what was going to happen, but he needed them with him.

Chapter 15: Discovery

"Blood reevers," Malsour said, his voice filled with certainty.

"What kind of creatures are those?" Anna asked from where she sat.

"They're similar to panthers. They have a Dark Affinity; they are extremely fast and strong. Some people tried to tame them to be their familiars but were largely unable to," Malsour said, not missing how Ursk seemed to pay more attention to his words.

"They drink the blood of their enemies to gain more power. They were originally creatures that followed behind the demons and angels across battlefields when the gods and goddesses of the Pantheon were actively fighting one another on Emerilia.

"They would absorb the life essence of those who they sucked dry. The stronger the person was before they died, the stronger they would become. In battlefields, there were plenty of strong and powerful creatures and people. They grew in strength and eventually stopped following armies and started to attack others. One of the things was that the fresher the kill, the more power remained within their blood.

"They became extremely powerful creatures that would enter battlefields in packs, waiting for an opportunity. In the middle of a battle, they would reveal themselves. While both sides were distracted, they would cut down their ranks, feasting on the dead."

"Well, they're creatures, right? Could they be controlled?" Ursk asked.

"They could, but the formation that would be needed would be hellishly complex and the will of those trying to subdue them must be greater than the blood reever's. Also, there will possibly be hundreds of them that appear. There needs to be enough masters to take command of them all," Malsour said.

Ursk grunted, looking thoughtful.

"Could it be done?" Deia looked to Dave and Malsour.

Dave and Malsour looked to each other; there was no need for them to share words at this point.

"Sure, the power requirements would be heavy indeed and we'd have to use some of the precious soul gem constructs," Dave said.

Malsour nodded beside him.

"If we do this, are you willing to trade with us?" Deia looked to Ursk.

Ursk held his chin and looked at them all. "If you do this for my clan, what will you ask for in return?" Ursk asked slowly. He might dress and look like some kind of barbarian, but Ursk was not some village idiot.

"Once you command the blood reevers, we ask that you join the Gudalo republic and support the Terra Alliance. As we help you here, others will need help in other nations and continents," Deia said.

Ursk was thoughtful for some time. "I accept your terms."

Screens appeared before her and Ursk to confirm the details of their agreement. Deia and Ursk were doing that when a prompt flashed across Dave's interface.

He opened the party chat request.

"Dave, I wasn't able to get a hold of Deia. Something appeared at Goblin Mountain. Get Party Zero back here as soon as possible!" Josh yelled.

"We're on our way." Dave stood.

The others looked to him as Dave accepted the attached image of the beast that had exited Goblin Mountain. He sent it to the other members of Party Zero as he opened up the party chat.

"We're needed back in the citadel right now. I just sent everyone an image of the creature that just appeared outside of Goblin Mountain," Dave said.

Deia and Ursk hurriedly talked to each other.

"Steve, I'm going to need you to make a soul gem construct for the orcs around the spawn point," Dave said over the party chat.

"Let me know what you need," Steve said, his normal joking tone subdued in the face of the disaster that had come down on the forces around Goblin Mountain.

***

Dwayne looked over the citadel's walls at the Nalheim.

The creature that hung in the sky was still too far away for anyone to figure out what it was; even the Aleph were having a hard time trying to figure it out.

"That floating jellyfish-looking thing is a Nerhoun. They're Level 2000 beasts. They are controlled by a king that rests within their scale-covered sack. It has the ability to float and fly. It can use its tentacles, disrupting attacks to destroy spells, as well as anything in its way. It can also create a massive Mana shield around its body. This can be used to cover Nalheim below; also, this is regulated by the Nerhoun, so those barrier busters aren't going to work," Anna said over the leadership channel.

Party Zero had just received the message from Josh and were now finishing up their discussion and racing back toward the nearest ono and through Terra to the citadel.

"Load plasma rounds!" the dwarven artillery commander called out

These rounds were the strongest that the dwarven artillery had, created by Dave with the inspiration coming from Deia and Induca's Plasma Cannon spell.

This wasn't just a simple artillery cannon round or grand working; this instead used special Magical Circuits around the artillery cannon.

Runes started to glow, forming lines made of characters that ran down the cannon. Artillery cannon rounds were loaded into the weapons.

When they were all ready, "Fire!" the artillery commander called out.

Around the barrels, blue sections of light seemed to cover the artillery cannon. They hovered around the gun and overlapped one another, extending past the barrel of the gun.

If someone was to see Deia and Induca's spell, they would understand that these different solid light-looking items were in fact condensed sheets of flame so contained, that heat didn't even seep out of them.

A magical circle appeared at the end of these condensed and overlapping plates of concentrated fire. The plates lit up from the base to where the magical circle appeared at the end of their reach.

The cannons recoiled as the magical circle disappeared. Multiple booms from the shells breaking through multiple sound barriers seemed to restrict the air around these guns.

The blue sheathing of blue plates continued to cover the artillery cannons.

As a new round was loaded, the magical circle would once again appear. All of its power drained into the artillery cannon to push it well beyond its limits, augmenting it with magical power.

The recoil was actually less but the rounds traveled much faster. With this, the cannons could fire much faster. These rounds didn't have much arc on them due to their speed as they screamed through the air.

These were the same as the solid-looking flames and spell formations that Deia and Induca made when casting their plasma cannons!

The plasma rounds smashed into a Mana barrier that seemed to grow out from the Nerhoun's head and expand down its massive body, encompassing all of the Nalheim in front of Goblin Mountain.

The plasma rounds arrived in cyan-colored explosions.

The Mana barrier quivered with the impacts of these hits but they weren't enough to destroy the Nerhoun's Mana barrier.

It sat there in midair, its tentacles killing the undead off and covering the Nalheim who were fighting below.

Those rounds made the barrier fluctuate slightly, taking power from the Nerhoun but its Mana pool was as massive as it was. These rounds might weaken it but even with a half-dozen, the barrier stayed strong.

More and more rounds hammered the Nerhoun; the barrier's color started to change.

The gryphons and sky screams within the barrier seemed to have received orders as they descended toward those on the ground. With their attacks, they greatly helped the Nalheim on the ground.

Slowly the Nerhoun started to move, the fighting following beneath it.

"Looks like the Nerhoun is headed for the eastern castle!" one of the observers called out.

Dwayne watched with cold eyes.

The Nalheim had cleared out a long path toward the south castle but now they were moving east. It seemed that with the Nerhoun's arrival, the strategy had changed.

There were fresh traps to the east but in the south, not only were there the two southern castles, there was also the citadel sitting in close support.

East was the closest castle and it only had one other defensive structure near it.

However, all of the castles could support it with their long-range artillery.

Artillery spells rained down on the Nerhoun. Its barriers started to change color once again with this mass of firepower raining on it. It might be a massive powerful creature, but it was also a massive target, covering a large area in an extremely powerful Mana barrier.

The dwarven artillery and the mages of the Terra Alliance were not weak.

Within ten minutes, the Nerhoun's barrier looked as if it was close to the end.

The Nalheim on the ground were in much better condition as they had finally finished off all of the undead that were roaming around. They started to pull themselves together as they moved toward the east.

Explosions went off as traps were found.

The Nalheim started to move into lines as they went.

"Seems that they got smarter when that Nerhoun came out, or that their commander that's within it cares more to win than about piling on honors," Dwayne said to himself. His eyes narrowed.

The Nerhoun's barrier continued to change color, becoming weaker and weaker under constant attack. The ability of the Nerhoun to have this much of a Mana reserve was incredible. It was as strong as some of the barriers used by the dwarves.

Dave and Party Zero finally arrived. Malsour, Dave, and Steve were all on the roof. They moved to the artillery cannons and looked to the Nerhoun.

Dave had a quick talk with the dwarven artillery commander. Dwayne couldn't hear it through all of the weapon fire.

Dave nodded, clapping the commander on the shoulder before he moved to the cannons where Malsour, Steve, and he had a conference.

Dwayne moved over to them and tapped them on the shoulder.

Dave saw him, quickly adding him to their private chat.

"Okay, so these rounds are pretty effective. If we were to use the grand working rounds that are sympathetic to the weapons, it will take maybe a hundred rounds to take one of these Nerhoun's barriers down. Right now, all of the dwarves are testing out the new flame-plate attachments. I say it's a good time for us to run our tests and see if we can improve them in any way." Dave sounded calm despite the war raging around the Nerhoun.

"What are you talking about—the rounds taking apart the barriers in a hundred rounds?" Dwayne asked.

"Right now, the cannons are using the simple Fire-based plasma artillery shells. There are grand working plasma artillery shells that have been custom made for the magical augmentation you see on the cannons. With it, the round is a hundred times stronger than what you're currently seeing. However, we only have a limited number of these shells. Making a grand working is more time-intensive than making a soul gem construct. You need to make the soul gem to hold the grand working, then you need someone to imprint their spell upon it. It's not simple to imprint it, either. Then you shoot it out of a cannon and all of that work blows up in destructive forces," Dave said.

"Whereas the simple shells that you see here, they're made by a factory that can spit out a hundred of them in an hour and a half," Malsour said.

Dwayne nodded. It made sense right now, even though there was a Nerhoun present. It was protecting the Nalheim, but it was moving slowly and wasn't a direct threat. Using the less powerful artillery shells on it made more sense than their limited supply of much more powerful rounds.

If another Nerhoun showed up at a crucial moment and they had used their rounds on the first one, it would be a great waste.

The Nerhoun's barriers continued to change colors before suddenly they disappeared. Rounds that had been intended for the barrier now hit the Nerhoun underneath.

It shuddered under the impacts against its armored top while tentacles that were struck by the plasma rounds were simply burnt through. The Nerhoun let out a pained screech as it pulled back and into Goblin Mountain, leaving the Nalheim uncovered once again but continuing on their path toward the south.

They were much faster than before and their formations were clear. The Nerhoun had brought order and allowed them to repel the attack from the undead.

Dwayne moved back to the citadel's crenellation wall, using a far sight spell to see the Nalheim up close.

The dwarven artillery commander ordered the shell types changed once again as barrier busters and Mana-based artillery spells took to the air.

The Nalheim fell, but now, those who were left wounded or dead had a spear shoved into each of their heads to make sure that they wouldn't rise again.

The tactic had worked once but it wouldn't happen a second time.

After about ten minutes, the Nalheim stopped trailing out of Goblin Mountain.

"The Nalheim have all but stopped coming out of Goblin Mountain, but we've more Nerhouns coming out," Josh yelled.

Once again, orders were passed among the artillery cannons as plasma rounds were readied.

Nerhouns tore out from Goblin Mountain, inflating to their full size. Hits smashed off their barriers as they slowly hovered over to the Nalheim, while their cone-like defenses covered those below.

The wounded Nerhoun sat in the middle of the four others, protected by them as it recovered its strength.

Each of the castles focused on just one Nerhoun but it would take another hour before they could take down its barrier. The Nalheim had found a way to resist the artillery attacks and now only had to deal with the traps of the ground.

Dwayne looked downward, his jaw working as the Nalheim front lines simply jabbed forward with their spears. It was similar to trying to walk through a minefield and shooting at the ground to make sure there was nothing there. Sometimes the magical traps were destroyed; sometimes they weren't. Other times they blew up immediately and killed those within a large area.

However, the Nalheim's losses weren't as great and all of the sky screams, gryphons, and war lizards were in straight and clean formations instead of rushing out to attack the enemy whenever they could.

A group of aerial forces moved in close to attack the Nerhouns and those under their protection.

The tentacles of the Nerhoun in question whipped out faster than a person's eye could track, cutting down dozens of the aerial fighters in just mere moments.

The aerial forces cut away hard and fast, trying to put distance between them and the Nerhoun. The aerial forces moved to attack from higher altitudes and drop Mana bombs.

"Josh, let's pull back our forces in the field. If they're under those barriers, they can hit the Nalheim, but those Nerhoun are just going to tear them apart," Dwayne said.

"Agreed. We'll move forces to reinforce the eastern castle," Josh said.

Dwayne cancelled his far sight spell, his eyes heavy. "They should arrive within no more than three or four hours."

The Nalheim had been largely gathering their strength; yes, they had trouble with advancing and most of their higher rank people were running around but now he saw what it was. They were scouting, figuring out what the people of Emerilia were going to do. With that information, as soon as the Nerhoun and its master came out, the army had started to move in a clear direction with a concrete strategy.

***

Within Terra, people stopped what they were doing to see as the forces under Esa's command that had been waiting within the city now started to move.

They marched through a teleport pad, leaving Terra and entering Eastern Castle One.

The castle commanders organized the fighting forces. All of them watched the Nerhoun and their protected Nalheim advancing for the castle.

From another teleport pad, Party Zero moved to join with the Stone Raiders within the force. There was a sense of excitement with the Stone Raiders but also a feeling of careful preparation. These were elite gamers; they might be excited to play, but they hadn't come here to lose.

The POE were stone-faced. They knew that they could die and that their opponent was strong, but they were here for the good of Terra and they wouldn't shirk their duty.

Chapter 16: Face-to-Face with a Nerhoun

Eastern Castle One had been filled up with fighters. Artillery cannons had been firing for two hours but the Nerhoun was getting closer and closer.

Deia looked at the floating beasts and the Nalheim who marched underneath them. They had moved across the battlefield practically unopposed. A number of them had died from the traps that were placed across the ground outside Goblin Mountain, but their losses didn't have a large impact on the Nalheim's forces.

"Switch to plasma cannon grand workings!" The dwarven artillery commander's words passed through the dwarven artillery and through the command channel.

Moments later, the first complete plasma round was fired off. It whizzed through the air. As it impacted the Nerhoun's barrier, it rapidly changed color.

Party Zero added in their firepower as the DCA's aerial forces moved all of their people from the ground and into the air. Mana spearheads projected from their hands as bombs dropped from their breastplates.

The Nalheim had been in the practice of rotating their weakest Nerhouns out of the outside of their formation to the inside, where they could regain their Mana and restore their barrier before switching out with another who was in the ring of four taking the majority of the hits from the castles.

It made it harder to destroy the Nerhoun's Mana barriers, but throughout their advance, the Nerhoun's average barriers had decreased in power. They were just prolonging the time they could stay active for.

Steve, Gurren, and Lox all raised their arms. The bands on their wrists rotated before Mana spears the size of Steve's head tore through the air and slammed into the Nerhoun.

Deia pulled back on her bow Firecracker's string. An arrow formed from the air; it glowed with blue and red fire but not even a bit of heat was released. As she pulled back, much like with the Mana cannons or her own plasma cannon spell, glowing panels appeared around her bow, conforming to it and extending along the length of the arrow. She released the arrow. It cut through the air, a blue-red streak. It impacted a Nerhoun with all of the force of Deia's plasma cannon spell.

However, Deia only needed to imbue the bow with a small amount of Mana and then use her strength to draw the bow.

This was the effect of a Weapon of Power.

Deia pulled back on the bow's string again. Her lips moved slightly; the blue of the arrow glowed brighter than before as she released it. With her increased strength of Fire spells when using the bow and their lower cost, she was able to increase her attack's power to terrifying new heights.

It slammed into the Mana barrier in a massive explosion that sent a ripple of power through the Nerhoun's barrier.

A black-looking magical circle appeared in front of Malsour's hand. Moments later, a truly massive magical circle appeared above the Nalheim formation.

Out of that inky dark magical circle, meteors started to appear, racing toward the Nerhoun below.

The Nerhoun's barriers shuddered under the incoming meteors' impacts.

The air around Induca was filled with floating panels that overlapped one another, creating a plasma cannon over her shoulder.

Every other second, a plasma round flashed through the air, impacting the Nerhoun barriers, only slightly weaker than Deia's own Fire arrows.

Suzy waved her hands. Her creations came together; there were just Air, Fire and metal creations. Above her, Lu Lu had expanded to fifteen meters in length. Her wings flapped to keep her hovering above the party as she unleashed blinding lightning attacks, one after another.

Suzy's Air creations created a massive air tunnel that seemed to pull all of the air within the castle through it. Lining this tunnel, there were metal constructs held in place by the Air constructs as well as Fire constructs heating up the air inside the tunnel, increasing the speed at which air was sucked through.

Behind them, there were a dozen or so metal creations with Air creations holding them at the mouth to the air tunnel.

All of the metal creations at the mouth to the tunnel had changed into what looked like sleek metal darts, or were in the process of it.

The suction of the Air creations increased as the first metal construction dart was hurled into the mouth of the tunnel. The metal constructs within the tunnel changed their polarity, pulling and pushing the dart along at incredible speeds.

Suzy had made a massive hybrid railgun. The Fire creations heated up the air that was pulled within the tunnel, speeding it up to an incredible speed while the metal creations within the tunnel attracted and then repelled the metal dart constructs.

The darts as big as a person howled through the skies.

LuLu let out a pleased screech as she opened her mouth, spitting lightning at the metal dart. The lightning covered the dart, writhing around it as if it were alive.

Moments later, the dart landed.

The barrier fluctuated. The attack wasn't as strong as Deia's arrows or Induca's cannon, nor was it as overbearing as Malsour's meteor rain.

The lightning increased the attack power of the dart, before a multi-colored ball of light seemed to appear around the dart and obliterated it.

Wild Mana tore against the Nerhoun's barrier, blasting in every direction. The Nerhoun's barrier quickly changed color. Tentacles rose up in defense, sending disrupting attacks at Party Zero.

The Mana barrier of the first eastern castle took the impacts head on.

An order must have been passed down to the other Nalheim, as at extreme range, the Nalheim not in the front ranks started to release their disrupting attacks from the tips of their spears once again.

Dave looked to Suzy, who looked slightly paler. The control needed to have that many creations working at once in such a complicated manner was high.

However, with the creations having their creation cores to hold them together and support them, as well as her staff of Hecate, she was able to hold the spell together and quickly recover as she fired out another creation.

Tentacles waved in the air, unleashing disrupting attacks and targeting the darts.

There was now only five hundred meters between the castle and the Nerhoun.

Malsour had lowered as he staggered slightly, panting from his exertions. The magical circle in the sky disappeared; the last meteors fell through and hit the Nerhoun. Their strength dissipated quickly as they started to dissolve.

Malsour downed a Mana potion, his face pale from his attacks.

Anna stood calmly on the wall, watching the fight, ready to step in at a moment's notice.

Dave tossed out grenades into the air. They flew off toward the Nalheim at great speed.

The true plasma round grand workings now started to impact against the Nerhoun, covering them in flames and destruction.

They were largely targeting the three Nerhouns who the eastern castle couldn't hit. Eastern Castles One and Two both had true plasma round grand workings. The Nerhoun's tentacles whipped out, sensing the power of these shells. The Nerhoun facing the eastern castles was able to cut down nearly a third of the shells while trying to fend off the various attacks from the mages and ranged attacks from Eastern Castle One.

Its barriers shuddered and turned a dangerous color. It was now within three hundred meters. More ranged attackers and those who had ranged weapons added their own attacks into the fight.

The other Nerhouns facing outward fared much better. They were able to destroy half to three-quarters of the incoming shells. Their barriers shook but they didn't reach the color of the leading Nerhoun's barrier.

Dave's grenades paused before the barrier, slowing down. Fast objects and magical spells couldn't enter a Mana barrier. The runes on the grenades seemed to turn off before hitting the Mana barrier. They passed through; once again their runes lit up as they descended toward the ground and spread out.

All at once, they dropped, reaching the Nalheim's head height before turning into bright explosions that overlapped one another.

A one-hundred-meter area was cleared of Nalheim in just a matter of seconds. War lizards and dismounted were obliterated. With one attack, Dave had managed to kill nearly two hundred of the Nalheim.

Dave looked at a prompt that appeared within his vision.

Level 239

You have reached Level 239; you have **5** stat points to use.

He smiled to himself and dismissed the screen. He looked to his Weapons Master quest.

Quest: Weapons Master Level 3

One handed and shield 1000/1000

Two handed 138/1000

Dual wielding 27/1000

Archery 541/1000

Rewards: Unlock Level 4 Quest

Increase to stats

Passive skills from other weapons increase from 25% to 50% when designated weapon is not equipped. (Example: While using Dual wield blades, one is able to gain 50% of the archery skill's abilities.)

Since he had been fighting much harder opponents, he had found that he was unable to greatly increase his various skills. Increasing the passive increases from the various skills was tempting indeed. However, fighting such powerful creatures, it was hard to kill many. Maybe if he was able to find some smaller and easier creatures, he could rapidly raise the classes' levels.

He dismissed the screen and tossed out more grenades.

Again they took off into the sky, turning off as they passed through the Mana barrier and descended upon the confused Nalheim.

Their barrier was still up but explosions continued to get in.

Dave watched as another hundred fell to his grenades. His eyes thinned as he threw out more of the grenades. *The external defensive strength of the Nerhoun is impressive, but what about up close?*

The Nerhoun was now within two hundred meters. Multiple explosions covered its Mana barriers as its disrupting tentacles blurred and flashed, attacking the castle's Mana barrier as well as trying to take out the most powerful attacks.

Dave could sense that the Nerhoun's barrier was quickly failing. Dave threw out more grenades that flew away.

Being so close to the eastern castle, the Nerhoun was unable to defeat many of the high-powered plasma cannon grand workings that were tearing its barrier apart with ease.

Still, it was capable of blocking Suzy's darts, which she was now detonating away from the Nerhoun's Mana barrier so as to at least affect it somewhat. However, that was becoming risky for her as the explosion of her creation's core could also hurt the castle's own Mana barrier. So many of her darts were being cut apart before they left the castle's barrier and reached the Nerhoun's.

Suddenly, the Nerhoun's barrier disappeared.

Dave didn't pause, increasing the speed of his grenades as the Nerhoun looked to retreat behind the center Nerhoun who had been waiting to switch out.

The unshielded Nerhoun took multiple hits. Its armored scale-covered head was able to take impact after impact. However, its powerful tentacles were easily cut apart by the high-powered attacks.

Dave had released nearly two hundred grenades. The Nerhoun or the Nalheim destroyed a hundred of them by accident or on purpose as they closed with the Nerhoun. Only ten were able to make it through the forest of tentacles and up toward the top of the Nerhoun.

Dave commanded them to fly with all speed upward.

Three more were destroyed by small inner tentacles before the seven remaining grenades touched the bottom of the Nerhoun's fleshy underside that lay within the scale-covered head.

The sound of their explosions wasn't even audible under the attacks that thundered through the air, tearing the very ground and air apart with their passage or destructive end.

The Nerhoun's flesh was actually weaker than the tentacles that drooped down from their head. The grenades tore deep holes in the Nerhoun, heating up the creature's internal liquids, which boiled at an incredible rate. The Nerhoun's brain was boiled within seconds as the Nalheim inside was cooked with it.

The Nerhoun's tentacles went slack. Smoke poured out from between its tentacles as it dropped toward the ground.

Nalheim moved to get out of the way of the falling Nerhoun. Dozens were crushed under the Nerhoun.

"Change target!" the Edon Kingdom commander who was in charge of the eastern castle yelled out.

A new objective was placed on the Nerhoun who had moved out from the center of the Nerhoun formation. Now there were just four of them left; there was no way for them to retreat and try to gain cover from the attacks.

However, the Nalheim had just reached the walls.

Howls came from the Nalheim's mouths as they charged toward the eastern castle. The gates that had been on the castle's walls had been removed, taking away with them the inherent weaker doors.

The Nalheim's spears flashed as they struck the Mana barrier that was just centimeters off the wall.

The Mana barrier shook with the impact of thousands of those disrupting attacks. The new Nerhoun who faced them also hammered against the Mana barrier as it started to turn a darker shade.

The war lizards didn't care to attack the walls; instead, they dug their talons into the walls and started to climb up.

The Terra Alliance fought back, hurling rocks down at them or sending down attack spells, arrows, and bolts. Here and there, they fell, but most continued to advance. The riders used their spears to break apart boulders and hit those who passed through the castle's Mana barrier to hit the attackers below.

The rider's shields and spears moved fluidly to defend and attack simultaneously as they moved.

Dave looked up. His face turned grim as gryphons, sky screams, and their masters rushed out from under the Nerhoun.

They attacked the Mana barrier, but it was clear that this was not their target. As they descended toward the ground, the sky screams let out their stun attack.

Many people were put off-balance by this attack. However, all of the anti-air repeater batteries were manned by Aleph automatons. They weren't organic and couldn't be stunned by an audible attack.

Some people were using just chats, but the majority of the fighting forces were actually people of Emerilia and they relied on their own voices instead of the party chats to command their forces.

Bolts tore through the air, trying to bring down the gryphons and sky screams. Both of these creatures had their own Mana barriers. They were nowhere close to the level of the Nerhoun's, but it was enough to deal with a few dozen impacts.

Sky screams fell here and there, but mostly the batteries made them cautious rather than decrease their numbers heavily. Their riders attacked from long range as they raced over the castle, killing maybe one or two people here and there, or luckily bringing their sky screams' claws to bear.

The gryphons targeted these batteries; whether they recognized them as a threat, or because they simply angered the gryphon riders, Dave didn't know.

Their Mana barriers failed but the gryphon's innate defense stopped the bolts from penetrating at long range, only lightly bruising them.

The gryphons descended out of the sky like golden flashes, their riders war gods as they let loose with disrupting attacks, hitting the walls of the castle tower and the various defenses. Rocks fell down, opening holes in walls and leaving craters where they struck.

Their gryphons' claws struck out, leaving deep grooves in the ground as they grabbed the repeaters and Aleph automatons, crushing them.

"Mages, get those gryphons!" Esa yelled out.

While the Nalheim could bring in air support with the gryphons and sky screams, the Terra Alliance had theirs continuously bombing the Nerhoun from above.

The Nerhoun's tentacles inspired fear within those ranks of aerial forces. They had easily gutted the four hundred DCA aerial force that had gone up against them before.

While the Nerhoun were at the walls of Eastern Castle One, the aerial forces didn't dare to help. To do so would be inviting their death.

This left the sky screams and gryphons largely to themselves.

"Zero, take out those Nerhouns!" Esa growled. In just minutes, Eastern Castle One had descended into chaos, with spells being hurled into the skies, lighting up the battlefield in front of the castle or along the walls.

A melee was underway between the war lizards atop the castle's walls and the defenders there.

Bolts continued to thrum, filling the air with their fire as gryphons roared and cleaved through defenders and repeater positions.

The replacement Nerhoun was almost in position. The dwarven artillery guns were mostly based next to the repeater batteries, both of them needing the greatest elevation in order to have the greatest range and impact on the battlefield.

Even as the gryphons continued to rake their positions, actually killing a number of the dwarven artillery crews, the dwarves continued on. Their rounds howled through the air and slammed into the Nerhoun's barriers.

Even under this onslaught, the Terra Alliance had hard faces filled with determination. This is what they had come together for, from all across Emerilia: to defend it against those who would see it burn.

"That's suicide!" the Edon Kingdom commander yelled at hearing Esa's words.

"No, that's Party Zero," Deia said. Flames appeared around her body; her hair waved behind her as she slowly rose into the air.

Induca was similarly covered in flames; a covering of white vicious Air blades formed around Anna. The shadows seemed to cover Malsour as a metal board appeared under his feet and the feet of Gurren, Lox, and Steve. Steve swung his massive axe in his hands as a massive dwarven shield and sword appeared in Gurren and Lox's hands. Their shields were covered in an earthen green aura as their swords were covered in an aura of Air.

Dave and Jung Lee simply rose into the air as if gravity had no bearing on them; Suzy's creations split apart from their hybrid formation. She held out her bag of holding, tossing out Earth creations over the wall. The metal and Fire creations in the air fell with them. The Air creations surrounded Anna, raising her up into the air as well.

Deia stepped over the edge of the castle's walls and dropped toward the ground below. The rest of Party Zero followed. Flames burst out from Deia's back, forming wings of flame as her fall turned into a glide over the Nalheim below and toward the Nerhoun.

Sky screams, seeing them leave the walls, dove to attack the party.

Lox and Gurren swung their swords, unleashing blades of Air. They weren't mages but with their Devastator armor enhancing their strength and the power of their conjured Air swords, making blades of Air wasn't hard for them.

These attacks smacked against Mana barriers but didn't pass through. Anna added in her attacks, cutting through the weakened Mana barriers and severely wounding the creatures hiding within them.

Deia fired out an arrow. This one arrow split into a hundred. As they hit, they erupted into concentrated Fire Mana, burning away shields and killing those who hid within. Without needing to pull out arrows from a quiver, Deia's speed had increased in leaps and bounds. As she fired at these oncoming creatures, the sky was filled with fiery arrows.

The sky screams, sensing the danger of Party Zero, tried to pull away, fighting their riders who attempted to spear them with their distorting attacks. These attacks hit a Mana barrier around Party Zero. The Mana barrier was grounded at orbs that seemed to appear from nothing.

Quickly, the party left the castle walls behind and entered the Nerhoun's Mana barrier. Tentacles attacked the Mana barrier with frantic and powerful attacks.

Dave grunted, keeping the barrier active.

Induca unleashed a firestorm around the Mana barrier. The Nerhoun let out a pained noise; its powerful but fragile tentacles were burnt as they passed through the powerful spell. Still its master continued to force it to attack even as its wounds became more severe.

Suzy's creations on the ground formed together, an earthen body with an arm of metal and an arm of fire. Together, the three different Affinitied creations worked as one symbiotic whole. Their strength was on par with a war lizard and its rider but more maneuverable. They started attacking the ranks below, weakening them and taking their attention away from Party Zero.

"Move!" Malsour yelled.

Around him, magical circles appeared; from them, spears of metal sped out—just faint blurs that tore into the Nerhoun's tentacles. Some of the spears were destroyed, but the others impacted the tentacles.

Lu Lu—now standing on Suzy's shoulder—unleashed her lightning attack. Her attacks were no weaker than they had been in her larger form.

The tentacles drew back and withered under the attacks but as Party Zero got closer, the attacks of the Nerhoun increased in speed and ferocity. Even if it was in pain, it seemed to understand the threat that Party Zero presented. It wasn't going to give up its life easily!

The last of the sky screams had fled from the party's attacks.

Around Deia, the air seemed to become increasingly heavy as threads of Fire Affinity Mana were pulled in from the world around her. The fire around her shrunk as she rose so that she faced the Nerhoun. "I'll open a path!" she yelled out to the rest of the party.

They focused on Deia, ready to act at a moment's notice.

Magical circles formed around her, and then in front of her bow in varying sizes. She let loose her arrow. It left the string of the bow; it looked no different than any other arrow except it was made from bright-red and blue materials.

However, one merely had to look at it to feel the terrifying power that was contained within.

Deia was a three-hundred-year-old mage who had long ago come to understand the power of archery. She had come to a high understanding of Fire magic and had the power of a Fire Affinity demi-god. With her mother and sister's guidance, her control over Fire Mana was close to the top. When she had fought while pregnant, she hadn't been unable to unleash her power at a high level for fear of harming her baby. It had taught her to refine her spells, increasing the power of her spells and decreasing the Mana cost.

Now she was able to unleash that power she had held onto, and combine it with the impressive control she had built up.

The Nerhoun, sensing the power of the arrows that sped through the air, turned. Its tentacles wrapped together, creating a drill underneath its body that faced the arrow. Its Mana barrier condensed, becoming more powerful and focused.

Artillery spells and shells hit the other Nerhoun and Nalheim below but this Nerhoun was wholly focused on the arrow that hit its shields. The weak-looking shields held for a few moments; the arrow became weaker and weaker as air seemed to distort around it as it spun at an incredible speed.

The Nerhoun unleashed disintegrating attacks along all of its tentacles, focused on the arrow that faded faster and faster.

The barrier rapidly changed colors before failing. It exploded with the sound of breaking glass. A shock wave of air blew out from where the arrow and barrier had been. The arrow exploded as the disintegrating attack of the tentacles that was focused upon it tore it apart.

Deia was under a cooldown time as her Mana worked to ready for the next.

The attack passed through where the arrow had been and struck Party Zero's Mana barrier.

Dave let out a grunt as he altered the barrier's strength and the power draw from the vault soul gem within his bag of holding. "Can't hold this more than three minutes!"

The Nerhoun's attack was still fairly wide and so passed around them, and struck the castle walls behind them, making the Mana barrier fluctuate wildly.

Induca fired a plasma round at the Nerhoun. It barely made it ten meters before it was destroyed by the Nerhoun's ongoing attack.

"Focus your attacks as we advance!" Deia called out as she held her hand out. A pillar of red light lanced out from her hand, impacting against the Nerhoun's attack.

Induca's attack melded with hers, pushing the distortion attack backward slightly as they all pushed forward. The attack was so powerful it actually slowed their forward progress.

No one tried to get close to Party Zero and their Mana barrier. The ripples of energy that were being thrown off around them were enough to severely wound a gryphon.

A stream of white was added to the other four when Anna joined in.

Lox, Gurren, and Steve put away their weapons and unleashed spearheads formed from Mana.

Slowly, they pushed forward; the Nerhoun's distorting attack was slowly pushed back.

Dave continued to alter the barrier to give the best coverage and reduce power usage. His right hand moved; his eyes glowed with gray light as runes lit up across his body.

The power of the mages' attacks was changed and altered, becoming one single stream. Dave felt the stress lessen on his body as he felt another presence helping him. He opened his eyes and looked to his side, where Jung Lee stood. His eyes glowed with similar gray light as gray smoke drifted away from his body.

Dave saw Jung Lee's smile. Dave looked back to the pillars of Mana that were fighting against the Nerhoun's attack.

Dave and Jung Lee solidified the attack made by the others, increasing its strength and allowing them to advance faster.

Jung Lee and Dave poured power into the combined spell formation. The power ripples coming from their fight with the Nerhoun increased as the Nerhoun frantically poured more power into its attack to fend off Party Zero.

"Fire!" This simple word barely registered in Dave's ear as his senses picked up a half-dozen plasma rounds flying through the air as one before hitting the Nerhoun.

The Nerhoun let out a pained shout.

Six of the dwarven artillery crews had been holding their rounds, waiting, ready to support Party Zero. Seeing their chance, they'd fired their plasma grand working rounds as one.

They hit the Nerhoun's tentacles. Without a barrier, the Nerhoun took the attack at full force. Its tentacles convulsed in pain. In that moment, its disrupting stream was broken.

Party Zero's combined attacks drilled through the flailing tentacles and through the fleshy interior of the Nerhoun's scaled head. The Nerhoun twitched a few times before going slack and dropping down toward the ground.

"Pull back!" Deia yelled to Party Zero.

They all followed her orders without hesitation. They moved back to the safety of the castle walls, which were filled with chaotic fighting as artillery now fired down directly onto those trying to advance for the walls.

The people of Eastern Castle One had no time to celebrate the defeat of the Nerhoun as they were all engaged in the fight of their lives.

"Split up and support people on the walls," Deia said as they landed, firing arrows as she spoke.

Lox and Gurren moved down the walls to their right, their sword and shields appearing.

Dave let out a breath of relief. The amplification Magical Circuit that was within the eastern castle allowed one to speed up their recovery of Health, Mana, and Stamina at nearly twice the rate.

Dave threw out grenades; explosions rippled down the walls, killing dozens. Gryphons moved to attack them. Anna and Jung Lee took to the skies in a flash, tearing through those who opposed them.

The wall shook as Dave stood in the air.

"They just broke through the wall!' Malsour called out.

"Well, that's pretty shitty." Steve wielded his massive axe in one hand, sparring against a Nalheim on a war lizard's back as he fired spearheads of Mana at sky screams.

Suzy's creations jumped onto the walls before they dropped into the courtyard below. Already the dismounted Nalheim were quickly advancing into the castle.

There were nearly three hundred thousand Nalheim outside of the eastern castle; there were but forty thousand people within the castle.

The disparity of forces was too great to overcome easily. When they had been fighting from the walls, they had bled the Nalheim. But now that they were inside, there might be a large amount of players and powerful POEs but the Nalheim were all powerful foes, not including their beasts and their abilities.

"POEs, pull back to the ono. Players, cover their retreat!" the Edon Kingdom commander yelled.

With an almost one-to-ten fight on their hands, it was clear that they were going to lose the castle. Pulling back was in their best interest to hold their strength in reserve. Losing people here in a battle that wasn't decisive was a quick and easy way to reduce the strength of the Terra Alliance.

Dave distorted the gravity around the Nalheim who had entered the castle while Malsour insta-cast a curse over the entrance to the castle. Anyone who came through the breach would be slightly weakened and more vulnerable. At the same time, Suzy's multiple Affinity creations rampaged through the open area.

Deia fired an arrow into the sky. It rose up, splitting as it did, turning and coming back down, speeding up as the arrows continued to split. They hammered down beyond the castle's walls, cutting down a number of Nalheim and wounding many others.

This attack wasn't meant to inflict massive casualties, but rather make it hard to enter the castle, giving the forces inside more time to get organized.

The sky screams and gryphons were becoming more bold as the majority of the repeater batteries had been destroyed. They came in, using their talons to cut people in half or knock them off walls as their beaks pierced through the defenders' bodies with ease.

The POEs pulled backward, the players taking over their positions as best as they could.

"Back to the castle!" Esa called out.

The POEs ran into the circular building that made up the main building within the castle walls. Many players and POEs lept from the walls, pulling backward as Nalheim flooded over those walls as another section of wall crumbled down.

Two of the remaining three Nerhoun reached the castle's Mana barrier. Their tentacles whipped against the barrier, quickly changing its color.

Party Zero all ran back toward the inner circular building from across the castle, throwing attacks behind them to slow down the Nerhoun who were following them.

Anna and Jung Lee floated above them, providing cover from the Nalheim in the sky.

Dave threw out hundreds of grenades as he formed a bow from his two conjuring rods. Gray arrows left a smoky trail behind as they threw dismounted Nalheim back with their force.

Lox and Gurren provided the rear-guard for POEs who were racing into the circular building, firing both of their armbands to at least slow the Nalheim's speed.

"Fuck, I hate squids!" Steve yelled over the fighting. He, too, was shooting Mana spearheads at the Nalheim.

"Agreed!" Dave yelled, hitting a dismounted Nalheim who was about to cut through a fleeing POE.

"Oh well, at least they're going to help with the destruction phase! I thought that the gray walls on glowing soul gems didn't really jive. Really was time this place had a facelift. Maybe go with some nice, fierce black and warriors white with just a hint of noble gold," Steve said.

"More running, less renovations talk!" Suzy yelled.

"You ever wonder who comes up with paint names? Like, how many ways are there to say white?" Steve continued.

"Seriously, that's what you're thinking about?" Induca let loose with a barrage of fireballs.

"Hate the paint game, not the painter!" Steve said.

Party Zero made it into the circular building. They were among the last. Already the POEs were rushing through the ono in orderly lines. None of them were happy with leaving Eastern Castle One, but this had been the plan of their leaders from the beginning.

Lox and Gurren took up the rear, covering Party Zero.

Once they made it into the castle proper, the Nalheim started to group together. But in the narrow halls it was hard for them to all fit. This meant that the Nalheim's progress was slowed. Only a few of them could get through the door and into the hall at one given time. Although Party Zero could hold them back, the Nalheim were opening up holes within the walls of the circular building, with more of them entering every minute.

The defenders in other halls weren't as strong as the Stone Raiders and couldn't hold out as long.

Deia continued to guide the party backward, careful to make sure that no one fell behind. If they didn't pull back, then the Nalheim from other halls and entrances could get in behind them and attack.

The POEs and players rushed through the ono in a flood, exiting and then heading right out and through a teleport pad, entering the second eastern castle.

The Stone Raiders held back the Nalheim as much as possible.

Dave ducked as the building shook. Using his senses, he was able to look through the castle and into the sky. "A Nerhoun is attacking the tower! Looks like it's going to come apart!"

The Nerhoun's tentacles smashed into the tower's walls. The impact took chunks out of the tower walls. Its disrupting attack only increased the damage that the Nerhoun did. The tower in the center of Eastern Castle Two shook; chunks of the tower came free, falling down and impacting on the circular building below. Holes started to appear on the upper floors. Rubble dust fell on those in the lower floors. Wounded were gathered up and rushed backward.

Lox, Gurren, and Steve threw up their hands. Spearheads in almost a solid line came from their hands. They hit the Nalheim disrupting attacks, and the Nalheim behind them, suppressing them fully.

The area they were in opened up. They were getting closer to the center of the castle. Here, all of the floors within the circular building were opened up in an interior courtyard that lay underneath the central tower.

In the middle of this courtyard, there was a Mana well on a pedestal of a soul gem construct, as well as an open ono that people were fleeing through. Most of the forces within the castle had already escaped, but now the fighting picked up in tempo with all of the last fighters at the entrances to this open area. They held their positions; they would all need to turn and run at the same time so that they weren't picked off in small groups.

"Party Zero, move to the ono. We'll cover the others' retreat!" Deia yelled to the party chat as well as the general chat.

Dave's Mana barrier orbs appeared once again, covering Party Zero as they moved back from their hallway. As they moved, the other members of Party Zero started to attack the Nalheim at the different entrances to the courtyard. They called out for different groups to pull back; they would rush backward as Party Zero held back the forces that they'd been fighting off.

Dave continuously threw out grenades as Malsour threw down hexes to weaken and slow the Nalheim. Induca and Deia hurled out Fire walls. These walls of flames covered over various entrances while Anna created air streams that increased the power of the flames and threw it back at those on the other side.

Jung Lee was by far the strongest of them all. He held off half of the corridors by himself, creating different walls made from every Affinity. Jekoni was next to him, assisting in the weaving of spells and looking out for his friend.

The castle shook as the tower was finally cut apart. Light streamed in from above as rubble fell down toward Party Zero and smashed into the soul gem-covered floor. Balconies and stone work were destroyed by the incoming rain of rubble. Dave's Mana barrier shook with the impacts from the rubble.

"Malsour, get the Mana well and turn the soul gem into a grand working!" Dave yelled.

Malsour appeared next to the Mana well in a flash. The last of the Stone Raiders made it into the ono as Dave restricted his Mana barrier to only cover the ono, Mana well, and Party Zero.

"I'm going to need some time!" Malsour yelled. His hand grew a metal blade that cut through the pedestal around the Mana well with ease; with a flick of his hand, the Mana well disappeared into his spatial ring. He pressed both of his hands against the pedestal made of soul gem. It glowed brighter as a spell formation appeared around Malsour.

The Nalheim pushed forward. A gryphon tore through a wall, leading a herd of war lizards. The general riding the gryphon stabbed out at Party Zero. Dave's Mana barrier took the impact.

An arrow tore through the air, breaking through the gryphon's barrier and hitting the gryphon. The general leaped free of their mount as the fire within the arrow was released, burning the gryphon from the inside.

The general landed heavily. War lizards rushed in from behind. The general jumped with ease onto a war lizard that stood on its rump. There was a cold look in the Nalheim general's eyes as it stared at the Party Zero Stone Raiders.

More generals on their gryphons broke through, leading the Nalheim forces. Sky screams rushed in through the tower that had been torn apart.

Lox, Steve, and Gurren pulled out their melee weapons. With a war cry, they met the Nalheim, their weapons flashing as they fought off war lizards and dismounted Nalheim.

A gryphon rushed into the Mana barrier.

The air shook as Anna took into the sky, an impact crater around where her feet had been. She deflected an attack made by the general at Malsour. She fought the general and the gryphon together in a fierce melee.

Dave was running low on grenades and he couldn't use many of his trump cards; to do that would cause the Jukal to start watching him closer.

He waved his hand. His two conjuring rods glowed with gray smoke as they combined with one another and landed in Dave's hand to reveal a monstrous two-handed blade. Dave held his blade and looked to his side.

Jung Lee had a small smile on his face as they looked to each other, Jung Lee with his hand on the hilt of his sword. Slowly his hands clasped over the blade.

Dave looked away; a cold smile appeared on his face.

Dave and Jung Lee shot forward at incredible speed.

Jung Lee was covered in gray smoke. Flashes of different colors appeared like lightning across his body. His sword came out with a piercing gray light that cut across the Nalheim in front of him. Dismounted were torn apart by the immaterial blade that passed through the air that Jung Lee's sword had cut through.

They supported Lox, Gurren, and Steve, holding back the Nalheim. All of the melee fighters were in a fierce melee. The Nalheim trained with a spear and shield to keep their enemy at range; all of the melee fighters with Party Zero liked to get up close and personal for close combat. Once they were able to get close to the Nalheim, they were able to use their greater strength and weapons to take them down.

In the corner of Dave's vision, he started to see a bar decreasing at a faster rate. A glowing circle appeared in the ground. The Nalheim were capturing the eastern castle!

"Malsour!" Deia yelled out. All of Party Zero did everything they could to make more time for Malsour.

"Nearly there! Ten more seconds!" Malsour called out. The spell formations around him moved faster and faster as more symbols were added to the glowing creation.

Dave switched from his two-handed claymore, tearing the blade apart as gray smoke covered the two conjuring poles and turned into twin wicked swords.

"Done!" Malsour said. The spell formation that was around him compressed and spread over the broken pedestal instead. A darkness spread out from the pedestal, spreading through the soul gem construct as if it were a virus.

"Pull back!" Deia yelled to Party Zero. Everyone moved backward to the ono.

A Fire wall erupted around the party.

They rushed through the ono as an unholy screeching came from within the castle. Malsour's spell that he had implanted into the castle's soul gem was being activated.

Dave waited at the ono, maintaining the Mana barrier. Suzy, Anna, Induca, Jung Lee, Malsour, and Lox made it through the ono when ten gryphons smashed through the magical defenses and passed through the Mana barrier.

A gryphon's claws reached out and latched onto Gurren in his Devastator armor.

"Yer not getting my friend!" Steve yelled, leaping into the air.

The general atop the gryphon hit him in the chest with a disrupting blast, opening up his armor and revealing the Mithril that lay underneath.

Steve swung his axe down, putting all of his strength in it. He left a deep groove in the general's shield. His deflected axe missed the general's leg but cut deep into the gryphon.

The gryphon let out a cry of pain and dropped Gurren in its efforts to try to escape the metal madman.

Gurren dropped to the ground and quickly got to his feet.

"Move!" Steve yelled, fighting two other gryphons as he tried to back up.

Gurren ran through the ono.

Dave altered the Mana barrier. Steve was getting hit with multiple high-powered disrupting attacks, taking apart his body. The gryphons were so close, it was hard for Dave to erect a Mana barrier between them.

"Lox! Grab them!" Steve yelled.

Lox reached through the ono, grabbing Dave and Deia and hauling them through the ono.

"What are you doing!" Deia yelled angrily.

Lox didn't say anything as he watched Steve swinging his axe and fighting.

"All right, now that the kids are out of the way, let's see what you've got!" Steve yelled at the Nalheim.

They surged forward from every direction. A shield covered the ono, not allowing them through and into the Terra as Steve fought them off. There was no way that he was going to make it to the ono. Still, Dave hoped for something—anything—to let Steve make it to the ono and escape.

Steve took hit after hit. Still, he continued to fight as his body started to fail him. His limbs came apart from the disrupting attacks; holes showed the gears and glowing runes underneath his metal armor.

His one arm dangled from his body. "'Tis but a scratch!" Steve laughed, fighting on with one arm. He got hit badly in the leg, making him limp. "Just a flesh wound!"

He took on war lizards, dismounted Nalheim, and gryphon generals. He couldn't fight them all at the same time; they were too strong.

Finally, he collapsed to the ground as his legs failed. A general hit him in the shoulder with a disrupting blast.

Steve hurled his axe through the ono. "Don't lose that!" Steve yelled and looked at the gryphon that now stood over him. Its head darted forward and into his head.

There was a screeching noise of metal on metal as the gryphon shook its head, turning Steve's head into nothing but warped metal.

Steve's runes across his body started to pulse with power, faster and faster, before everyone's vision went white.

The ono and the teleport it was connected to shut down their connection as everyone within Terra recovered their eyesight.

No one said anything, instead looking to the teleport pad opened to the second eastern castle. They ran forward and Gurren grabbed Steve's axe.

They exited the ono, quickly flying up the tower and onto the roof. Suzy's Air creations carried those who couldn't fly. They rushed to the wall that was closest to the first castle.

An explosion rocked the first eastern castle. The tower and inner castle exploded outward; half of the remaining tower turned into flying debris as the rest collapsed. Dust and debris covered the castle while Nerhouns moved to the area of the explosion.

Dave could make out massive groups of shadows that seemed to be moving within the leftovers from the explosion. "Are those darklings?"

"That was my spell, continuous darkling conjuration," Malsour said, his voice dead as they all stood there, looking at the castle.

"I don't feel his connection anymore," Suzy said in a small voice. The atmosphere seemed to darken as she confirmed their worst fears.

Chapter 17: Pulling Together

They watched as the Nerhoun started to fight against the darklings that Malsour had imprinted upon the soul gem construct within the castle.

The Nalheim had seen the end of the fight for the castle and had started to celebrate when Steve had ignited his soul gem and the power runes that led to it.

Then, as the shock of that was dimming, the darklings had crept out of the shadows, pooling together into beasts of darkness to pull down sky screams and cut through the Nalheim ranks before they broke apart, turning into shadows once again to avoid the Nalheim and attack from another direction. They were a fierce opponent and one that couldn't be pinned down by the Nalheim.

Still, the soul gem construct had its power reserves depleted with the castle's Mana barrier collapsing. There was only a limited time in which the darklings could act.

Slowly the darklings' actions decreased. The Nalheims and their beasts recovered from the initial shock and fought back against the darklings.

"I want all ranged defenders to report in by party within five minutes!" Esa demanded. Her voice made the members of Party Zero snap back into reality.

They looked to one another with hurt and somber faces. A hard edge started to fill them as they looked to Deia.

"Let's move to the front wall. Best we're ready for the Nalheim when they come," Deia said.

***

Josh looked away from the casualty lists. They might be playing in a fantasy world but there was a live updating stream on all of those who had died, from player to POE.

Later I can look at that. Right now I have an enemy to defeat.

He looked at the two new prompts in his vision.

Castle Conquest

You currently control (7/8) Castles

Earning: (7) conquest points per minute

Bonus: For controlling four of the Castles, you earn an additional (1) conquest point(s) per minute.

Total points: 48,067

Rights: Administrative (Can spend conquest points to upgrade Castle infrastructure and repair castles. Can also delete Castle infrastructure)

Eastern Castle 1

Status: Under Control by Nalheim Race

Earn: 1 conquest point per minute

Evolution: 1 (Second evolution 0%). Can increase evolution to Level 2 by paying (100,000) Conquest points.

Upgrades: Trebuchet, Increased combat abilities for defenders (Damaged), Soul Gem construct defenses (destroyed), Dwarven Artillery batteries (3/40), Aleph Repeater batteries (0/12)

Durability: 12,234/ 60,000

Castle Conquest

For controlling 4 conquest castles, you gain an extra conquest point (1) per minute

Castle Conquest

You have lost control of (1) castle(s); for not owning all of the castles, you do not gain an extra conquest point per minute.

"Looks like they're building siege weaponry," Josh said to himself.

The screen on the eastern castle stopped updating as it was fully captured by the Nalheim. The sounds of battle dissipated as they reorganized their forces.

The castle had a boost to its defenses slightly as soon as it was taken; now the dwarven artillery were slamming into the castle's Mana barrier that had appeared after the Nalheim took it. Right now the castle seemed as if it were invulnerable. None of the attacks were even lessening the strength of the barrier.

Still the dwarves kept one or two batteries firing, waiting to see when the shield barrier lessened in strength and they could start chipping it away.

Right now, every minute the Nalheim waited, they were getting organized and the Nerhoun started to recover their Mana so that they might be able to once again provide support to the Nalheim forces.

"How long will it take for the Nalheim to reach the second eastern castle?" Josh asked the command post.

"Put it at about an hour, maybe an hour and a half. The distance between the two is much farther than Goblin Mountain to the first castle and there aren't a bunch of traps in the way," Lucy said.

"We need something to take out those Nerhouns. If the Nalheim are left out in the open and without the overhead protection, we can rain hell down on them with artillery," the dwarven artillery commander added.

"I'll make a call and see if I can pull something together." Josh opened up a private chat.

"Josh?" Deia answered.

"Deia, if you and Party Zero were to go all out, could you take out those two remaining Nerhoun?" Josh asked.

"We could. If Induca or Malsour were to reveal their true nature, then they could deal with them," Deia said.

"Are you sure?" Josh asked, holding on the hope that Deia blessed him with.

"I'm sure." Deia's voice was unwavering.

"Okay, well, if they need to get away from the battle to change then they should go for it. We need to get rid of those Nerhoun as soon as they come out of the protection of the eastern castle. I will get the DCA and the aerial forces at our disposal to assist them," Josh said.

"Okay, I'll let them know what's going on and then let you know what their plan is."

"Thank you, Deia." Josh closed the channel. Party Zero was the trump card of the Stone Raiders. Both Malsour and Induca's repressed power as dragons made them fiercely powerful contestants who could compete one-on-one with the Nerhoun.

Having them appear might allow people to draw the conclusion that they were the same dragons as the two who were at Boranal's Citadel.

Some might think that they had the two as allies of some kind; a few might even figure out that they were Malsour and Induca or infer that the Stone Raiders were in an alliance with the dragons on Emerilia.

Got to pick which cards to use and when. We can't give all of our tricks away right now. If we do, then the people we're going to be going up against in the future will have an advantage over us. Although the Pantheon is quiet now, it's clear that the current state of things won't last for too long.

***

Ursk looked over the growing runes and magical runes that covered the inside of the defenses around the spawn point.

"Are you sure about this?" Ursk's brother asked from his side, his voice low so that no others could hear them.

Weakness in an orc tribe was stomped out quickly. Second-guessing one's decisions wasn't allowed. However, Ursk wasn't just a simple orc.

Although he might be headstrong and wouldn't back down from a decision, once he had made it, he kept to it. If he might have doubts, he only revealed it to those who he had absolute trust in.

"I'm not sure about it completely, but we've been given a chance here, one to increase our strength. Right now we are creating a republic of Gudalo that will see that our future generations will have chances that we can't even think about.

"With this larger strength behind us, then the other tribes and the other people who are becoming a part of this republic will treat us with a greater respect and be willing to negotiate with us as equals," Ursk said.

Ursk's brother nodded. He knew how Ursk saw the republic of Gudalo as a path toward a greater future for the tribe.

"Leader Ursk!" a gnome called out from atop of a blue-bellied snake.

"Report," Ursk said to the gnome scout.

"We have a party of summoners moving through the forest to our position. They have a large group of fighters with them. Seems that they were sent by the Terra Alliance and have people from the Gudalo republic committee with them." The gnome sounded confused by the last bits, but being a good scout, he knew not to leave out even the least significant detail.

Ursk looked to his brother thoughtfully before he looked to the gnome. "Go have one of the leaders meet with them. I will make my way over there to talk to them," Ursk said.

"Yes, Leader!" The gnome's snake turned and rushed off at speed through the swamp's mud and stagnant water.

Ursk took a moment to check his screen.

Spawn Point (Orcish Swamplands)

Days Hours Minutes Seconds

2 15 31 34

He didn't let his inner fears show as he walked confidently through his lands and toward where the group from the alliance was. As he got closer, he was surprised with the numbers that had assembled. The orcs never banded together for anything other than random beast attacks.

Otherwise, alliances were based on trade, not mutual defense. This was something that Ursk was looking forward to from the republic: a fighting force that would reinforce his tribe if it was needed in a time of war.

Still, although that was a future hope of his, he hadn't expected the alliance to do anything more than the soul gem construct around the spawn point. Even that, he could tell, took up a lot of precious resources that the various gnome and orc tribes within the swamps wouldn't be willing to give up to another tribe that they barely knew.

So when Ursk saw nearly ten thousand soldiers from different races riding atop of beasts that Ursk hadn't even heard of, his footsteps almost faltered. He quickly moved to where the leader of his scouts was conversing with a woman wearing robes that only allowed someone to see her eyes.

"Tribe Leader Ursk." The woman tilted her head in respect to Ursk.

He bowed his head to her as well, sensing the power that seemed to fill the air around this woman. He used his analysis on the woman by reflex.

Heroiu'quing

Human

Level 429

"My lady, I have heard that you have come on behalf of the Terra Alliance," Ursk said, in his most respectful tone. He was Level 357, the highest in all of his tribe, but this lady was nearly a hundred levels stronger than him.

The difference was immense. If she wanted to, Ursk didn't doubt that she could easily kill Ursk. He sensed that she was smiling before she continued onward to talk.

"Indeed, I was sent by the alliance. You can call me Quing. I am in charge of the group behind me. There are a number of summoners as well as beast tamers with my group. We were sent in order to help you with capturing and controlling the blood reevers that are supposed to be leaving the spawn point within your tribe lands."

Ursk looked to the people with their different animals. He realized that there were many more animals than there were people. With his instincts built up from a life of fighting, he saw a fierce intelligence in the eyes of those creatures as well as a strength born through their own power.

Animals were much easier to deal with when trying to estimate their power. Sentient races could hide their levels and their abilities through a number of ways; the creatures of Emerilia freely displayed their strength in order to scare off other predators or creatures that moved in on their territory.

To tame such powerful beasts not only required someone to be strong, it also meant that they were incredibly good at creating soul binding contracts that worked. These creatures wouldn't be subdued by anything but masterful beast tamers.

The stronger and stranger creatures glowed with magical auras or a strangeness that didn't seem to be associated with Emerilia; their soul binding masters gave off an even stronger aura. They had not only ripped open a passageway between realms, but afterward they had the strength and luck to soul bind these creatures to themselves.

Ursk hid his amazement and his jealousy well as he smiled to Quing. "We welcome any aid that you and your people might be able to provide." Ursk didn't have to force a smile as he felt a weight being lifted from his body with the arrival of this force.

They didn't need fighters, but people who could give them a higher chance of coming to make soul binding contracts with the blood reevers—they would be of greater aid.

***

Within Pandora's box, underneath a dust-covered tarp, a faint glow started to become brighter and brighter.

The room was filled with parts, soul gems, and sheets of runes. An interface that had been stuck to the wall showed an image of a roughly humanoid-looking creature covered in runes.

The air in the room was disturbed as a soul gem construct reached up from the floor underneath the tarp. The crystal grew, magical coding so packed together it looked like runic lines followed its growth.

It disappeared under the covering. A moment later, it stopped growing and power started to surge through the runes. More and more runic line covered crystals grew from the floor, all reaching up under the tarp and surging with power as they connected with whatever lay underneath.

The soul gem floor lit up with power underneath the tarp that was being tossed around with the powerful movement of Mana. There was a muffled noise from under the tarp as the light in the room continued to grow as the tarp tightened over what lay underneath.

"Blergh, aurgh, hremm!" came from under the tarp. "Elll ruck." A dejected noise followed shortly afterward. It sounded as if someone was trying to talk with a mouth full of marshmallows.

If Dave and Malsour had been in the room, they would have been alarmed at the amount of power that was being funneled into whatever lay under the tarp. Something pushed up against the tarp, raising it, to show a massive rune-covered table with something growing on top of it.

Suddenly, a half-formed hand made of soul gem grasped at the tarp. The hand took a few tries before its fumbling efforts resulted in it actually grabbing the tarp. The hand pulled on the tarp as the upper half of a man also made from soul gems sat up.

"Daddy's ho— Seriously, fuck off, tarp! Making this a pain in the ass, man!" the glowing soul gem man yelled. He only had one hand and was fighting the tarp still secured around the table.

The soul gem man fought with the tarp for a solid ten minutes before he let out a frustrated sigh and lay back down. "Would've been more epic if someone was here to see it," the man muttered.

He was fully formed from soul gems. Motes of light and power flooded through his body.

"Well, the Black Knight from Monty Python has nothing on me!" the man said. "Or was it the Green Knight? Hmm, I hope this whole growing a body thing isn't too slow."

The man tapped his half-formed finger against the table he was lying on. It was covered in magical coding as well as circuits and was formed from a soul gem construct. It was currently alight with power that was draining into the man, growing his missing limbs and half-formed body, bones of steel, veins of runic lines, muscles and body of soul gem crystal.

As time went on, all of these parts and the creation's facial features started to become more defined.

"Hah! It worked! This one's for the people who thought I could never pull myself together!" The man chuckled to himself before he let out a sigh. "Hope I'm not too late for the second fight."

Chapter 18: A Test of Will and Steel

After fifteen hours, Eastern Castle One's Mana barrier started to show fluctuations from the impacts by the dwarven artillery. It was immediately reported to the commanders of the alliance.

More shells were used and people were raised to alert as it was confirmed. The eastern castle now under the Nalheim control was no longer invulnerable.

They hadn't looked to repair the different parts of the castle at all. Instead, they had created siege weapons and were readying them within the castle, facing the walls that they would have to pass through to reach the second eastern castle.

In the fifteen hours the Terra Alliance had sent out the DCA and rangers into the dead ground between the two castles, they had been busy laying down all manner of traps. If they killed the Nalheim or slowed them in any way, then it would have been a good use of time.

Malsour and Induca were off within the Northwood. None of the creatures that called this area home had remained. As they sensed the power that had been unleashed in the fight for the first castle, they had all fled. Anything that tried to get close to Induca and Malsour were overwhelmed by their auras.

The Nalheim continued to make their siege weaponry from their conquest points.

"They must be getting more, or they got a bonus for taking the castle," Malsour said.

"I think it was a bonus for getting the castle. If it was a constant over time benefit, then I don't think that they'd have so many siege weapons as they do now." Induca looked over the battlefield.

They were perched on two massive trees in the Northwood. With their incredible eyesight, racial abilities, and spells, they could easily see what was happening at the eastern castle.

Malsour made a noise of agreement.

The two of them lapsed into silence as the dwarven artillery's tempo picked up as they peppered the Mana barrier with multiple impacts, taking down its strength. The three remaining Nerhoun floated into a formation above the castle, clearly readying themselves for the fight that was to come.

"Can't believe that he's gone," Induca said.

"Me either," Malsour said. Neither of them looked to the other. Even as they were hurting, now was not the time to grieve.

Induca's eyes narrowed as her body started to grow larger. Scales spread across her body; her eyes turned into vertical slits as she transformed into her dragon form. "This is for Steve," she said, her voice powerful enough to make animals in the immediate area cower in fear, hoping to be just looked over.

Malsour shook his head from side to side as he, too, grew into his dragon form. He was much larger than Induca and gave off an ancient and wise aura. His black scales shone in the cold early morning light. "The Mana barrier has failed," Malsour said. His deep voice passed to Induca's ears as he spread his wings out.

"Time to hunt," Induca said. The two of them flapped their wings, slowly rising straight up into the sky, their eyes focused on the Nerhoun who were now holding up Mana barriers around themselves and their fighters below.

The Nerhoun's tentacles whipped out, destroying the eastern wall that blocked their ground forces from the land between them and the next castle.

Scouts observed as the dismounted Nalheim moved forward, their spears once again unleashing their disrupting attack. The distorted blasts tore through the dust thrown up by the wall, striking the interior of the citadel and those unlucky few that lay in the path of the blasts.

The Nerhoun marched through the rubble clearing it out of the way for the war lizards. The war lizards moved in groups, towing siege weaponry.

From the dust and debris, siege towers and trebuchets started to appear as the Nalheim once again started to march. There were almost two hundred thousand Nalheim who marched, rode, or flew into the skies, under the protection of the Nerhouns.

Artillery shells were changed out to the limited reserves of the more powerful plasma cannon grand working rounds.

With the Nerhoun unable to switch out, they could do little but try to take down the attacks with their tentacles and disrupting attacks.

The second eastern castle had received the majority of the plasma grand working shells. With only a small distance between the Nerhoun and the second eastern castle, they had less time to react to try to block the shells before they hit their Mana barriers.

The dwarven artillery crews worked as if they were part of the gun that was under their control, mechanically loading, sighting, and firing their weapons before repeating the process over again.

Halos appeared around the guns repeatedly. All of the guns were ripple firing, so that there were constantly shells filling the skies.

Mages unleashed their own powerful artillery-classed spells, calling down lightning strikes and pillars of light from the sky, or creating air tornados in midair or a cutting whirlwind that screamed as its cutting blades impacted on the Nerhoun's Mana barrier.

The Nalheim took twenty minutes to leave the first eastern castle. A few had been hurt by the traps left behind but the majority were fine as they began to march as one toward the second eastern castle. The Nalheim's pace was quick as they would make it to the second castle's walls within an hour.

"They're clear of the first castle," Malkur reported to Deia.

She waved her hand to Party Zero and the forces behind them. They were nearly all made up of POE forces.

The teleport pad activated ahead of them.

"Move!" Deia yelled. Party Zero led the way back into Eastern Castle One.

They exited into a pile of rubble. The inner castle was barely standing: the tower had fallen over, smashing against one of the outer walls; debris littered the inner area of the castle while the circular castle base was open to the sky and looked as if it couldn't be saved. The walls had collapsed in places while there were holes in other areas.

Where the Nalheim had left, the wall was nothing but powder. Paths for the weapons moving through had been barely cleared.

Party Zero looked to a fifteen-meter-deep hole not too far from where the castle's ono lay. They didn't pause as they started to run over the rubble, getting higher and higher until they stood on the rubble of what had been an outer wall and looked at the Nalheim moving for the second castle.

Around them, the wall started to recover. Sections of the rubble moved with a black aura of a Dark mage around them as they shifted together like a game of Tetris, fusing into one wall and sliding into place with the wall.

Across Eastern Castle One, Dark mages used the rubble to repair the outer wall facing the Nalheim. Dwarven engineers cleared out different areas around the inner courtyard of the castle; others checked on the weapons in the castle as well as searched for possible resources to use and check the damage.

The walls facing the second eastern castle grew in width. The towers at the corners of the walls expanded as Air mages created air streams around dwarven artillery cannons, raising them up from the ground floor to these new positions.

Deia glanced to a screen that had appeared as soon as Party Zero had entered the eastern castle.

Castle Conquest

Progress: 12%

Every second, it was speeding up as the castle was being conquered by the Terra Alliance people who rushed to rebuild the castle enough to mount artillery on the walls and give them some defense.

Through the teleport pad, DCA aerial forces flew through and moved to the walls. They stayed away from standing atop the walls, instead hiding in the hallways underneath, watching the Nalheim.

Flying creatures with beast tamers and fighters mounted on their backs moved through the ono and spread out to the walls farthest from the second eastern castle.

Rubble continued to be picked up, and flowed into the growing defenses.

Party Zero was wholly focused on the Nalheim; their Mana freely circulated around their bodies as they waited. On Lox and Gurren's back there were Air creations, ready to help them fly forward when needed. Lu Lu seemed to sense the atmosphere, her eyes narrowed and predatory as she rested on Suzy's shoulders.

The Nalheim made it halfway to the second eastern castle, continuing on at a steady pace while their Nerhoun weathered the combined attacks from all of the castles.

The farthest castles had their shells easily defeated but it still meant that those tentacles couldn't easily defend against other shells that were coming in from closer artillery cannons.

"We're ready," Malsour said through the party chat.

"Let's move," Deia said to the party.

Their bodies seemed to turn blue as they rushed forward. Jung Lee looked as if he was running on the air itself as he climbed up into the sky. Dave floated as if gravity had no bearing on him. Suzy,

Gurren, and Lox all used Air creations to force their way higher and charge toward the Nerhoun.

Anna was a wind tempest as she cut through the air. Deia glowed with blue flames as she easily passed through the skies.

Deia and Dave held bows while Anna's sword hummed in the sky. Suzy held onto her staff while Jung Lee held the hilt of Jekoni's sword, ready to unleash it upon the world. Gurren and Lox's wrists glowed with runes, ready to unleash their Mana spearheads when necessary.

Behind them, the aerial forces took to the skies as the artillery cannons that had been re-positioned welcomed the Nalheim. They were loaded with special grand workings. The black shells raced through the skies. The Nerhoun didn't have time to smack the shells out of the sky before they impacted across their Mana barriers. The shells didn't do damage to the Mana barriers but instead massive black magical formations in the shape of magical circles appeared around where they had impacted. A faint black hue fell on all of the Nalheim in the area.

"The weakening hex is in place!" Deia confirmed as Party Zero raced forward. They had crossed the distance that had taken the Nalheim almost a half hour to reach within moments.

The Nalheim, now sensing danger from behind them, had one of their three Nerhouns move to greet the incoming party and the aerial forces that were forming up in the sky, well above the Nerhouns.

A roar that shook the very bones of the Party Zero members and sent chills down their spines inspired cold smiles on their faces as the Nalheim looked to the skies. Two dragons as large as a mansion plummeted toward the ground—one red, one black. Their eyes were focused on the two Nerhouns who were closest to the second eastern castle.

They opened their mouths. A pillar of darkness seemed to distort space as it reached out to one of the Nerhouns, hitting its Mana barrier with such force that the Nerhoun actually bobbed down slightly before it fought back up to its previous position.

A stream of blue flames pierced through the heavens from the red dragon. The second Nerhoun wasn't hit as hard as the first but it still took some time to recover from the attack.

The Nerhouns' barriers flickered and shuddered as they tried to defend against this powerful attack. They started to turn; their tentacles wrapped together to create their most powerful attacks.

Black streams appeared behind the black dragon's wings as he dove faster. Behind the red dragon, red streaks appeared as explosions sounded in the sky. The two dragons kept up their attacks as their speed continuously increased.

They were twin darts, only opening their wings moments before impact. They slammed into the Nerhouns' Mana barriers, cracking them. The black dragon's claws tore through the Nerhoun's scales with only slight difficulty. Pillars of stone rose up hundreds of feet, impaling the Nerhoun he was fighting as he continued to tear at the creature.

The red dragon was able to break the Nerhoun's defense but the impact from hitting the Mana barrier left her stunned for a moment as she flared out her wings, righting herself. She faced off against the Nerhoun she had picked as a target; it had started to wrap its tentacles together into a drill. Distorting attacks made the air shake as they slammed against the red dragon's Mana barrier.

She let out a roar. Red Fire essence from around the dragon pooled around her mouth, where a ball of red light turned blue, giving off an oppressive feeling for all who looked at it. The red dragon stabbed her head forward. Multiple magical circles appeared in front of her mouth and the ball of pure blue flame.

Induca's massive jaws opened and a blue pillar shot out from her mouth. The power of it was so intense that the light blinded anyone who looked close to it. Induca's timing was perfect because it slammed against the distorting attacks so hard that a shock wave exploded outward from where the two attacks met.

Creatures in the air near the point of impact were sent tumbling and spiraling to the ground below. A number of those below were crushed under the pressure alone. Induca's pillar of blue flame pushed the distorting attack back as the air around the attack seemed to become hazy with the heat and power that fought against one another.

In the air around the red dragon's target, a truly massive magical formation appeared. This massive multi-layered circle formation had the inner circles continue to turn. Thousands of flaming red arrows covered the sky and rained down on the Nerhoun. Many missed and covered the ground, killing Nalheim and their war lizards below.

The Nerhoun's tentacles took hits, making it warble in pain. The red dragon didn't give up on her pillar attack even as the Nerhoun weakened for just a moment before resuming, stronger than before. Sensing that if it failed it would die, the Nerhoun pushed back harder.

The second Nerhoun that had been pierced by hundreds of metal spears from the ground destroyed the spears with a twist of its body and lashed out at the black dragon who was tearing at its scales.

Malsour, still in his dragon form, let out an angered shout as the tentacles opened up his scales, making him start to bleed. With a powerful flap of his wings, he freed himself from the Nerhoun, sensing that if he were to become trapped within the Nerhoun's tentacles that it is a good chance that he would not survive.

The space under the Nerhoun distorted.

A black dome appeared over the Nalheim below. Pained screams and tortured noises could be heard across the battlefield, making event the veteran warriors cringe.

Tentacles made from oily darkness spread out, grabbing more and more of the surrounding Nalheim forces and pulling them into that darkness. None of them were seen again.

The Nerhoun expanded and shrunk, slamming into the black dragon with incredible speed.

The dark dragon yelled, but rushed back inward, its speed enough to break the very air as it slammed into the Nerhoun. Without the barrier, the Nerhoun was thrown back. Enraged, the Nerhoun lashed out, cutting the black dragon's scales open as its body took the impact of the dragon's claws. The Nerhoun hadn't been paying attention to its surroundings.

The dome of darkness had rapidly grown as massive tentacles came together. They shot out into the sky, reaching the Nerhoun who was trying to pool its tentacles together for its strongest attack.

The oily tentacles grabbed at the Nerhoun and pulled it downward, drawing it in towards the pitch black dome. Where the tentacles touched the Nerhoun, a faint black smoke appeared. The tentacles were dissolving the Nerhoun.

With an angered warble, the Nerhoun's attack turned to face the black dome.

Hundreds of distorting streams converged as one, tearing through the oily tentacles holding the Nerhoun and striking deep into the darkness below.

The darkness shuddered under the impacts, becoming less substantial as holes started to appear.

The distorting attacks could tear through material objects as well as spell formations with relative ease, turning the spell formation to shake and weaken.

The dome of darkness dissipated, as the Nerhoun recovered. Some of its tentacles were badly burned. Its scaly head bled from multiple claw hits and white marks from the burning oily tentacles still steamed slightly.

The sky darkened as dark mana gathered in front of Malsour's mouth. With a powerful breath the gathered mana shot out in a twisted pillar of darkness, cutting tens of tentacles apart within seconds. The Nerhoun contorted again, this time in pain and fear as it started rushing away with great speed.

Malsour rushed forwards, forcing it to slow and fight him.

Party Zero had finally arrived at the third Nerhoun.

Artillery cannons continued to fire, now raining down on the Nalheim below who had picked up the pace and were rushing toward the second castle.

The gryphons and sky screams' riders were lashing out into the sky with their lances, trying to fight back the mages' attack spells and the dwarven attacking spells. All of them felt that their attackers were weaker, the grand working made from Dark Mana still impacting their abilities.

Deia and Dave unleashed arrow after arrow at the Nerhoun, hitting its barriers and making them flash in multiple colors.

From Dave's bag of holding, grenades fell out, rushing ahead of the group at great speed. Jung Lee cast support spells on everyone, increasing the power of their spells and attacks.

Lox and Gurren had nearly constant streams of spearheads flying from their palms and hitting the Mana barrier.

Anna surged ahead in a white blur. The air in her passage congealed together into a terrifying tornado, with white wind blades on their exterior shining in the light.

Lu Lu added in her lightning attack, staying on Suzy's shoulders; her own speed wasn't enough to contend with the rest of Party Zero's. Her lightning formed into a spear that raced forward to hit the Nerhoun's shield, the Nerhoun shook with the impacts of Party Zero's attacks.

Anna let out a yell. Her sword extended ahead of her as the tornado of Air blades behind her compressed and rushed forward into a blinding white spear. The spear of Air slammed into the Nerhoun's barrier. A shock wave of force spread outward as the Mana barrier's color changed rapidly.

Under the weight of artillery spells from the mages and the dwarven artillery, the Nerhoun's barrier shook angrily.

The Nerhoun shot away from the ground and toward the oncoming Party Zero, its tentacles looking to grab and tear them apart.

Deia and Dave's arrows, flaming blue and cold gray, hit the Nerhoun's barrier. It shimmered briefly, as Party Zero slowed their speed.

The barrier started to crack as a magical formation appeared above the Nerhoun. Ice shards, as sharp as a spearhead, were spat from the magical formation, breaking the Mana barrier apart and hitting the Nerhoun underneath.

Anna raced through the sky, dodging between the raining ice shards. Her blade sang as tentacles rose to meet her. Covered in blood from multiple wounds across their length, Anna ruthlessly cut them apart.

Hundreds more shot forward to attack the rest of Party Zero.

Jung Lee, Lox, and Gurren stood in front. Lox and Gurren created massive shields attached to both of their arms and bigger than their Devastator armor. Jung Lee created a spiked wall from nothing that connected the shield wall and floated in front of his left hand, his right still holding the hilt of his sword.

They had barely formed it when it shook with the impact of the Nerhoun's tentacles. Party Zero couldn't see the Nerhoun on the other side but the sound of metal on metal rang out as Lox, Gurren, and Jung Lee were tossed back hundreds of meters.

Deia and Dave flew over them and unleashed arrows on the Nerhoun while Anna turned into a drill of Air, cutting through the prison of tentacles that surrounded her.

Induca let out a triumphant roar as she dodged the Nerhoun's disrupting spell it had been fighting. The distorting spell rushed through the air, hitting the Nerhoun who was fighting Malsour.

The Nerhoun fighting the black dragon faltered, a huge hole through its armored scales on its head.

Malsour seized on the opportunity, a pillar of black light pierced through the sky, hitting the Nerhoun directly.

It let out a moaning squeal as it was pushed back through the sky. Its tentacles burned away as it fell toward the ground. Malsour immediately turned and rushed toward the Nerhoun fighting with his sister.

Black magical circles appeared in the air. Spears of metal lanced through the Nerhoun's interwoven tentacles, smoking from corrosive damage as meteors appeared from another magical circle. Another rained down black arrows.

The Nerhoun's strongest attack was meant to kill one powerful creature at a time; now it found itself against two powerful dragons.

The red and black dragon worked perfectly together, coming in at an angle to each other. Blue flames and black light carved through scales and tentacles, burning them away or cutting them right off.

Party Zero didn't have time to watch the other battle or celebrate the victory that Malsour and Induca had won.

Anna was panting hard as she continued to stand upon the air, her Mana barrier from her armor showed a dark color from all the hits she'd taken. She'd underestimated the speed and attack power of the Nerhoun. Without the Abscondita armor, she would have been torn apart.

Gurren and Lox's armor had used up a lot of power maintaining a Mana barrier and blocking the Nerhoun's attack.

Deia was unleashing her most powerful arrow attacks, as was Dave. His grenades whittled away the number of tentacles they faced, or blocked them from hitting the party.

Jung Lee closed his hand; the conjured wall exploded forward. The metal shards burying themselves into the Nerhoun's body and tentacles. However, to the massive beast it was nothing but a flesh wound.

The Nerhoun attacked Party Zero with renewed energy and fury, sensing their tiredness and low power reserves.

As the barrier hit the Nerhoun, six powerful Affinity spirits left the metal and spread out through the Nerhoun's tentacles.

It let out a pained warble. It hadn't noticed the Free Affinity spirits that Jung Lee had used to reinforce the wall of metal, stopping the disrupting attack of the tentacles and now used as a Trojan horse.

These Free Affinity spirits were weak copies of the spirits that inhabited his body, but there were hundreds of them hidden within the metal shards

They consumed their limited power, the light wounds turning into catastrophic injuries as the Nerhoun cried out in shock and pain.

Not giving it time to think, Dave created a two-handed great sword and rushed forward. Gurren and Lox conjured shields and swords while Air creations poured from Suzy's bag and moved to cover her. Much like Anna's own sky guardian, a person of violent cutting white air formed in the shape of Suzy—a ten-meter-tall giant. This creation of amalgamated Air creations had no weapons as it punched forward. A single punch was enough to stagger the Nerhoun and kill off tens of its tentacles.

Suzy's speed was greater than the others in the party. She stepped in front of them, her Air-body taking on the tentacles' attacks and slashing them apart upon contact.

Air creations quickly used up their stored power. The cores fell to the ground as the remaining Air creations moved to cover over their loss.

Deia quietly muttered words to herself.

The Nerhoun, sensing the cage closing around it, once again grew and contracted, very much like a jellyfish would. It shot away by nearly a kilometer.

A pained warbling sounded out as Induca and Malsour, covered in wounds and the blood of Nerhouns, tore apart the other Nerhoun.

The last Nerhoun just needed to maintain distance and it could fight off the chasing Party Zero.

The Nalheim on the ground, even under the fire of the castles, used their remaining Mana barriers that were now being controlled by one—the Nerhoun's Nalheim master. That took that person out of the fight, but also made it impossible to destroy the barriers with the overloading barrier busters.

This allowed them great protection as they readied their trebuchets and continued to advance with their siege towers that would allow them to directly attack the top layer of the castle's outer defenses.

Around Deia, a red glow became brighter and brighter, her hair like ribbons of fire. She whispered a final word.

The ground itself shook. Cracks appeared as trees and siege engines fell over. Those on the ground had to try to reach out to stabilize themselves.

A pillar of red-hot magma erupted from the ground underneath the Nerhoun. Its tentacles were burnt away with ease as the magma made it inside and up into the Nerhoun's brain, killing it.

Deia stopped pouring power into her spell as the smoking corpse of the Nerhoun flopped to the ground.

The aerial forces that had exited the first eastern castle's ono were all in the air. Seeing the last Nerhoun fall, they charged forward, their eyes filled with cold fury. Those Nerhoun had stopped them from fighting the Nalheim directly, from helping to defend the first castle.

Now these aerial forces were filled with boundless fighting spirit as they rushed over the battlefield. Sky screams and gryphons were there to meet them as they collided in the air.

The DCA and those with different types of bombs came after this flying vanguard. They targeted the siege engines and big groups of Nalheim. Mana bombs lit up the Nalheim lines as they fell from the DCA aerial forces.

Grand workings fired from dwarven artillery broke upon the ground. Shades erupted out of portals in the midst of the Nalheim; the sounds of battle reached those in the air.

The Nalheim simply had too many numbers to be defeated so quickly. Even under these attacks, their Mana barriers held for the most part or they were able to fight off a good number of the shades.

They were not simple opponents.

Their trebuchets whirled as they unleashed their payloads. These rocks had been changed by the Nalheim: where they hit, a disrupting attack would obliterate anything within thirty meters.

The Mana barrier of the second eastern castle took hit after hit, shaking from the multiple and continuous hits. Gryphons and sky screams attacked the dwarven artillery and repeater batteries again if they could get free of the aerial forces.

The Nalheim simply had more people, so they could fight off the aerial forces and attack the castle at the same time.

War lizards, released of their burdens, charged forward. Some of them still pulled the remaining siege towers that hadn't been toppled. All of the Nalheim rushed forward under the fire of magical spells and ranged weaponry. Their hope lay in the Mana barrier that protected them from destruction.

"Move to the second castle!" Deia yelled, her spell already dying and leaving a small mass of cooling rock. Her party was better at fighting on the ground. If they were up in the air, the gryphons and sky screams could outmaneuver them and tear them apart.

Party Zero responded as one, rushing for the castle with all their speed.

The Nalheim aerial attackers noticed this and started to give chase. Disrupting attacks filled the air around them and struck their personal Mana barriers, taking a large amount of their Mana reserves with each successful hit.

Malsour and Induca took to the air.

Black and red magical formations appeared behind Party Zero. Arrows of flames and shadow tore through the pursuing forces as Malsour and Induca in their dragon form moved to either side of Party Zero.

Suzy's Air giant fell apart into Air creations that returned to her bag of holding.

Party Zero landed on the castle's walls, their weapons ready as they helped the defenders out against the oncoming Nalheim.

Suzy tossed out multiple cores, as well as their base materials. Creations made from multiple different Affinities jumped over the wall to fight the Nalheim below.

Malsour and Induca wheeled around the castle before coming to land on the north and south outer walls, facing west where the Nalheim were coming from.

Fire atronachs appeared around Induca; as a magical formation appeared in front of Malsour's mouth. As he turned his head, he projected out hundreds of black arrows, raking the Nalheim on the ground or those trying to attack the castle's defenses.

Anna, Gurren, Lox, and Jung Lee sent powerful attacks out at the trebuchets. The Mana barrier for the castle was quickly weakening under the Nalheim's attacks.

Dave fired arrow after arrow at the Nalheim war lizards and their riders who had climbed over the walls as the siege towers drew closer. He held up his hand; a ball of lightning formed before it shot out at a siege tower. The Mana barrier around the siege tower changed colors at a rapid pace before breaking through. Under the heat and power of that ball of lightning, the siege tower erupted into flames.

Still, there were tens of other siege towers and the Nalheim didn't have anyone in them for fear that what had happened to the first tower would happen to the Nalheim if they were in the others.

There was a sound of breaking glass as the Mana barrier finally broke.

Dave didn't even pause as he continued to unleash arrow after arrow. They hit their targets and exploded as he had conjured explosive runes within the arrows.

Although Dave was fast with the bow, Deia seemed as if she had been born with a bow in her hands. She moved across the castle wall, her flaming arrows pulling sky screams and gryphons from the sky one after another, not once losing her rhythm.

She used different Fire spells on her bow with ease. She fired arrows up into the sky; a rain of flaming arrows dropped from the sky a few moments later. Her arrows burrowed into the armored siege towers before exploding into flames that were powerful enough to set the towers on fire.

Even as they took out multiple siege towers, the Nalheim's ranged trebuchets and their Mana barriers stopped too many from falling to Party Zero and the Terra Alliance's attacks.

"Melee fighters, get ready! We hold them here!" Esa yelled out.

The player guilds and the POE pulled out their melee weapons, readying themselves for the coming battle.

A section of wall was destroyed by the disrupting boulder that had been hurled at the walls. It hit midway up the wall and the un-supported wall gave way. People screamed as they fell downward. Dark mages exerted their power, stopping the debris from falling on those who had been knocked off the wall and trying to rebuild the wall with the rubble.

The wounded were stabilized with healing potions and pulled back to the ono and Terra on the other side for further medical treatment if they were in a bad way.

"Incoming!" Suzy yelled.

Anna let out an angered shout. A spear of Air whipped out and impacted on the boulder, breaking it apart.

More and more hits were landing on the walls, breaking them apart.

Even the dismounted Nalheim only needed a few hits with their spears before they could make a hole in the thick wall.

"POE, pull back to the inner courtyard and castle!" the second eastern castle's commander called out.

The POEs pulled back as the players fought with everything they had.

***

A man made from soul gem crystals stood. He was covered in mag-ical coding that was so compact that it looked to be stylish lines all over his body. These lines glowed as the glass-like surface of the soul gems changed its color to black. The man was all one color, with soul gem eyes and glowing lines of code across his body.

"Well, should go get my axe back." The man moved to the door of the workshop. He opened the door and entered Pandora's laboratory. He exited, passing through the ono, and entered Terra.

People gave him odd looks as he took off in flight, headed across the city before he landed where there were a number of wounded coming out of a teleport pad.

"Unidentified life-form, state your name," Aleph automatons said as they moved from their alcoves around the teleport pad to confront the soul gem-made man.

"Dad, can I go out and play?" the man asked.

The Aleph automatons didn't do anything.

"Bet that crossed your circuits a bit, Shard. It's me, Steve. Going to get my axe back. See you in a bit!" Steve smiled, waved at the Aleph automatons, and flew through the teleport pad and out of the ono that lay within the second eastern castle.

He touched down and ran through the castle. As he ran, black armor started to cover his body as he grew taller. The armor looked like the Devastator armor that Lox and Gurren wore.

"Hope that they looked after Alex for me," Steve said as he left the castle.

A massive boulder slammed through the outside walls, breaking it apart.

Steve held up his arm. A shield of metal appeared along his arm, deflecting the debris from the boulder flying overhead; it slammed into the castle, destroying a part of the castle and opening up the third floor.

Steve's shield disappeared as he looked over the people around him.

"Nice, brought out the big guns," Steve said, seeing Induca and Malsour both in their dragon forms. "I lose one body and everyone goes on a kick-ass spree."

Steve looked at a halfling who was looking at him with confusion. "You leave for five minutes and everything goes to shit!" Steve shrugged as another section of wall exploded nearby from another trebuchet's hit.

"Y-yeah," the man said.

Steve looked up to where a group were still fighting on the wall. War lizards were climbing up the walls and fighting them directly.

"Should rename us Party Badass!" Steve laughed and shot off toward Party Zero.

***

Lox slammed his shield into a war lizard, throwing it and its rider off the wall he stood on. He turned; his shield took a disrupting attack and then a spearhead of another war lizard rider's spear. Lox's sword jabbed out, opening the war lizard's neck. The beast faltered, throwing the Nalheim off-balance.

Lox pushed sideways with his shield, making the Nalheim's spear go wide and leave them open as his sword stabbed outward again.

The two blows had been just seconds apart. The Nalheim looked at Lox with two faces filled with disbelief.

"The Prodigal Son returns! Bah bah baaaahhh!" someone said as they landed on the wall. A set of Devastator armor uppercut a war lizard in the face, forcing it upward before kicking it in the stomach and launching it into another coming over the wall. Both of them tumbled back over the wall.

"Pow—right in the kisser!" the armor said. The voice wasn't Gurren's.

"Who are you?" Lox asked.

"Dude, I'm hurt. Like truly, if I had a heart, it might be broken." The man casually slapped a war lizard head that raised over the wall and snarled at the man. "Talking here!" the man yelled at the war lizard that was tossed sideways because of the hit; its claws scrambled to find purchase as it fell toward the ground.

Lox fought off a war lizard and its rider who had leapt onto the wall. A sky scream landed, blasting Lox in the face with a stunning attack.

"Move, bitch!" The man grabbed a spear and hurled it through the sky scream and its rider with so much power that a fist-sized hole appeared through them both.

The man jumped forward in a blur, seeing the war lizard as it lurched forward, its mouth opened to bite down on Lox's head.

"Get out the way!" the man singsonged as he kicked the war lizard in the face.

It bit Lox's shoulder.

Lox recovered from the sky scream attack, moving his sword enough to deflect the Nalheim's spear. He punched one of the heads with the pommel of his sword, releasing it and opening his palm to the other. A Mana spearhead took the second in the face, removing its face. Lox did the same to the other head he'd punched.

"Lox, dude, where's Alex?" the man asked.

"You're fucking insane," Lox said, in his professional opinion.

"Ha ha, dude—good one. But seriously, where's my axe? I tossed it to you guys. Does Gurren have it?" the man said.

"I don't know what you're trying to pull but now isn't the time, buddy," Lox said through gritted teeth.

"Dude, it's me—it's Steve! I said 'tis nothing but a scratch before that asshole hit me in the face. Might have been better to tell you that I would come back in the new body that I was building, but eh, still good last words for the old get-up," Steve said.

Lox just looked at the faceless Devastator armor in front of him.

"So, where's my axe? Don't want to fight with my hands the entire time," Steve said.

"Gurren has it," Lox said blankly, his mind in a state of shock.

"Woo-hoo! Don't worry, baby! Daddy's home!" Steve said, running past.

Lox looked to the running Steve, or the man who said that he was Steve in Devastator armor.

A war lizard jumped onto the wall and Lox didn't have any more time to think about Steve coming back from the dead as he fought off the war lizard.

***

Gurren was covering archers who were firing arrow after arrow into the skies and the creatures that lay below. He had just killed off another war lizard and was watching a siege tower that was next to a wall. Tens of Nalheim were already clawing their way up the inner ladders within the tower, ready to charge up and through the doors and bridge that would drop into the castle, allowing them to surge onto the walls.

Then a fist tapped on his shoulder. He turned to find Lox.

"What you doing over here?" Gurren asked.

"Daddy needs his Alex," the man said, opening and closing his hand.

"Who are you?" Gurren demanded.

"Seriously, I blow myself up one friggin' time and you lose all sense of humor. Party Bummer might be better than bad ass," the man muttered to himself.

"I asked once—I don't want to ask again," Gurren growled.

"Gurren, gimme my axe! I tossed it to you lot and Lox didn't have it, so you've probably got it. Also, you know why Suzy doesn't have a soul binding contract with me anymore? Feels weird," Steve said.

"Steve?"

"Yup. Like the new look? I was thinking the Trio of Darkness? Too punk rock?" Steve asked.

"How? What?"

"I'm not flesh and bone like you dolts—more runes and power consumption. Axe?" Steve held out his hand.

"But the armor?"

"Oh, well, I made it—not permanent right now, just a construct from a soul gem. Need some more materials before I can make my own version," Steve said while Gurren stared at him and pulled out Steve's axe from his spatial ring.

"Oh, Alex, Daddy missed you!" Steve grabbed the axe and patted it lovingly. "I know, I know, I shouldn't have thrown you at the hard floor—look at you, all scuffed." Steve's hand swung out, holding the axe, taking off a war lizard's face with one blow before being cradled once more in Steve's arms. "There, there, see—you're perfectly fine now. Come on, Daddy's gotta go to work."

Another person joined the Party Zero chat.

"Hello, fellow mental patients! Miss me?" Steve said.

"What? How is this possible?" Suzy asked.

"Oh thanks. Seriously, you guys are the worst to surprise! Well, I kind of made a backup of myself within Pandora's box. When I broke my other body, it started a process to upload me to my replacement body. Gears and coding is cool and all, but soul gems and magical coding is much better!" Steve said.

"I wondered what the hell you were building in there," Dave said, sounding a bit emotional.

"Might have been nice to know," Malsour agreed.

"Well, I thought it would have been cooler this way, you mopey bastards." Steve laughed.

Gurren felt as if he were flying. He laughed, getting back his friend from the edge of death.

"Well, good to have you back. Now we need to bleed these Nalheim. We've got nearly forty thousand people here. There are about one hundred and fifty thousand Nalheim. We need to hold for a half hour per Josh's orders," Deia said.

"You people need to seriously talk to management about extended lunch breaks," Steve complained.

"Yeah, that's our Steve," Suzy said, her voice shaky but filled with happiness.

Chapter 19: On a Razor's Edge

Dwayne moved forward with the forces under his command. They had all gathered from the different castles that surrounded Goblin Mountain. There were aerial forces, dwarven warclans, and warriors who rode various beasts. They marched through the teleport pad within Terra and exited into the first eastern castle.

His notifications blinked at him but he dismissed them as he moved with the forces under his command. Kim was also with him.

As they exited, the fighting forces moved to the eastern wall, where the Dark mages had made massive openings in the walls for metal doors that swung outward to show the Nalheim and the second eastern castle.

Dwayne and his forces moved out of the castle gates. Dwarven warclans marched in cadence as the mounted riders moved with powerful grace upon their mounts. The dwarves formed into their warbands and warclans, making orderly lines beyond the walls, facing the rear of the Nalheim.

Kim and her mages moved to the walls. Dwarven artillery fired nonstop, making it hard to talk without using the party chat functions. The mages spread out over the different casting balconies.

In the distance, Dwayne could see the walls crumbling around the second eastern castle as well as the massive spells being hurled out by the defenders and the artillery shells that exploded upon impacting the Nalheim's Mana barriers.

Dwayne watched as the forces under his command moved with quick efficiency. His eyes continued to dart over to the second eastern castle as he saw Stone Raiders who were part of the fighting force push off the attacking Nalheim.

They were on par with the Nalheim. It was a fierce battle but the Stone Raiders Portal Purge, Fellox Guild and the rudimentary

Terra Alliance had a castle to defend. Players were willing to die for their friends, whether they happened to be POE or fellow players.

Even with the terrifying battle, Dwayne could see the excitement on these players' faces. *I wonder what they would think if they knew the truth.* He pushed those thoughts down, wishing for his forces to assemble quicker in order to lead their reinforcements into battle.

***

The teleport pad to the first eastern castle wasn't the only one that was in nearly constant use.

The ono within the second eastern castle was open as elves and DCA rushed outward and wounded were carried back into Terra.

The DCA and elves moved out, quickly reaching the top of the circular building. The elves ran in orderly lines; the DCA did the same on their opposite side, pulling out their mortars.

DCA observers called out ranges as mortar crews assembled their weapons. Those in the DCA who weren't trained with mortars rushed through the halls of the castle, their shields ready and their swords drawn. They ran as one unit, their eyes cold diamonds underneath their helmets. They rushed out of the castle like a stream overflowing its banks. They spread out in every direction, supporting the melee fighters who were holding their own within the open area between the outer walls and inner castle.

Overhead trebuchets continued to throw their boulders as the Terra Alliance's aerial forces clashed with the Nalheim's gryphons and sky screams.

Mana bombs rained down from the DCA in the sky, making Mana barriers change colors violently and creating craters in the ground.

The Nalheim attacked the oncoming DCA without a second thought. Their ranged disrupting attacks hit the DCA's personal

Mana barriers in a harsh display of colors. The Nalheim didn't have time to yell out in indignation as the DCA met them in battle.

The DCA soldiers were a little stronger in power than the Nalheim; however, they had been trained to the peak by their instructors. Their fighting abilities had been honed and refined over months and multiple battles with the Demon Horde or the creatures of the Ashal wilderness. They were meant to be a force that conducted lightning-fast raids, but they were also trained to defend a location, like the keeps that surrounded Devil's Crater.

Unlike the dwarves and the larger standing armies of Emerilia, the DCA didn't use standard tactics. They worked in small groups no larger than ten. They would use their swords and shields as easily as they would use their feet, their breastplates that could send out Mana bombs, grenades, or their coded bracelets. This was the power of the DCA: it wasn't their numbers or their innate strength, but their ability to use multiple tools to defeat an enemy.

Mana spearheads broke through the Nalheim's defenses as the DCA tossed out grenades. Their velocity was low enough that they could enter the Mana barriers, exploding within.

The DCA thrived in chaos. As they came to the battlefield, the Nalheim found that they had descended into hell and the demons and their fellows ruled.

The Nalheim were rigid in their fighting ways. They might be fast and great at defending themselves, but in the face of so many different attacks, they weren't prepared. A Mana-created spearhead could hit a Nalheim hard enough to send them flying, a grenade could roll under their feet: no matter what, the DCA made them hold their position by peppering them with physical spearheads.

A faint sound could be heard for a moment before arrows rose over the inner castle and the defenders, hitting Mana barriers and anyone who was unlucky enough to be caught out in the open. The rain of arrows seemed to be unending.

The elves would release their arrows, bend down and grab a new arrow; the second rank would fire; as they strung their arrow, the third would fire. As their arrows flew overhead, the first rank stood once again, pulling and releasing their arrows before ducking once again, the process repeating itself.

The surface of the castles was already covered with different dwarven artillery positions that were firing as fast as they could load the rounds in.

The DCA mortar teams called out to one another. Their weapons were simple tubes with a baseplate and supporting struts. The baseplate was similar to the Mana bomb chest plates of the aerial forces but with the repulsing code that was held within the ground forces' chest plates.

Phoump phoump phoump!

The mortars fired down the line. Glowing Mana bombs rose and then descended, arcing over the defenders and slamming against the attacking Nalheim.

***

Josh watched the battle at the second eastern castle. In his vision, he saw blinking notifications.

Castle Conquest

You have captured a contested castle!

Rewards:

2,000 Conquest points

Castle Conquest

You currently control (8/8) Castles

Earning: (8) conquest points per minute

Bonus: For controlling all of the Castles, you earn an additional (1) conquest point(s) per minute. For half of the Castles, you earn an additional (1) conquest point(s) per minute.

Total points: 33,487

Rights: Administrative (Can spend conquest points to upgrade Castle infrastructure and repair castles. Can also delete Castle infrastructure)

Weastern Castle 1

Status: Under Control by Terra Alliance

Earn: 1 conquest point per minute

Evolution: 1 (Second evolution 0%). Can increase evolution to Level 2 by paying (100,000) Conquest points.

Upgrades: Trebuchet, Siege Towers, Increased combat abilities for defenders (Damaged), Soul Gem construct defenses (destroyed), Dwarven Artillery batteries (3/40), Aleph Repeater batteries (0/12)

Durability: 21,548/ 60,000

Castle Conquest

For controlling 4 conquest castles, you gain an extra conquest point (1) per minute

Castle Conquest

For controlling 8 conquest castles, you gain an extra conquest point (1) per minute

His eyes moved to the interface screens that showed the battle within the second eastern castle in greater detail.

"The outer wall has been completely destroyed. The Nalheim are now firing their trebuchets over their forces, hitting the defenders in the open area between the outer wall and the castle. Also, the castle is being heavily damaged by the trebuchet's hits," Cassie said at Josh's elbow.

"What about Dwayne's forces?" Josh asked.

"They're nearly ready to move out. The aerial forces are moving through Terra at this time. They'll be ready to move within ten minutes," Cassie reported.

"Damn those Mana barriers," Josh hissed, slamming his fist down on the balcony. The Nalheim had smartened up about their Mana barriers when they'd stayed in the first eastern castle. Now the barrier busters were largely useless, making the dwarves have to burn through their offensive ammunition.

Malsour and Induca were opening up barriers with ease but there were hundreds of thousands of Nalheim warriors and only two of them.

A great roar came from the castle as Malsour flapped his wings, shooting into the air.

"Shit. Looks like those damned gryphons and sky screams finally got the balls to attack Malsour and Induca," Josh said.

Cassie put her hand on Josh's shoulder and squeezed it slightly. "The DCA are having a good effect on the ground— being light and mobile, they were easily able to reinforce the second eastern castle's forces. They're holding them back." Cassie tried to reassure him.

Josh patted her hand, smiling to her as he opened up his interface and watched streams from around the second eastern castle.

Party Zero stood in an island of calm where the wall had been. Around them, spells were constantly going off as Lox, Gurren, Jung Lee, Dave, and a third man in Devastator armor wielding Steve's axe held off the tide.

Even they couldn't resist all of the Nalheim as they were slowly pushed backward, linking up with the rest of the defenders.

Dave flew back, his Mana barrier faltering from a hit.

Flames, angry and cruel, flooded outward from Party Zero. Deia floated in midair, looking like a goddess of war. Her face was cold and filled with fury as the Nalheim were washed away in a flood of fire.

Josh's heart clenched, only relaxing slightly as he saw Dave get to his feet, moving backward; a swarm of grenades appeared around him and hurled out toward the Nalheim.

The ranks of Nalheim collapsed under the grenades' explosions.

Someone yelled out. The defenders raised their weapons in defiance and rushed forward to occupy the area that the Nalheim had held. They used the chaos and confusion to their advantage, killing all who tried to stop them and forcing the Nalheim back farther.

After a few moments, the Nalheim rallied but their losses had run a few hundred.

The Nalheim and the defenders were engaged in a wild melee. War lizards, their riders, and the dismounted Nalheim moved within their Mana barriers, their shields and spears clashing with the Terra Alliance's forces.

Arrows, spells, mortars, and dwarven artillery came down upon these ground forces that had pushed through the western walls of the eastern castle. Here and there, new sections of the castle's outer walls were destroyed by the combined efforts of the Nalheim's trebuchets and their own disrupting attacks.

As the castle walls crumbled, more and more of the Nalheim were able to join into battle, forcing the defenders to stretch out their lines to fight off these new threats.

The DCA had added much-needed strength to the defenders but the melee fighters who only numbered twenty-five thousand were up against a force nearly four times their strength.

The supporting fire was breaking Mana barriers but it took a lot of time and the Nalheim had secondary Mana barriers. The only way to defeat them seemed to be in straight-up combat.

Josh wanted to send more reinforcements through the ono but with much more defenders, it would become hard for the different commanders within the castle to organize a proper defense.

"Moving forward with what we've got," Dwayne said.

"Good luck." Josh knew that as soon as Dwayne joined into the battle with the Nalheim, the dwarven artillery would go silent. The chance that they would hit the advancing forces of the Terra Alliance was too high.

The battle would shortly be fought and resolved on the ground.

Josh turned from his balcony. He checked the twin daggers on his lower back and looked to Cassie.

"I'm coming with you," she said, equipping her sword and shield that appeared on her arm and her hip.

"Have I ever told you how sexy you are when you're about to go into a fight?"

"My boyfriend is so weird," Cassie muttered, shaking her head. A helmet appeared over her head and her hair disappeared into it.

***

Dave coughed. His Abscondita armor had run out of charge. He was currently charging it from a soul gem in his bag, but he was back from the front lines.

With maximizing his Intelligence out and not working on increasing his Strength or Vitality, once his Mana barrier of his armor was down, he was one of the squishiest people around. He was fast and agile, but the Nalheim packed together and with two heads instead of one, they were able to predict and move in a way that reduced Dave's chances of killing them easily.

They were much stronger than him and were able to push him back. Although they didn't land any hits that would kill him immediately, he'd taken a lot of hits on his Mana barrier, only to find out that the disrupting attacks were extremely good at breaking down Mana barriers.

"Cover me for a bit. I think if I can figure out how this spear works and their disrupting attacks, I'll be able to break down their barriers!" Dave yelled.

Deia had already ordered him to the rear. He felt useless in this battle. He could end it all with a wave of his hand but at the cost of setting off alarms with the monitoring AI and having the Jukal come down on him.

Still, the decision warred in his mind as he saw POEs being cut down.

Thankfully the defenders were mostly players and they could come back, though there was the occasional POE who also fell to the Nalheim's attacks.

Dave blocked that out as he sunk his Touch of the Land spell into the spear he'd pulled from a Nalheim's corpse. His eyes glowed with gray light; smoke pooled around him as he held the spear in his left and held out his right hand. An identical spear appeared in his hand. He jabbed upward, the same distorting attack coming from both.

The conjured spear faded away from existence while Dave tossed the Nalheim spear to the side.

Along Dave's right bracer, the steel was melted away by fierce blue flames. Dave closed his eyes; new coding appeared in the silver and ebony layers of the bracer.

People looked at the now revealed Mithril armband, many in jealousy as ebony and silver snaked over it, forming black and silver lines of tightly compacted lines or runes.

These runes lit up with power as Dave held up his hand and pointed it at the Nalheim not far away. The air changed, distorting until one could barely see through it. The distorting ray smashed into the Mana barrier surrounding the Nalheim. The barrier rapidly changed color under the fierce attack.

Dave held out his opposite hand. An orb appeared from midair and landed in his hand. The runes across the orb changed slightly as its surface moved quickly. The hundreds of layers that made up the orb changed into a new formation. Without a spell like Touch of the Land, one wouldn't even be able to understand the hundreds of changes that were taking place.

The Mana barrier that Dave had been attacking was broken as Dave's disrupting spell hit a Nalheim. Their shield warped and twisted before it exploded. The Nalheim cried out as their hand was hit by the ray. Their hand was destroyed in a matter of seconds.

"Highly effective against Mana barriers, not so good against armor. Effective against biological items," Dave said. The orb stopped changing in his hand.

He looked past the Nalheim with his senses, finding Dwayne and Kim's forces at the first eastern castle.

***

Dwayne was barely able to hide his frustration. He knew that his people were moving as fast as possible; still, he had wished that he could set out as soon as he exited the first eastern castle's ono.

"There's only the aerial forces left coming out of the ono," Kim said.

Dwayne looked to the dwarven commander in charge of the dwarven warbands. "We're ready."

The dwarven commander nodded. "Forrrward, march!" The dwarf's voice carried across the thirty thousand-strong force.

From within the warclans, the war drums started, the dwarves' footfalls landing in time with the drumbeat.

Dwayne walked forward with them.

To their flanks were massive groups of five thousand mounted. They rode leopards, wolves, horses, snakes, elephants, and rhinos.

The dwarves were the best unit to fight out in the open like they would be doing with the Nalheim. The Nalheim might fight in a similar way but the dwarves had honed their art over centuries. With their interlinking shields boosting their abilities and linking them together, a single dwarf's power was enough to topple a giant.

The Nalheim fought as if one person was a fighting unit; the dwarves all supported one another so that fighting one dwarf was like fighting them all. This was why the dwarves were said to be the marching mountains—able to get under their shields to defend themselves and take massive hits with ease.

The other forces had wanted to come but all of them understood that with the dwarves leading the battle, they would just be in the way.

The dwarves might be short, but they were powerful. The drums picked up pace and quickly the dwarves marched at their best speed toward the Nalheim, rank upon rank of identically armored and armed dwarves.

Dwayne felt the ground tremble in their passing as he rested his hand on his sword.

Behind the dwarves was a force of nearly ten thousand mages and ranged attackers. Archers walked in groups, spread out over a large area in order to protect the majority of the people to the front instead of just pockets.

Off to either side there were groups of summoners and necromancers talking to one another.

Dwayne's eyes looked forward at the Nalheim who stood in their way.

Once all of the aerial forces were ready within the first eastern castle, they took to the skies and moved to Kim and Dwayne's forces on the ground. They flew above them, ready to fight off threats from above. As they arrived, the group was just five minutes away from the Nalheim forces.

Yells went up as their gryphons and sky screams turned around, letting out battle cries and charging toward their new opponents.

The mass of aerial forces above the force moving from the first eastern castle also let out their own battle cries. They moved forward to meet the Nalheim in the air.

The aerial forces that had been fighting for hours pushed back to the first eastern castle. Their forces were weary; they had wounded and were pushed to their limits.

"Prepare the mounted forces! Tell the summoners and necros to be ready!" Dwayne yelled over the command chat.

"Support spells!" Kim called out. Mages unleashed spells on their own forces that would boost speed, defense, and the abilities of those within the Terra Alliance.

The mystical glow settled over their bodies as they charged forward.

"Healers, be ready!" Kim said moments later.

Healers glowed with their different-colored Manas and checked their various healing potions and remedies that they held.

The Nalheim who were at the rear turned to face the oncoming force, letting out excited yells.

"Release the mounted forces," Dwayne said.

War horns were blown as the mounted forces spread out from one another. Their mounts picked up speed, slowly at first before they became faster and faster.

There were supporting mages among them who cast spells among their forces and unleashed spells on the Nalheim, their barriers flashing angrily.

Dwayne saw something out of the corner of his eye: a rapid-moving silver blur. It stopped among the Nalheim. In a flash, the orb disappeared and a massive disrupting wave shot out in all directions.

There was no sound from the explosion as Mana barriers were torn apart and weakened the blast of the orb. Some unlucky Nalheim were turned into paste or their armor was twisted with them inside before exploding.

The wave of destruction was terrifying. There was no powerful rumbling or a dust cloud, just simple destruction as everything within a two-hundred-meter area was heavily distorted.

Artillery that had been falling now found Nalheim who weren't covered by a barrier anymore. They cried out in pain as they were torn apart. The Nalheim were in a state of confusion. The overhead artillery barrages ended but hundreds had died in just a few seconds.

The mounted forces hit the shocked Nalheim, riding through them. War lizards and beasts clawed at one another as their riders fought their own battles.

Massive magical formations formed at locations around the Nalheim. Creation summoners working together formed multiple creations from the materials they had that charged forward into the Nalheim lines.

The necromancers created rifts that appeared in midair, pulling out undead and other necromantic beasts from the undead realm.

Necromancers and summoners were very similar: One made living creatures from the living elements around them while summoning beasts from a different realm. The other made creatures from the dead and pulled from the undead realm.

The summoners usually soul bound themselves to the creatures that they summoned from other realms. The necromancers simply placed a command spell on them as their summoned creatures would decay after a few hours or days, depending on the strength of the beast and their own Mana supply.

Other summoners and necromancers pulled or poured out different items from various storage devices. Their minions formed from these items and the ranks of the summoners and necromancers tripled in seconds.

The marching mages chanted spells together and worked together in groups to create powerful spells that smashed into shields. Being so close, their spells didn't have time to weaken and the Nalheim didn't have much time to try to defeat them with their disrupting attacks.

Archers moved and fired. They were in an extended line across the rear of the dwarves.

Odd-numbered archers would fire as the even-numbered archers would draw an arrow back on their bow and release. By the time they had grabbed a new arrow, the other group had already fired, creating a continuous stream of arrows that descended upon the Nalheim.

The mounted forces disengaged from their attack, retreating.

The Nalheim picked some of them off with their ranged spear attacks; a few of the war lizards and their riders chased after, only to be cut down by the fleeing mounted.

Their mages and riding archers were more than enough to deal with the small groups of war lizards.

The majority of the Nalheim mounted on war lizards were already attacking the defenders of the second eastern castle.

"Shields!" the dwarven commander barked. The dwarves didn't even slow their pace as they took their shields off in one motion and presented them to their front. Their hands rested on the hilts of their swords, ready to draw at a moment's notice.

Mana barriers that surrounded the dwarves took multiple impacts from the Nalheim but it held.

The Nalheim charged forward with a yell.

"Shields up!"

The first line braced their shield, raising it higher, while the second rank raised their shields above their heads and held them over the first rank's heads, protecting them from any attacks that might come from above.

Rank by rank, shields were raised and interconnected. The dwarves disappeared under a sea of black shields.

"Half speed!" the commander barked out. The dwarves' pace slowed down; the Nalheim were now only fifty meters away.

The Nalheim war lizards that had arrived first slammed into the shield wall. Magical Circuits that were built within the dwarven shields lit up. These Magical Circuits were the same ones that Dave had worked with when he was training to be a dwarven master smith; these Magical Circuits were meant to boost the strength of the dwarven formation. Each additional shield reinforced the others, having a multiplying effect.

When the war lizards hit, Dwayne could see the confused looks on the war lizards as their limbs broke upon impact. It was as if they had run full speed into a metal wall.

The dwarves kept their pace moving forward.

"Swords!" Hundreds of swords were freed along the front rank as they moved like silver lightning and pierced the war lizards.

Some of the riders had been able to get free of the war lizards and jabbed at the dwarven shield wall, only to find it was covered with a Mana barrier. Others had actually landed on top of the shields of the later ranks.

The shields moved to the side. Swords shone in the light as the Nalheim was cut apart before they hit the dirt. The shields covered back over as if they had never opened in the first place.

The dwarves' swords flashed out to meet their attackers. The dwarven war council had sent some of their best veteran warclans and it showed.

They moved forward as if it were nothing more than a drill, relying on one another completely as the Nalheim encountered the impressive defense of the dwarves.

The dismounted Nalheim used to be a coordinated group; now they charged forward with abandon. For days they had been bombed, fighting their way out of Goblin Mountain and then across the plains, only to have to fight their way through a castle that blew up as soon as they gained some safety.

Now they were without their powerful Nerhoun and being attacked on both sides. Finally, they were able to engage the enemy in head-on fighting. The Nalheim were incredibly skilled with the spear and shield.

However, under the pressure of those behind them, they weren't able to use the reach of their spear as they were pinned against the wall of dwarven shields, only to be greeted by the dwarves' flashing swords.

The dwarves' line didn't buckle as they continued forward. Arrows and spells took out groups of Nalheim who tried to get organized, but even with their efforts, it was clear that the Nalheim were already rallying from their failed charge.

They moved into units. One of the generals, without his gryphon, marched down the lines, yelling out orders as the Nalheim rushed to obey.

"Kill me that general," Dwayne said to the leader of a group of rogues under his command.

"It will be done," the rogue said.

All of the rogues were players. They had immensely powerful attacks but they were only good for a few blows in fights, against a single powerful target that were distracted. When fighting a massive force, they were better at killing off leadership in the chaos of battle. In this case, taking out the general and hopefully messing up the enemy's coordination.

The chances of them landing a massive hit on the general, killing him and then getting away, were slim to none. They had impressive movement techniques, so Dwayne had some hope.

The summoners' and necromancers' creatures were all creating havoc along the sides of the enemy. They extended out from either flank of the dwarven formation, making it so that the Nalheim couldn't get around and hit them from the sides.

Mounted groups had broken down into their separate groups. Some were riding together to have greater impact as they rushed through the necros' and summoners' creatures, hammering the Nalheim before wheeling away. Their tactics were nearly identical to the ones used by the war lizards.

Above, the sky screams were in combat with the aerial forces. Occasionally they would dip down, attacking forces on the ground.

Support and healing spells covered Dwayne's forces, keeping them in the best condition possible.

Defensive spells flared up to cancel out the Nalheim attacks from the sky and the ground while offensive spells impacted against Mana barriers or landed upon the forces below.

"The Nalheim aerial forces are targeting the necromancers and summoners on the right flank!" an Aleph controller watching the battle and constantly updating the various commanders yelled out.

"Move to defend them, Kim!" Dwayne yelled. Losing a group of the summoners and necromancers would open up the flank that their creatures were protecting the dwarves and Dwayne's force from.

Panic rose into his chest as he saw the large force of sky screams led by a single gryphon-riding general ride at the right flank.

They unleashed their stunning attacks and their weapons unleashed disrupting attacks. Their summoned creatures and creations rose from around the right flank to greet the aerial forces. Only a few of the different minions were capable of flight; they were out of their element as their masters spent most of the time on the ground. In front of the Nalheim, they were just paper targets to be torn apart.

Kim's mages and the ranged fighters attacked the group with all they had but it wasn't enough to stop them.

A massive shadow fell over the ground as Dwayne looked up toward a whistling sound.

With an audible flap, Malsour's wings snapped outward, bringing him out of a dive, facing right at the Nalheim sky screams and gryphons that were attacking the right flank. A spell formation snapped up in front of Malsour's mouth as a ray of darkness cut through the Nalheim.

In the blink of an eye, half of them were removed, a massive hole in their formation. Instantly they split apart and raced away.

Malsour passed through the formation, wheeling around to hunt down one of the two halves of the attacking group.

"Where the hell did he come from?" Dwayne's heart thumped in his chest from Malsour's casual display of power. Matching up the Malsour from Party Zero and the massive ancient black dragon who was capable of wiping out tens of Nalheim fliers in a second was a hard task.

"He was being attacked by the fliers when he was on the northern side of the castle. He flew away to get rid of them and must have been flying above us, looking to see if anyone needed support." Kim sounded shaken up.

Malsour unleashed blasts of Dark Affinity fireballs. Wherever these flames hit the fliers, they burned, never being put out as the fliers and riders yelled out in agony.

Dwayne watched blurs race through the formation. Using the distraction of Malsour and the aerial battle, the rogues and high-damage fighters appeared around the dismounted general.

In a flash, blades came out and blood flew into the air.

The Nalheim around the general roared in rage, attacking the assassins who were now using every movement technique they knew to escape the Nalheim's ranks.

About a third of them made it back, better than what Dwayne had expected.

The Nalheim lost some of its form as they wildly attacked the dwarves once again, paying heavily for the attack.

With a powerful flap of her wings, Induca, too, flew into the skies. The Nalheim force in the skies hadn't been that large to begin with compared to their army; their numbers had been greatly reduced over the fighting and they were fighting tired while the Terra Alliance had fresh forces in the sky.

Induca went south and circled around. DCA aerial forces that had been moving up to the battle moved into formation to the side of Induca's wings. She slowed down to meet their speed as they came up and across the ground occupied by the Nalheim.

A powerful blue flame flashed through a number of spell formations before it hit the ground. It hit like an explosion, spreading outward, leaving a deep groove in the ground and turning the dirt and grass to glass.

Mana barriers turned angry colors. Here and there, they failed as behind Induca a magical formation followed. From this magical formation, hundreds of fireballs were dropped. They slammed into the ground and created two-meter-deep craters.

The DCA aerial forces unleashed their bombs from their breastplates and fired down with their bracelets, unleashing Mana-filled destruction behind.

Their bombs were more powerful than the ones that Induca was carpeting the ground with. The DCA aimed them to strike the weaker of the Mana barriers to open them up for the bombers after them to hammer those who had been hiding inside into oblivion.

Special attention was paid to the trebuchets. The siege towers had already been used and destroyed and were left alone. However, the trebuchets continued to open holes in the defenders' ranks and break down the inner castle's defenses.

***

Josh stood on the walls of the first eastern castle. The waves of destruction between the defenders and Dwayne's force that was falling directly on the Nalheim shook the very air with their impacts, even from where he stood.

"Dwayne, offer them the chance to surrender," Josh said.

"Understood," Dwayne said.

Josh knew that he wouldn't have offered this choice before. These Nalheim were from another planet and they were as much victims of Jukal as the humans. If they were willing to admit defeat, he would treat them as prisoners; if not, then he would destroy them. The event had only begun; he didn't want to leave people around who could hurt him and his alliance.

"To the Nalheim, if you surrender, you will be able to keep your lives as well as be treated with dignity! If you do not, then we will be forced to kill you off!" Dwayne yelled out.

Another voice started talking in the odd voices of the Nalheim, translating for them.

"Who is that?" Josh asked.

"Steve. Seems that he knows how to talk Nalheim," Deia said.

"Steve's alive?" Josh asked.

"It's...complicated," Deia said.

"Tell me later." Josh gave Cassie a look.

The both of them had perplexed but happy voices. They had become friends with Steve and were used to his quirky and rather odd sense of humor. Having him back was enough to make them smile in the face of all this destruction.

The Nalheim, seeing that the Terra Alliance had paused their attacks, regrouped their aerial forces above their ground forces.

One of the three remaining generals spoke out in the Nalheim's tongue.

Steve responded in the same language.

The three generals talked to one another.

Once again they talked to Steve. For a few minutes, this went on before one of the generals atop their golden gryphon moved forward to the second eastern castle.

A group stepped out of the first castle.

A giant man completely made from a black material wearing only shoes and pants of a darker shade than his body stepped forward. His eyes glittered and shone, drawing one's attention.

This man and Deia stepped forward.

"That must be Steve. Looks a little different," Josh said.

"Less like a gorilla of metal and more like a human giant made from ebony metal," Cassie agreed.

The general, Deia, and Steve talked for a few minutes.

"Josh, it seems that the Nalheim here rely on arid planets with lots of sunlight and heat in order to have their children. However, their home planet is getting colder and starting to go through an ice age. They came here to claim territory and find a place in which to live," Deia said.

Malsour came from the skies, his wings flapping, blowing wind past the general and at the Nalheim behind him.

The Nalheim all had their spears pointed at Malsour as he looked to the general. He talked to Steve, who talked to the Nalheim general.

The Nalheim said something back; both of its heads moved backward, its necks uncovered. A single slash now would be enough to open its necks and kill it.

"This race is honor and power based—to the strongest go the spoils. We have proved that we are the stronger. It seems that they are just looking for a place for them to have their children. Already they have massive battles with one another in order to try to gain areas that are warmer. Their population is only a few million," Deia said.

Malsour asked another question. The general seemed disbelieving that he had kept his life as he looked to the three in front of him. Deia snorted before relaying what was being said.

"The Nalheim's planet is about ten degrees centigrade around the equator, with everything else above and below being large ice fields. There are many beasts across it," Deia said. "They are willing to bow their head in servitude to the dragons that they respect as long as they are given some place to live."

Malsour said something else.

The general yelled to the forces behind him. The Nalheim took but a moment before shields and spears were dropped to the ground.

"They have officially surrendered but the terms for their surrender, they wish to discuss," Deia said.

Josh became aware of a dozen presences in the sky. He looked up, seeing multiple mage's guild overseers in the sky.

A man descended toward Josh with a faint smile on his face.

"Overseer Rendar, I didn't think that I would be seeing you again so soon," Josh said.

"We were originally sent in order to assist as best as we could. However, as the Nalheim, a sentient race, have surrendered, we believe that we can be of a greater assistance now than when the battle was ongoing," Rendar said.

Josh nodded. The overseers were a group that made sure that battles were done in accordance to the rules that the mage's guild and college passed down. They were acting as the scouts for the Terra Alliance; however, they also acted as a neutral party with conflicts between two groups to see whether a compromise could be found.

"Overseer Rendar, I think that Deia and Steve could use your help to learn more about the Nalheim and see if we can find a way to end this peacefully. I have a spawn point of blood reevers that are supposed to be arriving in less than thirty-six hours," Josh said.

"Of course. I will lend my talents if at all possible." Rendar smiled and headed off toward where the negotiations were taking place.

Chapter 20: A Change of Fates

The Nalheim sat in their ranks while Malsour, Steve, and Deia talked to the Nalheim general. Rendar was there, off to the side, acting as a neutral party and making sure that both sides followed the letter of the law that was held within the mage's guild's edicts on war.

Dwayne's forces were formed up, resting and waiting. Esa's forces within the castle were quickly and quietly charging the soul gem construct through the castle while they were also marshaling their forces.

Healers were moving through the people in the castles as well as casting area of effect healing spells on the Nalheim.

The Nalheim were stunned as their badly wounded started to recover as they were covered by these healing spells.

After all, the mage's guild had very similar rules regarding injured. No matter if they were allies or the enemy, they were supposed to receive the same care.

The Nalheim didn't have healers and let their wounded die; if a few of them died, then it would be easier on the rest of their people to survive.

"It looks like the Nalheim have come to pledge themselves to Malsour. They recognized his strength and see him as a worthy master." Deia sounded confused by it all. These proud warriors were willing to submit to Malsour in order to hopefully gain a place for their people to live and raise their young.

Josh frowned at Deia's information. "Okay, well, if you can make them our allies or keep them docile and helping out, then that's all we can do. Otherwise their people are just going to keep coming through the portal until we're having to fight children and the old," Josh said.

The Nalheim were in dire straits. In a few years, their people would no longer be able to have children. This was their last chance: either they would fight and win or die. Now, with the possibility of surrender, they were being given another possible option.

"How is the troop movement going?" Josh asked Cassie beside him.

"We have people from all of the castles moving through the onos back to Terra and then through to the orcish swamplands. We've got a number of fresh units moving out while others go to rest; they will make it to the swamplands in time. We've sent mages for the most part. Marching an army through the swamps would just get them stuck. However, the mages can get there in smaller groups and support the orcs and gnomes. The leader of the group of summoners and tamers is already at the spawn point. Heroiu'quing says that she believes that the orcs and gnomes will be able to soul bind the blood reevers to them. Also, she gained their promise to assist in the forming of the Gudalo republic and supporting the Terra Alliance," Cassie said.

Josh nodded. There was less than thirty-three hours until the spawn point in the orc and gnome swamplands opened. "Looks like everything is handled on that side of things."

"Still, you look like you've got something else weighing on your mind." Cassie used her interface as she talked.

Josh took a deep breath and his hands rested on the first eastern castle's walls. "By the end of one spawn point being activated, another is usually in place, but we have not been able to find out where this next spawn point is. It has to be out there somewhere."

Cassie stopped working on her interface. She, too, had these kinds of thoughts. "There's nothing we can do but keep out a watchful eye. We don't know what's coming or where it's coming, but we have the might of the Terra Alliance behind us. That is no simple thing," Cassie reminded him.

"Yes, but I can't shake the feeling that we're going to overextend ourselves dealing with all of these calamities, unable to last through it all or the battle that is coming with the angels."

Cassie didn't say anything else. In the past, she might have joked about it, but after finding out the reality of Emerilia and Earth, it was hard to joke around with matters that involved Emerilia.

***

The talks finally came to an end. It had taken nearly two days but finally an agreement that the mage's guild agreed to had been made.

"The Nalheim recognize Malsour Dracul as their king and will submit to becoming indentured servants to him. Malsour Dracul will allow them to live within the Densaou Ring of Fire. The Nalheim will no longer attack other races proactively, unless it is done in self-defense. They may allow another person to take on their indentured contract if they, Malsour Dracul, and the person taking the contract agree to the conditions. All of the Nalheim military will be indentured for five years. Their people will be brought from their homeland and moved to the Densaou Ring of Fire.

"As compensation, the planet Nal will be gifted to the Terra Alliance and Malsour Dracul," Steve said.

Rendar's eyebrows rose as he looked at Malsour, still in his dragon form, with a complicated look.

Steve then said the same agreement in the language of the Nalheim. Once he was finished, a prompt appeared in front of Malsour and the general. This was their binding contract. They both agreed to the conditions.

The general turned. Raising his voice, it cut through the silent battlefield. All of the Nalheim looked to him. They were willing to lay down their lives so that their people might get another chance to survive.

The general's words ended as the Nalheim's heads looked to one another. They might be from another species but Deia was able to see what she had come to see as their version of shock and the excitement that was held within their eyes.

Suddenly the Nalheim slapped their feet on the ground, faster and faster until the ground shook with the stomping. They started yelling, screaming, and moving their heads around wildly.

"Looks kind of like the New Zealand haka, but with a hell of a lot more heads," Steve said. "I hope it's not their war dance, but their greeting."

"Well, thanks for adding that little bit of doubt," Deia muttered.

"That's what I'm here for—keeping things interesting!" Steve laughed.

Deia snorted and shook her head. A small smile grew on her face.

The general joined in on the chant, facing Malsour and the negotiation group. It went on for about ten minutes before it finally started to settle down. They planted a fist in the ground and bent their bodies forward, lowering their heads.

"Tell them that first they are to gather up their people, to get them ready for the journey ahead. They have one week to be ready. They will wait inside Goblin Mountain. I will have some of the dragons come to meet them and guide them to the ring of fire. Right now I will take two of their people with me to check out the ring of fire," Malsour said.

Steve translated. A second general rode his gryphon to where Malsour and the first general was.

An Aleph scout appeared next to Malsour. "I have used Steve's language matrix on this automaton. It will be capable of translating for you." Shard's voice came from the automaton.

"Thank you, Shard," Malsour said. With a wave of his hand, the automaton disappeared into his storage ring. "Tell them to follow me."

Steve translated; the first general jumped onto his gryphon.

Malsour's massive wings flapped.

Deia and Rendar used Mana shields to stop the dust that was thrown up with Malsour's massive wing beats as he rose into the sky.

Deia felt her heart tremble as she smiled up at Malsour as he continued to rise into the sky. His aura was deep and incredibly powerful; it was almost as powerful as Deia's if she was to actually allow it out into the world.

The generals on their gryphons followed after their new king, not daring to be slow in anyway. Their gryphons followed their commands but it was clear that they had deference toward Malsour.

Deia looked to Rendar, who was still staring in the sky. Seeing a dragon or the mythical Nalheim was incredible; to be able to talk to a creature from another realm as well as a dragon was beyond any expectations. Rendar was still in a state of shock. Now that the negotiations were complete, he was left with his mind turning over.

"Rendar, we know that the truth of the dragons will come out at some time, but we hope to keep it a secret for as long as possible. After all, if others know, then our enemies will find out," Deia said.

Rendar looked to Deia. His gaze turned to Steve, understanding in his eyes.

Party Zero were famed throughout Emerilia. They were not people he wanted to annoy. Also, if he was to freely spread this information, then it might be used against the Stone Raiders and the dragons if they came in aide of Rendar's family or the mage's guild and college.

"I understand. Overseers know how to keep their lips closed," Rendar said with a reassuring smile.

Deia's hard expression fell away as Steve smiled.

"All right. Now, where's Dave? I need him to make me a set of armor!" Steve turned toward the castle.

Overseers moved down toward the Nalheim. Now that the agreement had been made, the Nalheim had stepped down and the overseers were to take over.

The Terra Alliance kept their people on alert even as they sent out healers with a large guard force to heal up those with the worst wounds who hadn't been completely healed by the large scale area of effect.

Deia found Party Zero waiting for her back in the castle. Already the mages were quickly repairing the castle from the inside.

"You metal-brained idiot!" Gurren moved to greet Steve.

"Hey! No more metal." Steve opened up his arms and turned side to side slightly.

"Hmm, a very interesting construct." Jekoni floated around Steve and inspected him.

"You're not possessing me!" Steve jumped away from Jekoni.

"How many times do I have to tell you I'm not that kind of spirit!" Jekoni complained.

Party Zero watched their antics, greeting Steve in his new form.

"A whole new planet." Dave moved to Deia with a smile.

"I had to get knocked up by the wanderlust explorer." Deia sighed.

"What? Don't tell me you don't want to explore it too." Dave grinned.

Deia pursed her lips; the corners of her mouth lifted upward.

"That's what I thought." Dave laughed with a knowing smile.

Deia elbowed his armor as Dave grunted slightly. "So, why is everything getting repaired? It's not like we're going to be using this place for long." Deia looked to the castle.

"Well, I wouldn't say that," Dave said.

"What are you planning?" Deia asked.

The others looked from their own conversation with Steve. If they knew one thing, it was that when Dave decided to do a project, it was going to be anything but simple.

"We're going to make citadels!" Dave looked at the castle with a large smile on his face.

***

"Prepare yourselves!" Ursk's deep and rough voice called out to the people who filled the defensive structures around the spawn point.

The area around the spawn point had changed wildly from when it had been visited by Party Zero.

Now their simple soul gem construct covered the entire area around the spawn point, extending outward to touch upon the surrounding defenses that the orcs and gnomes had built and then been improved upon by the various mages who had come just a day ago. Within a single day, they were able to raise stone and metal defenses, strengthening the defenses a hundredfold.

Ursk had heard of the abilities of these mages but without seeing them for himself, he had thought of them as wild tales.

The Air mages who had come had made complex runes on the various buildings and created a magical circle that had cleared the swamp's natural fog away from the spawn point. They could easily see the spawn point. Many of the orcs and gnomes had never been able to see this far in their lives.

This, even more than the metal and stone that had risen out of the ground, was enough to make the gnomes and orcs look at the mages with newfound respect.

The summoners had worked tirelessly together in order to figure out the best spell formations, magical circles, and summoning rituals they should combine in order to give the orcs and gnomes the greatest chance to bind with the blood reevers.

The beast tamers had done their best to figure out the type of creature that the blood reever was and also tell the gnomes and orcs what to expect. They had included ways in which to subdue different creatures. The summoners had also taught them how to activate the various magical formations and circles that they had created and made magical contracts with all of the orcs and gnomes.

They'd sorted people out from the strongest of Willpower and Ability to the weakest.

They had completely changed the orcs' and gnomes' ways of thinking toward beasts and controlling them. Still, all of this work was to give the orcs and gnomes a chance to take command of the blood reevers. It was up to them in order to complete the soul binding rituals.

Ursk had even been contacted by Josh Giles himself. He had discussed how he could move forces into the swamplands in order to help the gnomes and orcs to defend their territory.

Josh knew that as soon as an army made it into the swamplands, they would get bogged down. The work to get them to the defenses around the spawn point would be great.

Ursk had turned down his offer. The Terra Alliance had given them the tools and the abilities in order to turn the blood reevers from their enemy into their beasts.

It will be up to us if we win or fail. These were heavy thoughts but Ursk had an excitement in his eyes. He was an orc who lived on the edge of his axe; he had fought for his position, and then for territory, always pushing forward and growing his influence.

Now he once again faced a challenge that seemed impossible. This was what made him feel alive, what ignited the blood within his veins and raised his fighting spirit.

"The spawn point is activating!" someone called out.

Players who had come from all over Emerilia watched from the skies, trees, and around the defenses.

Ursk and his people had made it clear that the players were not to interfere. Only if the blood reevers weren't brought under the power of the soul binding contracts would they be free to kill and slaughter.

Ursk stepped onto a magical circle. The soul gem construct had multiple magical circles built into them, with one massive magical circle that surrounded the spawn point.

The gnomes and orcs all stood in their various magical circles. Their faces were grim and determined. This would be unlike any battle that they had ever fought before. But if they were able to win against the blood reevers, it would come with a victory that they couldn't even imagine in their entire lifetimes.

The counter for the spawn point hit zero. The various moving parts of the spawn point stopped moving. A second later, a flash of light made Ursk and the others who were looking in the direction of the spawn point raise their arms to try to block out that burning brightness.

Suddenly the area within the defensive circle and massive magical circle was filled with hundreds of creatures.

Blood reevers! Ursk thought excitedly. Blood reevers were wolves as large as a war horse. They had black fur that shimmered red slightly as they moved. Spit fell from their jaws as they looked at those surrounding them with black eyes.

Ursk felt his soul shiver as he looked into one of the blood reever's eyes. "Begin the soul binding!" Ursk yelled, pulling people out of their daze.

The reevers let out their howls, moving into packs as they started forward.

Magical circles around the spawn point lit up. Runes flared to life as they interacted with the massive magical circle that surrounded the reevers.

The reevers that were moving forward now looked as if the gravity underneath them had tripled. They bared their teeth. Their eyes found the eyes of those who were actively using the soul binding magical circle.

Ursk looked out at a massive reever. The magical circle was supposed to not only increase the power that he exerted, but weaken the power of the beasts within. It showed how great the power of the blood reevers was as they continued to resist the combined pressure that the orcs and gnomes put on them.

Ursk let out an angered yell as he slapped his chest. This was a battle of his will against the blood reevers. He was not going to lose!

Other orcs and gnomes yelled out their defiance. The blood reevers growled back.

Not all of the orcs and gnomes were as strong of spirit as they collapsed, cold sweat covering their bodies. With each who failed, the power of the reevers would increase.

The summoners, now with a better understanding of the blood reevers, changed the magical circles and formations that they had created. The pressure lessened as some of those who had collapsed once again stood in their positions and fought back.

The first reever bowed its head, lying down on the ground in submission.

A prompt appeared in front of one of the orcs, who let out a proud roar. They accepted the contract.

The blood reever, now under its new master's control, stood up easily. The Magical Circuit had no power over it now as it no longer resisted its master's commands. The reever moved out of the magical circle, lying down behind its new master.

Its master didn't even step out of his own magical circle. He had won control over his blood reever but there were still nearly two thousand left.

The battle of wills continued on. The beast tamers moved around, telling people of ways to increase the power of their will. Here and there, reevers bowed down in submission; a soul binding contract was burned up and a new reever left the magical circle.

However, sometimes this wasn't the case as a reever that had bowed down still had the strength to break the contract that was placed upon it.

New contracts were handed out. As the gnomes and orcs wore down the reevers, more and more contracts were formed.

Ursk felt the back and forth between the reevers, the pressure on his mind as he could do nothing but try to exert his own pressure upon their minds and endure the conflict of Willpower. The creature that he had been trying to create a soul binding contract with finally slipped up, their Willpower not as strong as Ursk's. He struck then, forcing his will upon the reever's.

It was as if a dam had broken and water was now flowing through freely. Ursk was the water while the reever's Willpower was the walls of the dam. Without pause, Ursk pulled out the soul binding contract, going through the motions that he had memorized long ago. Before the blood reever had time to even think of fighting back again, Ursk's soul binding contract fell over the beast.

Ursk was breathing heavily with ragged breaths. He felt a connection form in his mind; with a thought, the blood reever stood and walked toward Ursk, following his commands.

Ursk let out a relieved laugh. His body was covered in sweat but he had won the battle and claimed a blood reever!

With new energy, he once again pressured another reever. With two or more of the orcs and gnomes pressuring a reever, their ability to resist fell even faster. How could they, just one creature, hope to fight against two other minds, one of which had already brought one of its brothers or sisters under their will?

Contracts were thrown into the air as lights descended over the soul-bound beast and the soul binding master.

As more were free from their own soul binding, they turned to help others. Contracts were created faster and faster.

Ursk watched with growing hope as less than a fifth of the blood reevers were left trying to resist. Every couple of seconds, another contract would be formed and a reever would leave the magical circle around the spawn point.

Still, even seeing this sight, he once more focused on helping out the others who were still trying to form their soul binding contracts. Slowly and completely, the blood reevers were brought under the control of Ursk and his people.

Only when the last blood reever had submitted did Ursk let out a ragged laugh. His body was covered in sweat as he collapsed to the ground, his whole body shaking from muscle spasms.

"These fights of Willpower are much harder than fights of sword and shield," Ursk's brother said from beside Ursk, also on his hands and knees.

The two brothers laughed together. They had fought a battle harder than anything they had faced in the past and they had come out the victors.

The fight for control over the blood reevers had gone on for three days. Time held no bearing on those who were focused on soul binding the blood reevers.

Ursk looked behind him, where a large blood reever lay down. It looked at Ursk lazily with one eye. Seeing that Ursk was looking at it, it snorted and laid its head down to sleep.

Ursk felt a smile grow across his face as he looked at his blood reever. They had come back to kill and destroy, growing in strength and power, ravaging the swamplands. Instead, Ursk and his tribe had turned them into their soul-bound beasts.

Together they would defend the homes of their tribe.

He looked to the various mages, summoners, and beast tamers who were walking around. In his heart, Ursk knew that the debt he had with the Terra Alliance was great.

These blood reevers did not only mean that they would not be attacked today. It had made them stronger. The blood reevers could mate and create litters of more blood reevers for later generations.

Ursk had always dreamed of riding on something more than the great blue snakes of the swampland. Beasts were power and a symbol of strength; now he would face the world with a companion beside him at all times.

Maybe it's time to leave the swamplands, to move to the plains where we can ride, to learn how to fight with our blood reevers? Maybe we could unite the swamplands and the plains of the orc and gnome lands? This thought formed within Ursk's mind. A smile appeared on his face. He had once again faced a great challenge and now he thought of a greater one to aim toward.

"First I will pay my debt with the Terra Alliance and keep my word," Ursk vowed. He shakily got to his feet.

Quing, who was moving toward him, pulled out a potion and passed it to Ursk.

He took it, drinking it without a thought. Strength came back to his body as he smiled to Quing.

"It seems that the reevers were only a small obstacle to your tribe," Quing said.

Ursk heard the smile in her voice. "As you have helped my people, I will in turn honor my side of the agreement."

"Rest and recover first. The ono that is nearby will be placed in your village. With access to Terra, your people will grow stronger and you can be assured that your people will be safe as we fight for all of Emerilia." Quing sounded tense.

Although Ursk couldn't see her face, he had worked with Quing closely for a number of days and could easily read her emotions from her words or her eyes. "Something bothering you?"

"This is but the beginning of the event but no one has been able to find out where the next spawn point is, or what is coming," Quing explained.

Ursk nodded. "I feel that we will find out what is to come soon enough."

Chapter 21: Machinations

Dave opened up his interface to check out the notifications he'd ignored when he'd been fighting.

Quest: Weapons Master Level 3

One handed and shield 1000/1000

Two handed 218/1000

Dual wielding 61/1000

Archery 681/1000

Rewards: Unlock Level 4 Quest

Increase to stats

Passive skills from other weapons increase from 25% to 50% when designated weapon is not equipped. (Example: While using Dual wield blades, one is able to gain 50% of the archery skill's abilities.)

"Not bad. It's getting hard to fight people with the close-range melee weapons now." Dave sighed and moved to the next notification.

Level 240

You have reached Level **240**; you have **10** stat points to use.

Dave grinned as he looked at the stat points at his disposal. He opened up his character sheet.

Character Sheet

Name:	David Grahslagg	Gender:	Male
Level:	238	Class:	Dwarven Master Smith, Friend of the Grey God, Bleeder, Librarian, Aleph Engineer, Weapons Master, Champion Slayer, Skill Creator, Mine Manager, Master of Space and Time, Master of Gravitational Anomalies
Race:	Human/ Dwarf	Alignment:	Chaotic Neutral

Unspent points: 10

Health:	48,100	Regen:	24.02 /s
Mana:	15,780	Regen:	57.95 /s
Stamina:	5,320	Regen:	50.15 /s
Vitality:	481	Endurance:	1,201
Intelligence:	1,578	Willpower:	1,159
Strength:	532	Agility:	1,003

"I could put more into Vitality. Hell, I was damn close to losing all my hit points. I've gone all Mana- and barrier-based defenses. If those are gone, then I'm screwed. I've already dedicated myself to a max/min mage pretty much—I should keep that up. Either I kill the people before they get me, or they get me. If I start going back on what I have right now, then I'm just going to completely mess up the build that I've already got." Dave put in his new stat points and confirmed them.

Character Sheet

Name:	David Grahslagg	Gender:	Male
Level:	240	Class:	Dwarven Master Smith, Friend of the Grey God, Bleeder, Librarian, Aleph Engineer, Weapons Master, Champion Slayer, Skill Creator, Mine Manager, Master of Space and Time, Master of Gravitational Anomalies
Race:	Human/ Dwarf	Alignment:	Chaotic Neutral

Unspent points: 0

Health:	48,100	Regen:	24.02 /s
Mana:	15,830	Regen:	57.95 /s
Stamina:	5,320	Regen:	50.40 /s
Vitality:	481	Endurance:	1,201
Intelligence:	1,583	Willpower:	1,159
Strength:	532	Agility:	1,008

"Still squishy and badass as hell," Dave mocked. Just having ten stat points to use felt underwhelming as he put five into Intelligence and Agility.

"Are you insane yet?" Steve's voice carried through Pandora's box. Steve was in his room while Dave was out in the open laboratory.

"No?" Dave said.

"You're talking to yourself and I saw your plans for those citadels!" Steve retorted.

"Just because they're a bit ambitious doesn't make me insane!"

"Using five of our Mana wells for each citadel does!" Steve rolled out of his office on a chair.

"I wondered where that went," Dave muttered to himself.

"What? It was just laying around one day!" Steve defended, rubbing the armrest of the chair affectionately.

"It wasn't just laying around! I was working on shipyard one for five minutes and you took it and hid it in your workshop that you banned everyone from entering!" Dave yelled back.

"Ehh, semantics. So about that citadel. You're crazy."

"Changing the subject?" Dave accused Steve, who simply raised his hands and shrugged.

Dave rubbed his face. There was no winning with Steve and he had already made a replacement chair long ago. "So, what do you have a problem with?" Dave flopped into his own rolling spinny chair.

"I never said that I had a problem with it. I just said that it was bat shit crazy. Also, why is bat shit crazy?"

"I have no idea why bat shit is crazy." Dave looked to the ceiling as if asking some power in the universe to allow him to give him patience or strike him down.

As usual, nothing happened and Steve continued to open his mouth.

"It's indeed a rather complex question," Steve said seriously.

When he wants to know why bat shit is crazy, he's serious; when we're talking about a massive project that could help defend Emerilia, he has the attention of a five-year-old in a toy store.

"Back to the citadels. So you want to take these castles, slap a whole bunch of Mana wells to them as well as really complex soul gem constructs that will allow the castles to float. Taking the idea of the Per'Ush islands then applying it to the castles, filling them up with all the baddest and best weapons that we've thought up and fly them around Emerilia like they're bumper cars. It's brilliant, crazy as hell, but awesome!" Steve said with a smile that made Dave actually question his own sanity.

After all, if Steve's agreeing with it, I've probably taken a left turn into the land of crazy.

"The power consumption is going to be a pain in the ass. We damaged a few areas and then consumed the conquest points to repair them. The soul gem constructs in the walls and the magical formations we added were fixed as well. Using points, we can repair walls and the castle when in battle. They'll be the perfect launch platforms to deal with any large threats that we have to deal with. We simply move them across Emerilia, put them down where we want to defend or want to stage ourselves. Then we can use the onos to move people and resources around, giving us a base of operations with a ready fighting force anywhere in Emerilia," Dave said.

"Have you heard of his plans for the planet Nal yet?" Malsour entered Pandora's box.

"How did the trip go?" Dave looked to Malsour in his human form.

"It looks like they were really telling the truth. When they visited Densaou Ring of Fire, the two generals broke down. We are traveling to Nal in just an hour. I thought that you two would be interested in coming?" Malsour asked.

Dave and Steve jumped out of their chairs, sending them backward as they moved to Malsour.

"After you!" Steve pushed them both through the secret door that exited into the power station that kept Terra running.

They walked quickly through the power station.

"I heard that we're connecting up the first and second section of Terra soon," Malsour said.

"The runners are being inspected. We should start spinning the second section within a day or two. Once it's matched up in speed, we'll fuse the two sections together. In just a week, we'll double the size of Terra," Dave said with some pride.

"What about Nal?" Steve asked, interested now that Malsour had talked about it.

"Well, Nal right now is going through an ice age. It is also a planet that the Jukal Empire watches but they don't really care about. The Nalheim occupy the surface of the planet and they're dying off. The Jukal Empire are using the slow death of the Nalheim to create a bidding war between the races. None of them want to deal with an aggressive species on the planet. However, once they're all dead, it wouldn't be hard to change the planet's ecosystem to suit most of the sentient races.

"Right now, the only things that the Jukal Empire have watching over Nalheim are a few satellites used to check the weather of the planet, scan for resources and materials as well as record the number of Nalheim on the planet.

"These same satellites would have been used to record and send out imagery of the battles on the ground, as well as transmit the data from our interfaces back to the empire for their viewing pleasure. However, these satellites are spotty and there's not many of them. Compared to the measures that were taken here in Emerilia, it's not even worth commenting on their observation methods," Dave said.

"Okay, so the Jukal aren't watching as closely. So what?" Steve asked.

"There are seven planets in the system and thirteen moons. Many are resource rich. While the Jukal are watching the planet, they're not watching the rest of the system," Dave said. "We have a planet which is about to be devoid of life and a star system that has no one watching it. While we move the Nalheim out from Nal, we're going to dig deep into Nal. We're going to bury a portal in there and create a base under the planet's surface. From there, we can make a base for the star system. We can move in more portals, link to the different planets that have a bunch of resources; we funnel those resources into our projects. Already we've eaten through our resources that Bob had. We're also burning through the mining manager stuff at a massive rate with this event. We can't take out more resources from our stocks. The Jukal are going to start asking where the resources are coming from. The moonbase is pretty awesome but the fact is that there are nearly no resources there. Everything that we mine out for shipyard one, two, and the moonbase, all has to be covered by stealth runes to make sure that we're not discovered. With Nal, we get a step up." Dave's eyes shone. The faster their various projects could be completed, the faster that they could look to possibly getting out from under the Jukal.

They stepped through the power station's ono and stepped into Terra. The city was filled with people moving back and forth. The atmosphere was weird as the event had now descended. POEs were worried of what was to come while the players were excited for what was to come.

"You don't like to think small." Steve laughed.

Malsour smiled as well, looking to Dave.

"Got to get outside of the box once in a while," Dave said.

From Terra, they took a teleport pad connected to an ono, stepping out in Goblin Mountain where the Nalheim had first emerged and cleared the mountain of the original goblin inhabitants.

Now the Nalheim were wearing the clothes that usually rested under their armor. Malsour moved from the ono with confidence. The generals riding the gryphons inclined their heads slightly to Malsour. Only if someone was looking for it would they notice it.

Waiting was the rest of Party Zero, as well as an elite warclan of five thousand dwarves.

Ahead of them lay a portal.

Dave slowly stopped walking and looked at this portal.

For most of his adult life, he had built rockets to mine Sol, or at least what he thought of as Sol. He had wanted to build a spacefaring empire that would reach outward to touch other star systems. He had never dreamed that he would ever go to a system beyond Sol. He might reach Mars and he'd be happy with that.

Now, he stood on a planet that was tens of light-years away from where Sol had been. A prison meant to entertain an alien empire and destroy the aggressive species that they ran into.

He faced a portal that would allow him to cross over the vastness of space, to reach another planet in another star system. A planet that few humans had ever stepped on—if any.

It felt as if his soul made him stop to take this moment in.

"Ready?" Steve asked, his voice gentle as he sensed Dave's mood.

"Yeah." Dave nodded, looking from the portal to Steve and the rest of Party Zero behind him. He smiled to them all and moved to meet with Party Zero.

The group moved forward. The Nalheim generals, now indentured servants, passed through the portal first.

The dwarves marched forward, their shields up and ready as they moved through the portal.

Overseers as well as the Stone Raiders' leadership followed behind.

Party Zero followed afterward.

The portal showed a cold landscape. On the other side was a desolate plain with winds that cut at those who had stepped through the portal and at the ground. The wind and the temperature had scoured the ground free of any vegetation long ago.

Dave took a deep breath. Deia's fingers found his, holding his hand. He looked to her and the smile on her face. His heart was at ease as he smiled at her.

"Seems that I owe you a date." Dave stepped through the portal and pulled her with him. "How about another planet?"

Deia laughed at his antics before the wind cut through.

"Shit, that's cold!" Dave said.

"This is why your fiancée is a Fire mage." Deia created an area of warmth around the party.

"She's also one *hot* momma." Dave winked and squeezed her hand.

The others of Party Zero chuckled as Deia sighed. "You're going to pay for that one," she muttered.

Dave didn't say anything, smiling as they continued through the cold wasteland that was Nal.

"Seems that in these places, my Mana recovery is a quarter of what it usually is," Deia said.

"Without the 'natural' ley lines of Emerilia, there's a lot less natural Mana running around," Anna said.

The Nalheim continued to move forward. They quickly left the plains and entered the mountains. Here the wind died down slightly. The Nalheim led toward the mountain side. They called out in their language before continuing forward.

A massive gate could be seen, built into the mountain. Around this there were multiple fires that could be seen illuminating guard positions and windows.

The Nalheim called out again. The doors opened slowly.

Behind them, war lizards provided the strength to open the fifty-meter tall and forty-meter wide doors. They opened only enough to fit the group in, immediately closing behind them.

They passed through smaller gates, which were quickly sealed behind them. As they proceeded forward, the temperature rose quickly. They reached a large cavern that had been carved out from the rock. Nalheim stopped what they were doing and looked up at the stairs that led into their city, their eyes wide in shock at the races that they had never seen before in their life.

One of the generals roared out in the Nalheim's language; the Nalheim gathered closer, more coming from deeper in the city.

Dave looked to Deia and the rest of Party Zero.

"I'll translate. You two go set up the interspatial express," Steve said.

"That's not even close to being right," Dave said. He and Deia moved away from the group and moved down one of the side stairwells that led into the city.

They activated stealth, Dave sensing the Nalheim as Deia carved a path through Nalheim, her stealth skills much higher than his. Finally they reached a secluded spot that didn't seem to get much traffic.

Dave checked with his Touch of the Land spell again. "We're clear," Dave said over party chat with Deia and pressed his hands to the rock wall.

Quickly the rock started to be destroyed; a cave formed beyond. As soon as there was enough room, Dave and Deia moved inside.

Dave quickly pulled out pre-made soul gem constructs and put them around the doorway. From the outside, the cave disappeared; if someone was to use their sensing spells, it would be nearly impossible to detect the cave entrance.

Neither Dave nor Deia talked as they worked. Deia checked on the soul gem construct and Mana well, making sure it was operational before she started to pull out miners. The miners activated and then started to burrow into the farthest wall.

Both Dave and Deia had powerful sight that could easily cut through the darkness. With the soul gem construct that was spreading across the room, Deia was able to clearly see what Dave was working on.

Dave assembled panels with quick and precise movements. There were eight panels that connected to an octagon base plate. They were made from ebony-coded plates that had been infused with soul gems and had silver traced into them. This allowed the power to easily flow through the various components.

Dave pulled out an octagonal pillar, placing it down on the main base plate. The soul gem constructs of the different triangular panels that also connected to the base plate connected to this pillar that was covered in fins that were meant to disperse heat.

Dave checked over the different panels, then the base and the attached pillars. Satisfied, he pulled out a large ball from his bag of holding. It wasn't actually a perfect sphere but a soul gem ebony and silver construct that had so many faces on it that it was almost spherical.

Dave placed this on the top of the pillar.

There was a clicking noise as the different parts of the construct started to light up. Lines looking like the kind that you would find on computer chips lit up with power. These were soul gem and silver constructs that had been heavily coded. A person with a carver wouldn't have been able to carve the complex coding that made up these lines that moved in straight lines.

They flowed up from the bottom triangular panels, splitting as they moved higher before reaching the top of the pillar. The air around those heat-dispersing fans started to distort as heat started to flow away from the central pillar.

The multi-faced nearly sphere on top of the pillar glowed with an internal light. Lines of code like the kind that was traveling up the side of the pillar spread out from the center of the multi-faceted gem.

These lines were only as thick as a hair but they intersected and connected to one another, looking like hundreds of neurons within the brain lighting up all at once. The heat given off by the device only increased as Dave checked everything.

Dave pulled out a large Mirror of Communication and put it off to the side of the room. He pulled out a handheld Mirror of Communication and sent a message through it. It linked to the larger Mirror of Communication, using its much larger range in order to transmit the message.

Dave received a message back.

He took the rectangular mirror that was no bigger than a phone and placed it in a recess between the heat-dissipating fans on the body of the device.

The mirror was filled with lines of runes and information as coded lines reached, descended from the gem above, and spread around the Mirror of Communication.

Dave stepped backward and looked at the device.

"Come on, you can do it," Dave said, slightly bent over as he looked at the device, apprehension in his eyes.

"Dave, what is that?" Deia looked at the device that was giving off waves of energy.

"A portal anchor," Dave said with a nervous smile.

Deia's eye went wide. After all, she had expected that they would transport a portal to Nal through the supplies or wagons like they had done with the portal they'd gifted to the Aleph. "This…" Deia said. No words came to her mind.

"It's basically the same thing that we used on the moonbase, which was styled off of the drop plates. However, this is a hell of a lot more powerful and exact as we're not moving a portal around a planet or onto a moon of a planet nearby. We're attempting to move a portal from Emerilia directly to Nal," Dave said.

With that, Deia could understand just how hard this would be.

***

Bob was running from control panel to control panel.

A new panel had been added. This had a Mirror of Communication with glowing lines of code spreading out from it and into the console before spreading out around the room.

"Damn this science experiment!" Bob yelled as he checked the power outputs and the heat that was building within the various coded banks around the teleportation array.

In the middle of the room, there was a portal ready and waiting. Around it, the walls with their magically coded formations were moving and changing according to the information that they were receiving through the Mirror of Communication.

"Power levels are good, though it's going to take one hell of a bite out of the stored up power. I'm scared that these heat levels are going to just melt the coded plates in here." Bob nervously tapped on the console, trying to change things around in order to give the teleportation the best chances.

Heat built in the room as Mana filled the air.

Bob rushed out of the room.

"Where are they? Come on—disrupting tech, power enhancers, spatial items of holding," Bob muttered to himself as he ran through the laboratory, moving from table to table that was filled with various items.

"Gotcha! Heat exchangers!" Bob grabbed armfuls of the heat exchangers. "And Dave's duct tape." He grabbed a gray roll of duct tape as he rushed back to the room.

He was sweating as he grabbed a vault soul gem on the way. There were metal bands around the soul gem. He attuned the heat exchangers with the soul gem. Dropping the soul gem off by the consoles, he ran in with the heat exchangers.

The heat from the room started to decrease as the heat exchangers' coding activated and they started to convert that heat into Mana.

Bob hastily used the duct tape to stick the heat exchangers to places where the heat was the worst and where they wouldn't be in the way for the teleportation array when it was activated. It didn't take him long to put the different heat exchangers across the walls.

He rushed back to the consoles, sliding to a stop, using the consoles to stop himself as he looked to the Mirror of Communication console.

"Ninety percent," Bob said. Different sections of the teleportation array had locked into place as supercooled gases were released into the room in order to try to cool the area more.

Bob wiped sweat away as he checked his various settings.

The entire room hummed with power. The fusion plant had even picked up in pace, directly powering the teleportation array. Bob looked to his various screens that were telling him all manner of information on the teleportation array. Even as he rushed from console to console, his heart in his throat, he was filled with a sense of excitement.

He had been alive for hundreds of years. He had missed this sense of excitement. Dave had created this teleportation array, teaching Bob about the mysteries contained within it.

Now Bob stood there with his finger on the button, ready to push Dave's creation to the limit. This was the test—this was what science was about! Unraveling the mysteries of the universe and coming to understand it!

"One hundred percent." Bob smiled as finally the various components that made up the teleportation array were mostly in place. A few different items were constantly moving, keeping the teleportation array and the anchor that Dave had placed down in Nal synced up with each other.

A loud humming filled the room; there was an explosion of light. Bob ducked, the light burning into his eyes. He couldn't see a thing but he could hear the machinery within the room started to slow down.

He stood up slowly, using the console to help him keep his balance, blinking to try to get rid of the light spots. Slowly, his sight started to come back to him.

"It worked!" Dave's excited voice came over the party chat connected via the Mirror of Communication network.

Bob jumped in joy and let out an excited yell as he saw that there was no longer a portal within the teleportation array.

Still blinking heavily and half-blind, he grabbed the small Mirror of Communication that was no longer showing streaming runes but rather showing a room with a growing soul gem construct across the roof and walls.

Bob ran to the portals that were within the hub at the rear of the laboratory.

He was nearly hit by three different carts that were moving materials between the different connected areas. He made it past them all and reached the newest of the portals. Each of the portals rested on their own pedestal, with one side being the "entrance" to the portal and the other being the "exit." Each of these portals had clamps attached to their rings as well as a console on either side.

This console allowed them to power up and down the portals, as well as change which portal they would connect to and use the Mana shield that had been added to them all.

The last portal was already whirring with noise as the millions of runes that were arrayed within the rings were moving. Another portal was trying to establish a connection with it. It took some time before the different parts of the portal stopped turning around and locked into position.

Bob looked at the console as the portal activated.

"Looking good on our side. The portal is all dialed up," Dave said as the portal finished the last adjustments and connected to the one in Nal.

"I'm getting your signal nice and clear." Bob checked the information on the console. Power surged through the area; the soul gem dimmed slightly with the power that was used to connect the portals.

The portal activated with another flash of light.

"Wish these things wouldn't go off like a damn flash spell every time," Bob muttered to himself before he looked up.

"Hey, dude." Dave waved from the other side of the portal.

"Hey, Dave." Bob couldn't help but laugh as he deactivated the Mana shield. He moved around the console and moved to the portal.

It's been centuries since I've even seen a planet other than Emerilia. Bob took a shaky breath, a sad smile appearing on his face. He stepped through the portal without thinking of it and entered a dark room where Dave and Deia looked at Bob with large smiles. "Well, looks like it works. Seems that we've got a star system to colonize now." Bob grinned.

"We've got to get back to the rest of the party. You okay to take over the rest?" Dave asked.

"No worries. You guys have fun. I'll just manage a planet, a moonbase, and now a planetary base in another star system. Oh, and would you like me to set up a teleportation network across the star system as well?" Bob asked.

"That would be perfect. If you could start in the asteroid belt, we need some raw resources first of all. You know where the sensor units are, right?" Dave asked.

Bob let out a suffering sigh. "This is what I get for having a bleeder who's a damn rocket engineer." Bob shook his head.

Dave laughed. "Don't have all the fun without me. We'll be back soon enough."

"Not if I have anything to do with it!" Bob had a whole new star system that was open to play with. It was time to build!

Chapter 22: Quiet, Too Quiet

Josh, Lucy, and Koza, the leader of the Aleph security forces and their scouts, sat in Josh's office.

"We haven't been able to find any of the new spawn points," Koza said, a troubled look on his face.

"I haven't been able to find out anything through our different networks either," Lucy said. Both of them looked to Josh, who sat on the opposite couch with a frown on his face.

"Where the hell did they go? This can't be the last of the beings that came out of the prison," Josh thought out loud.

"We don't have a clear answer for that, but there is something odd going on." Lucy paused. Her eyebrows pinched together. She didn't like mysteries any more than the other two in the room. "It seems that while we haven't been able to find any spawn points that a number of quests have been appearing all over Emerilia of different kinds. Different towns and cities have been finding that they are having minor issues. When looking at just a few towns of elven kingdoms, then it doesn't seem to be too bad. However, when looking at all of Emerilia, there has been a sudden and large spike in odd issues coming up. I think that these different creatures and people who were imprisoned are being released in a totally random order. The frequency of these events has increased in number. I think that multiple spawn points are unleashing different prisoners across Emerilia."

"It is clear that the Jukal can activate the spawn points whenever they want to. They've only been putting the timer on them for interest. It wouldn't be hard for them to teleport people into Emerilia in sparse groups but all over the place. It would lead to multiple small confrontations. Reduce our numbers but make us stronger for the coming of the later groups," Koza said.

Josh sat forward in his seat, interlinking his fingers. "So our choices are to hold the Terra Alliance forces here, ready to react to something that might or might not come, or we let them go free for a bit to try to deal with all of these small quests?" Josh looked to the two who were the information leaders of the Terra Alliance.

"We've shown that in a fight we can pull together in a hurry. With all of these small issues, it's pulling people away from helping out the alliance and being ready for whatever might come next. If we let the guilds and the different people in the alliance go and deal with these quests, then they can help to reduce the pressure on the people of Emerilia," Lucy said.

Josh looked to his hands for a few minutes before he reached a decision.

"Okay, let the guilds run free and point them in the direction of the quests that deal with the biggest disturbances within Emerilia. All of this large war fighting hasn't allowed us to work in smaller party groups for some time. Will be good to have them do something different so that they're fresh when we have to fight larger groups," Josh said.

"I will have my people look into the different quests and we can see what we can do," Lucy promised.

"Good." Josh paused as a message appeared on his notifications. "Seems that Dave and Malsour are ready to spin up the second section of Terra. Want to go watch?"

"I have a lot of work to do," Lucy started.

"Look, we've been wrapped up in fights, planning, and getting all of this ready for months. What's five minutes to watch our little city grow a little bigger?" Josh asked.

Koza laughed. "When you put it that way, I would love to watch."

Lucy sighed and rolled her eyes. "I don't know how I get any work done around here. Sure, let's go and watch."

They headed out of the tower and toward where the second section of the city had been constructed.

"You going to see the second section?" Kim asked, seeing them along the way.

"Yeah. Cassie and Dwayne are there already with the rest of Party Zero and a bunch of others." Josh's smile came back as he was filled with excitement.

"It's really surprising how quickly you've been able to finish this second section of Terra," Koza said.

"Dave told me that the third section is going to be done even faster than the second," Kim added. "I'm stunned myself."

"Well, when we started on the second section, we had a lot more diggers and repair bots than we did with the first section. And we were also only starting to work with soul gem constructs. It's really a hybrid of Aleph ways of making a city and Dave's craziness matched with the soul gem constructs that have been turned into the different parts needed for the city. The third section will be much more simple, with soul gem constructs that go through the multiple outer layers of the rotating city. They will also take care of the different infrastructure needed within the city. We will have material supports to create the framework for them, but then they will grow over this superstructure to create towers, apartments, shops, gardens, power stations, and refineries. All of which will be capable of holding onto Mana. The entire city will be one massive battery," Lucy said.

"You don't ever like to think small, do you, Stone Raiders?" Koza laughed.

"Small is boring. World domination, however..." Kim said with an evil cackle.

"Seriously, if you're Brain, then who's going to be Pinky?" Josh asked.

"Ah, you look reasonably dumb and happy-go-lucky!" Kim grinned and winked.

"Thank you. I've always wanted to be compared to a cartoon mouse." Josh shook his head.

"Well, you made the reference." Kim waved to Dwayne, Jules, Esa, and Cassie, who were already waiting in a group next to the edge of the first section of the city.

"This doesn't look ominous at all," Josh said as they got closer. He walked up behind Cassie, who pulled his arms around her and leaned back into him.

Josh started sputtering.

"You okay?" Cassie looked back at him with a crooked eyebrow.

"Sorry, just—" Josh clawed at his tongue. "Tasting your hair. Is that a new conditioner?"

Cassie laughed, a mischievous light to her eyes as she turned and hit Josh in the face with her long white hair.

Josh tried to get the hair out of his face but Cassie continued to lean back into him and holding his arms around her, making it hard for him to get the hair out of his face. As he got some of it out of the way, she'd move her head again and get him in the face again.

"Mercy, mercy! I give up!" Josh said.

Cassie and the others laughed as their esteemed guildmaster was reduced to surrendering to his girlfriend's hair barrage.

Cassie flicked her hair out of Josh's face, turning so that she faced him. She put her mouth next to his ear and used a party chat so no one else could hear. "I love it when you beg." Cassie pressed up against him.

Josh looked around to make sure that no one had heard her as he looked down to her. "Well, little lady, what are you up to tonight?" Josh asked with a crooked smile.

"Hmm, well, I was looking to have some *fun,* but my boyfriend keeps on locking himself in his office." Cassie pouted and pulled at her lip.

Josh winced. He hadn't meant to but with the work that came with being the Stone Raiders' guildmaster, he had pushed Cassie away—not by choice, but it had still happened.

"Well, tonight I'm all yours." Josh tilted his head down as he put an arm around her back, pulling her close for a kiss as his other hand pushed away the hair on the right side of her face.

Their lips came together, heat spreading through their bodies. Josh opened his eyes to see an excited Cassie.

"Good!" She smiled, biting her lower lip in happiness as she turned around, once again leaning into Josh and holding his hands as they looked at what seemed to be nothing more than a cave.

"I still can't believe what Dave, Malsour, and Steve keep coming up with," Dwayne said as they continued to look into the darkness.

"With one move, we will double the size of Terra. Be nice to have some more room," Esa said.

"Don't think that it will be empty for long." Kim looked to Lucy.

"We've already got most of the units rented out and we're ready to purchase more teleport pads from the Aleph in order to place them down the length of Terra. Allowing people to move across Emerilia faster. We'll be able to allow more people to stay in Terra while also having more goods and more locations being connected more frequently," Lucy said.

"So it's going to remain a zoo for a while," Kim complained.

"I find it nice to have so many people in Terra—makes it feel more alive. I can't handle being all by myself with no one around," Jules said.

"My city girl." Esa smiled and grasped Jules's hand.

Josh watched them all as Party Zero joined them. They greeted one another. Josh couldn't help but keep looking at Steve. He now wore a simple set of hemp pants and shirt, with his massive Weapon of Power war axe on his back.

"So you thought to dim down the damn lighting?" Dwayne said upon seeing Steve. Instead of looking as if he were made from diamonds with swirling energy, he had made his body change colors until he now looked like a slightly tanned giant, but with faint tattoo-looking lines of compacted runes across his body and eyes that glowed with the power of the soul gems that made up his body.

"Well, I thought it might be for the best. Being a walking light show is a bit annoying," Steve said. "Disco anyone?"

"I swear, I'm still trying to blink out the light spots," Gurren complained. He and Lox were out of their Devastator armor. It was rare for them to leave it, but now that they were used to it, they spent more time outside of it, working on improving their own skills. Their own levels and abilities were amplified greatly by the armor, but it all relied on their own abilities. To take true advantage of their armor, they needed to continue to train past their limits.

"Is Malsour still off dealing with the Nalheim?" Kim asked.

"Yeah. Since they acknowledged him as the big shot, it seems that they're pretty hesitant to take orders from anyone else who hasn't proved their strength. The dragons, however, seem to have scared the ever-living shit out of them and have become the leaders of their race. It's going to be some time until they're all settled but they're loving the Densaou Ring of Fire. The dragons are trying to work to see that they value things other than their prowess and strength on the battlefield. It's going to be a long process but dragons are fine with playing the long game," Induca said.

"Bunch of big lizards with wings," Suzy said from beside her girlfriend, who bumped her with her hip.

Lights suddenly started to turn on within the second section of the city. The lights came on in groups as Mana flowed into the second section. A city was revealed, with different automated creations moving around to check various parts of the cylindrical city. The city seemed to be moving rather quickly.

"I didn't think that it would be rotating already," Josh said.

"It's not—we're rotating," Lucy said.

Josh looked to everyone, who had amused looks on their faces. "Oh," he said, connecting the dots. "I walked into that one, didn't I?"

"Little bit." Cassie smiled and looked up at Josh over her shoulder.

A deep rumbling could be felt as the second section of the city started to move. The pace at which the first section of the city moved seemed to slow down as the second section started to speed up.

Josh could sense the massive amount of Mana that was being expended in order to push the second city along.

It moved faster and faster, but to those in the already moving second city, it looked as if its rotation compared to the first city was only slowing down. The city sped up until it looked as though neither the first section nor the second section were actually moving as they rotated at the same speed.

Then the second section started to move slightly faster. The different streets and roads started to match up as well as the underground passages, sewer systems, and soul gem-coded pathways. The second section seemed to come to a stop, all of the roads and various parts matching up. There was still a two-foot gap between the rotating city sections.

As Josh watched, he saw the soul gem constructs and the different stone and metal grow out from their respective sections. It was like watching roots grow at high speed; they tangled themselves to-gether, fusing and becoming thicker and thicker.

The gap between the sections disappeared as the different link-ing materials, passages, and infrastructure connected and fused with one another. It took about ten minutes from beginning to end.

"You couldn't even tell that they were two different sections." Kim admired where the two massive city sections had been fused together.

Repair bots moved over the area, checking where the cities fused.

"That's one hell of a sight." Josh looked from the fuse point to the different parts of the second city that were coming alive.

The unfinished soul gem sections of the city were now drawing power from the soul gem constructs within the first section as well as the power generators and the power being transported from the power station facility.

He could see past the second section of the city and see the flashes that came from the drills made of light that were already cutting into what would be the third section of the city. There was no stopping progress and it looked as though Terra wasn't going to be slowing down anytime soon.

***

A few hours after the second section of Terra had been connected, the leaders of the Stone Raiders said that everyone was allowed to go out and take on whatever quest they desired. They had updat-ed their own quest boards. There were traders, mages, adventurers, kingdoms, empires, and even cities looking for Stone Raiders to carry out their various quests.

Malsour had taken a look at the different quests that were available within the guild as he walked to Pandora's box. It didn't take him long to reach the hidden laboratory.

Dave, Steve, and Bob were all looking at a star map that was projected in the middle of the laboratory. The different desks were the same organized chaos as always, with different workshops on either side of the main open laboratory. To the back right, there were the power sources and the rear had doors that would allow them to access the growing portal hub. Malsour, with his hearing, could pick out the carts that were moving from one portal to another, keeping their various projects going.

Getting the anchor to work in another system had allowed Dave to advance his Librarian as he had used his research to make the anchor, thus proving another theory.

Quest Completed: Librarian Level 5

Use research to prove a theory

Rewards: Unlock Level 6 Quest

+10 to all stats

500,000 Experience

Class: Librarian

Status: Level 4

       +40 to all stats

Effects: Read 5% faster

       Understand 10% more of the information that you read

Quest: Librarian Level 5

Use research to prove a theory (1/2)

Rewards: Unlock Level 5 Quest

Increase to stats

As such, his character sheet's stats had also increased.

Character Sheet

Name:	David Grahslagg	Gender:	Male
Level:	240	Class:	Dwarven Master Smith, Friend of the Grey God, Bleeder, Librarian, Aleph Engineer, Weapons Master, Champion Slayer, Skill Creator, Mine Manager, Master of Space and Time, Master of Gravitational Anomalies
Race:	Human/ Dwarf	Alignment:	Chaotic Neutral

Unspent points: 0

Health:	49,100	Regen:	24.22 /s
Mana:	15,930	Regen:	58.45 /s
Stamina:	5,420	Regen:	50.90 /s
Vitality:	491	Endurance:	1,211
Intelligence:	1,593	Willpower:	1,169
Strength:	542	Agility:	1,018

Although the extra stats were a nice boost, Dave was focused on the system that they had gained access to, rather than the fringe benefits of getting there.

"Hey, Malsour." Dave turned around slightly, playing with the beard at the end of his chin before he looked back to the map.

"What have you been up to?" Malsour looked at the projection.

"We're figuring out where to put our second portal within the Nalheim's home system," Bob said.

"So, this is their star system?" Malsour asked in an excited voice. He looked to the star system map that showed the orbiting planets and the sun at its center in real time.

"Yeah." Dave smiled, looking to Malsour, who looked at the hologram with rapt interest.

"Close your mouth—might have flies go in." Steve chuckled.

"So, we finally got scans of the system. What are we building first?" Malsour asked.

"That is the million-dollar question—well, billions or trillions if we get into the asteroid belt," Dave said.

"We need three things, really. One, we need metals to build various items and structures. Then we need organics to grow the soul gem constructs and we need helium-3 to be used as fuel within our reactors." Bob looked to Malsour and paused the star map.

"Here's the bind: we've got a gas planet here that we can pull multiple kinds of gas from and can refine out hydrogen. We need a hell of a lot of it to meet the demands for our fusion reactors. Right now, we don't have enough to keep the reactors we have going for more than four months. We've just expanded too quickly.

"We also need materials in order to keep up our production levels. Though there is a nice asteroid belt along the peripheral of the system that we can hide in to make all kinds of different projects, it's too far from the gas planet to make it feasible to get the needed hydrogen from it. Then we also need organic materials for different projects, including the project to grow those who are still within the Earth simulation," Dave said.

"And we can't get those organics from anywhere but Nal and some from the asteroids. But then that's going to require a lot of power and materials to make the coding to make sure that the Jukal don't see us," Steve said.

"Okay, so we do the gas planet first, get all of that going, then we start on the asteroids and then go back to Nal," Malsour said.

"That's what we're thinking but it also comes to our true issue." Dave looked to Malsour fully. "The Jukal have multiple different scanners looking into the gas planet. So we would have to use machines with massive stealth capacities and the ability to haul in that hydrogen, as well as a structure to hold the portal and power it while it's within the planet. We can't have machines going back and forth from the planet's orbit and back down. It would be easier to spot than hiding it within the gas cloud. We can program the factories to make what we need but it will take eight months before it's ready—and that's only with two harvesters as we don't have enough materials for more. Now, even with these two, we're going to get a lot of hydrogen."

"It'll be enough to keep the power on for another year at least," Bob interjected.

"Yes, but it's risky as hell," Dave said.

Malsour sensed that they had been arguing about this for a long time.

"Our second option is to put a portal on the true ice planet within the Nal system," Steve said to Malsour. "There's nothing watching it and it's stable, so that we don't need to create a structure to hold the portal in place. Also, we can use our miners that we have with some modifications in order to harvest the frozen hydrogen. It's much closer to the asteroids around the peripheral for mutual support at certain times of its orbit. There is a chance that we can maybe get some organics from the ice ball."

"However, it hasn't been scanned, so we're not sure how dense the hydrogen is going to be. So, we'd have to put a portal down, which would take up a month's stored energy to do, then scan the place," Bob said.

"From our spectral analysis, Steve's been getting decent readings of hydrogen being on the planet," Dave rebutted.

"However, this is a spectral analysis; I wasn't looking at specific regions of the planet, so it might be that we put down the portal in the middle of an area that is barren of the hydrogen we need," Steve said.

"So, it's a shot in the dark: we take months and most of our power and resources to hopefully mine the gas planet and possibly get caught, or we mine an ice planet using up most of our power for no guarantee of the materials we need." Malsour rubbed his neck. "Dealing with the Nalheim was easier than this."

"The ice planet is lower risk to our security and has the possibility of getting something. Steve, if you had more time and more information on the planet, could you maybe find us a decent region to land in?" Dave asked.

"I can get it within a few thousand kilometers probably," Steve said.

Dave looked to Bob and Malsour.

"It really is a shot in the dark, but with the gas planet, there's just too many things that might go wrong." Malsour looked to Bob.

Bob nodded and sighed. "Okay, well, it looks like we have our decision. Now let's see about putting a plan together." Bob knew that they weren't trying to gang up on him but rather using their own reasoning to work through the same problem as him. Now that a decision had been made, it was time for them to put all of their effort into seeing it through.

"Well, first, we need to make a teleportation array in Nal. Going to be a hell of a lot cheaper power-wise to move things from Nal than here in Emerilia," Dave said.

"I swear, these teleports are trying to make me blind," Bob muttered.

Malsour looked at Bob oddly before he shook his head. "All right, I'll help you out," Malsour said.

"I'll see if I can find a region with a high possibility of having hydrogen within it," Steve said.

With that, they got to work. Dave, Malsour, and Bob all went to the different factories, getting as many parts of the teleportation array made as possible. But still, some of them had to be made by hand so it wasn't long till they were at a table with carvers at hand with ebony sheets and molten silver in front of them.

"So, how are things going with the Nalheim?" Dave asked as they worked. The noise of carvers filled the laboratory as they worked.

"Slowly. They're aggressive as hell, but we can work on it. Right now they understand that they're not as strong as us so they're not acting out; however, it isn't abnormal for them to fight over the smallest of things. We're trying to introduce the idea of bartering and work, so that we can cut down on all of the fighting. That said, they've already started to build their homes and are working to bring back their race. They have broods instead of just single births, similar to dragons, so their population should swell up within a few months and take a few years for them to start being able to do more than just survive. They've made it clear that they want to fight beside me and that would mean that they would have to join the Terra Alliance. I'm not against it; it's their choice. But their race is really weak right now." Malsour sighed.

"As you said, this is their decision, not yours," Bob said. "We can lead people along what we see as the right path, but as to if they'll take our advice and go down that path? No one can predict that."

For a time, only the carvers could be heard as they moved through hand-carved sheet after hand-crafted sheet.

"So, what are our plans for the Nalheim home system?" Malsour asked.

"Set up an industrial node," Dave said.

"There we don't have to deal with things like building items on a planet or a planetary body. When we're building items in space, it will speed it up a lot more. Without the need for so much security, we can speed up all of the projects there and take the pressure off the projects we have going on in Emerilia." Bob smiled.

"We can also work to link the systems together more and, if at all possible, we can start making bases there that will be able to sustain the people we send to them," Dave said.

"We're thinking of waking up the people in the Earth simulation earlier," Bob said.

"What?" Malsour ruined the rune he had been making as he looked to the other two.

"Look, right now there's just us three who are running the tech and logistics of this all. Sure, the leaders of the Stone Raiders know what's going on and the Aleph have figured out that the Jukal are the real people running this world, but we need more people on our side. If we have people who are players right now or even people of Emerilia, then they're going to think that we're nuts. What we need is a group of people we can come to rely on. We also need to start getting people ready to fight a battle in space to hold Emerilia, not just one where we fight hand-to-hand," Dave said.

"So, you're going to wake them up? What about Sato and all of his people?" Malsour demanded. Waking up the people who were in the simulation was a risky idea. Sure, it could pay off and he wanted to free them of that prison that was called Earth. Though, just like putting a portal in the gas planet, it could throw all of their plans into jeopardy. And right now, Emerilia wasn't exactly the safest place; adding in the threat of the Jukal raining down hell on their heads did not instill him with confidence.

"Sato and his people seem to have been making leaps and advances. However, we don't know where the hell they are and it doesn't look like they're going to be of much help to us. They've been hiding for hundreds of years. Expecting them to come to our aid—I don't think it's something that we can rely on." Dave shrugged.

"I hope that you have some way of covering this up? So that you don't trip the AIs that are running the Earth simulation?" Malsour asked.

"Well, that is something that Bob came up with." Dave looked to the gnome, who had a crafty smile on his face.

"It's rather easy. We make the computers all think that all of the people are just like Dave and his Austin counterpart in the simulation," Bob said.

Malsour frowned. Having all the same person would just make the world ridiculous. "Huh?"

"What Bob means is that he can take the data surrounding me and Suzy to trick the AIs in the other simulations to create bleeders. They will automatically start controlling our avatars in order to maintain stability. They would just be tricking themselves into thinking that every person is still within the simulation as they're simulating it themselves," Dave said.

"Wouldn't that, you know, trip something?" Malsour asked.

"Well, I'm still here and they haven't figured out that I'm not going back to Earth, or that Suzy is, for that fact," Dave said.

Malsour frowned as he thought it over. It was one hell of a plan. *Though is he right that he and Suzy haven't been discovered? Will it hold up with so many people?* "It might be a good idea to do it at a slow pace at first."

"Agreed. Well, we couldn't pull them all out at the same time anyway," Bob said. "Remember that organic matter? Well, we need a hell of a lot of it before we can even think about having more people being born."

"How are we going to educate them and let them know about all of this?" Malsour waved his hands to encapsulate all of Emerilia.

"We'll show them what's going on and what happened to them; then we see if we can get Sato to help us out. We get them to understand what's going on and then we allow them access to the Mirror of Communication schools. We teach them everything and anything. We give them a purpose and a way to fight against the Jukal. They will also have interfaces. However, if they die, then they will be just like the POE—they'll be gone."

"We don't know enough about the Altars of Rebirth to totally recreate them. With their first body, we're just printing a body around a brain—much easier than creating it all from scratch and inserting all the right bits so that it's seamless," Bob said.

Malsour shook his head. Bob said it as if it were the most natural thing in the world, but the sheer scope of what they were trying to do was finally starting to seep into Malsour's mind. "Okay, so, what's going to happen with the people who don't want to help out?"

"Well, that's part of the reason that we need to get those materials. We need to make a ship that can travel across Jukal space and find a system far outside. We can set up an outpost there. It will be connected by a portal that can be destroyed by either side. This way, people can have the time that they need to decompress from finding out everything about their lives and the lie of what they thought was Earth. Also, if they make products that are useful to us, then we can trade with them. Having people who are motivated to help out are the best. If someone hates what they're doing, then they're not going to be putting their best effort forward. We're not here to make it so that we force them into doing something they don't want to. After all, that's what the Jukal have been doing," Dave said.

"However, these people have been conditioned for years—they've been raised by the AI to be adventurous to want to play video games. If you were given the option of being in your very own video game world or to just hide out somewhere, what would you do?" Bob asked.

Dave scratched his head, thinking on Bob's words.

"We've seen it with players that roughly ten percent of them *don't* want to actually get involved in a game. The other ninety percent get so into it that they usually become E-heads within the thirty years that they're in the game for. They're more prone to be impulsive; however, they think through their actions to a high degree and they are fine with violence as long as it serves a purpose or it fits with their ideals and interests. So, while you think that there might be a large portion of the people who try to get away from it all, the fact of the matter is that I think you'll be surprised with the number of people who actually get involved and are driven to help out with fighting the Jukal," Bob finished.

"What you say makes a lot of sense, but it makes me feel as if we're using them," Dave said.

"As Bob said, this is their life. Once they're out here in Emerilia, then they can start to figure out what they want to do," Malsour said.

"In the meantime, this new teleportation array isn't going to make itself! Let's get to it!" Bob said, filled with excitement.

"I think I found the area with the highest possibility of having hydrogen on the planet. However, I'm just running off a simple spectral analysis, which, while it is good, the images that we do have aren't the best quality," Steve said.

Malsour tried to clamp down on his excitement. But if they could get that hydrogen—well, then they would be set to move on with the rest of their plans!

"Well, we could use a hand with putting the rest of this teleportation array together," Dave said.

"There really is no end to this all with you lot." Steve moved to the table they were working at.

"Have you told the rest of Party Zero and the Stone Raiders' leadership about everything in the Nal system and the various bases?" Bob asked.

"We've gone over it in general terms but we haven't gotten in-depth into it all," Dave said.

"We trust them, but the fact is that we have a lot of secrets right now. If one of them gets out, then the whole thing will come back on us," Steve said.

Malsour nodded in agreement.

"I understand. Reminds me that we should have a talk with Sato and his people," Bob said.

"I'm interested what they've gotten up to with all the information on the soul gem constructs. Hey, we could run our spectral analysis through their systems to see if they can figure out where that hydrogen is," Dave said.

"Saying I'm not enough?" Steve huffed. "Though, they've probably got way more computing power than I do, so it makes sense."

Malsour rolled his eyes. "Once we've got the portals and the different items into place, there's not much for us to do. I think that the rest of Party Zero is interested in going and doing some of the quests available to the guild."

"Been awhile since we've carried out a quest. Be kind of nice to do a low-level quest. Hell, I'd be fine with a fetch quest or a simple clearing one," Dave said.

"Anything that gets me out of this padded room with you lot, I'm in for," Steve said.

"Thanks, Steve," Bob drawled.

***

Jekoni floated at the edge of the training arena; a book floated in front of him, the pages moving with a wave of his hand. Jung Lee was in the middle of the arena, moving through different positions. His sword flashed in different colors as he moved.

Deia cleared her throat as she entered the sparring area. Little Koi was in the crook of her arm, looking around the arena with wide eyes, trying to see everything, and her mouth open as her head moved from side to side in starts.

Induca was with her.

"Deia, Induca," Jung Lee said in greeting to the two, a smile on his face as he looked at little Koi. He waved for them to join him at a bench near Jekoni.

The archmage looked up, his hat waving before he looked back down at his book.

"Jung Lee, it seems that you've become a part of Party Zero rather easily, but we've realized that we haven't talked about what you want to do. We've just been kind of rolling with everything," Deia said.

"There hasn't been much time to take a break," Jung Lee agreed with a small smile.

Deia returned the smile as she shifted Koi around a bit.

"We're planning on going to try out some of these quests that are popping up all over Emerilia and we wanted to see what you wanted to do—if you wanted to stay with the party or go do something on your own. Even if you want to do something on your own and still remain part of the party, that would be fine. We've done plenty of things with just a few people from the party—we don't always need to be with one another," Induca said.

Jung Lee tilted his head, looking into the distance, thinking. "My levels are very high and so is my power. However, I still haven't been able to come to understand it all. Jekoni has been helping me to understand the power of the Free Affinity spirits that have submitted to my command. While he is able to help me in controlling the powers and understanding them, my fighting style is primarily with the sword and with potions. I have focused on these aspects rather than coming to understand magic." Jung Lee's face wrinkled in frustration. "There is also the fact that the Affinity spirits, while they can supply me with their magic and help to augment my abilities, they are essentially creatures under my command. Much like how Lu Lu is under Suzy's control."

"So, you're having an issue with understanding your new abilities?" Deia asked, wanting to confirm.

"Precisely." Jung Lee nodded.

Induca and Deia looked to each other as Koi started to try to grab her mother's hair.

"As for fighting with Affinities through weapons, you, Ela-Gal, and Anna would be the best. Then, for coming to understand the Free Affinity spirits, well, we can probably ask Suzy, or one of the summoners, beast tamers, or necromancers," Induca said.

Deia nodded, rescuing her hair from Koi before she started to pull on it.

"Anna is back in Devil's Crater again, looking over the DCA. She would be the best as she not only has wind magic but a greater understanding of other magic types. With her analytical mind, she can probably figure out what Jung Lee needs help in the most," Deia agreed before she turned back to Jung Lee. "Okay, so that should sort out training, but training isn't everything. What else do you want to do? Do you want to stay with Party Zero or make your position within the Stone Raiders official or do you want to do your own thing?"

"I like being with the Stone Raiders. You've accepted me without a second thought and Party Zero has helped me out more than I could hope for. I would like to become a Stone Raider and stay with Party Zero, if at all possible. However, I have a passion for alchemy and creating potions. To this end, I wanted to see if I could meet with the healers of the Stone Raiders as well as visit the mage's college to see how far potion making has come." An excited smile covered Jung Lee's face as his eyes seemed to shine.

Deia laughed. "We're just your party, not your parents. You can do whatever you want to do! If you want to make potions, go for it! I know that Jules would be happy to have a master potion maker helping her out with her various potion stores."

"And the markets in Terra have the best ingredients one could desire. It wouldn't be hard for you to make whatever kind of potions you desired," Induca added.

Jekoni cleared his throat and gave Jung Lee a pointed look.

Jung Lee had an embarrassed look on his face as he averted his eyes from the two ladies.

"Is something the matter?" Deia looked from Jekoni to Jung Lee.

"You going to tell her or will I?" Jekoni said.

"I will, you old coot." Jung Lee waved Jekoni away.

"Hey, I'm only a few decades older than you!" Jekoni complained. His hat flopped down. "Don't you start, too!" Jekoni started to berate and fight with his hat as it flopped all over the place while Jekoni whizzed through the courtyard.

"The problem is that I have no money," Jung Lee said, as if Jekoni and his hat fighting around the courtyard wasn't happening.

"Well, we could loan it to you." Induca shrugged.

"I don't like to borrow money from other people." Jung Lee winced slightly.

"Damn stubborn idiotic honor-bound jackass! And you can piss off and all, hat!" Jekoni flew by, still in a valiant fight with his hat.

Deia and Induca looked to each other and shrugged. They'd seen weirder things than a spiritual projection of a long dead archmage fighting with his magical and sentient hat.

"Well, there is no need to borrow from us. We can get Lucy to confirm your acceptance into the Stone Raiders. From there, you will be allowed access to all of the Stone Raiders' resources, including the quest board. We're going to Ecora, a city that's part of the Strabon kingdom on the Ashal continent. There's a quest to look into missing people. The reward is pretty good—should be enough to get you some supplies. If you don't feel like doing that, then there are many fetch quests, or even transporting goods. With the Stone Raiders' reduced fee for their members when using the teleport pads and onos, traders are willing to pay a good price for Stone Raiders to transport their goods for them," Deia said.

Jung Lee nodded. They might not be the most glamorous jobs but if he could grind a number of them out, then he could purchase the various ingredients that he would need and be able to support his profession.

"Yeah, with more and more of the sea creatures showing up, trade by water is decreasing. I'm glad we got that second section of the city. We've got so many people moving goods through Terra it's getting a bit crazy," Induca said.

"You've given me a lot to think on. I will look into this quest board." Jung Lee was relieved now that he had picked a path toward his future goals.

"Everything is calm right now, but remember that things can change in an instant," Induca warned.

"Indeed, it does feel like things have been a little too calm in the last few weeks," Jung Lee said with a troubled expression.

The atmosphere grew cold.

Koi ruined it and started to cry.

"Seems that someone is hungry." Deia scratched under Koi's chin. Koi continued to cry, as if in agreement. "Well, I'll see you both later. Seems this little miss won't take no for an answer!"

"See you later," Induca and Jung Lee said.

***

A man-shaped statue that seemed to have been carved from trees, rocks, and dirt sat on top of a throne made from interwoven trees.

A green glow filled the room, creating a series of magical formations that filled the air. A hobgoblin adorned with feathers, bracelets, and other ornaments bowed in front of the statue.

The statue shifted and opened his eyes. It was the Earth Lord!

The hobgoblin didn't dare to raise his head or talk in the presence of this god.

"The preparations are complete?" The Earth Lord looked to the hobgoblin.

It chittered in the positive, still not raising its head.

"Good. We will start with Quidil." From the ground, flowers seemed to bloom. The flowers opened to reveal sprites inside.

These sprites were made from green, almost emerald material. Their bodies looked like corded wood pushed into a human shape. Each of them were around three meters tall and wore darker green armor that covered their bodies, only allowing their glowing green eyes to be visible. They had axes, swords, bows, and magical staffs.

"Go support the conquest. Raise your levels and power. If you are going to die, flee—do not keep fighting. Report to me when you need more support. I will send more sprites to join you and level up," the Earth Lord said to his sprites, cutting the hobgoblin off so that he couldn't hear his words.

The sprites all bowed, unable to talk naturally.

The Earth Lord raised his hand. Spell formations appeared around the sprites and the hobgoblin leader. "Go!" With a wave of his hand, green light formed over the eleven creatures. As the light disappeared, the cavern once again returned to silence. The Earth Lord gazed into a pool of water off to the side of the cavern surrounded by trees that moved out of the way.

Through the water, he could see the vision of hundreds of creatures racing through forests or engaged in battle.

The Dark Lord and Lady of Light might be reassured in their forces. I will let them fight it out at the end of this war as I collect my lost power.

The Earth Lord's bulk shifted slightly as he rested his head against his hand, gazing into the pool. A horde of goblins appeared in a number of the different ripples that made up the viewing pool.

***

"I am free!" a woman yelled as she raised her hands up into the air in excitement. Her eyes glowed red as her teeth extended into spikes and her hands into claws as wings sprouted from her back. She was a beautiful woman, in her prime and with looks that would draw anyone's eye.

Behind her, nearly a hundred other people wearing black clothes accented in red appeared. All of them had red eyes, as well as wings and claws. Their eyes flicked around before settling down. Seeing that they were safe, their features reverted, making them appear almost human. Each of them was stunningly beautiful and handsome; they looked like a family of models. Each of them had a noble and powerful aura about them, as if they totally controlled the space in which they were in.

"Mother, what shall we do?" a sturdily built man with rippling muscles that augmented his looks instead of making him look hefty asked.

"We will move slow. It might have been a day since we were caught in that prison; it might be a millennia," the woman addressed as "Mother" said.

"We will stay here?" One of the women looked in disgust at the surrounding area. They were within some city's sewer system.

"We were banished once and we have been given a chance. We must move slowly and cautiously to regain our lost power and position." Their mother looked to the others.

These noble-looking people nodded assent, all of them looking to please their "mother."

"Now go, and find out what this world has to offer. Gilez, Durnst—stay."

The nearly one hundred pale-looking individuals turned into shadows, disappearing in moments.

Only three people remained: the mother, Gilez, and Durnst, the large man who had spoken first.

"Durnst, I sense another powerful practitioner of the Dark arts. Go look for them and see what their desires are. We are weak right now and must recover our strength quickly."

"Yes, Mother." Durnst bowed slightly, shadows wrapping around him. It seemed he had teleported as the shadows disappeared, as did any sign of him.

"Gilez, we will make a home here," the mother said.

Gilez nodded. The two of them looked like sisters with looks that would make many people's minds go blank.

Dark Mana circulated around them as they directed their power at the area around them. The sewer walls started to firm up, the cracks and breaks fusing back together into one solid whole. A doorway appeared in one of the walls. Gilez threw out Mana torches that landed in holders on either side of the doorway. Past the doorway, they created a long corridor of stone.

It stopped at some solid gates of metal before continuing past and branching into various rooms. They walked through what they had created, adding torches as they reached the weaving corridors.

With a wave of their hands, stone and metal bent to their will, expanding outward to create a truly massive open underground area. Gilez and the mother were both panting as they completed this area. They had moved thousands of tons of material in just a few short minutes. They had also had to work to push the material not just upward but outward so that a massive hill didn't just appear in the ground.

"I have burned a lot of my remaining blood essence," Gilez said.

"This is the strength and weakness of our people. With enough blood essence, we can use it to manipulate our Dark Mana to carry out spells and actions well above our level, but we burn blood essence to live and to carry out our magic. We will have to try to harvest some more blood essence in the near future." The mother pulled out a ruby-colored stone that she passed to Gilez and popped another in her own mouth, swallowing it down.

Her power increased a hundred times with swallowing that gem. Gilez, too, stood a bit taller, her vitality returning to her as her eyes flashed red for a moment.

In the stone cavern, metal and stone started to spiral out of the ground and formed into a massive castle that reached up to the top of the open space and was rooted deep below the floor of the area.

By the end of it, Gilez was slightly sweating, her pale features becoming clammy.

The castle was something that only people on Malsour's level could make in one sitting. However, these two had been able to make it in one shot, speaking of their innate power.

"Looks just like our old home," Gilez said, sadness in her voice.

"Do not worry, Gilez. This time we will not be broken apart and hunted down like dogs. We were cursed with the affliction of needing blood essence to survive; we will not allow it to be the root of our destruction," the mother said. "When the others return, I want you to lead hunting parties to hunt down creatures for their blood essence."

"Mother, the creatures might be strong but few of them are as powerful as the players and the people of Emerilia." Gilez was one of the few who would dare to even possibly sound as if she disagreed with the mother.

"Our hunting and feeding on people is what led to them turning against us and hunting us down, turning into a war between us and the people of Emerilia. The Dark Lord might have supported us in a limited way, but make no mistake—it was only as he hoped to gain more power from us," the mother said.

"You want us to ally ourselves with the people of Emerilia?" Gilez asked.

"I want to see if this time we don't need to fight one another. I do not wish to see any more of my family lost to wars and battles that could be avoided." The mother moved toward the large castle, its massive gates opening before her.

The mother and her clan were not the only people to return to Emerilia, but the majority of them decided to lay low in order to try to figure out what had happened to Emerilia while they were gone.

Chapter 23: Sightings

Lucy finished reading the report in front of her. "It looks like I was right." She sighed to herself as she dismissed the screen and opened up a private chat with Josh.

"What's up?" Josh answered a few moments later.

"The creatures and people are being released into Emerilia still. They look to be centered around cities for the most part. Many of them are being hidden away in different corners. Looks like the Jukal game masters didn't like us getting to the spawn points early and cutting down on the collateral damage," Lucy said.

"What happened?" Josh's voice hardened as he braced himself for the news.

"At Emkari, there had been a number of reported missing people in the surrounding areas. It seems that there were a large number of wraiths that had spawned around the town. At night, they attacked the outlying communes, farms, and travelers. In the day, they hid. Last night, they swarmed in toward the main city. Thankfully, someone saw them early on and they figured out what they were. A big fight ensued but the wraiths barely passed by the walls, making it through and descending upon the civilians of the town to devour their life force and build up their own strength.

"The city was able to kill them off, but there is only a third of the population left in the town," Lucy said.

"Shit," Josh said. Neither of them spoke for a while.

"There's nothing that we could have done. By the time we knew what was going on, the people of Emkari were already fighting off the wraith," Lucy said, trying to console him.

"We have all of these fighters here but we weren't even able to stop a flood of wraiths." Josh let out a heavy breath.

"Well, it makes it clear that people's defenses aren't as good as they could be. Already people are working to reinforce their cities. They can't rely on us all the time," Lucy said.

"I know, but I still feel responsible," Josh said.

"Well, stop. We've got our own battles to fight and trying to put out every little fire is just going to tear the alliance apart."

"Thanks, Lucy. I needed to hear someone say it, but these decisions aren't easy," Josh said with a dry laugh.

***

Dave frowned at Deia as he bounced Koi in his arms. "I know that there's no way in hell that I can stop you from going out on a quest, and I'm wrapped up in things here so I can't leave." Dave's features softened as he smiled and put out his hand.

Deia held it, a relieved smile on her face. She didn't want to have a fight with Dave but she wanted to get stronger and do something. Quests were good for experience and it got her out of Terra for a bit.

"Take care."

"I will," she promised, kissing Dave quickly.

"And try not to get into too much trouble!"

"Me? Get into trouble? I don't even want to know half of the things you're doing down in Pandora's that could get you in trouble." Deia snorted.

Dave smiled sheepishly.

"I'll see you in a few days hopefully." Deia grabbed her bag of holding and put it on her back.

"Okay." Dave smiled.

She gave him another kiss and gently kissed Koi, who was sleeping on her father's shoulder. With that, she quickly left the apartment and headed out to meet the rest of Party Zero who were joining her on the quest.

She felt butterflies in her stomach as she left behind Dave and Koi. She was happy to be around them but she also wanted adventure. While Dave was working on whatever he was doing in Pandora's box, he could also look after Koi.

"Okay, let's go see what's happening in Ecora!" Deia said.

Induca, Gurren, and Lox were all waiting in their various armors with their various items of holding filled and ready to go.

"To Strabon kingdom!" Gurren, in his Devastator armor, raised his fist into the air in a valiant manner as they walked through Terra and toward the teleport pad that would take them to the city of Ecora.

***

Party Zero immediately drew stares as they exited the ono in Ecora. The teleportation network was still growing. Its cost was extremely high and although the Aleph were faster than anyone else, it still took them a lot of time to create the onos.

"Looks like we have to go to the city manor and talk to the mayor's steward to get this quest." Deia checked her quest log.

"Lead on," Induca said.

They moved out from where the ono was located. Ecora was a decent sized town, based in the Strabon kingdom on Ashal. The city was a base for people and players who were looking to venture into the Ashal wilderness in order to harvest the precious materials of the land—from herbs and spices to ores and trees or to fight the great beasts of the wilderness, selling their meat, bones and hide at Ecora.

The city was filled with high-leveled people. Most of them had a rugged, hardy look to them. It took a certain kind of person to come out to Ashal in order to try to make a living. Unlike many of the other towns that were on the other continents, there weren't many children around. Instead, there were taverns, blacksmiths, traders, and the three main guilds.

Food that was sold here was dried and salted for people who were headed out into the wilderness again. All of the farming took place within the city walls, taking up most of the space. If these farms were to be outside of the city walls, then those who tended to them would be killed off by the beasts that roamed around long ago.

There were only two gates out of the city. One led to Iudarai, the capital of the Strabon kingdom. The other led to Iagadas, the port city where the first settlers of the Strabon kingdom had landed. With the arrival of the various sea beasts, sea travel had become harder and harder, making it so that the travel to Iagadas had decreased.

With the ono in both Iagadas and Ecora, there was little need to make the dangerous trek to Iudarai to transport their goods to different continents in order to make a higher profit. The area around the ono had the heaviest traffic in the town.

Most of the houses within Ecora were made from stone, as were their walls. This made their city much more expensive material-wise compared to other cities, but also easier to defend as there were fewer items to be burnt, and they offered greater protection. The beasts of Ashal didn't just move along the ground. They could come from the skies; having a beast unleash Air or Fire attacks from above wasn't uncommon.

Massive defensive works and twin gates ringed the town. The small town had defenses that could compare to the walls around Nadorf, the capital of Opheir.

People talked to one another, watching Party Zero. In Ashal, strength was praised and weakness shunned. Many of the people in Ecora could tell that they were a strong party. Even if they had lower levels than those that grinded out experience. They had an aura that made others treat them with respect.

It didn't take them long to reach the city manor. It was built more like a miniature castle than a government building. In fact, all of the larger homes within Ecora were also like small castles, even having their own defensive walls.

Guards watched them with cold eyes as they went into the manor.

"Hello. We're here from the Stone Raiders' guild to take on a quest given out by the city's mayor." Deia moved to the main desk within the front of the castle.

To Deia's eye, she could see this desk might also be used as a barricade for archers to fire over or melee types to use to defend their legs.

A beefy-looking man studied them all before he let out a grunt of praise. "There is no need to see the mayor. I can award you the quest myself," the man said in a deep voice.

I would think that he would make more sense to be a guard captain leader than a secretary. There really are none who are faint of heart in the Ashal continent.

Even though Party Zero and the Stone Raiders had been on the Ashal continent for some time, they had been dealing with the Six Affinities Temple or Devil's Crater; they hadn't had time to go to the other nations or cities on the continent.

A screen appeared in front of Deia and the rest of Party Zero.

Quest: Sightings and Disappearances

Animals have been going missing from around town and there have been fewer creatures in the wilderness around Ecora. A number of people who were drinking have also disappeared; people in cloaks have been seen moving through the forests outside of Ecora.

Find out what is taking these people and animals and report it to the Ecora Mayor for his decision.

Failure:

All of the party dies without completing the quest

Do not find the cause of the disturbances

Rewards: 15,000 Gold

Experience

Strabon Kingdom's Favor

"What's this Strabon kingdom's favor?" Deia looked up from the quest.

"It's a token that you can use to enter any city within the kingdom for free. It will also give you a discount at many of the businesses within the Strabon kingdom and their cities," the secretary said, not sounding interested in the slightest.

"Do you have somewhere that we could start looking for information on these disappearances?" Induca asked.

"The farmers and maybe the people who work in the sewers. Though the farmers are more likely to give you an earful of not much use. They lost their animals and they're all annoyed about it." The secretary rolled his eyes. "Trust me, they're just going to tell you the same crap and demand someone pays for the animals they lost."

"Thanks for the advice," Gurren said.

"No worries. Hopefully you can stop them from annoying me about their prize-winning bear hog." The secretary snorted.

"Thank you for the information. Hopefully we should have this sorted out quickly," Deia said.

"Good luck." The secretary returned to his work as Party Zero turned around and started to leave the city manor, now with markers on their map that highlighted the farmers and the people who went into the city sewers a lot. The sewers were the only place someone might be able to hide within the city. If they weren't there, then they must be outside of the city, which would make Party Zero's work harder.

"Okay, so off to see the people who work in the sewers?" Lox asked.

"Just a moment. Dave taught me his Touch of the Land spell. My version isn't as strong as his, but I want to test it out," Deia said.

"Well, let's go to somewhere that doesn't have so many people in it," Induca said.

They quickly moved away from the main roads and to an alleyway out of the way. Gurren and Lox blocked off either side so that Deia could concentrate.

She muttered a few words as a spell formation formed a sphere around her. It seemed to solidify before expanding outward. It only went a few feet before the lights for the spell formation seemed to dissipate. Although the formation couldn't be seen, Deia now saw the world in a completely different view.

She let out a breath. She could see and sense everything within three hundred meters of her. This kind of information overload, the power that she felt at seeing this all, was similar to when she tapped into her true magical power.

It was almost god-like.

She looked into the sewers, unable to find anything significant.

"Let's go around the city so that I can build up a map of this place," Deia said. Right now their map only consisted of the maps that they had combined. By using Deia's own findings from her

Touch of the Land, they'd be able to get a clear picture of not only the city but everything underneath it.

Night descended by the time they had completed mapping out the city.

"Looks like there are a number of ways in and out of the city through the sewers. Maybe the people who work in the sewers can help us out," Deia said.

"Just so happens that they're all in taverns for the most part," Gurren said, as if a wise sage passing on priceless knowledge.

"Indeed, it does seem that way," Lox said. A split seemed to appear in the back of his Devastator armor as he stepped out and onto the ground. With a wave of his hand, his armor disappeared into a spatial ring he wore.

Deia didn't say anything as Lox and Gurren, now out of their armor, followed them toward where the sewer workers were hanging out in the taverns. They entered the tavern Deia was supposed to meet with the sewer workers at.

"They're haunted, I tell you—flickering lights, whispering voices. Place gives me the chills. Need to get a different job," one of the sewer workers confided to Deia. She filed it away as they moved to another tavern with more sewer workers.

"Ah, I can show you the sewers if you want, lass, but I know there's something else you want." One of them grabbed between his legs and shook his hips at Deia.

He didn't see Induca's punch that hit him in the face like a freight train. His teeth flew out as he fell to the ground.

People cheered around the room. Seemed they didn't like a braggart trying to pull one over on a lady either.

The rest, cowed by Induca's actions, said that they'd heard odd things, whispers and the like, or thought that there were others down there, but nothing out of the ordinary.

They left the taverns, Lox and Gurren singing songs. Induca and Deia moved to the residential areas. They went to four different homes where the workers lived; two were asleep while the others said things similar to the ones in the tavern.

"One last sewer worker to go," Induca said.

"Why the hell is he so far away from everyone else?" Gurren complained as they moved through the streets.

Deia frowned as they reached their destination.

"You're saying that our sewer dude is in there?" Lox said as they looked at a stone warehouse. They didn't pause to look at it, instead following Deia, who continue to walk past.

"With the Touch of the Land spell, I can see a crude entrance to the sewers. I think there's a bit more going on here," Deia said.

"Lox, Gurren—you get into one of the other buildings and keep a watch. Induca and I will use stealth to try to check out the inside of this place and see what's going on," Deia said.

"Can do." Lox and Gurren headed off to find a perch around the warehouse.

Deia and Induca activated stealth and their stealth spells, and moved back toward the warehouse where the sewer worker was.

"What do you think, boss?" a thin man asked, his face and body covered in scars, as he looked at the man with a hovering way point above him.

"Good," the sewer worker who had been called boss said.

There were twenty or so others, all of them looking excitedly at the boss, who was looking over small vials of purple liquid.

He tossed one of the vials to the thin man, who eagerly caught it, a look of happiness on his face. Immediately the man opened the vial and drank deeply from it. He finished the vial in one go as the boss closed the case of vials.

The thin man shook from his head to his toes, a look of ecstasy on his face.

"Make sure that this gets to Iudarai. Everything that goes through Terra is checked by those damn Stone Raiders." The boss man looked to the others within the room.

"Yes, boss!" the others replied. Within the warehouse were three trader's carts with various items of holding adorning them.

"So, what's our play?" Induca asked, using their party chat so no one else could hear them.

"Well, seems that this is illegal in some kind of way. I say that we get our hands on that sewer worker, ask him a few questions and figure out what the hell is going on here," Deia said.

"What's up?" Lox asked through the party chat, unable to see what they were seeing.

"The sewer worker seems to be in charge of a gang of some kind that is moving what looks like to be illegal potions from here to Iudarai," Induca said.

They waited above the warehouse. The gang members moved more crates from the hole that was in the corner of the warehouse that led down to the sewers. These were loaded onto the carts that were attached to horses. It took a few hours. As this was going on, the sewer worker left the warehouse, leaving the final preparations to the others.

He had two bodyguards following him. They wore simple clothes and could be thought of as his friends for anyone who wasn't watching them carefully.

"Lox, Gurren—make sure that those two don't escape and warn the others." Deia and Induca moved along the rooftops, while Lox and Gurren, in their armor, moved up an adjacent street.

"Got it," Lox said.

"Okay, let's do this." Deia launched herself into the air. Induca followed her as Lox and Gurren ran through an alleyway.

One of the guards looked upward and saw Deia. He let out a warning yell as he tried to pull a weapon from inside his cloak.

A fireball exploded, the pressure from the explosion directed at the guard, sending them flying backward. As Deia landed, she blocked the leader's punch with her forearm. Her other hand moved so fast that the man didn't have any time to react as it smashed into his face, making him take a dazed step backward. She pivoted on her foot; her leg swept up and hit the man in the ribs with a crunch.

Lox backhanded the guard who Deia's fireball had propelled sideways while Induca created an explosion behind the other guard, throwing them forward and at her. Her fist jabbed outward and hit the man in the head. He dropped to the ground, rolling a bit, knocked out cold from her hit.

Lox and Gurren quickly bound the guards and gagged them. Deia did the same to their boss. They collected up their prisoners and headed to an empty warehouse a few blocks away.

It was a few minutes after they had secured the guards and their boss in the warehouse before they started to show signs of coming around.

The "sewer worker" looked at them with anger and smug confidence in his eyes.

Induca pulled the rag from his mouth.

He laughed at seeing them all. "You don't know what you've all done. Once my master learns of this, you'll all die!" the man said with complete confidence, an ugly look upon his face.

"Who is your master?" Deia asked.

"Not who, but what." The man sneered.

"What are they?" Induca asked.

"You will see soon enough!" the man said, a crazed light in his eyes.

Deia looked to Induca. She put the gag back into the man's mouth none too gently.

"We need to find out what's in those carts," Deia said in party chat.

"Nothing to do but steal one of them. We need more proof of what's going on before we can take this to the mayor," Lox said.

"Fine," Deia said. "Lox, Induca—stay here. Gurren, you're with me."

They returned to the warehouse only to find that the carts were gone.

"Crap, the sun is coming up. They must have moved toward the city gates. Use the Touch of the Land spell!" Gurren said.

Deia cast the spell but she couldn't find the carts. "I can't find them. Let's move toward the gate that leads to Iudarai." She and Gurren ran toward the gate.

"I found them!" Deia yelled excitedly, finding the cart after her third Touch of the Land she had cast.

The carts were just a few of a multi-cart procession that was moving from Ecora to Iudarai.

"Okay, I'll get in and see if I can steal a bag of holding with the vials in it," Deia said.

"I'll wait in an alley if you need help," Gurren said. The two of them split up.

Deia quickly made her way to the courtyard where the caravan was getting ready to move out from. All of the various traders were checking their goods and making sure that they were secured for the ride.

Deia slowed her pace. Her heart beat fiercely as she moved through the carts and started toward one of the ones she had seen in the warehouse. She checked no one was looking as she moved through the caravan, easily slipping between people, horses, and different items. She reached the cart and touched one of the hidden items of holding that carried the vials.

She quickly accessed the bag of holding, stealing the vials from the item of holding. She only barely paused before continuing on her way. Her heart beat rapidly the entire time as she exited the courtyard, expecting for someone to call out to her at any moment.

No one called out and she left the courtyard quickly.

"Okay, I've got it. Let's head back to the warehouse and find out just what this stuff is," Deia said.

All of them were looking at the box; the guards and the leader were all off to the side, watching them.

Deia opened the box. Inside there were nearly a hundred vials, each of them made from a purple-looking elixir.

"Looks like purple drank to me," Gurren said.

Everyone looked to him with frowns.

"Sorry, too much time around Steve." Gurren's armor shrugged.

Induca picked up one of the vials and tilted it around, looking at the contents. "Is that a worm?" She looked closer as she shook the vial, trying to see what was inside better.

"It looks like it." Deia grabbed another one of the vials. "There's a worm in here too. What are worms doing in drugs?"

No one seemed to have any answers.

"Okay, well, let's see if Jung Lee can help us out." Deia pulled out a small Mirror of Communication. She used it to make a video link to Jung Lee's Mirror of Communication and linked him into the party chat.

A few moments later, he appeared on the other side. "Deia, is there something that I can help you with?" He'd been using the time to learn about what had happened to Emerilia, work on alchemy and do the things that he had wanted to do in the hundreds of years he'd been captured for.

"We've broken up a drug ring of some kind, but they're peddling this." Deia showed the vial. "It seems that there is a worm inside it."

"A worm? Has anyone ingested it?" Jung Lee's normally calm voice became panicky.

"One of the thugs. Why?"

"Because when I was dealing with the Elsoom spores, I looked up all kinds of diseases or other affiliations that were similar to the Elsoom spores. One of them being worm's control," Jung Lee said. "The worms spread through water systems and entered people and creatures. They would lay dormant for a time before they were activated. The worms would take over people's bodies, leaving them conscious. They could only watch as their bodies were controlled for the purpose of killing or infecting others."

"Well, this idiot was trying to get them to Iudarai," Induca said.

"Do you have something that could examine him, maybe a spell of some kind? Look at his brain stem, along the back of his neck. He might already be controlled by the worm. There are two stages to the worms: one where they can suggest things to people by releasing chemicals, or the second where they burrow into the spinal cord and take over the host's nervous system. There are also multiple kinds of infected, from those who are simply controlled to the ones who have been infected with multiple worms and turn into mobile breeding farms for the worms," Jung Lee said.

"Well, none of that sounds good," Lox said.

"No, but that's not the worst part," Jung Lee said, his face grim. "The worms are only used to control other people—they are just following the commands of their queen. Their queen is also smart."

"So this queen commands the worms that are spread out across a large area, takes over the creatures or people in the area and lives it up," Gurren said.

"Pretty much. However, this one seems smarter than average as she's taken over this sewer worker and seen that her worms could be hidden in drugs and smuggled into larger cities. She is looking to create an empire, not just simple control of her surrounding territory," Jung Lee said.

Deia cast her Touch of the Land spell to study the leader and his two guards. They all had worms coiled around their spinal cords where it became the brain stem. "Okay, it looks like all of these people have been infected by the worms." A screen popped up into her view.

Quest Completed: Sightings and Disappearances

You have found out the reason that people and creatures have been disappearing; they were controlled by worms.

Objectives:

Go to the Mayor's office to collect your rewards

Rewards: 15,000 Gold

Experience

Strabon Kingdom's Favor

Quest: A Worm's Power (Of Myths and Legends sub-quest)

A Worm Queen that was banned from Emerilia has returned and is starting her domination with the city of Ecora; however, you have learned about the plot before she has had time to carry out her plan.

Kill her to stop her from taking over the people of Ecora.

Failure:

All of the party dies without completing the quest

Allow the city Ecora to fall under the control of the Worm Queen

Rewards: Experience

Unknown

Deia dismissed the screens.

"So it's hunting time?" A big axe appeared in Gurren's hands as he held it over his shoulder.

"Of course." Deia smiled. Controlling queens, a plot to take over the Strabon kingdom, and a creature that was part of the

Myths and Legends Quest group: Deia's blood boiled with excitement.

They checked the bonds on the three and then headed out through the city. The gates were still closed but it was easy for the four to slip out over the city walls.

If they were to attack the carts, it would warn the others and they might escape. However, if they could get the leaders and then cut down the carts, then they could destroy the whole operation.

Jung Lee sent them all the information he had on the worm queen and they set off. Deia had been a ranger for decades; as soon as she stepped into the forest surrounding Ecora, she felt at home.

The other three followed as she moved through the forest, using the skills she had built up through her life to look for signs of the queen.

***

It took a number of hours before Deia was able to pick up a trail but Lox had every confidence in her.

Nothing escapes ranger Deia's eyes. He proudly remembered the times that Deia and his warband had worked together in the Kufo'tel forest and the forest that surrounded the Mithsia Mountains. It felt as if it had been a lifetime ago, so many things had changed since then.

Deia suddenly stopped and looked over the ground. She cast Touch of the Land; moments later, a way point appeared on the party's map.

"Looks like we found her lair. It's kind of set up like an ants' nest. There are multiple entrances all over the place—some of them connecting to the surface, others going deep into the ground and connected to the sewers of Ecora.

"There's all kinds of creatures that are expanding the nest. The tunnels are confusing as hell too," Deia said, a frustrated note to her voice.

Lox brought up his map and looked at the section of the nest that the Touch of the Land had been able to penetrate. "Looks like a mess," Lox said disdainfully. As a dwarf, he liked clean lines and things to be laid out in a straightforward manner. The crazed way that the nest seemed to have holes all the way through it made him frown in annoyance. Fighting in such an area was going to be difficult.

"That's what I was thinking, but, who says that we have to follow their plan?" A blue flame appeared in Deia's hand.

"What's the plan, boss?" Gurren asked, excitement in his voice.

Lox also grinned inside his armor. It had been some time since he had been out on his own, completing a quest with no back-up—enticing rewards that he wanted to get as well as a powerful enemy that could defeat him and his if he wasn't careful. It was dangerous, crazy, and it made Lox feel alive in a way he didn't feel doing other things.

"I will burn us a tunnel through the ground, right into the heart of the nest where the queen should be. While we're tunneling, Induca, I want you to pour every Fire spell you know into the nest's entrances. Don't get stuck in any fights. That way, when we reach the nest then they'll all be up on the surface trying to fight you instead of running around in the chaotic underground," Deia said. "Lox, you're with Induca, and Gurren with me."

"Simple, just the way I like it," Induca said with approval.

"Okay, then let's go kill us a queen," Lox said.

It was only a few minutes later that Lox and Induca had crept up to one of the larger entrances into the nest that seemed to go deep into the heart of the worm's home. Deia had used Touch of the Land a few more times so that now they had a clear picture of the nest. The queen also had a way point on her as she rested in the middle of the nest.

"Well, looks like it's time for a barbecue," Induca said.

"Ready when you are," Lox said. A shield appeared over his arm and a sword in his hand. He knelt in the underbrush of the forest, looking for anything that might threaten Induca. A number of way points marked other entrances that went deep into the nest in case they were swarmed and needed to change positions.

The wind in the area seemed to pick up as faint magical formations appeared around Induca, gaining in strength as red streams seemed to be drawn in from the world and toward Induca's hands.

The creatures in the forest went quiet as a sense of dread filled them.

A shimmering blue ball appeared in Induca's hands. It looked almost like a gem, not a hint of heat escaping from it. The ball grew to be five foot in diameter before shrinking suddenly to a ball no bigger than a tennis ball.

Lox's eyes were focused on that gem-looking ball and broke out into a cold sweat as he felt his scalp tingle.

With a casual toss, that blue ball disappeared into the three-foot-wide hole that led into the nest. The ball quickly disappeared as Induca sat down in a meditative position, her eyes closed.

Lox kept watch for any threat in the area as Induca continued to sit there without any care. *Looks like she's been working on making a new spell,* Lox thought with approval. Someone who didn't spend much time around mages who dealt in Fire might have thought that Induca was just unleashing a complicated fireball spell. However, Lox had spent most of the last couple of years around Deia and Induca; he had come to understand Fire magic to a much greater degree than he had in the past.

That spell that Induca had unleashed, it was something that he had never seen before and it was extremely powerful. Coming to his senses, he realized something. *Why does it feel colder around here?* Lox frowned to himself but continued to keep watch.

"Knock knock." Induca's face looked a little pale but she wore a triumphant smile on her face.

***

Queen Holum frowned. As she looked from her throne, she felt cold air seeping into her nest. She was in her human form with gem-like eyes and two antenna that stuck out of the top of her head. Her body moved oddly and with a grace that no normal human was capable of.

She stretched out her senses. One of her skills was land control. By seeding her worms all over an area, she could take control of it. She could "sense" everything that happened within her worms' range.

Now she felt an incredibly cold force traveling through her tunnels and headed for her. She had battled mages and warriors in the hundreds when she had been at the height of her power, turning them all into her slaves. She was well versed in the ways of magic.

"Attack!" She let out a screech.

The calm nest turned into a hive of activity as beasts that had come under her command as well as people who had been brought into the fold started to move. The people were at the depths of the nest; they moved the worms and the vials from the nest to Ecora, spreading out her parasites.

It would take time for them to arrive.

However, she had brought hundreds of creatures under her command. The Ashal wilderness might be filled with great predators, but didn't all animals need to drink? She'd easily taken command of powerful beasts that now moved toward that ice attack.

More of her forces charged through the nest, headed to the surface and where the ice attack had come through.

Her first creatures met the attack head on.

"What? They were burned?" Holum was shocked. With her connection, she could clearly sense what was happening to those under her direct control.

The ice attack seemed to pick up in speed, cooling more and more of the area around it as it shot forward. Its strength weakened somewhat as it seemed to burn holes through any that lay in its path.

Holum ordered her creatures to make a wall to reduce the strength of the spell as she transformed into a ten-meter-long worm with purple gem-like eyes and twin antenna on the top of her head.

In her natural form, just like with dragons, her power was greatly increased!

She saw the blue gem-like ball as it continued to speed downward toward the heart of her nest. Her body shook in anger at the loss of her beasts. "I created an empire out of the slaves I controlled but now this mage wishes to finish me off with one attack!" Angered, Holum dove into a wall. Her land control allowed her to sense where Induca was.

She would tear this attacker limb from limb!

Walls of fire appeared at dozens of entrances to the nest, badly burning anything that tried to leave them. Holum changed her path to move around these firewalls, her eyes filled with cold anger.

The blue gem-like ball had reduced from the size of a tennis ball to that of a golf ball. If Holum were to see it with her own eyes, she would have realized the incredible power held within it.

It finally reached the center of the nest. It looked beautiful as it rested in front of the throne. All around it, creatures were charging to weaken the spell and reduce the damage that it would bring down on the nest.

The blue gem didn't seem to care as it reduced to the size of a marble. In an instant, it exploded outward in a ripple of pure Fire Mana.

The surrounding area was turned to magma as the spell went off in a massive explosion. Tunnels collapsed and creatures were incinerated. In the face of the blue gem's blast wave, the nest was torn apart as if it were made of nothing but paper.

Holum's eyes went wide as she increased her speed. *That incredibly cold attack was actually Fire based! To come to this level of mastery—they will be a powerful slave!*

Holum, confident in her own abilities, didn't even think of fleeing. She had been a queen of an empire. She had nothing to fear; even after being banished, she had come back. Nothing had stopped her in the past and nothing would stop her in the future.

Behind her, the tunnel that she had created was being ripped apart by the explosion. Blue flames chased her. These flames burnt everything in their path, turning the dirt to glass that would explode under the massive heat.

The inside of the nest was carnage as Holum raced out of the ground, appearing just fifteen meters from Induca. Her eyes locked onto the human sitting down on the ground. Holum raced forward, a look of excitement on her face.

"Little human, it seems that you have used up all of your Mana. Why don't you just submit to my command?" Holum gave a cold smile as her body rushed forward.

Holum sensed danger. Relying on her instincts, she moved her body slightly as a massive armored man wielding a sword and shield appeared from behind the mage. His sword cut through the air that Holum had just occupied.

Seems that she didn't come alone. Holum spat at the warrior. A purple substance hit the man's shield, hardening in seconds.

The man threw his shield away that seemed to disappear, even as he closed with Holum.

She didn't notice the shield seemed to disintegrate as it left his hand. "It has been some time since someone dared to challenge me!" Holum yelled out. Her tail whipped out toward the warrior.

A shield appeared on his arm, blocking her attack even as he was sent flying five meters. He dug his sword in the ground, flipped his body around, his feet digging into the ground. Green light swarmed up lines across his legs while white light illuminated his arms and weapons. He jumped forward without pause. The ground underneath his feet turned into a crater as he let out a yell.

She spat hardening goop at the warrior. His shield was covered with those geometric lines, lit with red power. The shield burned through the goop before it could harden.

What is this? Holum should be able to easily bring this man under control but he was resisting her to the point that she would have to wear him down before she could implant him with a worm. *Still, there's that mage. If I can bring her under my control, then she should be able to help me defeat this creature and I have more of my slaves coming from the nest.*

Induca's firewall spells couldn't last forever and although her attack had been powerful, with the chaotic nature of the nest, the full power of her attack had been redirected and dissipated in a number of places.

From holes that lined the belly of Holum, worms buried themselves in the ground, traveling at high speed underground toward the mage. Her power was not in fighting people head on, but her ability to bring them under her command.

She pulled back slightly so that the warrior's sword didn't connect with her as her tail once again shot forward and smashed into the warrior and sent him into the air. *What can you do when you have nothing to slow you—WHAT!?*

White light lines covered the man's armor as he paused in midair. His weapons disappeared as lines raced from his shoulders to his wrists and over his hand, creating a circle in the palm of his hands. From the circles on his hands, Mana bolts raced forward.

What is this? He's able to create Mana bolts, but he's not a mage!

Holum was hit with multiple Mana bolts. Her body shook with the impacts but none of them made it through. A Mana barrier appeared around her, stopping the Mana bolts. Her eyes glowed with cold fury. "You dare?" she yelled out.

"Yup," the warrior said flippantly.

Her body shot forward like an arrow from a bow. Rage filled her as she hit the man. She moved too fast for him to react.

"Dammit." The man sounded more annoyed than scared as he shot toward the ground, smashing into it and creating a crater where he landed. He flew away from where he had impacted as Holum's tail drilled into the ground where he had been moments before.

Once again they faced each other, one in the air blasting out Mana bolts that flared across her barrier and the other resting on the ground.

"Come into my service and I won't kill you," Holum yelled.

"Serve you? Do I look like an idiot?" the man yelled back, not letting up on his attacks.

Holum's face turned savage as she looked at the mage. They were just a few meters apart. The human was too deep in Mana fatigue to do anything. Worms jumped up from the ground in a blur, all headed toward the mage.

"Really?" a powerful voice called out, sounding almost bored as the air distorted around the mage. All of the worms were incinerated before they could make it close to the mage, who floated upward, stretching out her legs so that she stood.

To be able to have such Mana reserves to carry out these attacks and have more left over... Holum immediately jumped back twenty meters. "Who are you people?" Holum looked to the two people. The armored one was still sending out Mana bolts, but they didn't have the power to do more than distort her Mana shields. Her personal attacks might not be strong, but Holum had confidence in her defenses.

"Lox and Induca of Party Zero," Induca said, with an extravagant bow and a cocky smile.

"Why did you attack me?" Holum asked.

"We're just the distraction." The warrior chuckled.

"Distraction?" Holum asked, a look of confusion on her face until she felt a scorching heat from underneath her body.

A woman wreathed in flames, looking like a goddess born of fire, tore through the ground right underneath Holum, cutting through her side.

Another warrior in identical armor to the first let go of the fire goddess's foot. A sword seven meters tall formed in his hands as white lines covered his armor.

Holum barely had time to move, howling in pain from the first attack landing when the second attack from within her Mana barrier cut through the side of her belly. The blade pierced through her sides, unleashing multiple Air blades within Holum. She cried out in pain. Her Health points dropped off with the critical hit that Gurren had landed.

Lox had rushed forward as soon as Deia had erupted from the ground. A massive war hammer appeared in his hands; his body was covered in white lines while his arms were lit with a light green.

He swung his hammer in a savage arc, unleashing all of his strength—the two titans in the Devastator armor against the massive Queen Holum.

His blow connected with a crunch as his war hammer crushed Holum's head.

Holum's vision went blank, not understanding what had happened or how she, a person who had been at the peak of power on Emerilia for nearly a decade, could be defeated by these three people.

***

Deia saw as Lox landed the final hit, ending Queen Holum.

The massive worm queen dropped to the ground, her Health at zero as a tombstone appeared over her body.

Both Lox and Gurren's armor was covered in the green blood of the worm queen.

"Well, that's one hell of a way to do pest control," Gurren said.

Induca let out a pained sigh as Deia cast Touch of the Land.

"Well, it seems that it worked. All of the creatures and people under her control have collapsed," Deia said. A screen appeared in her vision.

Quest: A Worm's Power (Of Myths and Legends sub-quest)

You have killed the Worm Queen Holum

Rewards: 20,000 Gold

120,000 Experience

Quest Completed: Sightings and Disappearances

You have found out the reason that people and creatures have been disappearing; they were controlled by worms. You have killed off the threat that was Queen Holum. Report your findings to the Mayor.

Objectives:

Go to the Mayor's office to collect your rewards

Rewards: 15,000 Gold

Experience

Strabon Kingdom's Favor

"Let's get the people who were controlled out of there and then head back to Ecora," Deia said.

"Could you have maybe toned down the destruction?" Gurren said as they looked at the smoking crater that had been the nest. With Induca's attack, the nest had been destroyed from the inside and caved in. Now smoke was still rising from various openings as heat seemed to radiate out from the melted and broken mass of nest.

"Whoops?" Induca shrugged, a smile on her face.

"So, anyone up for another quest after this?" Lox asked.

"Someone's eager to start clearing the board," Deia joked.

"Well, there's plenty to do and as much as I do love a big-scale battle, sometimes going on a quest and going around Emerilia is more fun," Lox said.

"Well, I don't have anything else that I need to do," Induca said.

"Me either, other than try to figure out a way into this nest," Gurren said.

"Dave should be able to handle Koi for a couple more days and he can drop her off with my parents," Deia thought aloud.

"Come on—it's going to be a lot of fun," Induca said.

"Fine, all right—I'm in," Deia said.

Chapter 24: Odd Request

Sato looked to Dave and then back to the information that he had given him.

"You want me to have our AI look over these images and see if they can pinpoint down to a small area through spectral analysis where there is a large concentration of hydrogen?" Sato repeated back Dave's request.

"Essentially, yes." Dave nodded.

"Might I ask why?" Sato shifted in his seat.

"Well, we need hydrogen and we've essentially got one shot. If we can find hydrogen in the location that you provide, then we'll be good. If we don't, within three months we're going to be barely keeping all of our projects running." Dave smiled.

"Well, you're good at hiding your nerves," Sato said, sensing Dave's nervousness even though he showed no outward sign of it. "Okay, this is one of the more odd requests that you've given me but I'll see if Edwards or someone can look into this and make it their highest priority."

Although Sato couldn't give any direct help, this supporting was one way that he could assist. Dave and the people of Emerilia had given them so much and helped his system and his people to grow in power. He wanted to help out more, but the issue was they just simply couldn't go and directly help them without knowing that their plan would work out.

He had been watching the feeds that came from Emerilia; he'd watched the fighting happening on the Ashal continent between the Terra Alliance and the Nalheim. He'd never seen that kind of fighting except on recordings of ancient battles. He knew that the people he had been watching were in a true life-or-death battle for the most part. Only a few of the people who had been in that battle were players who could come back from the dead.

The universe has changed more in the last couple of years since I've come to know Dave than in the centuries since humanity lost the Sol system.

"Thank you, Sato. If we can get past this hurdle then we can truly start to prepare for the fight with the Jukal and work in regaining the humans of Emerilia's freedom back," Dave said. A pop up appeared in his vision.

"If you'll excuse me. Seems that Uncle Malsour has realized that his niece filled up her diaper." Dave sighed.

"Niece?" Sato asked.

"My daughter Koi," Dave said with a proud smile.

"You have a daughter now?"

"Ahh, yes, well, we really just talk about projects, the two of us." Dave laughed. "Yeah, I've got a daughter. She's just a few months old. Her name's Koi."

"Koi— that's a good name." Sato couldn't resist smiling at seeing the joy on Dave's face.

"I thought so, too." Dave laughed. "All right, well, I'll see you later. Thanks for looking into this for me."

"Least we can do to help."

"Oh, and we figured out those heavy duty inertia compensators as well!" With that, Dave disconnected from the Mirror of Communication conference room.

"Good," Sato said. "Based on those plans, if they can get those ships operational, they're going to be a right pain in the ass for the Jukal to deal with."

Sato disconnected from the Mirror of Communication, taking the file that Dave had given him and sending it to Edwards.

***

"Here you go." Jung Lee smiled and handed over a half-dozen different types of potions.

The vendor laughed out loud as he happily took the potions. "Mister Jung, I didn't think that it would only take you a day to make these potions. You truly are a potion master! As agreed, please select any ingredients you desire worth up to three thousand gold," the vendor said.

"Thank you."

Quest: Potions for ingredients

You have successfully turned the ingredients given to you by the vendor Faruk and turned them into the specified Potions.

Rewards: 32,000 Experience

Pick up to 3,000 gold worth of ingredients

He dismissed the quest screen that appeared in his vision and moved around the store to pick out various ingredients before he brought them back to the counter.

The vendor looked at the ingredients with interest; they were all rather simple ingredients and in large numbers. If it had been another potion maker, then he might have pointed out that they might want to get some other ingredients. However, he had not seen someone with Jung Lee's skill before and held onto his words.

"This comes to around twenty-seven hundred gold, leaving you with a credit of two hundred and thirty-four gold remaining." The vendor smiled.

"Thank you." Jung Lee put the items into a pouch of holding that was on his belt.

"Please come by whenever you need ingredients, Mister Jung!" the vendor said.

Jung Lee nodded slightly to the vendor before he left the store. He patted his pouch, smiling to himself. He could create impressive potions that could boost a person's abilities for a short while or could poison Level 500 creatures. However, all of these were potions that took up many expensive ingredients and took a long time to create.

What Jung Lee needed right now was gold so that he could pursue his passion in potion making. He had bought simple and low-cost ingredients of just a few kinds. His reasoning was simple. Using his skills, he could use the ingredients to make a number of simple but useful potions, ones that most people could afford—minor healing, Stamina and Mana regeneration. The ingredients for a single potion might be worth two gold, but he could sell them for nearly twelve in Terra!

With the ingredients he had purchased, he could sell all of his potions for nearly sixteen thousand gold. He could repeat the process for similar kinds of potions and increase his profits. It was true that potion makers were some of the richest people in all of Emerilia!

"Most people would be depressed or annoyed with how long it will take for them to gain the money they need to pursue their passion." Jekoni looked at Jung Lee as he floated in the air.

"Having been locked up in the Six Affinities Temple for so long, it feels good to be challenged once again. To have little to nothing and fight for my passion." Jung Lee's eyes shone.

"The final product is only a reflection of the path that one has taken to reach it." Jekoni smiled.

"Right! Now let's go and make some potions!" Jung Lee laughed as they hurried off toward the Stone Raiders' towers, their home and where Jung Lee's laboratory was located.

It was a number of hours until Jung Lee left his room-turned-laboratory. He had a big smile on his face even as his eyes looked tired. He didn't need to sleep for nearly a week at a time, but still, working on the potions was not simple. It took care and hard work. Even though these had been simple potions, Jung Lee had poured his heart and soul into them. Potion making was his passion, after all.

He quickly moved through the tower and to the areas where the healers and the hospital for Terra was located through one of the soul gem constructs that crisscrossed the underground city.

"Hi, I'm looking for Jules." Jung Lee moved to one of the healers who stood around in the hallways.

"She's a pretty busy lady. What's your name and affiliation?" The healers came from all over Emerilia and not all of them were Stone Raiders. In a city as big as Terra, they needed more than just the Stone Raider guild members to fill all the positions needed to keep the city running.

There were now nearly four thousand Stone Raider guild members. Most of them were fighters and the types to go out and do quests. Only a few of them were part of the trading organizations or the groups that looked after Terra and the guild's matters.

Most of the healers, when there wasn't a massive battle going on, were with their parties on their own adventures.

"Jung Lee, Party Zero, I guess." He smiled.

"Party Zero? And I'm the king of the Edon Kingdom."

"Watch your tone, lady." Jekoni appeared out of midair. "Jules is up three floors." With that, Jekoni disappeared again.

The healer frowned and gave Jung Lee an annoyed glance.

"Sorry about Jekoni," Jung Lee said. He was in too good of a mood to ruin it as he quickly moved away and toward a set of stairs. He got three floors up and spread out his senses as he sent a message to Jules.

She sent him back a way point. With a relieved smile, he quickly moved to their meeting point.

"Okay and watch out—that break is still healing. It will take a week to get back to its full strength," Jules said, talking to a person she was guiding out of an examination room.

"Thanks, Doc." The large orc smiled, looking at his arm in a cast and sling.

"Ah, the famous Mister Jung Lee. Deia said that I should be expecting you." Jules smiled. It was clear that she was tired but she had a sort of irascible energy about her that seemed to come out, making Jung Lee feel welcomed.

"Jules, I've heard a great number of things about you as well." Jung Lee bowed his head slightly, a wide smile on his face.

"Please, let's go to my office." Jules waved for him to join her as they started to walk through the hospital's halls. "Deia said that you are a potion maker."

"Yes, well, I was. I haven't done it for a while and I'm looking forward to once again turning my hands toward it." Jung Lee smiled.

"Your face seems familiar, as if I saw it somewhere before. Are you a streamer?"

Jung Lee chuckled. "No, I'm not a streamer. I'm a person from Emerilia but you might remember me from the Six Affinities Temple."

Within Terra there was little fear that the Jukal would be able to record what people were doing. Dave and Party Zero didn't trust this security that much, which was why they talked in party chat or within Pandora's box and similarly "stealthed" areas that the Jukal wouldn't be able to access.

"The Six Affinities Temple," Jules said, a thoughtful look on her face. "The guy on the throne looked similar." Jules glanced at Jung Lee again. "Can't be, though."

"It can be if Party Zero helps you out." Jung Lee laughed slightly. Still, when he thought about it, their rescue and the way in which they had helped him to regain control over his various Free Affinity spirits that were vying to take over his soul, he was reminded of how impossible it all seemed.

Jules looked at him with a shocked expression. "That must have been one hell of a time," Jules said with feeling.

Jung Lee felt a familiar weight in the back of his mind, a fear that he had carried with him since he had gained his freedom—that it would once again be ripped away from him and he would be stuck, with no one around, helpless once again.

"It was hell," Jung Lee said. His normally joyful face dimmed slightly as his eyes seemed to lose their luster. "But now I'm free and I can once again pursue my passions."

Once again, the smiling and eager Jung Lee reappeared.

Jules laughed and patted Jung Lee on the back. "I know that sometimes people bottle up the hardest crap and try to just shrug it off. Sometimes we can't. Feel free to come and talk to me if you need to, or talk to someone about it. Those demons on your shoulders can grow." Jules's eyes held Jung Lee's.

Maybe it would be good to talk to someone about it all. "Thank you," Jung Lee said.

"No worries. Now about these potions—what are you thinking of doing or creating, I guess?" Jules laughed as they reached her office. She opened the office and guided him inside. There was a desk and two seats in front of it; she took one of the seats in front.

Jung Lee sat in the one opposite. "I am able to make a number of high-level potions. I can also help in the training of others to make lower-grade potions. After being trapped for so long, this was my deepest regret—not that I would die but that I would take with me a number of potions and different ways to make potions to my grave. Now that I have been given this second life, I do not wish to waste it and hope to pass this knowledge on," Jung Lee said. "I was told that you would be the best person to talk about getting supplies for alchemy and also pass on my knowledge."

"Well, as for passing on the information, then going to the Mirror of Communication school would be for the best. You would gain tokens from the various guilds and groups that you can redeem for various items. As for making potions—well, the Stone

Raiders are always burning through them. We have multiple quests and orders open for potions. If you can demonstrate your skills, then we can open up our vaults of ingredients to you. If you want any ingredients we don't have in the vaults, then Florence can acquire them. If it's for the guild, we will take on the cost. But if it's for personal experimentation, you can get them at a reduced price. She still operates out of Verlun and she has a number of rare and interesting items that she sells there. If you were willing to offer your services or came into an agreement with her for making potions, I think she would be happy to pay you in gold or ingredients." Jules tapped her chin in thought.

"That would be great!" Jung Lee said. Not only would he be able to work on his more ambitious potions that he had thought up while he had been stuck in the Six Affinities Temple, if Florence was to use his services then he could make many different kinds of potions.

"If you could send me in the direction of Florence, that would be great," Jung Lee said.

"I'll let her know that you're on your way."

"Thank you." Jung Lee smiled. While he was in Verlun, he could also sell the potions he had made last night.

They quickly said their good-byes and Jung Lee headed for the teleport pad that would take him to Verlun.

***

The mother looked out over the castle that she and Gilez had made; below she could hear the noises of celebration.

They had escaped their imprisonment and Gilez, with her hunting parties, had been able to kill many powerful creatures and drain them of their blood essence.

The mother and her children couldn't eat normal food and drink. However, if they consumed a lot of blood essence, then it moved from feeling euphoric to making them drunk. It was similar to drugs that humans used on Earth.

The mother frowned as Durnst moved to return to the castle. Alarms started to ring out.

"Mother, the other entity is a pack of hell fiends!" Durnst said through their party chat. "Their leader is a woman who took interest in me. She and her family members put me under their spell for nearly a week. I was unable to escape her power until she started to play games that would lead to my death. I was able to escape her shackles. None of the others were strong enough to control me. However, they have strong Fire attacks and are good at fighting with their spears!"

"The rest of you, be ready to receive the hell fiends! Cast protections against being dominated!" The mother's voice was cold as she rose off the balcony she was in, slowly descending in front of her castle. The shadows behind her dissipated to reveal her children casting spells. Their eyes were red, ready to meet the oncoming threat.

"They also command a large host of people who have made contracts on their souls for items that the fiends have promised," Durnst added.

The mother felt her heart clench. *It is one thing to destroy those who attacked my son, but if we are forced to fight against the people of Emerilia, what will be the result?*

Her eyes glowed in anger. No matter who it was, if they dared to attack her family then she would destroy them. She didn't want to make enemies of the Emerilian people; however, she would if she had to.

***

After completing the worm queen quest and the disappearances of the people in Ecora, the Strabon kingdom immediately seized the caravan filled with worms. The people who had been under the control of the worm queen collapsed into a coma as the worms in their bodies died off. A few hours later, they awoke with memories of what they had done but in a haze.

All of them had been bent to the queen's will and weren't accountable for their actions. The sewer worker Party Zero had captured repeatedly apologized and thanked Deia, Induca, Lox, and Gurren. He had been under the most influence.

Now they were in the city-state Imend, part of the Orun Free States. They had accepted another quest. There had been talks of gatherings and powerful good-looking people starting to build up an army out of the weaker members of the town.

Deia looked to the quest window.

Quest: A Rebellion Rising

Handsome and beautiful people who seem to come from another plane have been seen gathering the poor and weaker people of Imend. The Lord Governor of the city has become apprehensive and has asked you to look into it.

Find out what the goal of these people are.

Inform the Lord Governor of their plans.

Failure:

All of the party dies without completing the quest

Allow the city Imend to fall

Kill citizens of Imend

Rewards: Experience

15,000 Gold

The gold wasn't all that much but they were here more to have fun than to earn gold. All of Party Zero were rather wealthy themselves. They had little need for more wealth and poured all of it into Pandora's box.

Induca stopped her head, whipping to the side as her eyes thinned. "There's a massive battle going on underground!"

The rest of the party looked to one another.

"Sounds like my kind of party!" Gurren laughed.

Deia's eyes glowed with Mana. Her sight passed through buildings as she saw the massive flares of power that emanated from a huge area underneath a hill outside of the city-state.

The scale of the cavern was massive. The Mana from the battle lit up the interior, showing a massive open area with various underground vegetation and a massive castle against one wall. On one side, a half-dozen people unleashed fire and melee attacks, staying in the rear of a five-hundred-person-strong-group that were wildly attacking a group of nearly one hundred who were using Dark magic.

Deia's understanding of magic had come to the level where at a glance she could identify the different spells that were being used in a fight.

The half-dozen attackers with the army were unleashing Fire spells as well as manipulation spells. They were also redirecting attacks. Any truly powerful magic, they reflected back to the casters.

The defenders attacked these leaders but tried to restrain rather than kill the soldiers in the army.

"Let's go and check it out." Deia had confidence in their forces that they would be able to at least flee if they needed to.

Induca and Deia took to the skies, their bodies covered in flames. White lines appeared on Gurren and Lox's armor as they chased after the other two.

People looked in shock. Their minor display of power was enough for most of those in the surrounding area to get a good idea of their power.

***

The mother let out an enraged scream as she fought off another attempt by the hell fiends to take command over her.

"Come, pet, don't worry. It is all a matter of time before you come under my command. Once you do, I'll let you kill each and every one of your fellows off." A woman wearing an armored dress laughed joyously, enjoying the mother's struggle.

The mother had powerful spells at her disposal but the hell fiends had the ability to return the magical attacks sent at them back to the casters.

A number of the mother's children had been injured so badly that they had been brought to the brink of death.

The only way to deal with the hell fiends was in close combat. But they had their army of nearly five hundred clustered around them. Their abilities with their own melee weapons and their controlling attacks were actually stronger the closer they were to their victim.

A number of her children were fighting in bodies of stone and metal that had wrapped around them, throwing out shadows and materials to secure the soldiers of the hell fiends' army.

I don't want to kill them off, but under the control of the hell fiends there is little that I can do.

The hell fiends could only charm someone for a day and then it would run out for a few hours before they could charm them again. Their army wasn't charmed but instead filled with hope at the promises that the hell fiends had made with them.

It truly was a hellish battle with only the mother and her side getting abused. If it wasn't for the five-hundred-strong army, then they could directly deal with the hell fiends without worry.

The mother looked upward in alarm as something disturbed her senses. *Someone is coming down?*

She wasn't the only one to look as the female leading the hell fiends looked upward.

The ceiling melted, revealing a hole that extended up to the surface. Standing in midair, there were two women and two massive suits of armor with white lines on them.

"Greetings! My name is Zeli, leader of this group of hell fiends. We're always looking for more people to join our cause," the leader of the hell fiends said as the fighting came to a pause.

"Quickly—recover your strength," the mother said over her family's chat. They all hurriedly took their blood essence gems, their strength and their bodies recovering quickly. They didn't know whether the four had come to help or harm them.

"If we can't win in the next battle, be ready to flee. We will meet at our old home," the mother continued.

"Are you the group that has been inviting the people from Imend to join your cause?" one of the women in midair asked casually.

"Yes. We've needed protection against the rabble that is trying to harm them." Zeli cast a solemn gaze at the mother and her children.

"We haven't harmed a single person of Emerilia!" the mother yelled out.

"Hmm, interesting. Vampires and hell fiends," one of the people in armor said.

"They must have both have been prisoners," the other woman said. Clearly the first woman to talk was their leader.

"Hmm, it does look like that they are part of the Myths and Legends quest line," the first woman said.

"Okay, well, here's the deal. You release any of those you've charmed and let these people of Emerilia leave your service and publicly announce yourselves," the woman said to the hell fiend. "As for the vampires."

"We prefer to be called Blood Kin," one of the mother's children said.

"Very well. Blood Kin, you also must announce yourselves and—" The woman's face distorted as a spell landed on her.

The mother's eyes went wide. Zeli had sneak attacked with her charm; all of her subordinates had also attacked at the same time.

Zeli laughed as the two women in midair struggled. "Should have kept your guard up," Zeli said with a mocking smile.

"Mistress!" one of the other hell fiends said as the lines across the two armored warriors turned gray. A powerful aura that made the mother step back in fear spread across the room.

A sword and a shield wreathed in gray smoke appeared in both of the warriors' hands.

"I'm really starting to hate this mind magic bullshit," one of them said.

"Well, as I see it, they're not going to repent," the other replied.

No one had time to say anything when the two sets of armor moved in gray blurs.

A hell fiend unleashed their flame ray. The warrior's shield blocked it, throwing the light outward and making them look like a meteor as their shield plowed through that ray and hit the fiend.

With a lightning-fast strike, the hell fiend was torn apart; the warrior blurred once again. The Emerilian fighters didn't have time to react to the warrior as they headed for their next target.

The hell fiends unleashed their Fire ray attacks constantly. Red beams hit the warriors' Mana barriers around their bodies.

They're only Level 150 creatures...how is this possible? The mother didn't know that Gurren and Lox in their armor had fought Level 400 beasts in Ashal's wilderness to get used to how they worked.

Fire rays illuminated the air within the massive cavern, hitting the gray blurs. Two more auras erupted and the Fire rays were cut off immediately.

"Well, that wasn't pleasant," the female leader in the sky said.

Zeli was looking at shock at the two warriors who had killed three of her people already. There was only five left, including her. "I didn't mean to—"

"You prey on the weak and use them for your own means. What kind of person would I be to let you stay in Emerilia, where my child lives?" The leader casually lifted her hand, casting Fire ray.

It cut through the sky.

Zeli used her own Fire ray spell but with a wave of the leader's hand, it dissipated. Zeli could only scream out as the Fire ray blasted through her.

The leader and the other woman in the sky fired off their own Fire rays, killing off the remaining hell fiends. They had shown their true colors and these two knew that to show mercy to those who liked to see others suffering was asking for them to cause trouble later.

"For those of you remaining, you are all now prisoners of war," the female leader said.

"But we're not part of an army!" one yelled out.

"Well, you're stupid enough to join a group that wants nothing more than to turn this city into a battlefield for their own enjoyment. Don't tell me you didn't know what the hell fiends did in the past?" one of the warriors yelled back.

"If you want to keep fighting, we'll happily greet you," the other warrior said.

With that, the Emerilian forces quickly laid down their weapons.

"Good. I've sent a message to the mage's guild. They're sending an overseer here." The female leader descended from the sky. Her aura retracted as she moved to where the mother and her family was.

"Sorry about that. Before I was interrupted, I was giving you terms," the woman said with a kind smile. It was hard to think that just moments ago she had killed off the hell fiends.

The mother bowed slightly, feeling that unless she had a lot more blood essence she wouldn't be able to fight off this woman and her people.

"So, right, you got released from prison and you're back on Emerilia."

"That's one kick-ass castle," one of the warriors said.

"Heh, Malsour would probably try to outdo it," the other woman said.

"Gurren, Induca—time and place." The woman sighed. "Sorry. Though it is a cool castle. Impressive for you to make it. Oh, and my name is Deia." Deia smiled.

"I am called Yemi, though many refer to me as the mother," Yemi said with a slight smile. "My daughter, Gilez, and I made the castle."

"Impressive, though they're not as strong as Malsour. How did you do it?" the last warrior asked. As Yemi looked to him, his name, Lox, appeared above his head.

"We have our ways. We don't want to give away all our secrets to people, sorry," Yemi said.

Lox laughed. "No worries. Us dwarves are used to having a few secrets, too."

Dwarf? But his armor is massive! Yemi shook her head. *A lot has changed since we were banished from Emerilia.*

"Okay, well, as I was saying, we haven't had any reports of you doing anything really. Heard that there were less animals in the area and I can sense that there are animals within your castle. Those blood-red gems you had were made from blood, so I'm guessing you're using animals to get that essence?" Deia asked.

"Yes," Yemi said, not daring to lie.

"Well, okay, so as long as you keep doing that then I think everything should be fine." Deia shrugged.

"Uh, Deia, I sent a message to Malsour about who we'd found. Bob sent a message back." Induca passed over a Mirror of Communication.

Deia checked the message on the Mirror of Communication. "Okay, so it seems that my husband and his friends would also like to offer you or your people a job if they would be interested?"

"A job?" Yemi asked, hesitant.

"Malsour seems to know quite a bit about your race. He says that you're some of the strongest manipulators of the Dark arts if you have enough blood essence. We have an underground city called Terra and other facilities underground that we're looking to expand. We have drills, but there's always a place for those skilled in manipulating rock and other Dark materials," Deia said.

"Terra, as in the place controlled by the Stone Raiders?" Yemi said. Her children had been able to gather a good amount of information on Emerilia. One of the things that most people talked about was the underground city Terra and the Stone Raiders.

"You're probably hesitant about it all, so we can offer for a few of you to come and check out Terra and meet with the others if some of you are interested. If you do agree to help us, then you will be given a residence within Terra. It's a lot less dangerous than being here. We've got all kinds of races and people, so you should be fine. There are people selling all manner of goods so it would be easier for you to acquire blood essence," Deia said.

"I feel that you would make a lot of money if you were a trader in any market," Yemi said.

Deia laughed, her eyes shining.

"I will travel with you to Terra with a number of others," Yemi said.

"Okay, well, we need to get the overseer to look after this mess." Deia pointed at the Emerilians that had followed the hell fiends and were now sitting on the ground. "And then hand in our quest to the Lord Governor and we can head off for Terra."

"Okay." Yemi nodded.

In a rush of air, several mages dropped through the hole in the roof of their cavern. They looked around for a moment before they headed to where Yemi and Deia were.

"Lady Oson, we came as fast as possible," one of the mages said in greeting to Deia.

"Thank you for coming. Seems we have some judgement to pass down on this lot." Deia waved at the Emerilians.

Chapter 25: Ground Breaking

"You're sure?" Sato looked to Edwards. They were inside Edwards's new sprawling research and development area that took up part of the newest shipyard.

In here, Edwards and his people were performing miracles every day. However, they had all turned their focus onto the information that Sato had given them.

"I'm sure that this is the best location, down to around a hundred kilometers," Edwards said.

Sato nodded. "Okay, good." He took the information chip from Edwards.

"Though some of us while this was going through the servers went and looked up just what this planet is, and well, we kind of found a match," Edwards said, as if judging how Sato would react to the news.

"Oh?" Sato said, interested.

"Well, using this, we figured out the planet's composition. Using that, we checked it against the planets and systems that humanity knew of; there weren't any that matched within the eightieth percentile. So, we moved to the information that Bob gave us on various systems. We found that there were two possible systems. One of them was close enough to some of the stealth sensor systems that Admiral Adams and her crew put into place that we could verify the data. We checked the information and found that it wasn't a match, so we checked our telescope data. We have recordings of the second possible system's location.

"We worked through the data through spectral analysis—we had a hit of almost ninety percent. It's called the Nal system. It's populated by the Nalheim race, an aggressive species that was dying off. We pulled up a profile of them. They're the same creatures that the Terra Alliance was fighting in central Ashal," Edwards said excitedly. "It was actually through those images that we were able to clear up the information that Dave gave us and find out the best location. It seems that somehow Dave and Party Zero are expanding into another star system. This one doesn't have much more than a few satellites in it and it's two-thirds the distance that it would be from De'qual to Emerilia."

"So, the hydrogen—he must be making those fusion reactors," Sato said.

"Exactly what I was thinking. I wonder what he's going to do there."

"Why wonder? Let's see if Adams can redirect one of the scouts to put a drone in-system so we can look over what's happening." Sato pulled out a data pad and tapped out a message.

"We can do that?" Edwards asked.

"Seems that the commander of the Deq'ual system's armed forces has just approved it, isn't that odd?" Sato's mystified look on his face quickly turned into a smile.

"The other thing that I wanted to get you over here for is about this information Dave gave us on teleportation. The servers and my people are working through it but it's clear that Dave hasn't given us everything about portals," Edwards said.

"Why would he do that?" Sato frowned.

"So that we can come to appreciate how awesome and powerful it is? This technology is only known by the Jukal. Dave might know how it works but it's some complicated stuff. If we just fed it into a computer, then we wouldn't understand just how powerful this is. The teleport pads are pretty easy, but portals can allow you to cross entire star systems. That must be how the Nalheim were able to reach Emerilia over a distance of tens of light-years. A journey that would take months using our normal faster-than-light space drives," Edwards said.

"So, he's basically given us the guide but then is letting us work through it so that we're not like a kid with a gun," Sato said. It made sense to him.

"Pretty much," Edwards said. "Though, if we can get this working, then we can start to set up bases all across known space with much less risk of the Jukal ever detecting us, unless they're purposefully looking for portals."

"And if they think that they're still the only people who have portals, then why would they go looking for them?" Sato's eyes lit up.

"Well, I didn't think that way but it makes sense," Edwards agreed.

"Thanks for letting me know. I'll go and get this information to Dave, and hopefully Adams and her scouts can get us a view of this Nal system."

***

Malsour, Bob, and Steve were checking the last parts of the teleportation array.

All of the Nalheim had moved out of the mountain system that they called home.

"Looks like the last of the Nalheim have passed through the portal," Steve said, linked through the Mirror of Communication to the Aleph scouts that were watching the process from within Goblin Mountain.

"Huh, what the hell?" Steve said.

"What is it?" Malsour asked as he looked to Steve, who had stopped working.

"As soon as the last person was through the portal, it disappeared," Steve said.

"Hmm, let me check something." Bob pulled out a Mirror of Communication and opened an interface on it.

"Looks like it was recalled back to that moon where the Jukal military are stationed," Bob said. "Most of it is automated but there's still at least one carrier and two battleships located there at all times."

"They can actually recall them?" Steve asked.

"The portals are some of the most important technology to the Jukal. Now that the Nalheim are not here, people are probably going crazy to bid on living on Nal. If they left the portal, then someone might take it. Also, they need to be recharged before they can be used. There is only one recharging station within the same star system as Emerilia," Bob said.

"So, people will probably be coming to Nal. Doesn't that mean that we should leave?" Malsour sounded hopeless.

"Leave? The bidding has only just started in earnest. It will probably be another hundred years before the Jukal pick out someone for this planet and then they have to organize everything for the rest of the system. It will take centuries for people to reach here unless they have Jukal drives." Bob laughed. "They also need to build their own portals here so that they can establish control over whoever comes here."

This is the power the Jukal hold: they can auction off planets; they have the ability to move from one system to another instantly. Even as someone takes control of this system, it's no more than they're leasing it from the Jukal, who can take it back at any time, otherwise denying them ships that can travel faster than light or threatening them with a Jukal fleet. It truly is an unfair system. Malsour let out a sigh as his hope returned. If they had a few centuries, that would be more than enough time!

"Woo-hoo!" Dave yelled, jumping up from where he had been sitting in front of a Mirror of Communication.

Koi, who had been sleeping nearby, let out a cry, annoyed at her father.

"Oh, no, it's all okay, Koi," Dave said. No news he had was more precious than his own daughter. He picked up the crying little Koi, bouncing her slightly as he made comforting noises. "You want to sleep again?" Dave asked Koi, who started to calm down a few minutes later.

Malsour, Steve, and Bob were all smiles as they finished off the teleportation array that filled the middle of the open area. A glowing portal showed Pandora's box on the other side and carts moving various items from portal to portal.

Koi, who was now awake, was sleepily looking around, moving her lips oddly as she stared at the different glowing mage lights.

"So, what was the good news?" Bob asked.

"Sato and Edwards were able to find a place where there's a high concentration of hydrogen in an area about one hundred kilometers wide." Dave opened his interface and shared the information with them.

All of them looked at the planetary map as well as a big arrow saying "Hydrogen be here!" with a big red area and a cross over it.

"Looks like a crappy treasure map," Bob said.

"Classy," Steve said with approval.

"A few more tests and we can check it out," Malsour said.

"Hope you brought your snow shoes!" Steve said.

"It's an ice planet, Steve. How is there going to be snow on an ice planet?" Dave asked.

"Umm, if Deia starts to melt it a bit?" Steve asked.

"She would be melting for centuries to try to change the atmosphere so that it would produce snow!" Dave complained.

"It would still make snow." Steve shrugged.

"Let's get these tests done," Dave said in defeat.

Malsour watched as the teleportation array went through start-up tests. Steve and Dave talked to each other, with Bob looking over their shoulder as they worked to figure out the best coordinates for the teleportation array to create a wormhole.

The teleportation array was more impressive than a portal in many ways as it could teleport items from one location to another over distances as large as a star system. The power usage was hellish, but the portals could only connect to other portals and needed to have the exact positional data between each of them before they could make one connection.

Dave changed Koi's nappies and fed her some formula. He quickly finished up his fatherly duties, making childish noises that made Koi wave her feet and legs in joy while giggling.

"That's my princess," Dave said with a wide smile, picking up Koi to burp her on his shoulder.

"Teleport array is ready to go," Malsour said.

"Coordinates are in," Bob said.

"Who's a cute little girl—yes, you are!" Steve said, behind Dave as he waved his finger at Koi, who laughed happily.

"The anchor is ready too." Bob looked to the device that they had used to connect the teleport array in Emerilia to Nal and drop in the first portal.

All of the feet that extended from the base of the anchor had been folded upward, making it look like some kind of missile.

"Well, let's fire it up," Dave said as Steve continued to play with Koi, who grasped at his finger.

Bob and Malsour moved to the consoles. The soul gem construct surrounding them and the vault soul gems glowed with power before quickly dimming. The power leeched from them and flowed into the teleportation array.

Runes lit up as the various components of the teleportation array came to life. The heat within the room started to increase before heat exchangers took in the heat, changing it into Mana and feeding it right into the teleportation array once again.

The massive banks of coded sheets started to hum and shake with the power going through them. The runes on the floor in a circular formation started to light up; section by section, they powered up as they reached toward the center of the teleportation array.

Everything was powered up with heat radiating from the teleportation array and the last parts of the runed floor coming to life. Power flowed outward. It was incomparable to the power that had been circulating around the room earlier.

A wormhole appeared above the magical circles. It wasn't large, about four foot tall and three wide. On the other side, there was a barren landscape of ice.

With a wave of his hand, Dave picked up the anchor with his gravity manipulation. He wasn't able to do this on Emerilia for fear that the Jukal would see it.

With a flick, the anchor headed through the wormhole that had been created.

It flew through and landed on the other side. As it hit the ground, the feet clamped onto the ground and the runes lit up the body of the anchor. The portal closed as the heat exchangers continued to pull the heat out of the room they were in.

Malsour and Bob were bent over their consoles, glancing at another console with a Mirror of Communication on it. Information was being fed from the anchor through the Mirror of Communication and back to the teleportation array.

Dave pointed to a modified portal that was off to the side of the room. In total, there were three portals in the room: one connected to Pandora's box, and two others—one of which would stay in this room and the other that would be put on the ice planet in the Nal system. This last portal was moved into the center of the teleportation array.

"We've got a connection!" Bob said as his and Malsour's hands moved over the consoles.

Power once again surged through the room as the remaining vault soul gems dimmed with the power output. This time, the power-up process was a lot more simple with less of the coded banks being connected as the teleportation array wasn't doing all the work, but the anchor was helping out.

The portal disappeared in a flash.

Malsour smacked a button. "Establishing connection to the ice planet!" Malsour said as the dormant portal started to whir with power, its complicated inner runes and circuits quickly changing over.

It took less than a minute but to everyone in that room it seemed like an hour. If they were to make it to the ice planet, they would still have to hope that they would find hydrogen. If they didn't or this portal didn't connect, then it would be impossible for them to continue their ongoing projects.

This was their only hope to continue their work.

The portal's main components stopped moving as a wormhole event horizon appeared in the center of the portal's ring. An ice planet was visible on the other side.

Everyone in the room whooped and yelled for joy. Koi looked around at her crazy uncles and father.

All of them moved to the portal and stopped before it.

"We're going to be the first sentient people in the history of the known universe to step on this planet," Bob said. All of them looked at the portal with shining eyes.

All of them, even Steve, had taken ideas, theories, and hopes throughout their lives and their time on Emerilia. Through their hard work, they had created and done things that many would have thought of as impossible.

Now they were once again standing at the doorway to the next part of their future.

Even Steve stood there solemnly. All of them thought of the path they had traveled up till this point and the distance they still had to go in order to bring their plans to fruition.

"Well, let's go and check it out." Dave smiled and looked to Steve and Malsour—his friends, his family, his brothers. His eyes moved to Bob and that mischievous look in his eyes and the pride that was on his face.

Bob had guided Dave, helped him to break free from the lie that was Earth; he was closer to Dave than his father on Earth had ever been.

With faces filled with smiles, they created Mana shields around themselves to trap in the air as they looked toward the portal and walked through the event horizon.

They exited the portal to a barren wasteland. There were ice tornados that sparkled in the limited light that made it to the planet. They were larger than entire towns as they moved lazily across the skies.

The land wasn't even and flat. Crevasses, gorges, and peaks made of frozen materials as well as stone and metals created a breathtaking view. They all stopped to look out over the untouched planet, never having seen anything like it in their lives.

Dave cocked his head to the side as he detected something with his Touch of the Land. Since he had trained with it so many years ago on Cliff-Hill, he cast the spell nearly automatically. "Well, looks like Edwards was right on the money." Dave laughed as he pulled out a large cylinder on a spike.

He threw it up in the air, halting its movement with his hand before lowering his hand quickly. The spike dug deep into the ice; the cylinder started to rotate in small sections. If one was to use their arcane sight, they would see that it emitted massive pulses that mapped out the area, similar to the Touch of the Land spell that Dave had modified.

"What do you mean?" Bob asked.

"I think I've detected a vein of hydrogen nearby, though the sensor unit will let us know soon enough. For now, let's get this base established. I'm going to drop Koi off with her grandmother and then I'll come back to help you all," Dave said.

"It's building time!" Steve clapped his hands together.

Koi let out a miserable cry, not liking the noise.

"Oh, sorry, little Koi. Uncle Steve didn't mean it." Steve went from hardy crystal man to apologetic uncle in a split second.

"Well, it's about time that I used my power." Bob held out his hands, his palms facing upward, closed his eyes and tilted his head back slightly.

The ground shook as a tunnel appeared. A mountain of ice in blocks appeared on the surface of the planet as the ground beneath their feet started to move. Bob didn't use his power on Emerilia, or even in the different secret bases they had. But here on an ice planet, without anyone watching, he was free to do as he wanted.

He floated into the air, looking like God in the middle of his domain.

Dave's face went pale as everyone looked at Bob in awe.

There weren't many changes to the surface of the planet but underneath. He wasn't creating just a simple facility. He was creating a city. From his hand, a soul gem construct appeared, racing off into the tunnel that had been created.

He pulled metal and stone from the surrounding area, pulling them through the ice and forming it around the area he had hollowed out. He created a square city with spikes reaching outward to stick out into the surrounding ice.

From the metal and stone that was gathering, he made the superstructure for different areas.

A hydrogen and elemental refinery formed, as well as an area for the portal to sit in. There was housing as well as laboratories and space for more portals to be positioned. There were fusion reactor rooms and tunnels appeared that dug deep into the ice. Anything that wasn't needed was compressed into ice blocks and pushed to the surface.

Even if they didn't get hydrogen from these materials, they could use the other elements for their other projects or store them for later.

Bob reached out his hand and power surged out of his body. His unleashed aura was dominating, many times more powerful than Fire's. He poured power in the soul gem construct within the city. It was wrapping around the stone and metal structure that would be the refinery.

The soul gem expanded rapidly, quickly filling out. It wasn't able to grow as fast as Bob put power into the soul gem, instead storing it. He'd provided enough power to get the refinery built from the soul gem construct and start on the other facilities.

"I didn't think..." Malsour said.

"What—that I practiced magic?" Bob laughed. "I might not do quests or go out and destroy things. However, I have been studying it for an incredibly long time and using the information that the people of Emerilia have come up with to make my own spells and develop my own magic. How did you think that I kept the *Datskun* running with just that one fusion reactor? I had a whole hell of a lot more portals than it could sustain."

"You were using your own power to fuel portals?" Steve asked.

"Yup," Bob said with a sly grin.

Dave shook his head. This power—he'd never expected that Bob would be this powerful. "Do you have access to a divine well?" Dave asked suddenly.

"No, I don't. This power is all from my own reserves. However, I have been storing my power in the portals on my ship as well as the vault soul gems that you made," Bob said.

A way point appeared in everyone's vision, including a prompt.

Dave clicked on the prompt.

Hydrogen found!

In your scan, a vein of frozen hydrogen has been found. For a list of other materials found, please refer to your sensor unit's menu.

Malsour let out a laugh as the others smiled.

"Seems that I will be able to send you back with a gift," Bob said.

Once again, the ice shook; however, the ground under Malsour, Steve, and Dave's feet didn't move an inch.

Gray smoke wrapped around Bob. Lines of highly compressed runes covered his body, gray smoke wafting off them. Bob's outreached hand shook; runic lines covered his face as his eyes were a dark gray.

"Rise!" Bob's voice carried with it an incomparable power. Dave went pale as the vein of frozen hydrogen moved through the ice. A tunnel appeared above it as it flowed out from where it had rested for unknown millions of years. It was pulled up from the ground and formed into one-foot by one-foot by one-foot boxes that rapidly flew from the small opening toward the group.

The control, the power—it left the others in shock as the blocks formed an orderly line.

"Open your bag of holding," Bob said.

"Steve, take Koi," Dave said.

Steve's hands changed so that they were smaller—he was now able to change his crystal body however he wanted to—gently taking Koi as if she were his own child.

Dave pulled off his bag of holding as hydrogen blocks waited in the air. He opened the top and the blocks flew into the bag.

Another line of blocks rushed down into the tunnel toward the city that Bob was building, moving to the refinery that was still growing.

The stream of hydrogen blocks into Dave's bag stopped.

"When you go back, send over some of the carts. I'll be back in a bit. It's been some time since I've been able to test out my magic. I want to see how much I can do," Bob said with a wide smile.

"Okay." Dave had a big smile on his face at the hydrogen blocks in his bag. They could get hopefully a few more months of hydrogen from it all. Their power consumption was truly too massive.

Now, however, they had gained themselves time. Within just a half hour, they'd found a decent vein. Dave hoped that they could find another dozen like it so they would no longer have to worry about power. Dave slung his bag over his shoulders.

"Well, I don't think that there's much use in me staying around either. So, I'm gonna go see what the rest of Party Zero is up to," Steve said.

"I'll stay here," Malsour said.

"All right, well, let's head back then," Dave said. Steve was still cradling Koi, who was now having a hard time keeping her eyes open.

Dave looked around once more. There wasn't much to tell what they had done but through his Touch of the Land, he could feel the growing city.

Once again they would be free to work on their projects. *Now we just need to mine a few asteroids. Good thing I did it before in a past life.* With a smile on his face, he and Steve walked back through the teleport pad, reaching Nal, and then through the other portal back to Pandora's box.

***

Dave arrived in the Densaou Ring of Fire using the teleportation array. With Fire's stealth runes, the Jukal could no longer see what was going on inside.

There was a lot of movement going on in the normally sedate area around the volcanoes that the dragons called their home. That was due to the growing Nalheim cities.

"Dave!" Oson'Mal called out from the living room where he was reading a book and watching over his son. Desmond was in a cart, currently playing around with the baubles mounted to the wheeled contraption.

"Hey, Mal, could you look after Koi for a bit? I've got some work to do," Dave said. He'd passed off the block of hydrogen to one of the moving carts at Pandora's box, which had taken them directly to one of the refineries.

Dave was filled with excitement but what they were doing was dangerous so he didn't want to have Koi with him for the entire thing.

"Another one wouldn't be a problem." The corners of Mal's eyes wrinkled as he stood and looked to his sleeping granddaughter.

Dave gently passed her over to Mal as a burst of silent flames formed into a person.

"Hey, Fire." Dave smiled.

"Dave, you seem pretty excited," Fire said with an amused look. The goddess of Fire probably wasn't used to being greeted so familiarly.

"Well, we just got a portal to the ice planet in the Nal system sorted out and we got enough hydrogen to hopefully run our reactors for a few more weeks, possibly a couple of months!" Dave said excitedly.

"Oh, the ice planet, already?" Fire said, her shock clear. "Well, would you be interested in taking Water with you?"

"Water? Why would he want to come?" Dave asked.

"Well, he's pretty much reached the end of what he can learn from the Per'Ush islands, and he really wants to try out his powers but not reveal them to the rest of the Pantheon," Fire said.

"Sure. If he wants to come, he's welcome to do so," Dave said.

"I'll let him know and send him to you." Fire opened her interface.

Dave got a request for a party chat; he accessed it. "Hey, babe." Dave smiled.

"Hi, Dave," Deia said. He could tell that she was smiling as she was talking. "Where are you?"

"I'm at your mom and dad's, though I'm heading back to Pandora as soon as possible. What's up?" Dave asked.

"I'm bringing a bunch of people who are apparently really good at working with Dark Mana. I was thinking that they could help out you and the others in making the third section of the city, or with your other jobs that are underground. I've talked to Malsour and he's excited by the idea. He's going to meet with them first."

Dave's smile grew wider. "The good and the bad do come in groups."

"What was that?" Deia asked.

"Nothing." Dave laughed. "I have something to show you."

"Okay, I'll meet you at the Densaou Ring. I want to see Koi before we go off."

From her voice, Dave could tell how much Deia had missed their daughter.

"I can wait around for a bit," Dave said.

"Try not to drink all the whiskey," Deia muttered.

"Sorry—you're breaking up. I'll talk to you later." Dave cut the chat.

"So, want to celebrate reaching another planet?" Mal asked with a wide smile.

"Well, if you have some of that fine dwarven whiskey around, I might be able to add you onto this little trip," Dave said.

"I'm coming as well—never seen another planet," Fire said.

"Who's going to watch the kids?" Dave asked.

"That would be me." Denur's voice passed through the room as she glided toward the apartment. She shrunk in size, turning into her human form as she touched down on the balcony outside of the apartment. Denur had a happy expression on her face as she looked over the sleeping Koi and playing Desmond.

"All right, well, I'll go get some of that whiskey," Mal said.

***

Yemi stepped out of Imend and into Terra. With her senses, she could "see" the masses of people moving through the city. Her eyes went wide as people moved out of the way of Deia and her party.

They greeted a few people, waving and joking as they passed.

These are the people who defeated nearly ten hell fiends all by themselves as if they were nothing. Yet here they act as nothing more than normal people.

One of the Blood Kin gasped as they left the teleport's hub, coming outside to see the massive sprawling city of Terra with buildings on every surface of the massive cylindrical city.

Deia led them onward through the city, past the moving people. Yemi and her family members got a few curious glances but many people weren't all that interested. In the crowds, there were people from nearly every race—eating, bartering, having a drink, or working on something or just admiring the stores and city.

Lights hovered in the skies, illuminating the city.

Yemi closed her eyes, taking in the feeling of the warm sun without it burning her. She coughed a few times, as her eyes went wet. It had been so long since she had last seen the sun. It must have been before the experiments that were run on her by a mage group trying to find everlasting life.

When she had escaped that hellish life of being an experiment, she'd raced toward the exit of the cave they'd kept her in. As soon as she'd been touched by the sun, her skin started to burn and peel, causing her immense pain and making her retreat.

Here, she could stand under this fake sun and take in its rays without fear.

The rest of her family looked up at the sun with curious gazes, removing their veils and other covering headdresses that stopped them from getting too burned by the sun.

"Welcome to Terra," Deia said as they continued to lead them through the city and toward the larger towers that dominated the landscape.

A man riding a surfboard of metal appeared over the rooftops and leapt off a roof. Metal came to meet him before he hit the street, speeding up as he charged toward Yemi and her group.

Yemi and the other Blood Kins' eyes went wide. The control that the man had over Dark Mana was impressive, much stronger than they had unless they had consumed an impressive amount of blood essence.

The man came to a stop and turned his surfboard to the side. "Hey guys!" The man grinned.

"You know how to make one hell of an entrance, Malsour!" Gurren laughed.

"Hey, I'm a busy guy. Jump up?" Malsour's surfboard rose above the people on the ground, widening as a set of stairs grew up to the surfboard.

The others stepped onto the surfboard. After a few moments, Yemi and her family followed.

"Hello, Yemi, is it? My name is Malsour." The man took her hand in his as he shook it, a big smile on his face.

The other Blood Kins' fangs elongated as well as their hands, their eyes turning red in anger.

Malsour looked to them but didn't seem to pay them any heed.

Yemi herself was stunned by his actions. It had been centuries since anyone had touched her, let alone a man. She pushed a smile onto her face. Malsour looked genuinely confused but not alarmed. From his eyes, Yemi could tell that he was a kind man.

"You must be Malsour, Induca's brother," Yemi said, awkwardly shaking his hand.

"Right!" Malsour smiled and looked to Induca before he released Yemi's hand. The surfboard flew forward over the city as Malsour stepped back a bit.

"You're all really Blood Kin? I've heard so many fascinating stories about you all!" Malsour rubbed his hands together, a look of excitement on his face.

Yemi smiled slightly, thinking that a few of those stories weren't that good.

"As long as you don't go around killing people for their blood essences, we won't have any troubles. Otherwise, we're in need of people who are skilled in using Dark Mana, and we'll pay for it. I'll show you what we're working on," Malsour said. His surfboard moved faster than anything in Terra; he'd created a Mana shield around them so that the air wasn't fighting them.

They quickly passed the second section and headed into the third section.

"You all have high night vision, right?" Malsour looked to the Blood Kin.

"It is good enough," Yemi said, not telling more than she had to.

"Good. Take a look." Malsour's surfboard moved downward before it stopped in the middle of what looked like a cave.

Yemi looked around at the half carved out structures and the various repair bots and drills that were working on the city.

"This is the third section of the Terra City project. It will be as big as the first two sections that we passed over; however, this will be made from soul gem constructs built over metal superstructures. Now, we have drills to do the biggest sections and the repair bots for the small stuff, but we all know that a good Dark mage can do the work of fifteen drills easily. We have other projects that we need these drills and repair bots for. We want to hire you so that we can speed up the building of this section and get those machines to use in other places," Malsour said.

Yemi looked at the scale of the project. It was truly massive. There was so much to do that it could take weeks with her family working together. It was a challenge but it would be incredible—as would living down here with a fake sun and with people who didn't seem to care what they looked like.

As long as they keep to their end of the bargain, we'll keep to ours. We should request blood essence so that we have more than what we need so that we're not caught off guard.

"We're interested but we will need blood essence to stay strong," Yemi said.

"Well, that would be easy enough. We could pay you and you could buy it from the people here. I know one potion master who could refine it for you. Otherwise, you can make a request on the quest board. We have a lot of adventurers who come through here. If you commission it, then the adventurer's guild or the Stone Raiders will make sure that the agreement is followed through. The people who kill animals will probably be more than willing to collect the blood essences of the creatures that they've killed—to them it would be easy, just a little something extra," Malsour said.

Yemi had a thoughtful look on her face.

"We've got plenty of jobs to work on that are underground. We need more facilities like power stations that would go a lot faster with your help," Malsour said.

"We're interested but we would need more information. And we would like to see your city in more detail," Yemi said.

"Okay, that's fine. I can drop you off somewhere, give you some cash as a token of goodwill and you can check out Terra. I really hope that you do join us. We need the skilled workers!"

***

Deia looked at her notifications as she waited for the portal to activate.

Event: Of Myths and Legends

You have defeated a pride of: Hell Fiends.

Objectives:

Defeat the Hell Fiends

Rescue those under their control

Rewards:

250,000 Experience

Increased standing in the Terra Alliance

Event: Of Myths and Legends

You have created an alliance with the Blood Kin.

Objectives:

Created alliance with Blood Kin.

Rewards:

250,000 Experience (+500,000 for completing harder objective)

Blood Kin now view you as: Ally

Increased standing in the Terra Alliance

Quest: A Rebellion Rising (Events of Myths and Legends subquest)

You have killed the Hell Fiend Pride.

Rewards:

30,000 Experience

15,000 Gold

Deia smiled to herself, dismissing the screens as the portal finished connecting.

She stepped forwards and through the portal's event horizon and into the small city. Carts were already moving through the massive facility. A refinery grew to one side, the portal facing it and storage facilities next to the refinery with superstructures for housing units off to the other side of the city.

It wasn't the cylindrical city of Terra but set up like any other surface city. However, it was under nearly seven hundred meters of ice, with carts shifting back frozen materials from drills that were expanding the facility and working to dig out the veins of hydrogen that the sensor system had already found.

"It's beautiful." Deia held Dave's hand from within a Mana shield. There was no atmosphere in the city yet, but Bob was working in one of the living areas turned greenhouse to fix that problem.

There was already another portal just a small distance away from the first.

"Want to go see the stars?" Dave asked.

"What do you mean?" Deia asked.

"He means that it's time to set up another portal to the asteroid belt to start harvesting asteroids," Suzy said from behind them. Behind them, all of Party Zero was following and checking out what Bob, Steve, and Dave had been up to.

"It's only been two days since this place was established," Deia said in shock.

"Well, I'm not that patient." Dave smiled.

"Oh, I think our daughter would agree," Deia muttered.

"No matter if we're married or not, I still love you no matter what." Dave looked deep into Deia's eyes. His words made her heart flutter and she blushed, feeling like nothing more than a pining teenager.

Dave laughed and kissed her quickly. Deia let out a giggle, looking away from the others in embarrassment.

"Ready?" Bob looked to everyone, a large smile on his face.

The others smiled and nodded in agreement.

He led them to the second portal in the city. As he reached it, he pressed a button on a console off to the side.

The portal started to power up, its internal runes and circuits moving into position. It took a few minutes as everyone looked at the portal.

Dave looked to Bob. "You already placed the anchor?"

"Yeah, well, I had a bunch of time and everyone was doing other things. Once we got that fusion reactor online here, I've had plenty of energy to make progress on the city and store up plenty to keep these portals running for two months. Though I'm thinking that it might just be a better idea to have greenhouses here instead of keeping anything on Nal. There are satellites there and we can't go to the surface. Here we're not going back up to the surface but with all of the frozen elements around, we can easily combine them together to make different materials," Bob said. "I didn't just put an anchor on the asteroid—I also sent a portal over there."

Dave shook his head. "Well, looks like you've been busy. As for the rest, I agree—we'll work that out later."

Holding a portal open took a lot of power; connecting the portal on the ice planet to a portal in Pandora's box and then removing the portal on Nal would reduce their power consumption.

Deia gripped his hand tighter as the portal's main circuits locked into position, different runes lighting up. The portal's runes finished lighting up; the hum of power died down as through the portal an inky darkness was revealed.

"We're connected to the asteroid." Bob checked his readings, his solemn face splitting in an excited grin. "Make sure to keep those Mana shields up to keep in the oxygen. Dave, you're going to have to make a gravity field so that everyone can stay rooted on the asteroid."

Bob stepped forward and into that inky darkness. A light appeared above him as he threw out mage lights.

Dave and the others followed. Dave's hand tightened on Deia's. He had mined the asteroids around simulated Earth and had developments on Mars and the Moon. However, he had never left Earth himself. He had now been on three planets that weren't Earth, that weren't even in Sol system.

He had always imagined space as that darkness that called to his soul, that called for him to wander between those stars and dream, dream big.

It was that drive that had pushed him as far as he had gone; it was what continued to drive him. For his daughter, for any other children he would have, he would push toward that future, to that unlimited freedom and possibility of discovery across the stars.

They all stepped through the portal, finding themselves in a deep gorge. Dave had created a gravity field that made the asteroid that they were on have enough gravity so that every step didn't send them flying off.

"Look up." Bob smiled.

They looked upward, gasping as they saw through the vastness of space the lights of the Nal sun and the uncountable stars that lit up space.

For a long time, they were silent with their own thoughts.

We're so small in this universe, barely a speck of dust on the universe's vastness.

Dave took a heavy breath. Many might be disheartened by these thoughts, but Dave found them oddly relaxing as he smiled, looking up at that vast universe. It was massive and beautiful. Dave felt gratitude deep in his soul. No matter the struggles and what he had gone through his life, at least he had existed—to have been alive to have this life, to see the sights he'd seen, to meet the people he'd met.

Dave pulled Deia close, standing behind her, his head next to hers as they looked up at that universe together.

"Looks like no matter where you are, you'll always be a miner," Deia said into Dave's ear.

Dave chuckled and kissed the side of her head. "Must be my dwarven half."

Chapter 26: Epilogue

"Open them," the Jukal emperor said. A faint mist fell on his frog-like body as various creatures from all across the universe tended to his needs, making sure that he wanted for nothing as he laid on his chair, looking almost asleep.

"Yes, my emperor." His aide opened their interface and sent out the required orders.

"It is past due that those portals were opened. I want to see what will happen when the aggressive species enter Emerilia," the Jukal emperor said.

Wanting for nothing, his only interest was in the Emerilia games.

"The portals across Emerilia will be opened within a few weeks." The aide bowed.

"Good, good." The Jukal emperor waved his hand and dismissed the aide.

Emerilia will be continued in Of Myths and Legends.

As a self published author I live for reviews! If you've enjoyed Emerilia, please leave a review!

Hope you have a great Day! ☺

Want a bigger map of Emerilia and the continents? Check out **http://theeternalwriter.deviantart.com/**

You can check out my other books, what I'm working on and upcoming releases through the following means:

Website: **http://michaelchatfield.com/**

Twitter: **@chatfieldsbooks**[1]

Facebook: **Michael Chatfield**[2]

Goodreads: **Goodreads.com/michaelchatfield**[3]

Thanks again for reading! ☺

Interested in more LitRPG? Check out **https://www.facebook.com/groups/LitRPGsociety/**

Continue on for Character Sheet!

---

1. https://twitter.com/chatfieldsbooks

2. https://www.facebook.com/michaelchatfieldsbooks/?ref=hl

3. https://www.goodreads.com/author/show/14055550.Michael_Chatfield

In Alphabetical order
Ankol

Dwarf

Dwarven Master Smith. Smithing Art: Metal Spinner. Lives in Grorart Mountain.

Boran-Al

Lich

One of the Dark Lord's Champions. Works directly under the Dark Lord. Creates Creatures of Power and carry's out the Dark Lord's orders. His Citadel was destroyed.

Alastair Montgoa

Arch Lich, aka former Lord Vailyn. Gave up his fellow Aleph to have everlasting life; used the centuries to build strength and knowledge

Barry

Dwarf

Dwarven Master Smith. Smithing Art: Unknown. Wandering smith.

Cassie

Elf/Human Halfling

Holy warrior. Leader of the Golden Sabres. In a relationship with Josh Giles.

Dark Lord

God

Embodiment of the Dark affinity. Created Demons. Normally an ally with the Earth Lord. Always looking for a way to tip the power balance of Emerilia in his favor.

Dasano

Dwarf

Dwarven Master Smith. Smithing Art: Metal Press. Lives in Grorart Mountain.

Akatol Dracul

Dragon

Water Mage. Was the second Dragon, Denur's husband. Went mad and started a genocide, disappeared.

Denur Dracul

Dragon

Fire Mage Hailed as 'Mother of Dragons'. First of her race, a Creature of Power created by the Lady of Fire. Seen as her daughter. Sister to Oson' Deia.

Gelimah Dracul

Dragon
  Dark Mage. Brother to Induca, Louna and Malsour

Fornau Dracul

Dragon

Earth Mage. Quindar's mate, Malsour and Induca's grand-nephew.

Induca Dracul

Dragon

Fire Mage. One of the youngest from the first generation of Dragons. Sister to Malsour, daughter of Denur, aunt to Quindar, great aunt to Fornau. Member of the Stone Raiders and Party Zero.

Kinal Dracul

Dragon

Louna Dracul

Dragon
Induca, Gelimah and Malsour's sister.

Deceased.
Malsour Dracul

Dragon

Dark Mage. One of the oldest Dragons in existence, first born of Denur. Deia and Induca's Guardian, Stone Raider and Party Zero member. Brother to Induca. Great Uncle to Fornau Dracul and Uncle to Quindar Dracul.

Quindar Dracul

Dragon
Wind Mage, wife to Fornau, niece to Induca and Malsour.

Wokui Dracul

Dragon
    Water Mage

Xednai Dracul

Dragon

    One of the first Dragons, had several Dragons. Her son is Fornau.

Gorpal Dunsk

Dwarf

    Dwarven Master Smith, lives in Aldamire Mountain, created 3 Weapons of Power - Mace of Fury, Tower Shield, Boots of Smash. Smithing Art: Paint Copy

Earth Lord

God
Embodiment of the Dark affinity. Created Earth Sprites.

Edmur

Dwarf

Dwarven Master Smith. Had been in the Dwarven War Bands as a Shield Bearer. Former pupil of Quino's Brother to Endur. Smithing Art: Metal's Song

Edwards

Human. Military scientist within the Deq'ual System. Friend of
Sato's

Edwin

Beast Kin. Beast Kin representative on ruling council.

Endur

Dwarf

Dwarven Master Smith. Had been in the Dwarven War Bands as a Shield Bearer. Former pupil of Quino's, brother to Edmur, lives in Zolu Mountain. Smithing Art: Hammer Blows

Esa

Human

Melee fighter. Member of Mikal and Jule's party. Fought at Boranl-Al's Citadel.

Member of the Stone Raiders. Going out with Jules. Works under Dwayne as a fighter. Being trained for a leadership position under Dwayne.

Lord Esamael

Human.

Lord of Emaren within the Gudalo Kingdom.

Ela-Gal

High Elf.

Warrior living in Aleph, married to Ela'Dorn. Persecuted by High Elves as heretic.

Ela-Dorn

Orc.

Researcher and professor at Aleph College. Aleph Council Member. Married to Ela-Gal

Fend

Dwarf
Lord Under the Mithsia Mountains.

Geswald

Human.

Trader's Guild Chapter head in Emaren.

David Grahslagg

Dwarf/Human Halfling, in-game character of Austin Zane. Dwarven Master Smith, Resident of Cliff Hill, member of Party Zero and the Stone Raider's Guild. Other names: Austin Zane

Josh Giles

Human

Rogue. Leader of the Stone Raiders. Was an investment broker on Earth, became an E-head. In a relationship with Cassie from the Golden Sabres.

Gimel

Human
   Warrior.
   Fellox Guild Master.

Gorrund

Dwarf

Dwarven Master Smith in Benvari Mountain with Jesal, teaching four apprentices. Smithing Art: Blood Bender.

Goula

Demon
    On the Ruling council for Devil's Crater.

Gurren

Dwarf

Shield bearer, member of Dwarven War Band under Lox's command, sent to guide people to Cliff-Hill. Friend of David Grahslagg, Kol's Grandson. Member of the Stone Raiders.

Helick

Dwarf

Dwarven Master Smith. Smithing Art: Unknown.

Kim Isdola

Human

Cleric/alchemist. Lieutenant in Stone Raiders.

Ishox

Demon
> On the Ruling council for Devil's Crater.

Archmage Jekoni

Human/item

Over 2,000 years old Weapons of Power. Current form of a blade, able to leave the blade as a spiritual projection, accompanied by his minion 'Hat'. Friend and weapon of Jung Lee.

Jeeves

AI

Made by Bob to assist the Dwarven Master Smiths.

Jeremy

Human
Fellox Guild member.

Jesal

Dwarf

Dwarven Master Smith, Dave's Master Smith trainer. Smithing art: Nature's Guide

Joko

Dwarf

Shield bearer, member of Dwarven War Band under Lox's command, sent to guide people to Cliff-Hill. Friend and trainer of David Grahslagg.

Deceased.
Jules

Human

Healer. Member of Mikal and Esa's party. Fought at Boranl-Al's Citadel.

Member of the Stone Raiders. Used to be an army medic, E-head without legs IRL. Going out with Esa. Works under Lucy as support; leads the healers of the Stone Raiders.

Jung Lee

Human

Alchemist/potion maker.

Was possessed by six affinity free spirits and held within the affinity temple in Ashal for centuries.

Escaped with the help of Party Zero, gained control over the possessing free affinity spirits and joined the Stone Raiders and Party Zero. Wields Jekoni's vessel in the form of a sword.

Anna'Kal

Wolf Beast Kin/Administrator AI24681

Air mage. Originally a program meant to assist Lo'kal with the running of Emerilia. Anna was uploaded to a Player body and inserted into Emerilia. She became emotionally attached with her charges. When the Beast Kin people were wiped out from Emerilia, she went into cold storage, waiting for her father to awaken her when a chance came to fight Member of the Stone Raiders against the prison they had created.

and Party Zero. Daughter of Bob.

Lo'kal

Jukal

Scientist, created Emerilia. Awarded the position of the Gray God, maintaining Emerilia, its people and Players. Other names: Bob, Bobby McMahnon, The Balancer, Gray God.

Kino

Demon
> On the Ruling Council for Devil's Crater.

Kol

Dwarf

Dwarven Master Smith. Gurren's grandfather. Resides in Cliff-Hill. Taught Dave how to Smith. Runs his Smithies. Smithing art: Blind Man's Touch

Lady of Air

Goddess

Embodiment of the Affinity Air. Known for causing mischief. Her Champions act as spies and information brokers, tilting the balance of Emerilia.

Lady of Fire

Goddess

Created Dragons, Mages Guild and College. Gave gift of 'knowledge' to the People of Emerilia. Mother to Deia, Lover of Oson'Mal and best friend with Bob.

Other Names: Ignil

Lady of Light

Goddess

Sent Players to kill/capture Dragons to make her own Creatures of Power. Created the race known as Angels. Large rivalry with the Dark Lord.

Lena

Demon

On the Ruling Council of Devil's Crater. Wife to Vrexu.

Lovan

Dwarf
Mithsia Mountain Warclan leader

Lox

Dwarf

Shield bearer. Was the commander of the War Band sent to guide people to Cliff-Hill. Friend of David Grahslagg. Member of the Stone Raiders.

Suzy Markell

Human (IRL)

High Elf (Emerilia)

Austin Zane's secretary and best friend. David Grahslagg's best friend and assistant with running Grahslagg industries. Summoning Mage. Steven's contractor, member of Party Zero and the Stone Raiders.

Max

Dwarf

Shield bearer, member of Dwarven War Band under Lox's command, sent to guide people to Cliff-Hill. Friend of David Grahslagg.

Deceased.
Meda

Dwarf/Elf

Aleph Council member. Deals with the food within Aleph cities and facilities

Melanie

Human
Archmage Alamos' Wife.

Melhoun

Water snake made by the Water Lord.
Sealed away.

Mikal

Human

Rogue. Jules and Esa's party member. Member of the Stone Raiders. Friends with Party Zero.

Oson'Deia

Elf/Demi God Halfling

Elven Ranger and Fire Mage. Daughter of Oson'Mal and Lady Fire of the Affinity Pantheon. Resident of Cliff Hill and member of the Stone Raider's Guild, Leader of Party Zero.

Other names: Ouluv'Deia

Penelope

Human

Fellox Guild member.

Pete

Human
Geswald's secretary.

Queen Farun

High Elf
    Queen of Raolor.

Queen Mendari Selhi

Human
Queen of Selhi.

Quino

Dwarf

Dwarven Master Smith, lives in Zolu Mountain. Trained the brothers Endur and Edmur. Smithing Art: Internal Cutting.

Rola

Dwarf

Dwarven Master Smith. Smithing Art: Puppeteer. Lives in Aldamire Mountain.

Sato/Communications Officer Sato

Human

Lives in De'qual system.

Communications Officer, becomes Vice Commander of Deq'ual military forces. Grandfather original settler.

Emperor Talis

Human.

Ruler of the Xeugrera Empire, located in the Ashal Continent.

Tounk

Dwarf

Shield bearer, member of Dwarven War Band under Lox's command, sent to guide people to Cliff-Hill. Friend of David Grahslagg.

Deceased.

Demon Prince Alkao/Alkao Travezar

Aerial Demon

Melee fighter. Commander of the Third Demon Horde and leader of Xerzit lands. Oldest of the five remaining Demon Prince's of Devil's Crater. Current King of Devil's Crater

Dwayne Trebault

Human

Melee fighter. Lieutenant in Stone Raiders. Leads and trains the melee fighters in the Stone Raiders.

Venfik

Elf
Lady Air's advisor.

Lucy Vernia

Wood Elf/Human

Lieutenant in Stone Raiders. Spy master, deals with supporting the Stone Raiders and paperwork.

Vrexu

Demon

One of the seven Demon Princes. General in the Devil's Crater Army. Married to Lena, the youngest of the five remaining Demon Princes.

Water Lord

God

Embodiment of the Water Affinity. Created the Merpeople and water creatures. Created the Water Serpent Melhoun. Rival to the Lady of Fire.

Austin Zane

CEO of Rock Breaker's Corporation. Engineer specializing in space vehicles. Background in Astro physics. Other names: David Grahslagg

Wis'Zel

Wood Elf

Bard. Works for David Grahslagg, managing his Ceramics factories in Cliff Hill.